WINDSWEPT

[signature] 1942

By MARY ELLEN CHASE

DAWN IN LYONESSE

A GOODLY FELLOWSHIP

MARY PETERS

SILAS CROCKETT

THIS ENGLAND

WINDSWEPT

WINDSWEPT

BY

MARY ELLEN CHASE

NEW YORK

THE MACMILLAN COMPANY · 1941

Reprinted October, 1941; November, 1941;
December, 1941.

PRINTED IN THE UNITED STATES OF AMERICA
AMERICAN BOOK—STRATFORD PRESS, INC., NEW YORK

Life is a pure flame, and we live by an invisible sun within us.

SIR THOMAS BROWNE
in *Urn Burial*

TO

ELEANOR GODDARD DANIELS

IN GRATITUDE

IN ORDER to forestall the many questions which are often asked of novelists as to the settings of their novels and as to the characters who live in the places described, I wish to say at the outset that the setting of this novel has no exact location on any exact portion of the coast of Maine. Windswept is a wholly fictitious house placed in eastern Maine, anywhere between Schoodic Point and Passamaquoddy. Readers may, therefore, place it where they like, on any headland of those wide and long spaces of land which mark the eastern Maine coast as distinct from the Mt. Desert region and from the many-harboured central and western coastline. Since the character and personality of this portion of Maine interest me more than those of any other part of my native state, I have chosen to place my novel here. I may say also that the endpapers are suggestive rather than in any way accurate.

Novelists, I believe, do not copy characters or settings. They are creators rather than copyists. Although I hope that my descriptions are true to this Maine coast as I know it, any curious reader will search in vain for the house described, the exact surroundings portrayed, or the characters created.

MARY ELLEN CHASE

Petit Manan Point, Maine.
September, 1941

CONTENTS

PROLOGUE   1

THE INHERITANCE   17

THE POSSESSION

    1881–1883   79

    1891–1907   211

    1918–1939   311

PROLOGUE

ON AN AFTERNOON in September in the year 1938 two women were driving through the open country of southwest Germany. Their destination was the town of Freudenstadt in the Black Forest; their way, over the black, well-paved roads that cut the fertile valley between the Rhine and the tributaries of the Upper Danube. The blue peaks of the Tyrol above Innsbruck, which they had left that morning, were far from sight behind them; the slim, dark trees of the Schwarzwald had not yet begun to shadow the bright horizon to the northwest. The day was fine; the sunlight warm and rich; the slightly rolling farmland yellow with cut harvest or suddenly green here and there with the fierce new green of winter grain, freshly planted and waiting rain and snow. For miles no villages had marked their route. There were no workers in the fields, no passing of cars or wagons on the road; and, except for an occasional group of farm buildings in the distance, no sign of life anywhere at all. One wondered over the whereabouts of ownership, the source of labour which had planted, nurtured, and gathered in. This seemed a dream country, suspended, drowsy, deserted, and content.

The women in the car were markedly of different age. One, the driver, was young, twenty, perhaps; the other

3

in the mid-forties; yet there existed between them that
rare harmony which, unhampered by the confusing reservations and expectations of blood relationship, sometimes exists between women of disparate ages. Theirs had
been a long association, begun under the strangest of circumstances when the girl was a child of ten in a black
dress buttoned sedately down the front over her flat little
chest, begun on the wildest of autumn nights in a place
far away from this sleeping German countryside; and the
years between then and now had been woven so closely,
so inextricably with knowledge and experience common
to both, with persons and thoughts and places, and, above
all, with one place which was not merely a place, that
they had lost all identity as years.

Both women were Americans, but in the features
of the younger there was evident a vivacity, even a restlessness, which was not apparent in the face of the older,
and which was attributable not merely to the difference
in age. It was shown in that mobility of expression and
line, which, difficult to describe, is nevertheless unmistakable in those of nearer European background and inheritance. It was evident, too, in the way the girl's expres-
sive hands held the wheel, in their sure, yet light and
almost fragile management of the car. She seemed a part
of its speed, its power, the light, soaring way in which,
under her nervous hands, it took the few rises of the
land, swooping downward again, rounding a curve, skim-
ming almost noiselessly over the smooth road. One knew
that under the hands of the older woman it would have
been secure and obedient, yet harnessed, impatient, not
itself.

They had been driving for some time in silence, enjoying the drowsy, unoccupied country, the warmth of the sun, even the almost imperceptible purr of the engine. It was one of those days when time seems graciously to halt, when a sense of waiting is welcome and inevitable, when the concerns of the world are not so much distant as completely absent, and when an odd security enfolds one. The finished, completed harvest, the still, yellow fields, gathered and garnered, bore out the impression. Even the new green of the winter grain seemed unambitious and idle, conscious that there was time enough for growth after its long sleep beneath the cold and snow. Perhaps it was this half-unconscious sense of a momentary truce with life which caused the older woman to break the silence between them.

"Why so fast, Julie? After all, there's no hurry. It's really too lovely for tearing along so, don't you think?"

The girl lightened the pressure of her foot on the accelerator, laughing as she did so as one sometimes laughs when awakened suddenly from sleep.

"Were we fast?"

"Oh, a little matter of sixty or more."

"Sorry. I hadn't noticed. I've been miles away with one of Rod's old poets. You know that thing he was always saying on still days at Windswept about 'the landscape inspiring perfect ease'.

'O pleasing land of drowsyhed it was,
Of dreams that wave before the half-shut eye.'
That's where I've been. Where's it from?"

"Thomson, I think."

"I never know the source of anything, do I? But it's like that here."

"Yes, it is."

"There isn't a sound. Nothing's awake. It makes you want to live on forever just like this. But I suppose we'd come to hate it after a time."

"I'm not so sure."

They descended a hill and at its foot swung around a curve. Just ahead a road from the east cut their own, the intersection marked by signs, neat black letters on white metal. Westward the land dropped to a tiny valley with sheep and cattle cropping a field by a quiet stream.

"Shall we stop for a cigarette?" asked the girl. "After all, as you say, there's no hurry, and those sheep and cows are nice to watch. They're the only sign of life we've seen for miles, and they're half asleep, I think."

She took her hands from the wheel, turned off the engine, secured the brake, lighted the cigarettes with quick, deft fingers.

"Freudenstadt, 60 kilometers. I never see these kilometer signs without thinking of Sister Sainte Geneviève and how she beat metrics into our stupid little heads when we were barely nine. She said we'd need them one day, God rest her soul! But I never have. You do divide by 8 and multiply by 5, don't you? Then Freudenstadt's—I can't do it—anyhow on a day like this. Let's say one-half the way we always do. Thirty, plus a few more miles which don't matter at all."

They smoked slowly and quietly. The clock on the dashboard said four o'clock. The sun was still high and warm. The land still lay in silence.

Then suddenly from somewhere distant on the road eastward came a confused rumble, growing constantly heavier in volume, shattering the silence of the land like an approaching earthquake. They looked questioningly at each other and then along the road at their right which stretched firm and straight for miles through the shorn fields. There was nothing in sight, but the sound continued, the rumble increasing now to a steady throbbing, punctuated by quick explosive beats. Great, quickly moving blurs now began to fill the distant reaches of the black road, taking shape every moment, now becoming clearly defined as gigantic motor lorries in swift procession, shaking the countryside with the throbbing of their engines. The quick, explosive beats rose in ever-heightening staccato, thumping the quiet air. They were the beats of motorcycles, which soon burst into full view, a contingent of five ahead, mounted by swift, swooping Centaurs in goggles and steel helmets.

Now the lorries were hurtling past, one by one, in mathematical precision, in exact speed, none faster, none slower, none deviating an inch toward left or right from the one ahead. Between every two of them thudded a motorcycle, like a period following a unit of heavy, lumbering prose, a period exactly placed, only marking no completion, thudding on and on.

Each lorry, thundering across the intersection to descend into the little valley and startle the sheep and cows into frightened excitement, was filled with soldiers. They sat in two rows facing one another, the elbows of each man braced in exact placement against the back of the seat, knees firm, feet gripping the floor. There were twenty soldiers to each lorry. They were all young, fresh-faced boys in steel helmets, all at the same angle and strapped below their chins; and as they rode on and on, the eyes of each boy stared straight ahead into some grim foreground with no perceptible recognition either of their own whereabouts or of the car with its occupants halted at right angles to their line of march.

The two women, half in fear, half in fascination, stared at them as lorry after lorry, cycle after cycle, roared past with no deviation in speed or position, with no apparent perception of time or of place, the fields, the sunlight, the finished work of men's patient hands. They were the very embodiment of blind, mechanized force, impersonal, insensate, careless, a force outside the world of thought and longing, a force which, knowing neither, was scornful of both.

"There are maneuvers near the Rhine," explained the older woman. "I read about them at Innsbruck this morning."

"Watch their eyes," said the younger. "I'm trying to get even half a glance, but I guess I'm beaten. We're really not bad-looking, and I always thought soldiers everywhere had eyes for women. The French do, and think how our own army would be behaving."

Yet there were no glances right or left, no sign of recognition. No new, long-lined American car was apparently at the crossroads; its occupants were not even an apparition. Ten minutes passed before the nearer thundering of lorries and cycles ceased; five more before the blurred shapes rumbling westward were absorbed by the bright distance.

When the shattered silence had reassembled itself and again lay over the land, the girl at the wheel of the car made no movement toward starting it again. She and her companion sat motionless, without speaking. Between them there was no need for comment or question, but comment and question at that moment lay far away from the mind of each. Each was suddenly elsewhere, in the same place, in a stretch of country old from the beginning, yet in a New World. And each had suddenly returned there, not through any conscious volition or desire of her own, not in any conscious attempt at escape, but because the direct and complete antithesis of what had just passed before their eyes had risen before them and claimed them both.

This power and force, this compulsion and violence, this sacrifice of the one to the mass movement of the many, had begotten in each, in an uncomprehended instant, the necessity for freedom and security. Out of danger had sprung the involuntary need for safety, out of foreboding and fear, the need of confidence and courage, out of suspicion, the need of faith. This terror which had swept seemingly from nowhere across a still, peaceful land had swept them elsewhere; and they had returned in instinctive adherence to all those things which had shaped and anchored their thoughts for many years and from which, for them, there could be no release.

Yet the manner of this return was different, dictated by a difference in years and even more by an unequal span of experience. The younger, once taken back to those familiar scenes which had nurtured her childhood and adolescence, was now recalling consciously by the act

of memory persons she had known and loved, pastimes,
moments and hours of days and weeks, as one turns the
pages of a book of pictures, lingering upon this one, skim-
ming others quickly, pausing again to gaze upon a favour-
ite. She saw quickly children running in the wind above
the sea, their hair blown, their clothes slapping against
their brown legs, dogs leaping and barking, and a flock
of curlews circling and calling. She lingered over the
memory of a little girl, herself, in a black convent dress,
sobbing miserably on a great red rock against which the
surf crashed, feeling again the strange helplessness of
being with new people, who, kind though they were, had
odd manners and ways, and of being in a new place which
terrified her by its isolation and loneliness, its lack of
restraint, of tidy, snug days when one did as one was told
and because of that knew no fear. She summoned before
her and as quickly let them go the smell of wild strawberries in the unkempt July grass; the shock of cold
water as she raced down white sand into it, afraid of the
taunts of the boy who ran with her if she should hesitate;
the chugging of lobster fishermen in the early morning,
the crazy careening of their boats beside the brightly
painted buoys, as they hauled, baited, threw back, and
chugged on again; a thousand hours of sun and storm
and wind, a thousand fleeting memories merging with
one another, a bright tapestry, a magic carpet, woven of
the reds and blacks, gold and grays, of returns and wel-
comes and farewells, of noise and silence, anger and remorse, laughter and resentment, tears swift and painless,
tears slow and never really quenched.

She lingered over the picture of a small, excited boy,

dipping his hands into a rusted iron pot and bringing them up filled with tarnished bits of foreign gold. She saw herself rubbing one of the coins with the corner of her cotton dress, which she had moistened in her mouth, and remembered the onrush of pride, engulfing her there on that dim path in the deep woods, when she told the astonished boy what the strange words said, summoning back now and holding closely for long moments the healing which his discovery had brought her, better than the gold coins, the knowledge that those of her own tongue had once long ago penetrated that very wilderness, gazed upon that very sea. She could never forget that moment or the miracle it had wrought through days and years.

More swift turning of leaves, more sights and sounds and smells. Blueberries ripening in the sun; ospreys screaming and circling above their nest in the top of a tall, dead pine; the red of cranberries like drops of fresh blood, millions upon millions of drops against the green of their tiny spiralling leaves matting the high, rocky slopes of miles of unfenced land.

The cranberries held her memory longest, longer even than that of her first knowledge of death and its relentless, intruding, sickening grasp. The cranberries, she thought, are red now, ready to be picked and winnowed in the sun and wind. I'm willing to bet, she thought, that Rod is thinking of them, too, even in Cambridge, even in his musty old rooms above the gardens of Emmanuel with their dahlias and chrysanthemums and Michaelmas daisies, and swans floating in the garden pool, even in the market-place with its book-stalls, even as he looks upon the pinnacles of King's and the old cloister of Queen's, even as he punts up the river to Grantchester and tea in the Orchard. I know he remembers them, she thought, and how for years we picked and winnowed them. I couldn't be more certain of anything than that Rod remembers them.

She saw a tall boy, growing taller with every September, rangy and gangling and untidy before his bones and muscles at last found their proper relationship and decided to live together amicably. Standing in the high wind, his white shirt flattened against his chest and billowing behind his back, he held a bucket of cranberries above his head and poured them slowly into a big wicker basket on the ground. She saw the red stream catching the sunlight as it fell through the bright air, heard the quick, sharp tapping of the first berries as they struck, the succeeding patter, the soft, muted thudding as the basket filled. She saw the bits of grass and straw, leaves and twig fragments blown away through the air to fall spent and indistinguishable upon the rough, unkempt ground. Rod was always laughing as he winnowed, she remembered. It was the winnowing of the cranberries that he liked best of anything at all at Windswept.

The memory of the older woman had nothing to do with a conscious act of will. She summoned nothing from the past, re-created nothing, re-lived nothing. What was holding her so securely in its grasp seemed, in fact, hardly memory at all. Or was this memory as it ought to be but is not? She was experiencing the odd, half-frightening sensation of being momentarily freed from the shackles of time, its half-truths, its importunities, its confusion.

The present with its rudely awakened sense of dread and disaster was not; the future which that present darkly foretold held for the moment no terror. It was as though some bright hour had been suddenly salvaged from the dark night of time and that she was secure within it, safe from the uncomprehended movement of days and weeks and years. Or as though streaming northern lights had suddenly swept across a dark sky, blotting out its mysteries with their effulgence. Or as though the great, revolving lamp, far beyond the rugged, rockstrewn point at Windswept, had ceased its rhythmical shining east and west, north and south, and now shone on her alone, clear and steady.

Was it that the gods, jealous of the possible little triumphs of men, the comfort of their dreams, the assurance of their fancies, had from their ramparts beyond the world made this time, this dark, unfathomable pool of the past, this instantaneous waterfall of the present, this ocean of the future, only to baffle the living and silence the dead? Was this sudden halting of it in which one knew things and people for what they were rather than for what they had seemed—this light over years that had gone, this golden branch among the shadows, this quickening to the life immortal—a gift, or an accident, or a discovery? For in this bright hour she was re-capturing time; the past had returned to her in all its fullness, its plenitude, its meaning. Why or how she did not know, but here it was. The persons of that past, whom she was now seeing as though for the first time, were sharpened by her awakened sense of that which had given them life: that stooped man digging a grave on a hillside in the late November sun; that nun standing by a blazing fire, her black, austere shadow stretching high across the wall; those black oxen breaking a snowy road for a sledge with laughing people in the bitter cold; those blue iris in countless thousands filling the marshes, encircling a pond with a brilliant band of colour, flowering so close to the tide line above a rocky beach that they sometimes caught the spray from the incoming surges; those stars so bright on September nights that the Milky Way in contrast was as though swept with surf across the sky;—all these had risen again, revealing now through their outward and visible signs their inward and spiritual grace, their sure and simple answers to the questions of life, their balm in Gilead, their springs in the Valley of Baca.

She had known them all, and yet never known them, loved them all and yet never loved them. They had been fibre and tissue, bone and muscle and blood of her being for forty years and more, yet they had seemingly until now never been truly known. They had their counterparts in countless thousands of places, she thought, in countless thousands of minds, out of sight and anchored in the dark pool of the past, unapprehended in the quick stream of the present, unable to make themselves known through conscious memory alone, through the quick passage of circumstance or even through the love they had engendered. They waited, she knew now, for some means of revelation, for some momentary experience in the present, some quick sense of grief, some realization of transcending pain or pleasure, some long-forgotten sight or sound, smell or taste or touch, some cruel onrush of terror like this roar of power and might which she had just now heard and seen.

Must they always thus wait upon chance, she wondered, to rise thus from the dead? Were fleeting glimpses of life all that one could hope for, glimpses like those realities in dreams which one searches for upon awakening, clinging to fast-fading perceptions, helpless before their absorption into oblivion? Could life be apprehended only as the flashes of fireflies over a dark meadow or as a shower of sparks on a windy night? Or was it, instead, a pure flame as the poets and saints and prophets had known, and not for themselves alone but for all men everywhere, in whose light the rich might value their riches aright, in whose warmth the poor might be rich? Were the slow sorrows and quick joys of life doomed then to be spent and wasted, engulfed and submerged in time, or was there some long slow process of building the human mind and spirit so that they might be understood by the many and not only by the few, so that the prose and poetry of time and place and circumstance might be read and discovered, not merely caught as in the stray notes of a passing song and lost in a moment? Had she herself not known that building through many years, that long, slow process of becoming, and yet not until now completely apprehended it?

The girl at her side was speaking, and she came back suddenly to the knowledge that she was in a car, in Germany, by a crossroads with neat sign-posts, that the clock on the dash-board said five o'clock, that the sun was less warm.

"Where have you been?" the girl was asking. "I've been

winnowing the cranberries at Windswept with Rod. What will you bet he's not thinking of them now in spite of his Cambridge?"

"I've been—well, to sound completely pious, darling, I think I've been on the road to Damascus," she said.

The girl started the car. They swept across the intersection, over the stream, and away toward the northwest through more quiet fields.

"Well, you're on the road to Freudenstadt now—the city of joy. This special sort of Fatherland needs a good bit of joy, if you ask me. I'll not be sorry to leave it. Tomorrow there's France,—Strassburg and Verdun, wine and good food with people laughing for a change, and the next day there's Beauvais and Havre, and the ship. On we go!"

THE INHERITANCE

1

JOHN MARSTON first came into possession of Windswept, its hundreds of rough, unkempt acres, its miles of high, rockstrewn coast, its one precipitous headland, cut by the fierce tides into almost a semi-circle within which his house was later to be built, on Advent Sunday in the year 1880. He was fourteen years old at the time. The day, in fact, chanced to be his birthday.

Sixty years then have passed since that day of his sudden, puzzling, even awful inheritance and legacy; yet Advent Sunday has always been so inextricably associated with Windswept that it seems fitting, perhaps even inevitable, that its story should be undertaken on this special November Sunday. Today the snow is deep there and, according to this morning's weather report, the cold intense and bitter. Today the blueberry fields are discernible only as white mounds tumbling steadily downward toward the wooded point three miles eastward from the house; the tips of the alders, leafless and stiff, shudder in the wind; the clumps of dark, ungainly firs and spruces at each corner of the house and on the slope behind the barn, stand black against the snow, their shadows purple in the sunlight. Today the sea is a purplish gray; surf foams like thick suds about the treeless islands; the distant summit of Cadillac cuts the western sky, sharp and keen as a new

knife blade; the spruces of Schoodic are jet-black above
the tossing water; and southward the open ocean is ridged
with white at the breaking of the swells, uninhabited now,
as it is so often even in summer, by a solitary sail.

It is safe to assume that there is no sound there this
morning except those of the wind and water. There is
surely no human sound. The caretaker does his needless
inspecting on Saturdays from the village eight miles away.
If there are hunters about, they are miles eastward in the
woods and marshes. The snow has discouraged any birds
that there might be. The gulls have gone into the bays
where there is chance of food. The curlews have long
since gone now that the blueberries are gathered. Crows
do not often cry above so treeless a piece of land as Windswept.

But the sea thunders against the high, gaunt boulders
and pounds the shingle below the headland, pulling back
the smaller stones with a roar, hurling them forward
again, forever rounding and polishing them. It reverber-
ates in the fissures and openings among the rocks with a
roll of drumbeats throbbing for miles as the surging tide
madly inundates each hollow and crevice of the massive,
uneven coastline. And as for the wind, there is no stopping it either in sound or in volume. It blusters across the
snow, sweeping out of sight with the smallest fraction of
its breath the button-holing of the rabbits, the feather-
stitching of the mice. It booms against the face of the
headland, bangs against the closed shutters of the house,
distorts the black branches of the trees. It is not *in* the air.
It *is* the air. It is air swollen to great bulk, heavy with
pressure and power, might and force.

Yet there are still days at Windswept, rare summer and autumn days when the sea at dawn is the colour of thin milk and motionless except for the breaking of the long swells in frail white lace about the rocks, days when the sun is pale yellow and one can stare at it without the least sense of being blinded, when a haze fills the air and sails hang languid above the water. It was, in fact, on such a day that John Marston at fourteen came into his inheritance.

There had been a long succession of such days in late November in the year 1880. For such early and heavy snow as this which has just fallen is unusual even to New England, even to the far eastern coast of Maine. November often grants its benison of Indian Summer, nowhere more lovely than at Windswept. The reds and purples of the blueberry leaves hardly fade completely before the heavier frosts begin, so that the whole great extent of rough, uncultivated land from the house itself to the end of Sieur de Monts Point is sometimes almost as swept with colour in November as in October.

2

John Marston received his inheritance on that Advent Sunday from his father, Philip Marston, who was buried at Windswept on that day. Philip Marston had been born in the valley of the Kennebec, of a family known in the eighteenth century as one of strong Loyalist and Church sympathies and in the nineteenth as one which provided good ship-masters in the foreign trade. His grandfathers on both sides had owned extensive docks at the mouth of

that most lovely of Maine rivers. His father had com-
manded his own square-rigged ship for twenty of the fifty
years allotted to him. Had he himself been born even a
generation earlier, he would doubtless have rounded Java
Head, weathered the Sunda Straits, and torn through the
roaring forties with the best of them. As it was, he had
sailed as a boy in the great days of the late 1850's, leaving
Harvard College because he could not bear the uneasiness
in his mind and body, and shipping to Sydney and Singa-
pore and the Mediterranean before the mast as others of
his family had done in their way up to officers' papers and
at last to a master's berth. He was twenty when the War
broke out and young men left both college and forecastle
to defend and keep the Union. And when it was over and
had taken its toll of shipping, when no more American
clippers were racing around Cape Horn to the Golden
Gate, when tariffs and steam and railroad building and
the opening of the Great West had dealt to sail its ultimate death blow, he had succumbed none too willingly
to the demands of time and circumstance and entered a
firm of marine engineers located in New York, a firm
soon to be known as Marston, Cobb, and Lassiter. He
married young and, as it proved, unhappily. John Marston was his only child.

Philip Marston was an odd American for his day and
generation. In him the strong Loyalist traits of his ancestors had not resulted either in conservatism or in a devotion to tradition and a fear of change. His interest in the
influx of foreign labour in the late sixties and the seventies was at once absorbing and intelligent. Contrary to
most of his contemporaries and associates, he believed

honestly and ardently in the manifold contributions which northern and even southern Europe were making to the tapestry of American life, its manners, its colour, and its thought. Perhaps he had won from his few voyages to far countries more vision than usual with those who sailed. At all events he believed in the future of the foreigners flocking in such numbers to New York, manning the mills of New England, penetrating to the Great West and taking up its boundless acres of homesteading land. He saw in America not so much their creditor as in the long run their debtor; and to those puzzled, hopeful men from the regions south of central Europe whom he employed— dark-eyed Greeks and Italians, broad-faced, gray-eyed Slavs—he was always more a friend than a master.

It was, in fact, to this vision and faith, this humour and imagination and vitality of Philip Marston, that Windswept owed Jan and Anton and the others who took from it in such measure and gave to it in even greater.

3

Jan and Anton were two Bohemians whom Philip Marston met on shipboard in 1871, when he was returning from a business trip to London and Hamburg. In those days of open steerage the odd human cargoes in the lowest decks of ocean liners were a source of speculation and suspicion in the minds of passengers travelling in comfort, if, indeed, they were aware, as many were not, of those inhabiting the cramped quarters below them. It was characteristic of Philip Marston that he was not only aware of their presence but filled with consuming interest in those many-tongued hundreds of men, women, and children, who quarrelled and fought, laughed and wept, were clean or filthy, hopeful or sad, loquacious or silent, within the narrow boundaries of the deck just above the water line. He went the rounds with the harassed under-officers and stewards, who strove to keep some semblance of order and decency among their charges, who quelled brawls with fists or even with clubs when necessity arose, acted as mid-wives or as undertakers on more than one occasion, and became with every voyage, perhaps with good reason so far as their own experience was concerned, more hard-headed and hard-hearted toward the human race in general.

In 1871 as in the years immediately preceding and following the immigrants flocking to America were in large proportion of Northern European stock, Germans, Dutch, and Scandinavians, decent, cleanly people with the hope of new and free land in their blue eyes on this first, seemingly interminable stage of their long journey to Iowa or Minnesota, Wisconsin or Nebraska. They themselves suffered from the noisier, dirtier, more voluble and inflammable Jews and Italians, Greeks, Rumanians, Poles and Czechs, who ate and slept among them, jostled and fought, and were sick wherever they happened to be. Yet even among these Philip Marston saw interest and drama, suffering, tragedy, and triumph.

Jan Pisek and Anton Karel were boys of sixteen and seventeen from peasant families in Bohemia. They were travelling with and under the guardianship of a Bohemian priest on his way to the Czech colony in Milwaukee. The two boys had served him at the altar in his church at home, and their parents, hearing and reading of the vast and unlimited opportunities which America offered to the foreigner, had consented with prayers and dreams to their sons accompanying him. On his first eager descent into the steerage quarters Philip Marston had spied the priest, whom he liked upon sight. He was a young man with intelligent gray eyes well set in his wide Slavic face, a face which, if not genial in expression, made up in kindliness and strength what it lacked in vivacity. His name was Father Urban. Philip Marston saw that he was neat and clean, that his manners were gentle, and that he exacted decent behaviour from the two boys under his care. He soon learned that the priest spoke a competent, if limited, English, which he had learned in expectation of his long journey and new life, and that he had taught Jan and Anton the rudiments of their new tongue. Philip Marston fell into the habit of talking with the three, who mingled little with the other steerage passengers, and before the voyage was half over, had with his usual friendliness offered help with the necessary formalities and instructions in New York before they should start upon their journey westward to Wisconsin.

Father Urban was killed two days from New York by an infuriated young Italian in a brawl over a Rumanian girl, whose favours had been sought by a dozen men throughout the voyage. She was young and beautiful with black eyes, a full figure, and sinuous, voluptuous ways. As she moved about the deck, laughing at this man and that, she became the center of attraction and the cause of numberless embroilments and controversies, terminating daily in noisy quarrels and even in fist fights. The harassed

stewards and under-officers had more than once hauled
her bodily away from where she lay stretched out in the
sun on the hatchway, laughing into the eyes of some man
who lounged beside her and who for his share came in
for kicks and cuffs and the threat of confinement below
if he did not leave the woman alone.

In this last encounter, which occurred late at night, the
Italian had drawn a knife against another of his countrymen who was engaging the girl in a dark corner of the
deck. The priest, who was saying his night prayers under
the stars, was foolish and decent enough to interfere in
the unsavoury mess. He received a knife thrust in the
neck for his pains and promptly bled to death before the
ship's doctor could reach him. The bewildered, heart-
broken Jan and Anton fell as promptly into Philip Marston's hands.

When the ship had docked in New York, he took the
two Bohemian boys to his home on West 28th Street,
much to the discomfiture of his wife, who did not share
either his views or his kindliness and who remained after
six years of marriage to him as unprepared as at the start
for his chimerical behaviour. After a few days from which
no member of the household, except five-year-old John
Marston, gained anything save discomfort and embarrassment, he obtained lodging for them in the Bohemian settlement between Houston and 8th Streets, prevailed upon
his skeptical and astonished partners to employ them as
errand boys, and took quite easily upon his shoulders the
rôle of guide, philosopher, and friend.

John Marston always remembered their unexpected
and unannounced arrival in the over-furnished drawing-

room of the house on West 28th Street, how he as a little boy in a black velvet suit with a white lace collar stood by the fluted white marble columns, which upheld the mantel above the fireplace, and stared at them and at their strange assortment of disreputable luggage on the red, rose-strewn carpet. They were shock-headed boys, he said, seeming old to him, and they fingered dirty cloth caps in great red hands far below their jacket sleeves. One of them was crying, he could not remember which, and the other sullen and sad. He did not see them long at this first meeting, for his mother swept him from the room and up the winding staircase. But he saw that his father put his arm around the crying one, so that, as his mother pulled him hastily away, he did not know whether to feel jealousy or pity. And during the few days while the boys stayed in a basement room belonging to the coachman (who was moved, protesting, to the top floor) and ate with the scornful servants in the kitchen, he was not allowed to seek them out or to talk with them on pain of punishment from his nurse and his mother.

But after his mother died, when he was eight years old, and he and his father were alone with a benign old housekeeper, his nurse banished in favour of a day school for boys on University Place, he began to know Jan and Anton. They were no longer with Marston, Cobb, and Lassiter. His father had set them up for themselves in a shoe-shining parlour on 12th Street instead of allowing them to work with the Czech cigar makers on Attorney or Canal Streets, rolling "smokers" as so many of their countrymen did. Jan and Anton proved to be wonderfully skillful at shining shoes and at repairing them as well. They prospered, slowly paying back to his father his original investment on their behalf. They would not allow John and Philip Marston to sit on their high chairs with their feet extended before them, but instead either Jan or Anton came weekly to the house to collect the boots and shoes, which they returned mended and shining. John Marston sometimes took his school friends to the shoe-shining parlour, although Jan and Anton clearly thought it was not the thing for a young gentleman to do; but they smiled nevertheless, and on afternoons when business was dull, they sang Czech songs and told a fabulous, terrible Bohemian story about a monstrous white snake—a story which two later generations of young Marstons were to hear from Jan by the great fireplace at Windswept.

4

The best of John Marston's evenings as a boy in New York, he used to say, were those when he went with his father and Jan and Anton to the Národní Budova on East 5th Street. This was the National Hall of the Czechs, where they held their theatricals, concerts, and meetings of all kinds. Whenever they gave a play, Jan and Anton invited Philip Marston and John, and they saw enacted there the dramas of the kings and queens of old Bohemia, Libussa and Premysl, Wenceslas and Vratislav.

Anton never liked to take part in the plays. He was self-conscious and feared people laughing at him. He could not be someone different from himself. But Jan was a good actor. He loved to play the part of Premysl, who was

a peasant until the soothsayer and queen, Libussa, had
seen him in a vision ploughing in his field with his two
oxen and had sent for him to be her husband and the
king of Bohemia. Jan himself would have made a very
good king, John Marston thought. There was an odd
something in his voice that made one listen to him, a rise
and a fall like the rise and fall of poetry, and a fervour
which stayed in one's mind. There was a warmth in Jan,
a glow, which surrounded all that he did and said with
liveliness and light. And yet, thought John, thinking it
over at night, a bit puzzled in his bed at home, Jan was
far more quiet and slow in all his ways than Anton.

There was always a Christmas play at the Národní Budova, which they never failed to see, and in which John
Marston strove to catch the Bohemian words and phrases
which Jan and Anton had taught him. But with all the
sentences he missed there was always the fervour of the
acting, the knowledge of a strange land beyond the sea
which these people loved and in which many of them still
lived although they were far away; and he learned to
catch the frequent invectives hurled at the Austrians and
Germans with which the plays were interspersed and
which never failed to bring forth shouts of hatred and defiance from the crowded room. There were choral singings, too, which he liked almost better than the plays.
There were no people who sang as the Czechs sang, their
voices rising in loneliness and anguish, faith and hope, joy
and misery and courage.

When he and his father left the stifling Národní Budova to walk the twenty blocks and more up Fifth Avenue
to their house in the cold of winter nights and saw the

carriages of people whom they knew returning from din-
ners and parties, he felt often queerly out of place. New
York was not New York only as his friends at school and
their families knew it. Coming out of the Národní Budova, its doors and windows, were thoughts and feelings
and aspirations of which most New Yorkers knew nothing at all. There was something old there, stretching back
through centuries, seen in the tears which sometimes ran
down the faces of the aged, in gestures and in the rhythm
of voices, in hatred and homesickness, grief and memory.
There was something new in bewilderment and courage,
in the sense of comradeship, and in the hope common to
them all. And above all there was something real, something more alive and stirring than anything he knew in
his school, where all the boys came from the same sort of
homes and looked forward to the same sort of holidays.
Since he could not put into words what he always felt in
the Národní Budova, he said simply to his father as they
walked home:

"I'm glad we know Jan and Anton and the others,
aren't you, father?"

Philip Marston was glad, and said so through all the
years in the seventies when he and his son went together
to the Národní Budova and walked home up the Avenue.
He said other wise things, how Jan and Anton, and Palda,
the Czech tailor on 7th Street, whose daughter now worked
in the Marston kitchen and was beginning to be an American girl rather than a Bohemian, and Tony, the Italian,
who sold fruit from his wagon, had things to give to
America in the years that were coming. He said that how
much they gave and how they gave it would depend on

the vision and intelligence of men like him and his son.
He said that these new people could give for evil or give
for good, for destruction or for construction. Or that they
might not give at all if, cut off from the life of their old
country, they did not come into contact with the best in
their new. If, blinded by the prejudice and lack of understanding which so many Americans felt toward them, they
saw only the striving after material success, then they
would give nothing of the gifts they had brought, for they
would have lost alike the gifts and the power of giving.

"That's what we're facing," said Philip Marston to his
son, "with every immigrant ship that docks."

5

Before he left his school in New York at thirteen to go
to St. Paul's in Concord, John Marston had grown more
aware of the difference between Jan and Anton. He saw
that, although Jan was the younger, he had many things
which Anton had not, things never quite understood but
nevertheless there. There was a strange kind of excitement about Jan. It shut people away from him, and yet it
somehow revealed more to them, not perhaps about Jan
himself, but about those long, deep things behind him,
years and old griefs, the crest and summit of days old and
new, lived not only by Jan himself but by the few men
like him everywhere. Anton forgot; Jan remembered.
Anton used life; Jan created it.

It was easy to forget in New York. New things came
crowding one by one, new habits, new ideas, new demands. Time was quick in New York, not slow as in the

old country. And as the children who had come with their
parents and those who were born in New York grew older
and went to American schools, the forgetting became almost inevitable. The children began to speak the English of the school in their homes. Some of them despised
the language of their parents, refusing to speak it. They
took on American ways with their American clothes. Only
the old remembered and the few young men and women
like Jan.

It was not so much that Jan remembered the *things* of
the past: the wide plains reaching to the distant mountains; the hollyhocks in the angles of his father's white
cottage; the mushrooms in the deep woods; the snow and
cold and hunger. Rather he remembered what these things
had done to him, the effect they had had upon him in
quick moments of sorrow or anger or affection, which
after all is the reward and meaning of memory to those
who have the gift of understanding it. Time had pulled
no dark curtain between the past and the present for Jan
as it had done for Anton. There was no sharp distinction
between the old and the new for him.

Anton was quicker than Jan about his work, and he was
an artist at shining shoes. How deftly he cleaned the
soiled, dull leather of the boots or shoes extended before
him, wielded his heavy brushes, rubbed in the polish with
his bare fingers, again wielded his brushes, swinging them
carelessly from one hand to the other just to prove his
skill! How he snapped his stout cloth in the final touches,
stood away to inspect, snapped and cracked the cloth
again in the last triumphant retouching, now with force,
now gently and quickly with a rhythm like that of an old

dance in the fields at home! He was vastly proud of his work, and so was Jan.

"Anton," Jan said more than once, half in fun, half in earnest, "the shoes which you polish, they are not for this earth. They are for Heaven before the throne of God."

Anton idolized Jan, seeing in him dimly those things which others saw and could not name; and yet Jan's slow, quiet ways often irritated him. They lived together in the Czech settlement in one room with a sputtering gas jet over which they cooked. They saved their money. Anton carried the dirty bills and coins every Saturday morning to the bank, watched them with some misgiving at first being put into the till and the amount entered in a small black book, which he always carried in the upper pocket of his vest. He did this upon the explanation and advice of Philip Marston. Otherwise he would have stuffed the money inside their mattress or hidden it beneath a board in their room. Every month they sent some of the money home to Bohemia, going together to the post-office nearest them, leaving the money and signing a blue paper, which in some mysterious way was the money itself. Anton would have sent less than Jan if he had dared, but he never did.

Long before John Marston went to New Hampshire to school, Anton had met Anna. Anna was a Polish girl who worked in a hat factory. She and Anton had dreams of leaving New York some day and having a farm of their own. They had nearer dreams of getting married. On Sunday Anton took Anna with him to the church of Saints Cyril and Method on East 4th Street. Jan went by himself, and more often than on Sunday.

Had Father Urban not so absurdly given his life for a moral value, in the existence of which no one concerned, except himself, believed at all or even recognized, he would doubtless have made a priest of Jan. Jan, then, after his years at the seminary, could have stood before the altar of some hideous church in Milwaukee, or Racine, or Chicago. He would have turned to his congregation, mumbling their rosaries, and said the *Dominus vobiscum* or the *Domine, non sum dignus* in such a way that they would have waked up for a moment. As it was, Jan had no interest in the Annas or the Yulkas or the Olgas, who flashed their red stockings and swung their white petticoats in the plays and dancings and singings in the Národní Budova and on spring evenings on the streets of the settlement. He had his memories and his odd, bright thoughts. He was married to life, loving it, understanding it, bringing forth from his union with it new life. With all its pain it could never hurt him as his incomplete marriage with Anna or Olga or Yulka would have done.

Even at fourteen John Marston felt glad that it was Jan and not Anton who buried his father at Windswept on Advent Sunday in November, 1880.

6

Philip Marston bought a ketch for his son when he was ten and old enough to learn to sail it. They kept it on the Sound at New Haven, and every summer they cruised for a month in the waters off the Maine coast. They took Jan along as an extra hand on these summer voyages, and

from the money which Philip Marston paid him Jan engaged Anna's brother Ambroz to help Anton with the
shoes. For two summers Anton, too, was induced to take
a holiday, but even with business slack he was restless over
the shop. After two weeks with Anton aboard they had to
make a sizable harbour, Portland, or Rockland or Bath,
so that he could catch a train back to New York.

Jan spent the happiest days of his life on the ketch,
which John Marston named *The Sea Hawk*. They formed
a bright pool of memory for the long winter evenings
when he sat alone in his room in New York. He learned
to sail well, not so well as Anton, who was agile and quick,
but well enough. Philip Marston bought him a blue coat
with brass buttons and a yachtsman's cap, and he wore
both with consuming pride. He loved the coast of Maine,
the dark hills of Camden, the islands of Eggemoggin, the
small, unnamed capes jutting into the water with firs and
spruces clinging to their red rocks, the coves where the
great blue herons stood. He loved those rare days when
they dawdled, more than the brisk days when they sped
before the wind, those mornings and afternoons when the
sails hung listless and languid, when the sun dried the
clean deck, and the porpoises sometimes whirled rhythmi-
cally above the sea, dripping laziness and peace.

He and John studied water birds under Philip Marston's teaching, loons and cormorants, gulls and herons,
hawks and terns, and the plovers which sometimes cried
at night in thin, whimpering cries while they lay at anchor. Jan loved those still nights in a hundred lonely coves
and backwaters from Cape Porpoise to the St. Croix,

when, after they had eaten their supper, which he was good at preparing, they lay stretched out on the hatch and watched the darkness stealing over the land and sea. He knew the stars. He was not much of a talker, but there was about him an odd quality which made John Marston miss him when Jan was forward playing his mouth organ and John only the length of the deck away. Sometimes when the unforeseen and sudden happened, the mad cry of a loon cutting the darkness into little quivering pieces, the fog coming upon them unawares as it sometimes does, rising from sea and land alike and blotting out faces and even hands, he would bring something up from the bottom of his mind, where it lay, making him what he was, and give it words. John Marston always remembered such a fog off Cape Split, how the shrouds dripped onto the wet deck, how each was alone though close together, and how Jan's voice came from out the clinging mist:

"In the old country when I was little there were fogs. They rose in the night from the heat in the fields, and when my mother went to work they were there, thick like this. My mother carried me on her back in a basket, bent over, trying to see her way to the fields, waiting for the light. She had to work early, not to miss the time. The time, it meant bread. When we got there, to the fields, she went on her knees on the wet ground in the mist and waited till she could see the light so she could begin to work. We waited there till it was light enough for my mother to work in the field. She often sang to me there in the fog above the earth so that I could finish my sleep while we waited. 'Jesus, Mary's son, give us bread,' she sang. I was very small, but I remember."

7

In October, when John Marston was unwillingly at school, his father and Jan again sailed *The Sea Hawk* far beyond Mt. Desert after ducks. Sometimes Philip Marston took a friend along; more often he and Jan managed by themselves, to Jan's infinite satisfaction. Philip Marston liked those untenanted reaches of the eastern Maine coast, those wide, almost treeless stretches beyond Schoodic and Gouldsboro, better than he liked the more beautiful, more romantic outlines of mountain and high shore, of headlands and islands, of inlets and bays, which were in a few years to lure so many thousands to Camden and Mt. Desert, Penobscot Bay and Eggemoggin, Christmas Cove and Pemaquid. There was something that reminded him of Europe, of the Scottish, or Cornish, or Breton moors, in those wide, unfenced tracts of land that lay east of Frenchman's Bay: land rough with squat alders and bayberry, sumach and raspberry, and with unmeasured acres of blueberries, then quite untended and, for the most part, even ungathered; land low with marshes, or black with rockstrewn, treeless pastures, or rising now and then to windy promontories high above the sea.

It seems, indeed, an older land than that westward. Here the coast is less cut by bays and snug harbours rimmed by hills. The open sea is close; one can catch cod and haddock but a mile or two from shore; the tides are higher and more ruthless as they swell eastward toward the great depths of Fundy.

Even today this portion of the coast is relatively unfrequented by native and sojourner alike. The desire to live within easily circumscribed harbours, to look out upon the security of boundaries is characteristic of most persons. Few wish to sail, either in body or in mind, far beyond the Pillars of Hercules. But Philip Marston liked the less beautiful, more unkempt character of this far eastern coast, those trackless stretches over which the darkness settled more heavily and the dawn came more quickly, those tumbling, uneven pastures, those ragged wastes which faced the open sea, those rocky coves of deep swirling water into which one edged warily with the knowledge of the full force of the Atlantic behind one's back.

In the late summer of 1880 John Marston was kept from school by a severe attack of scarlet fever, which left him so weak and thin that all thought of a return to Concord was deferred until after the Christmas holidays. In October the thought of accompanying Jan and his father on their annual hunting jaunt began to put flesh on his bones and strength into his legs. He could not have asked for a better dealing from the unreliable hands of Circumstance. They started in mid-October. The killing frosts that year were late in coming, and the colour was still brilliant as they sailed eastward in the fine, firm weather which held for days.

The Maine coast had never been so lovely, Philip Marston thought. He had for years been toying with the notion of buying some hundreds of wild acres which he and Jan had tramped for four autumns. They lay east of Mt. Desert and Schoodic, miles southward from the small villages along the one road leading from Eastport to the more considerable towns west, a road later to be known as Route 1 and desecrated along its more populous reaches by any number of hideous means of catching tourist money.

This half-fledged notion of buying land for himself and John took form and shape as the good weather held and they neared their destination. It was further strengthened by a surprise which he had with difficulty throughout the summer kept secret from Jan and his son. They had been curious over two journeys which he had taken by train in June and July to some unknown place and by the prescribed nature of their August cruising, which had been strictly limited to the farthest reaches of Penobscot Bay. Now as they slipped out of Bar Harbor after seven days of sailing, well stocked with provisions for what seemed an indefinite stay, and swung eastward, both John Marston and Jan knew that the momentous secret was about to be revealed.

It proved better than the best of dreams and surmises. When they had dropped anchor late in the same afternoon off the one sandy beach which that portion of the coast afforded and rowed ashore in the dory, Philip Marston led them half a mile through bayberry and juniper to a log cabin, which he had had built during the summer on a rocky ledge a few feet from the sea. It stood in a clump of firs and spruces, almost out of sight, complete with rude furnishings in one large room and a mammoth fireplace. The actual ownership of the land itself being a matter of uncertainty through lapsed taxes and a succession of run-out deeds, there had been no objection raised by the authorities of the nearest village to Philip Marston's odd request, although why anyone should wish to erect even the flimsiest of shelters in a spot miles from anywhere at all remained a matter of astonished conjecture.

As they sat that evening by their own roaring fire with the rising tide swirling against the ledges outside, Philip Marston made up his mind once and for all. He would buy as many acres as he could get of that land which stretched eastward toward the great light beyond Sieur de Monts Point. There were miles of it, desolate and treeless above the sea, great wastes across which one could make paths along the edge of the high shore. Beyond the Point itself the strong tides had swept inland, hollowing out the shore in a vast half-circle, cutting it farther and farther away, hurling in years gone by such masses of rock and driftwood that a massive sea-wall had been built. He remembered how the gulls clustered on this wall, rimming it with a long line of white and silver. Behind and beyond the wall sand dunes rolled backward to a fresh-water pond, encircled by marshes, where the ducks lingered in October and the herons stood on still summer days. And beyond the pond, once the marsh grass and soggy pools of black water gave way to stumpage, the woods began, damp at first even in the dryest seasons, mossy underfoot, until the land rose into dark ranks of spruces and pines and at last gave way again to the long, treeless wastes above the sea with their blueberry bushes and alders.

Philip Marston framed his plan to its last, finest detail long after his son and Jan had gone to bed in their wall-bunks, which smelled of fresh wood. He threw more spruce logs and great, ungainly pieces of driftwood on the fire until far into the night. Unless he was mistaken, this especial portion of the earth had been peculiarly set apart for him and for those who should come after him. During the years he had known it, the four Octobers when he and Jan had tramped its open reaches on their way to the pond where the ducks would take wing, in the two visits he had made to it in the summer just past, he had become aware of its spell, even unable to escape from it when far away.

He was still a young man, barely forty. There were many years left to him, and here he could live them as he had seemingly been unable to live the past. With the symmetry and orderliness of his life here through the long summer and autumn and the memories he would take back to the city, he could so cover up the confusion and disappointments of his marriage that in time they would be out of sight and forgotten. There was healing here for unhappiness and failure, faith for disillusionment, peace for the pain of self-reproach. Here one would not need to make impossible adjustments to men and manners, or to conceal from others, and even from oneself, the things and the thoughts by which one lived. Here one could safely entrust one's son to the better instruction of sea and sky and of this bare and sturdy land.

Old Numa had been right, he thought, in recognizing the gods who inhabit the surface of the earth, the sea, and the air, and who cast their spells upon it for evil or for good. The spirits of this place, the *genii loci*, were benevolent spirits. Of that he felt certain. They must be lonely now for companionship after all these years of tenantless space.

8

In the morning early they set out to fulfill his quest, sacrificing even those tense, watchful hours in the marsh grass at the pond behind the sea-wall. They sailed the ketch four miles, beyond the point which the great light guarded, and northward into Heron Cove, following from there the rude road which, after a five-mile tramp, brought them to the nearest village and a lawyer's office. The astonished lawyer warned them that it might take weeks to accomplish their purpose. The very ownership of part of the land which Philip Marston wanted was in question, to say nothing of the uncertain boundaries of the rest. Yet if the owners could be ascertained and found, he did not doubt of their willingness to part with their property, unless, indeed, they were shocked to death by the mere notion of a purchaser. As for himself, he had never thought there was much away out there except ducks, an occasional deer, and, of course, scenery. He had not set foot on the place in years, he said, and he did not know of many who had. But he would get to work at once.

October gave place to November as they waited. The good weather still held after a rainy day or two which they enjoyed indoors. Philip Marston wrote his firm that his absence from it was indefinite, and Anton sent a laborious letter in pencil to Jan saying that he was doing fine with the help of Ambroz and others as he needed them. John Marston never once thought of school.

A boy by the name of Daniel Perkins brought their mail every afternoon to Heron Cove, and they went in

The Sea Hawk to fetch it. He brought also any news which the lawyer might have for them. He had orders to leave the newspaper and letters under a designated stone high up on the beach in case they missed him or a sudden storm might make it inadvisable to man the ketch. They used the stone very seldom, however, as Daniel Perkins' teacher let him out early from school so that he might be at Heron Cove at four o'clock, and his curiosity made him punctual. He was a lanky, red-haired boy of thirteen with long, bare freckled legs. He felt his importance keenly.

9

John Marston had never, he thought, been so happy as during those long, slow weeks. Contentment here became a veritable excitement. He was glad of the delay in some remote court-house over musty deeds and mortgages and tax-record sheets. It was strange how this new place seemed old and familiar almost from the moment of their setting foot upon it, stranger how, nevertheless, it was somehow always holding something back from their knowledge of it, strangest how it decreed one's hours and ordered one's thoughts.

The short days succeeded one another, growing shorter as the November frosts sobered the reds of blueberry bushes and sumach. The October drone of the crickets died from the air. The rime whitened the ground in early morning and made the rocks, wet from the surf of the receding tide, slippery as he clambered down over them and across the shingly beach to haul in the dory from its mooring. He longed for snow to enclose the three of them even more completely from a world which he had almost forgotten.

But the snow did not come. By ten o'clock the sun was warm, and seven hours of daylight lay before them. A short walk from their cabin among the spruces led them away from the strip of sand, which afforded safe anchorage for the ketch, and brought them in a quarter of an hour to that high, treeless promontory above the open sea where the land which was to be their own began its uneven slope eastward. This, Philip Marston decided daily with increased pleasure in each identical decision, was to be the site of the house which they would begin to build in the spring.

Every morning they went there, leaving the path among the spruces, skirting a high pasture, which rose higher as they walked, until they had reached the summit. Behind them lay the sandy anchorage, flanked by its protecting ledges; on their right, beyond two rocky points of mainland rose the distant Mt. Desert hills; before them some treeless, jagged islands caught the surf even on quiet days; beyond the islands there was nothing but sea and sky and the vast, shimmering space between them.

It was here on this vast, dun headland, cut into a great semi-circle by the strong tides seventy feet below, that one best caught the character of the place, here that its fascination most held one. The promontory was not, strictly speaking, a cliff, for in spite of the huge boulders at its base, it was not itself formed of rock but rather of tough clay and sand, so tough from the interlacing of grass roots, the pounding of by-gone tides which for centuries had been at work upon it, and from the buffeting of the wind which drove straight on from the open ocean, that it had taken upon itself the solidity, even the appearance, of stone. There it had remained, permanent and impregnable, its unbroken, almost flat summit extending back for fully a mile before a high wooded hill shut it from whatever of lesser attraction might lie beyond. Upon its right, between it and the nearest point of land westward, the sea extended into the quiet anchorage; upon its left more land like itself, decreasing gradually in height, sloped eastward, a vast expanse of land, open to the sky, swept by the wind, its high shoreline constantly receiving the pounding of the surf upon the giant rocks below.

The place to many might have seemed desolate, bleak and barren enough, sinister, sullen, even foreboding, especially in November. For it was a somber region, even at noon when the sun lay full upon it. The very absence of trees, the swarthy monotony of its mounds and hollows made by the clumps of blueberry and alder scattered upon its shaggy surface, gave to it a grave and solemn simplicity, a naked reality which struck upon the mind as well as upon the sight of the sensitive observer. There was mystery in its very emptiness, and grandeur in its severity. It might have been some ancient highway between sea and sky in the earliest ages of the world before creation had begun to embellish itself and thus to obscure its simpler glory. The gods might still waken here at dawn and evening. There was room here in these unenclosed, pathless spaces for their long and varied processionals by day, their recessionals by night.

Nothing commonplace could happen here, Philip Marston thought, nothing mediocre or mean. Perhaps that was why men had shunned it as a dwelling-place, having been made vaguely uncomfortable by its nobility and dignity as well as fearful by its solitude. Events could not pass here into the nadir of forgetfulness. Whatever dramas were enacted here upon this stage, against these settings, behind this orchestra of wind and surf, should by right call forth in those who played their parts only constancy and honour.

Here, even sadness must be sharpened and refined to understanding and acceptance; here, Earth was still the ancient life-giver, increasing joy. Here, away from the roar of the world and the confusion of themselves men might grow into heroic mould as in those early ages of the world, their spirits chastened and cured, seeing in these bare and rugged outlines the sure and simple design made for them in the beginning of things. For this was an old and a wise land, a long uninhabited and forgotten spur of a new world, which elsewhere seemed to grow newer instead of older. Here, Philip Marston thought, one could, if he would, catch something of that wisdom which life in most places and under most circumstances leaves unfinished, even undiscovered.

10

Every morning while they waited, they grew more at home. The naming of their longed-for property increased their confidence in their ultimate possession of it. Although some days were calm and soundless, and the dark, brooding land seemed asleep, on most the wind was strong and ruthless. It swept over the promontory with such might that they lay face downward in the grass and blueberries to escape its full, relentless force. It seemed the breath of the land, the evidence of its life and power.

"We will name this place Windswept," said Philip Marston one morning as he bent over a pad of white drawing-paper on the uneven ground before him. "Both the land itself and the house shall be called Windswept."

Although his words were oracular, his manner of saying them seemed incidental, even casual. It was as though he were communicating to Jan and to John Marston a name which someone else had thought of.

"That is the right name," said Jan. "There could be no other name for here. This is an old land, like my country, and the name is old. I heard the wind last night while you were asleep. It filled our house with sound. At once it made me think of the great wind which was the Holy Ghost of God. You remember, at Pentecost, like the Bible says."

Philip Marston glanced quickly at Jan before he went on with his drawing.

"We will place the house right here," he said, "right where we are now. Get some stakes, Jan, so we'll not forget the exact spot. A hundred feet from the edge is about right. It will be long and low, like this, with two wings folded back at right angles to the front. These will make a kind of open court at the back where we can have a flower garden, if we want, well out of the wind. The big chimney will go up in this court, like this, an outside chimney of our own stones. We'll lay some more stones, flat ones, in front for a long, wide terrace. And beyond in the pasture, here, we'll build a big barn, low like the house. I think we'll shingle both and let the wind and weather colour them. It won't take long before they are as gray as those clouds there or as the wings of these gulls. We want our house to belong to the place, not to stand out away from it."

11

In the afternoons they went to the pond, tramping the three miles along the edge of the high land above the sea, entering the woods beyond a rocky cove into which the sea swirled and crashed, and coming at last through waist-high bayberry and coarse marsh grass to the pond itself, where they kept a small skiff moored. The ducks were plentiful. They had only to lie for a few minutes among the grass and stumpage, as still as the sheet of dark water, before black flocks of them would rise and fly straight and low toward the sea-wall with a great whirr of wings. The sudden reports of their guns shattered the silence and seemed to echo not only over the pond itself but beyond the sea-wall and out across the open water.

John Marston had received in advance of his birthday his first shotgun, to take the place of the small rifle which he had been entrusted with two years before; and under the instruction of his father he was learning to use it with expertness and pride. Occasionally other hunters penetrated their solitude, coming from the village eight miles away by the road through the woods or by sea from the settlements farther east; but for the most part they were alone and undisturbed. One day, after they had been to see the lawyer and to stock up with more provisions from the village store, they asked Daniel Perkins' father to hunt with them. He was the carpenter who had built their cabin in the summer, and Philip Marston wanted to talk with him about their plans for the house to be built in the spring. He came on Saturday through the woods with Dan to Heron Cove to meet them there in *The Sea Hawk.*

Daniel's father, Caleb Perkins, was a tall, friendly man whom they all liked. He had long, strong legs and tremendous strength in his hands. Unlike the lawyer he had a feeling for this land which they so much wanted. He had often hunted here, he said, ever since he was a boy. He had a quick eye for signs in the weather, and he knew the habits of water birds. He was a fine shot, but after he had brought down more ducks than all of them together, he said a bit self-consciously that he did not really like to kill them.

"I do it," he said, "I suppose because I'm a man and they're only birds. But, mind you, I don't take to it. They have their place same as I have mine."

Since the same feeling had been growing in them, too, they liked him for giving it words.

He knew something of local history and more of local tradition, and he told them what he knew and had heard about the land for which they were so anxiously waiting.

"So far as I know," he said, "there's been no one livin' here for years and years back. Way beyond your cabin there's an old cellar hole. I discovered it once when I was a boy and had landed on the beach there after raspberries. There must ha' been a family there once in a sizable kind of house, but no one in town recalls who they were or when, how they came or why they left. You see there ain't much here to live on except blueberries and ducks and a deer once in a while. The land's poor, and there's no near market for fish. The sea's a risky one off these rocks with the wind blowin' the way it does three hundred days out o' the year. But it's my private notion that most folks shun tracts of outlyin' land like this. They don't feel to home in wild places, that's the truth of it. They get queer fancies, and things sort of go to their heads. I know lots o' men who don't even like to hunt about here except in threes and fours. Ask them why not and they look sort of foolish. They don't exactly know, but it's there all the same.

"My father used to tell me when I was just a little shaver about some women who came out here to pick berries once when he was a boy. The berries are always prime here in August, barrels of 'em for the pickin'. Well, about half a dozen of these women came by the road for a long day of pickin'. It seems the fog caught 'em unawares, the way these fogs sometimes do, and they got plumb lost and couldn't find their way. Fogs are nerve-rackin' things. I don't fancy fogs myself. When they didn't come home, some men started out with lanterns after 'em, but they'd wandered so far it was mornin' before they were found. It's lonesome out here in the dark with the wind blowin' and the surf crashin' against the rocks and the danger of these high shores. My father went along as a boy with his father, and he said they were well-nigh crazy, all of 'em, once they were found. They told wild stories of all the terrible things they'd heard and seen, nonsense, of course, but it was real to them. And one of them, they say, a young girl she was, never got over it, but went off into a kind of slow decline and died. It's nonsense, of course, but stories like that get attached to a place and make folks scared of it. I don't take any stock in 'em myself. I must say I've found folks a heap sight more scarey to a man than any kind of country. The wilder the place is, the better I like it."

They took Caleb Perkins and Dan home with them that afternoon and kept them for supper and the night. John and Dan stretched out before the fire on their stomachs and listened to their fathers' voices until they fell asleep there in the warmth and snugness. Jan washed up the dishes and then took his seat by the fire, keeping it well supplied with driftwood he had gathered from the shore. It burned with brilliant colours of green and rose and blue.

"I never saw so much wood on any shore," Philip Marston said. "It's hurled way above the tide line, and there are logs and hunks of it ten feet back in the grass. I can't imagine where it all came from or how it got away up there over these high banks."

"You haven't seen a winter storm here yet," said Caleb Perkins, "and there ain't many that have. No one stands here lookin' at 'em who doesn't have to. Or a spring tide on a full moon with a high wind blowin'. These winds and tides out here can work miracles with logs o' wood. As to where it all comes from, I've often wondered myself. Folks used to say wreckage from ships, and I suppose there's still some o' that left over from the old sailin' days on a coast like this. But we don't get many wrecks these days even in the worst storms. I take it some comes from the lumber schooners workin' along toward Boston and New York. I shipped in one once when I was a boy, and I remember we threw a lot over the side when we found ourselves too heavy in a gale o' wind. And some just drifts around from one place to another. The sea takes back as well as brings, and there's a heap o' shiftin' about that comes natural.

"The French were along these shores in the real old days comin' from the St. Croix and points east where they'd made settlements. And even before that, so I've read, Champlain sailed to Mt. Desert and gave names to a lot o' these points and islands that keep their French names still, though folks who know say that we don't pronounce 'em right. It's an old coast, this is. I like to think about it myself. They say the French had tradin'-posts up and down here to buy fur from the Indians. And once, a lot o' years back before I was born at all, a farmer about ten miles further east from here dug up a sheet o' brass with his plough that had some Latin words on it. That's true as gospel. The schoolmaster could read it out and found it to be the corner-stone of a Catholic Chapel. He said the words told how it was a chapel dedicated to the Virgin Mary. So we know the French were around here once upon a time."

John Marston and Daniel Perkins wished they had been around here then, too. Before they took their guests back to Heron Cove on Sunday morning, John gave Dan the rifle which he had had for two years and which his new shotgun had displaced in value. He liked Dan, his

blue eyes and shock of red hair, his freckled face and
shy, friendly ways, and wanted to show him that he did.
Dan was delighted with the gift, and so was his father.

12

As October wore on and November began, they formed
the habit almost unconsciously of walking after supper
through the darkness to see how the site of their house
felt to them after night had fallen. The path through the
spruces had grown so familiar to their feet that they could
manage now with a minimum of stumbling; the pasture
afforded no obstacles at all; and once they were upon the
high, windswept promontory, the ground was solid and
clear.

Sometimes the nights were black with no stars at all.
The sky was as though it were not; and only the sound
of the sea below them gave evidence of its presence. Except for the gleaming or flashing of light-houses in the
distance, the one thing visible on such nights was the wind
itself, streaming in torrents of darkness about and above
them. On such nights they were shut away even from
space.

There were nights of stars in countless thousands. The
planets and constellations seemed close to the dark earth
on which they lay. The Milky Way in contrast to their
brilliance was a band of white, as though it were swept
by some mysterious surf on the upper air. On these
nights they moved through space as though the headland
were the prow of some mighty ship speeding them on

toward remote, celestial shores, the sound of the sea their
steerage-way as they sailed on and on, beating into the
wind.

There were nights of northern lights streaming across
the sky like the expanding wings of the seraphim, piercing
the clouds with radiance, dimming the stars. With these
it was impossible not to see the wind as companion, even
as master, the power behind those shooting, soaring paths
of flame, clearing the way, thought Philip Marston, for
the streets of the New Jerusalem, blazing with topaz and
emerald.

When the great hunter's moon rose in early November
and the wind moved in shadowy gusts across the clear
outlines of the land eastward, they could see the shining
white of the swells sweeping shoreward like the manes
of gigantic horses bounding over the rocks, thudding the
high shore with the thunder of their hoofs.

13

The last week of November marked an odd return to
Indian Summer. The wind died; and there came a succession of early autumn days, warm and still. A haze hung
over the land in the morning, softening its rugged outlines, giving to it the aspect of quiet waiting, undisturbed,
unexpectant. The sun at noon was almost hot.

Philip Marston had completed his drawings of the
house, outside and within. They were now transferred
from his large drawing pad to long, professional-looking
sheets of blue paper which had been sent from New York.
Now only the long-deferred assurance of ownership was

wanted before he should hand these over to Caleb Perkins
and return with Jan and John, who was once again brown
and well.

An excited Daniel was waiting at Heron Cove on Friday, the 26th of November. He bore news from the
lawyer that at last the titles were sufficiently clear and
that all arrangements for immediate purchase and trans-
fer had been completed. There remained only the necessary signing of documents and the payment of money.
For this, his father, Dan said, would come in his wagon
early the next morning through the wood road to the
Cove and transport them all to the village and the lawyer's office.

The news was less a surprise to them than it was the
inevitable consummation of expectation and assurance.
As they sailed slowly homeward, adroitly catching all the
wind there was, past their own darkening shores, beneath
the high, overhanging site of their house, and into the
bay toward their sandy anchorage, they realized suddenly
how perplexed and mystified they would have felt had
the purchase not been possible. They would have been
more unconvinced than disappointed.

"This land could be no one's but ours," said Jan, as
he swung the dory alongside. "It has been ours for years.
It is only that we have been late to find it."

On Saturday when the papers were at last signed and
the money paid, a small amount of money, Philip Marston thought, for so many hundreds of acres, they took
Daniel and his father back with them, Dan with his
cherished rifle, his father with some necessary tools of his
trade, pencils and compasses, measuring-rods and rolls of

white paper. Although he would not begin with his men to break ground until the spring, he wanted a day with Philip Marston to talk over plans and receive instructions. On Sunday they would sail the ketch far around the point and the great light to her winter moorings, which they had decided upon, and that night board the train for New York at the station fifteen miles east.

Saturday was as lovely a day as the ones preceding it, weather breeders, all, Caleb Perkins said.

"When this breaks," he said, "it'll break plenty. Mark my words. You're gettin' out just in time."

Jan prepared a late lunch for them which they ate on what was to be in the following summer the long terrace of stone before their front door. The sea stretching before them was like some vast sheet of pale gray satin. Only by the line of white where it broke upon the rocks eastward could they detect its motion.

"It's gettin' ready for trouble," said Caleb Perkins again. "See the tails of those clouds there, swishin' around. We call them mares' tails hereabouts. They're a bad sign. I'll give this spell o' weather one more day. Monday'll see a change in things, and not so good a change either. They tell me there's storm warnin's out already down along."

After they had eaten their lunch, the boys took their guns and started down the long slope toward the distant woods. They had a bet on as to who could get the more rabbits. Dan had a secret plan in his head about making a fur cap for John Marston from his rabbit skins. He was not sure that boys wore such caps in New York, but he would like to do something by himself for this boy from the city who had been friendly to him. He knew a trapper who would show him how to sew the skins in just the right way and how to complete the cap in a jaunty manner by fastening two white scuts on it, one in front, the other in back.

Their fathers watched them go along the edge of the high shore above the sea. They were thin, rangy boys, tall for their age. There was an unexpressed bond between their fathers, for Philip Marston had discovered that Daniel's mother had died the preceding winter. He and his father shifted for themselves in their house in the village.

"Your boy's been awful kind to Dan'l," Caleb Perkins said, "givin' him the rifle and all. Seems like Dan'l can't talk about nothin' else at home, and I'm sure he's a braggin' nuisance at school."

"Dan's a fine boy," said Philip Marston in his turn. "John liked giving him the rifle, 'twas his own idea, and he says Dan's getting to be a good shot with it. He'll be a good companion for John once we get settled in here. I hope we'll see a lot of him and of you, too."

"You will," Daniel's father promised. "We don't see many folks from away, down around here. They're good for us, give us a kind o' new slant on things." He paused and puffed a bit nervously on his pipe. It was not easy for him to say things, but since it was harder for him to write them down on paper, he had decided to tell Philip Marston of his gratitude in the best way he could. "And I'd like to thank you before you start for home for givin' me a job like this. I've never had one of this size in my life. Work's scarce down here, and folks haven't money to do things beyond repairin', shinglin', and such like. If I ever do get a house to put up, it's a mean, spindly thing. Most folks hereabout don't have ideas,—they're set on a roof to cover 'em, and they don't care much about the *looks* of a house. I've always wanted to put up a big, fine one that would look right, before I die—just to show myself what I could do if I had the chance. It's mighty prime of you to trust a plain country carpenter like me to do your job for you when you might ha' got a city man who's more up to date and all. I'd like you to know before you go back that I value what you've done."

Philip Marston knocked out his pipe on a rock as he rose to his feet.

"I know a good man when I see one," he said quietly. "I don't like business that's just business. A man can do a better job if he has his heart in it. I want my house to be built by someone who will have a feeling for my own piece of land here so that he can make the house fit the place. Now let's get to work."

14

It was nearly three o'clock when the two men with Jan's help had finished their job. The stakes were driven, the measuring completed, the blue sheets of paper studied one by one to the minutest detail. The placing of the barn had been agreed upon, and the site of a well discussed, subject to the tappings and prophesying of a dowser, who lived on the outskirts of the village and whom Caleb Perkins would bring to Windswept before the final decision could be safely made

"Funny about these dowsin' men," he said. "They seem plumb crazy pacin' around a piece o' land, across it one way, across it the other, tappin' away with a bit of ash or willow. Some use ash and some use willow, and what they use, they use, and they won't place faith in nothin' else. Seems as though they have a queer sort o' knowledge not given to the rest of us, for they don't often fail, and that's a fact. I've never been sure whether dowsin's a trade or a bit o' witchcraft left over from the old days, but that there's a lot to it there's no gainsayin'.

"I knew a fellow once years back—he's gone now—who was the best dowser in all Washington County. The wells he dowsed for are deep down in the earth all over the place, from Eastport to Sullivan, and not one of 'em has failed so far as I know, no matter what sort o' drought hits us. Once twenty years back I watched him dowse over a field where they was goin' to dig a well. The land was springy like with surface water on a lot of it, and every man of us thought he was plumb daft when after a lot o' tappin' he said he felt his stick jump-like on a sort of a knoll with no sign o' water anywhere near it and the ground dry as pipe-clay. 'Dig here,' he says. 'Here's your place.' 'You're crazy,' they said. 'You're plumb out o' your head. It'll cost twice as much to dig there,' they said. 'All right,' he says, throwin' down his stick. 'Have it your own way,' he says, 'but you'll pay me all the same for your ill luck.' And off he went down the road with his crazy old stick.

"Well, they begun to dig, and 'twas just as he said. The water petered out after a few feet down, and all their work was for nothin'. So they closed up after they'd paid a couple o' men for half a day's work and started on the knoll just as he said they should. They struck signs o' water after ten feet and at twenty a fine vein, and there's no better well hereabouts.

"This dowser of ours is a kind o' slack-twisted fellow with a no-account wife and a parcel o' measley children that are apt to pick up what don't belong to 'em if they get the chance. He don't know much of anythin' else, digs clams and fishes a mite for a livin'. No one puts any stock in him at all except for his dowsin'. But I wouldn't take it on myself to say dig here or dig there on this land without his say so, I vum I wouldn't. Some men have one sort o' knowledge, and others another, and some none at all, at least to all appearances."

The afternoon continued warm and soft. The thick swirling clouds, which Caleb Perkins knew were sinister in prophecy, did not obscure the sun, now journeyed lower in the west. There was no sign of the two boys, no sound of their guns.

"We might walk down a bit," Philip Marston said. "We may not get a day like this tomorrow, and besides there'll be packing to do then. I'd like to feel my own land beneath my feet once more before I have to leave it. We might go down toward the woods and give the boys a shout or two. It's time they were back."

The three of them started in long strides across the rough, shaggy land. It had never seemed so still. The fine, feathery lines of the clouds, now tinged with approaching sunset and sweeping across the pale blue November sky, the pale yellow of the late afternoon light, lent to it, with its fading russets and browns, a golden colour like the faintly tarnished gold of old paintings. He had seen those same fawn-coloured browns, Philip Marston thought, in walks across Umbrian hills, without warmth and yet warm, without colour and yet with it, the colour of age and history.

The land seemed to drowse there behind the quiet sea with its fragile lace-work of surf upon the russet ledges and along the shingly beach. Some gulls were circling lazily above the water; others were standing still with folded silver wings on the rocks above the full tide.

15

They entered the wood road just beyond the rocky cove where it curved sharply on its way to the pond and the sea-wall. There was a sudden crash through the underbrush on their left, and a deer leapt across the path almost directly before them. A rifle shot burst in the quiet air, and in another moment the deer had bounded away among the sumachs and alders toward the shore. Philip Marston had fallen to the ground with the bullet from his son's gift to Daniel Perkins in his side.

John Marston never clearly remembered all that happened then, after he and Dan had sprung into the path from their hiding-place among the trees. He had a confused memory of Dan, running back toward the open land, screaming for someone to come from where no one was; of Caleb Perkins and Jan making a stretcher of some poles with their coats tied to them, and of himself trying to staunch the blood with his shirt which he had pulled off. He knew that somehow they all stumbled out of the growing twilight and darkness of the woods into the open where there was still light and warmth, and that his father was asking to be taken back to the headland where their house was to be built. He heard Caleb Perkins calling to Dan, who still ran screaming on up the uneven slope toward the headland. And all the time he knew with sickening horror that there was no help to be had, and that the first bitter harvest of this land which they had loved and wanted would be his father's death.

Once they had reached the open land, it was Jan who caught Dan and sent him, still sobbing and screaming, through the overgrown path to Heron Cove where one of the fishermen there could ride Caleb Perkins' horse to the village and a doctor. But John Marston knew, even as Dan's sobs came back to them through the still air before the silence fell again behind them, that the doctor would come too late. He knew it by the quiet, desperate way in which they went about things and by something equally quiet and fateful in the fast-gathering twilight over the land.

His knowledge justified itself. They got his father to the headland since he wanted it so much, but at a sacrifice of blood and strength and of their own better judgment. Philip Marston had time up there in the stillness and in the fading light over land and sea to tell them to be kind to Dan and to say that the house was still to be built. He had time, too, to say that he had got from his land precisely what he had all his life wanted, and that it would give to his son, to Jan and to the others, still in the mists of the future, all that it had given to him and more. If the doctor should not, perhaps, come in time, he said, saying this lightly for the sake of John who was holding his hand, he would like to be buried beyond the site of the house on the pasture slope. He made Jan promise that it should be done.

"I won't bother anyone here, except perhaps your dowser," he said, with a smile for Caleb Perkins.

The first stars were coming out as he died. It grew cold suddenly up there in the darkness. They sat for a few minutes in the glow of the lantern, which Jan had brought from the cabin, a small pool of glimmering, uncertain light in a suddenly created world of terrifying certainty. Then they went back over the pasture slope and through the path among the spruces to the cabin, John Marston ahead with the lantern, Jan and Caleb Perkins carrying Philip Marston's body. When the doctor came three hours later with the others whom he had brought to give what help they could, there was nothing to be done but to say on paper what they all knew too well already.

16

John Marston never forgot that night in the cabin among the spruces above the dark, swirling water. Nor did those who came after and because of him ever forget it. They were always being brought up sharply by the difficult truth that not one of them had actually been there; and yet the reality of it became so much a part of their conscious experience from the beginning that they never really believed that truth, much as it reproved them. Eileen Marston, once she had come to Windswept, found her presence in the cabin on that night the easiest

part to play of all the parts in all the dramas she was forever playing. Ann Marston still believes that she was
there. Young Philip Marston was all his short life so
much there that Jan's face in that firelight was the last
thing he saw as he died in Belleau Wood. Rod even
placed the dogs there with him, Giles and Friday and
Pippin; and when he was at last convinced after years of
bickering that Julie had as much right to the claim of
her presence there as he had of his own, he grudgingly
allowed her a place there also. For from out of the bright
and dark moments of that night Windswept and all those
who make its story came. Without those moments neither
they nor their story would have been.

Jan made hot coffee and sandwiches in the lean-to,
which served as a kitchen. There was a small, squat stove
there with the date 1850 on its oven door. They had been
saying, through all the weeks that they had cooked upon
it, what a merry-looking stove it was. Tonight the small
pieces of soft wood with which Jan filled it snapped and
crackled as they had always done and made bright rings
of light around the black covers. Jan made them eat the
sandwiches and drink the scalding coffee. He would not
send the doctor and the men, who had come to help, back
through the woods to Heron Cove and the village road
until they were all warmed and fed. They stood, awkward and silent and sorry, about the kitchen, their shadows reaching across the ceiling in the light of the swinging lamp overhead.

When they had gone, Jan built up the fire in the great
fireplace, throwing great hunks of driftwood upon it and
big logs of spruce. Then he drew Dan from the far cor-

ner of the room where he had been crouching away from them and made him lie down before the fire beside John Marston. John suddenly placed his arm around Dan's shoulders, and they lay there together, with Jan in his chair on one side of the fire and Dan's father in his chair on the other side.

Jan began to talk then.

"Suppose I tell you boys some stories, you, John, and you, Daniel, about myself when I was at your age. Good? Yes, I will do so. I will tell you first about where I lived when I was at your age, and then I will tell you about how I went to the great city of Praha, which you call Prague. It is a great city of Bohemia, my own country, very old with many palaces and castles, and many hun, dreds of bells all sounding at once. Well, to begin when I was at your age.

"When I was at your age, I lived in a little white house with a brown roof of thatch, and lime trees near. You do not know lime trees? They have many little white flowers in the summer that smell very sweet when they hang on the trees and when they fall into the green grass. They smell like music, like old songs. We were poor when I was at your age and littler, always poor. My mother and father, my sisters and brothers, we all worked in the fields of potatoes and beets and paprika and oats. My brothers they were two, Kaspar and Rudolph, and my sisters were two, Olga and Philomena. It was Philomena I loved best. She was my twin sister. Some day I go back to bring Philomena to this good country. She waits for me to get enough money to go back for her.

"Well, as I said, we were always poor. Sometimes we

did not have enough to eat. But we had good times, too, and when the times were very merry and good, we forgot that we were hungry. What did we do, you say, on our good times? In the summer, when we were not so hungry because there were fruits and berries to gather, we went for walks over the plain toward where we could see the high mountains more close. Often on Sundays we did this, after Mass, for all day. We picked all kinds of flowers, many like you have here, many different. There were daisies and wild roses like you have here and one flower like you do not have. In my country we call it Our Lady's tears.

"It is a red flower with magic in it. For if you gather it and pray for all those who have broken hearts while you do so, they will all be healed of their broken hearts. One flower, one prayer, one broken heart made mended, they used to say in my country. But one day I and my friend Anton, who shines shoes with me in New York, Dan, gathered many of the flowers called Our Lady's tears, too many. Our hands were full, and we forgot to pray for the broken hearts. This is a sin, I said to myself, and I told the priest about it, and how Anton and me did not know of enough broken hearts when we remembered to pray. But the priest said, 'We will pray now for all the broken hearts in Bohemia and for all the broken hearts in all the world. They are very many,' he said. 'That will make it right,' he said. That was a wise man, that priest.

"Well, on those good summer days we rolled hoops when we had them. The blacksmith, who was a kind man, sometimes gave us the rims of wheels which were worn out. We mended them, and they were fine, great hoops to roll. Or we flew many kites, which we made out of paper and pieces of wood which the shop-keeper gave us from his boxes. It is a fine sight, yes? to see a kite with a coloured tail up in the air and to hold the string, running fast over the fields. The priest near us was a great master in making kites, and he had much paper from packages sent to him. My friend Anton, who shines shoes with me in New York,—he and I went with the priest to fly our kites after we had helped him to say Mass at the altar in the church. Sometimes he would take lunch with him—enough for us all—bread and cheese, and sometimes even meat, and sweet cakes called *kolache*. Those were the fine days.

"In the winter when it was not too cold we built forts of snow. Then we drew lots, for some of us had to be the Germans or the Austrians, which we did not like to be. We had fights then, and the boys who must be the Germans or the Austrians mostly let themselves be beaten. Or we slid down hills on pieces of boards, which were our sleds, or on a shovel, or just some days on ourselves."

Jan laughed then, his laugh resounding suddenly in the big, quiet room, with its living and its dead together. He waited for Daniel Perkins and John Marston to smile back at him. Then he said:

"Now I will tell you how I once went to Praha, or Prague, as you say. John knows about Prague, but, Dan, you do not, so listen well while I tell you this good story. And, John, you listen well, too, because you must have forgotten a great deal since I told you the last time. Well, when I was at your age, our house was from Prague twenty miles away, and I had never seen that great city. We had a neighbour, richer than us. His name was Jonas —Jonas Jurka was his name—and he was, what you say, close with his money. Well, one fine summer day, very early, before the sun was up, he come to our house and he said, 'One of my sons is sick, and the other son, he is to be married tomorrow and not want to work. Will you and Anton,' he says, 'go with me to Prague with a great load of wood for the market, to help me?' he says. I ran to Anton's house. What joy we felt to see the city of Prague which we had not before seen, ever!

"Well, we began to go, Jonas Jurka, Anton, and me, with the cart piled up with wood. Jonas had two oxen that drew the cart. They were great red oxen, and they were named for kings of Bohemia in the old days, one Krok and the other Ottokar. Now Ottokar was a good, gentle ox, but Krok was a bad one. Jonas said the devil lived right inside that ox's skin. He bellowed and lashed his tail, and he would not draw his half of the heavy load. Sometimes he stopped and would not go on at all. We had to prick him with the goad and crack a whip above him.

" 'I mean to sell that Krok in the market of Prague,' Jonas said to Anton and me. 'I will not tell of his bad tricks, and I will get much money for him, for he looks well and is strong. I will save my money, for I tell you, boys, one good ox is better for a poor man than one good ox and one bad one together.' That was what Jonas said. So we went on to Prague.

"Long before we got there we could see many tall

towers shining in the sun and high steeples of the many churches. It was a fine sight to me and Anton. We grew much excited. Our breaths came quick, our eyes shone. When we got nearer, we heard bells, hundreds of bells. It was a feast day, and all the bells in all the steeples and all the towers were ringing, and all the hundreds of people were going to Mass and then to the market. We had never seen so many people, Anton and me, and all in their bright clothes for the feast day.

"What a place the market in Prague was! Flowers and vegetables and geese dead and geese alive, and ducks and chickens in pens, and people buying and people selling, and all calling and talking at once. We boys helped Jonas unload the wood and tie it in bundles to sell. It was good wood and it sold fine. When Jonas had put the money in his leather bag, he said to Anton and me,

" 'Now I will sell that Krok, if the devil will for a time leave his skin.'

"So he took Krok away from the cart and put a paper on his back that said in the Czech language, 'A good, kind ox to sell cheap.' And he gave Krok hay to eat so he would be still and good. Well, first came up a peasant woman to look at him. She walked around him and felt his back with her hands. And what did that Krok do but lift his tail quick and splash her with his dirt!"

Jan laughed again here and waited for Dan and John Marston to laugh over the plight of the peasant woman and the vulgar trick that Krok had played upon her. From his corner by the fire Caleb Perkins suddenly added his laugh, which lent Jan courage.

"My! Was that peasant woman mad? She was very

mad. Her face grew redder and redder as the people laughed at her.

" 'See how your stupid ox has spoiled my holiday dress!' she cried. 'You will pay me silver for his dirt,' she cried. And Jonas had to give her a piece of silver to make her stop her screams.

"Then up came a farmer with his little boy. Jonas knew that farmer, that he was rich, and he began to tell him how strong Krok was and what a gentle ox. I do believe that that Krok heard those lies of Jonas, for all at once he swung his horns about quick and hit the farmer's boy in the head and tore his face so that the blood came out. Then the farmer yelled at Jonas.

" 'You foolish Honza!' he cried, which in Czech means, *you stupid man,* 'you lying mule, you gabbling gander! You will pay me well for the hole your ox has made in my boy's face!' And Jonas had to pay more silver from his bag.

"Then no one would buy Krok, for all had seen that the devil was under his skin, and by and by, when the sun was low, we began to go home once more. What an angry man was Jonas! He swore bad words at Anton and me. He said we had brought ill luck to him, but we sat on the back of the empty cart and watched all the towers and steeples of Prague fade away out of sight, and did not mind his curses and bad words.

"Jonas was so angry that he struck Krok more and more with his leather whip and pricked him with the goad, and suddenly Krok made a great jump and sprang away from Ottokar and the pole that held them together.

Then he ran leaping and bellowing across the road and through a field of grain. Another angry man was the farmer who owned that grain. He came running from his barn and he said to Jonas,

" 'You will pay me for my grain that your ox has trampled down, or I will go to the law!' So Jonas had to pay him, too. And by now Anton and me, we had to hold our faces tight not to laugh.

"By now it was night, and the moon was coming up in the sky, big and round. The farmer, who was a kind man after he had Jonas' money in his own leather bag, let us leave Ottokar and the cart in his farmyard while we went to hunt for Krok. He said, too, that he would mend Jonas' cart for him. There was a little river below the farmer's house and across another field, and by that river there were gypsies. There are many gypsies in my country, more than here. Well, down we went to the gypsies. They were sitting around a big fire with an iron pot on it full of something that smelled very good to Anton and me, for Jonas gave no money to us in Prague, and we had had only some bread in our pockets since the early morning. Jonas swore at the gypsies, who only laughed and said things in their language which we could not know.

"By and by Jonas found Krok hid in some trees by the river, but the gypsies would not let him go. They all made a circle around Jonas and laughed at him until his face was red with madness. Then one of them began to speak in Czech, which he could speak all along only he wanted to make Jonas more mad.

" 'The ox,' he said, 'ran away from you and came to

us. So he is ours. Is not findings keepings?' he said, just as you boys say when you find things. 'What comes to us is ours, is it not right, brothers?' And all the gypsies laughed loud and screamed that it was right. 'You will give us coins for our ox,' the gypsy man said, 'or we will keep him. We are more than you, and we keep this good ox.' Then Jonas had to give them coins all around their circle, and they danced about him and laughed in his red face.

"But one of the gypsy women was good to Anton and me. She gave us each a big tin cup full of that stew in the iron pot while the men laughed and danced around Jonas. All my life, Daniel and John, I have remembered what was in that tin cup, meat and thick gravy and bits of corn and peppers and mushrooms like what we used to gather in the woods after a rain and dry to cook in the winter. It was hot and sweet, and it made a warm feeling in our stomachs. All my life I have remembered how good was that tin cup of gypsy food.

"The sun was rising again when we got back home with Krok and Ottokar. A very, very angry man was that Jonas. He would not speak a word to our fathers and mothers and all the others when they ran down the road to give us good-day. And he would not give so much as the smallest coin of silver to Anton and me. But our fathers and mothers, they laughed when Anton and I told them about that wicked Krok. And my father, he said, 'Well, sometimes the devil, he does good and right things.' I always remember my father saying that. And that, Daniel and John, was the way I saw the great city of Prague."

17

John Marston and Daniel Perkins must have fallen asleep when Jan had finished his stories, or perhaps even before. In the morning they were on the rug by the dying fire with pillows beneath their heads and blankets over them. It was full daylight when they awoke. Jan and Daniel's father were not in the cabin. Neither was Philip Marston's body, as John discovered when he had at last summoned courage enough to look toward his father's bed in the far corner of the room.

When he and Dan had hurried out-of-doors to get away from the awful silence of the room, they found that another day was soft and warm, although the clouds were closer to the earth, the sun was less bright, and there were longer, higher swells breaking on the rocks. Once out of the dark path through the spruces and into the pasture, they saw Jan standing on the high pasture land just before it gave place to the stretch of headland above the sea.

John Marston always remembered Jan standing there beneath the milk-white sky with the brown land stretching before him and the sea beyond. He was leaning upon his spade before a mound of brown earth. His coat and cap lay on the ground, and as he stood there in the wide, bare space with his broad shoulders and his short, stocky body, he gave the impression of strength as well as of loneliness. There was something of the very nature of the land itself in his still figure there beneath the whitening sky. It was some minutes before he saw the boys watching him from the slope below. When he did, he left his spade standing in the pile of soil and came down the hill toward them.

There was a little knot of men gathered farther down the land eastward. They had come through the woods from Heron Cove before dawn, bringing lengths of new lumber with them. Caleb Perkins had made Philip Marston's coffin from the fresh boards, while Jan with others of the men to help him had dug his grave in the hours after dawn.

The men went back to breakfast with them. There were six of them, tall, lanky men, fishermen and farmers with brown faces and hard-worked hands. They helped out things immeasurably although they said almost nothing. Two of them helped Jan with the bread and eggs and coffee, and the others, under Caleb Perkins' direction, got things in readiness for them to leave. Then when breakfast was ready, they all sat around the big table and ate so hungrily that it was easier for Daniel and John to eat their breakfast, too.

After breakfast was over, two of the men took Dan with them across the beach to the anchorage to help in getting things aboard the ketch. The others followed Caleb Perkins from the cabin, leaving Jan and John Marston together. Then Jan went to John's bed and took from the shelf above it his small black prayer-book which he used at school. John standing by the fire, stared at him, uncomprehending, until Jan said in his slow, quiet way:

"It is not easy for you, what I shall say, but it has come, and we must do as your father said. We must not leave him here without a prayer to God. I cannot read the words straight and right, and there is no man here who knows this book. You must read them yourself. You will be glad some day that you did. My own book says it is, what you say, Advent Sunday, the time of the Lord's coming to this earth. I found the place last night in your book, and the other place where it says *The Burial of the Dead.* I know you cannot read much, but you must read a little. I have marked the places, here and here." He gave the book to the boy, who stood white and still beside the dead fire, and remained beside him for a moment without speaking. Then he said, "We are sad now, but we shall not always be sad. Some day we shall be joyful on this land that your father wanted we should have."

His words sounded in the still room like the words of ancient prophecy. Then they went out together toward Philip Marston's grave.

Caleb Perkins and the other men were waiting for them there. Everything was ready. The youngest of the men came forward a little to meet them, undoing a parcel of brown paper as he did so. There were some scarlet geraniums in the parcel, and he held them out awkwardly to young John Marston.

"My wife sent these," he said. "They ain't much, but she hadn't no others, and she wanted there should be a flower or two."

Then they all stood together by the open grave, and John Marston read the words that Jan had marked in his book.

It was the collect for Advent Sunday. In all the years afterward that they read it in the chapel at Windswept, which they were later to build, its prayer for grace to cast away the works of darkness and to put upon us all the armour of light now in the time of this mortal life, they were to see that little group of men standing about John Marston on that vast brown summit of land beneath that whitening sky. They were to hear his voice sounding clear and strong in the still air, as Jan told them it had sounded, reading the words about the quick and the dead, about rising to the life immortal, about corruption and incorruption, the Resurrection and the Life.

The sun came suddenly out, bright and warm, as John Marston finished his reading. It made the red flowers, which Jan had held in his hand, glow above the brown earth. It made the wide waste of sea before them blue; it sharpened the islands and purpled the distant Mt. Desert hills.

Then they all repeated together the Lord's Prayer, which Caleb Perkins started, and when they had finished, Jan drew John Marston away, down the pasture slope toward the path through the trees to the cabin. Just before they entered the path, they looked suddenly back and saw that the men were still standing there with their hats in their hands. The sun made their shadows long across the high brown land, stretching still and bright upon it. They both always remembered how the men waited quietly there until they should be out of sight.

18

Before noon they were ready to go. The men had gone back through the woods to Heron Cove and on to the

village. Caleb Perkins and Daniel were to sail with them
down the coast to the harbour where *The Sea Hawk*
would be hauled up for the winter.

A wind had risen, blowing from the southwest, increasing steadily minute by minute. It was just the wind they
wanted, Caleb Perkins said. Before it swung into the
northeast, as it was bound to do before nightfall, they
would be secure and safe in the harbour eastward.

Once they had left the anchorage bay and rounded the
headland, they caught the full force of the wind. The
ketch lay over, her sails filled, and she cut the water with
a fine speed. Dan held the sheet with Jan beside him to
tell him when to let out, when to draw in. Caleb Perkins leaned against the main hatchway, smoking his pipe,
scanning the weather. John Marston went forward and
stretched himself along the prow above the sea.

The wind blew steadily on. The sea was making up
before it. Already the surf was strong and high against
the shore and the swells white long before they cut them.
Sailing and sorrow, John Marston thought, do not go
together. It was for all the world as though they were
upon a pleasure trip rather than upon a sad return.

He would not look back upon the headland, he
thought, as he lay with his face buried in his arms. He
would not look at anything at all until they had rounded
the point, passed the great light, and were swinging
north toward other land. He would not look, he thought,
because, if he did, he might be tempted to return to this
place where life had ended for him. And that, he thought,
he could never do in spite of his father's wish and Jan's
stupid prophecy. Then the rise and fall of the ketch as

she took the waves, the wind in the sail above him, the distant roar of the surf against the rocks, merged into a soothing monotone of half-perceived sound, and he fell asleep.

When he awoke, they were nearing the point and the great light. The sun had gone, and the sea was steel gray beneath him. Soon they would swing northward, and Windswept would be gone from sight.

He must look back, he thought. It would not be right to leave his father there without looking back. It would be as though a black curtain had been let fall between yesterday and today, between the morning and the afternoon, between things that had gone and things which were to come. He could not return to school knowing that he had not looked back. If he could make himself look back, only once, for the most fleeting of moments, it might summon his father again from that dark, lonely summit of land where he lay.

He rose and stood in the prow, looking first at the great rocks of the point over which the gulls screamed and circled, then back along the high shore, past the cove where the surf crashed, past the entrance to the woods, up and up along the miles of dark, empty land, climbing higher and higher, until at last his eyes saw the promontory, circling back above the sea.

THE POSSESSION

1881–1883

1

IT WAS ALWAYS a matter of grateful wonder to young Philip Marston and Ann and later to Roderick and even to Julie that the house at Windswept was ever built; that Jan and John Marston and Caleb Perkins ever triumphed over the bulwarks of opposition in New York and in the old Marston home in Gardiner above the Kennebec. Whenever they returned to it in later years, from school or college, from holidays or sojourns or visits elsewhere, they were always to feel surprise by the simple fact that it was there after its narrow escape from nothingness. Jan, whose life was to span three generations of Marstons like some long, strong bridge upheld by columns across a wide river, never allowed them to forget the perils which had beset its building. And together with this tenacious hold upon its past was the almost incredible sight of the house itself after miles of untenanted wilderness or across as many miles of open water. It held, moreover, that mystery which the completely familiar often holds and which the strange and unfamiliar often lacks. It was like that wise saying of one of the ancients: it was true because it was impossible.

Philip Marston, with the foresight characteristic of him, had, two years before his death, named as guardian of his son until he should come of age his partner, James

Lassiter. He had done this in the knowledge that James Lassiter was honest, sound, and conservative where business was concerned and one of the kindest of men. He had done it also, of course, with the tacit reservation that James Lassiter's services would never be required anyway. Persons abounding in the vitality of Philip Marston often possess such forethought; not liking things at loose ends, they are forever tidying up their personal affairs; yet at the same time death to them is as remote a possibility as famine, pestilence, or a World War. Philip Marston's act had been performed partly out of courtesy to his partner, whom he liked and admired, partly as a half-humorous sop to Chance, partly because he was the sort of man who likes to feel that he has not in the least particular neglected his responsibilities.

There was doubtless also another reason lurking in the background of his mind which out of a decent loyalty to his family he did not bring boldly out into the light of day. His mother, Ellen Marston, then seventy-five years old, still lived in the family home above the Kennebec. She was a self-possessed old woman with clean-cut, well-entrenched ideas. She made quick, impregnable decisions and, although most of them had been made in the past and never altered, Philip Marston had been long aware that she was capable, whenever necessary, of making new ones. She disapproved of New York, which she had never seen, despised and feared all foreigners, and contended that the only reputable places in Maine for one to live in were Portland and the historic Anglican towns on the Kennebec. Bangor was an upstart place of crude lumberjacks and grasping speculators. East and north of it there was nothing whatsoever. While other women of more adventuresome, if less pretentious, families had sailed with their husbands to the far corners of the earth, she had with better sense and far better decorum remained at home. She was tenacious of her son, whom she had never known, and jealous of the affection of her only grandson, which she had, as a matter of fact, never possessed. Her grief over Philip Marston's death had been modified, even inundated, by resentment that she had not been informed of it before he was buried, and by an outraged sense of propriety in that he had been laid away with no rites of the Church in some wild piece of country of which no one whom she knew had even so much as heard.

Beyond the necessity of a brief visit twice a year to his grandmother, to which his father always lent the support of his uneasy presence, John Marston was for the greater part of his time quite oblivious to her existence. The visits to Gardiner were occasions which had to be endured. Once weathered, they were hurriedly and gratefully forgotten until a distasteful foreboding warned him that another was imminent. He hated the big house, which his grandfather had built of bricks painted gray and topped by a mansard roof. It had a porte-cochere, and a coach-house in the rear and, standing upon a hill above the river, it was as much out of place in its present surroundings as was Ellen Marston herself. He hated the formal, dutiful greetings once they had been driven from the station, the interminable breakfasts in the dark dining-room with his grandmother imperturbable behind the coffee-urn, the sense that each of them (he and his father counting as one) suspected the other, the quick, pointed questions of his grandmother and his father's evasive replies, the veiled references to his mother, and the sadness which seemed to rest always on his father's face for all the days that they were there.

They never stayed any longer than they had to, although getting away was almost more costly than lingering. The announcement that they must go always seemed to come as a distasteful surprise in spite of the fact that his father had carefully and well in advance stated the exact hour of their departure. His grandmother never quite brought herself to say that they could easily stay longer if they really wanted to; but the truth of it was so obvious to everyone that he sometimes thought it would be a relief if it were brought out into the open, expressed in her clear, cold voice, and candidly admitted by the three of them.

There was rarely anything to do in Gardiner except to endure whatever happened and to feel like someone else in one's own clothes. Whenever he read, his grandmother thought he read too much; whenever he sat without reading, she thought he was wasting his time; whenever he sat with his book while his father and grandmother were talking, she thought he was impolite. She thought and said that his manners were not what she had always insisted his father's should be when he was a boy.

Whenever he could manage it, he slipped down the dark back stairs, through the kitchen, out the back door, and down the hill behind the house for a walk along the Kennebec. He loved the river flowing wide and deep between high slopes on its way to Merry Meeting Bay where it would join the Androscoggin at the sea. He liked the fresh smell of newly cut lumber, the rasping, peremptory slash of the saws, the wet brown lengths of the logs, tethered in gigantic geometrical patterns in the water, awaiting the mills or the decks of broad-beamed schooners, the golden pyramids of pulp-wood catching the sunlight. He liked to watch the agile balancing of the men who walked the logs, turning them with their long cant-hooks, calling to one another in their quick French *patois*. They often wore red coats or shirts and made splashes of vivid, moving colour against the brown or green of the hills and the deep blue of the river.

Sarah, his grandmother's elderly maid, who had been with her for forty querulous years and whose face was always frightened and enduring, connived with him in these secret escapes, signaling to him from parlour or hall when the time seemed ripe for action, and procuring for him from the patient cook some doughnuts or hermits in a white paper bag striped with green, purple, and red lines. He and Sarah had a silent understanding between them, evident and oddly comforting when she brought his clean clothes to his room or played Chessindia or dominoes with him sometimes in the evening.

Sometimes his walks were open and above board, suggested by his father and reluctantly assented to by his grandmother. But on these occasions she warned him against loitering about the mill and lumber yards. No one knew, she said, what he might pick up, in disease or worse, from the awful people who worked in Gardiner nowadays.

"It takes every ounce of strength and faith I have,"

she was always saying, "not to worry myself to death over the future of this town. And the worst of it is that no one seems to *do* anything about it."

On their last visit, when she said this at breakfast, his father had answered her to his own peril.

"I'm wondering what there is to do about it," he said quietly. "The country's changing, New England like the rest, and we may as well get used to it. What would *you* do?"

His grandmother became so agitated then that she spilled some coffee on her immaculate white fichu which she wore over her lavender morning dress.

"Do?" she cried. "Do? I'd send all these ignorant French and Irish back where they came from. We don't have to have them here, do we? Buying our decent old homes and ruining our schools? Setting up their horrid churches on our old streets? Why doesn't the President of this country and the Congress say they can't come?"

"I'm afraid it's not so simple as that," said Philip Marston.

Together with the coffee stain (for Ellen Marston was always immaculate) and her son's treachery, she completely lost her decorum.

"It's perfectly simple," she said, her words icy and bitter, while young John Marston kept his eyes on his plate. "It's just that men like you condone it all. And, what's more, you encourage it, having immigrants in your house to corrupt your son's mind, taking them in your boat in place of decent people, and setting them up in business as though they belonged here. You never tell *me* what you do, but—I have ways of finding out. I know far more than you think I know about the way you and John live in New York, and the things you let him do."

"I don't think we'd better talk any more about it," Philip Marston said. "John and I don't see it from your point of view."

The inclusion of him in his father's thoughts, proud as it made John Marston, was a fatal step. It had resulted in the most embarrassing day he had ever remembered and in the indefinite postponement of other visits to Gardiner.

But now with Philip Marston dead and his own world in confusion, John Marston knew that his grandmother was a power to be reckoned with. The house in Gardiner with its high, clean rooms filled with old, dark furniture, with family portraits, with glass and silver and china from across the seas, and with the echoes of bitter words, usually unspoken but always lingering there, now emerged from the obscurity where he had always before managed to consign it and loomed darkly upon the horizon of his mind. He knew too well his grandmother's tenacious, ugly sense of duty. Now it could not fail to be directed toward him as the only surviving member of her immediate family. Fears of holidays in Gardiner became terrors so real and depleting that James Lassiter wrote to Ellen Marston at Christmas time refusing to countenance the boy's departure from New York.

Jan stayed with him on West 28th Street through December. They built ship models in the basement workroom in the evenings or sometimes went for long walks. Anton joined them now and then. Awkward and fumbling in his speech and ways as Anton was, he was sorry for John Marston and did what he could. The puzzled housekeeper at last grew used to Jan's presence at the table in the big dining-room (upon which John had insisted in spite of Jan's own protests) and to his sleeping in the room next John's. He was clean and quiet, bathing and changing his clothes each night as he came from work. He said little, but he was there, and it always seemed, the housekeeper thought, as though there were more there than just Jan's stocky frame and slow, kind ways.

On the evenings that James Lassiter came to talk with his ward about the future, Jan was there. He rarely took part in the uneasy conversations, but in an odd way James Lassiter knew that he was behind and through whatever answers he himself managed to draw forth from John. He wanted to dislike Jan but somehow could not manage to do it. Failing in dislike, he took refuge in suspicion, but that also vanished before Jan's direct gaze and John Marston's confidence. Moreover, he had the memory constantly assailing him of Jan's service for Marston, Cobb, and Lassiter during the two years following his arrival in New York. He had often said to Philip Marston during those years that his partner's mad insistence upon employing Jan and Anton had more than justified itself. They had both given good measure, but Jan in particular had proved to be the Gibraltar among all the errand boys.

After he had reiterated his reasons for disapproving of the house at Windswept, the distance, the loneliness of the place, the impossibility of a young boy's knowing how to manage a home of his own, the cost of the building and the upkeep and the wisdom of investing money securely against possible hard times, the manifest social advantages to be gained by John Marston's spending his summers with other boys, his own, for example, Jan had only one reply to make. It was vastly irritating to James Lassiter that it was always made in the same words.

"John's father wanted the house should be built," said Jan. "He is dead. We were there when he died, and we heard what he said."

It was Ellen Marston's frequent letters to James Lassiter which began slowly to over-rule his own well-founded objections to the house at Windswept. They came on Wednesdays and Saturdays throughout December, directed to his firm until she had been informed of the unwelcome news of his guardianship, thereafter addressed personally to him. Ann Marston has these letters today and often reads them. One, dated December 12th, 1880 and written in a strong, bold hand on black-edged, heavily lined paper, speaks eloquently of her great-grandmother:

James Lassiter, Esq.,
   New York.
Dear Sir:
   Yours of the 10th instant has been received and its contents most carefully noted. I am relieved to know that my grandson is bearing manfully the tragic death of his father, which has been a blow not easily sustained. Since I have not received any word from him since his father's death, will you kindly direct him to write to his grandmother?
   The information that you were two years ago appointed as the boy's guardian was naturally received by me with some

measure of surprise. I had not until then realized so acutely
my son's tacit admission of my age and incompetence. Surely
he must have been aware of my deep interest in my one
grandson and my sense of duty and responsibility toward
him.

My son has never entrusted me with any information as to
his financial condition. I regret to say that I know less than
nothing of his affairs. I assume that he was a man of com-
petence, if not of wealth. Upon his coming of age he received
from his father, my late husband, substantial securities, which
I trust have not been allowed to diminish in value. I should
appreciate at your earliest convenience information relative
to these matters.

Had I not been stricken with illness, which has without
doubt been accentuated and increased by the shock of this
sad event, I should, of course, have come immediately to
New York and remained over the Christmas season, which
will inevitably be a season of grief and unmitigated sorrow.
You will, of course, see that my grandson comes to me here
in response to my invitation already forwarded to him but
not as yet acknowledged.

I shall thank you to tell me also at an early date of the
household arrangements now in force at my son's home. I
trust that some elderly woman has been caring for my grandson in my own unavoidable absence from him, and especially
that he has not been left to the care of servants, of whom at
one time my son kept a strange collection.

Although you are evidently to be in charge of John's material necessities, I am sure you will not esteem it in any way
an intrusion if I take upon myself his moral and spiritual
welfare and watch over his education. I am writing to the
Reverend Dr. Coit at St. Paul's School as to these urgent
matters. I assume that the boy, if he has not already been
sent, will be despatched at once to school, even though the
term draws to a close. Nothing can so assuage grief as the

faithful performance of one's regular duties. I am sure you are aware of this fact.

I assume also that my son's house will be sold as soon as possible. My grandson will, of course, make his home with me in the town which his forefathers founded and in which so many of his family have grown up.

There is one last matter upon which I wish to consult you. Can there be any possible reason for respecting my son's odd request, made at a time when he was surely not himself, that he should be buried in a distant and isolated tract of land, the purchase of which, as now so tragically proved, was the whim of a moment and a sad mistake? The members of his family, both men and women, have for generations been buried in the churchyard here next the church which they themselves built. I cannot endure the thought that he should not rest among them.

May I hear from you, my dear Sir, as promptly as may be concerning these matters so close to my mind and heart?

Yours very truly,
Ellen Marston

P.S. John will go from Concord to Boston on the 21st of December, thence on the 5:00 P.M. train to Gardiner. He will be met at the station. I have so informed him, but I fear that he is notoriously careless of details. I shall also so inform his school.

A series of letters such as this, together with the total lack of headway made in numberless advisory conversations with his ward, was slowly winning James Lassiter over to the absurd notion of retaining Windswept and building a house there. His tardy decision was finally clinched by a visit from Ellen Marston, who suddenly announced her intention of coming to New York early in January before her grandson's prolonged holidays should be at an end. A veiled allusion in one of James Lassiter's letters to Philip Marston's purchase of the land in Maine and to his wish concerning it had thrown her into indescribable confusion, and resulted in her immediate determination to straighten out minds in New York more confused than her own and to put at once to rout any such intolerable notion. Upon her visit to New York hung the fate of Windswept; from her subsequent defeat came its possession.

Ann and the second Philip Marston never passed through Gardiner on the train on their way to and from Windswept without gazing upon the house high upon the hill above the railway and wondering by just which window their great-grandmother had sat while she read James Lassiter's letter and sprang to her momentous decision. They could see her at any one of them, quivering with angry fear, which she mistook for righteous indignation. And even now when Ann Marston drives through the high streets of Gardiner, going out of her way only to pass the old house, she plays the same game with her fancy. Now the house is cut into flats for its new occupants, the French Canadians and Irish who work in the mills and factories. Are these present occupants, she wonders, ever assailed by baffling, half-fledged notions of vehement ghosts, which haunt the broad staircase, the white wainscotings? Are they ever aware of shadowy hatreds and suspicions as, returning from work at night, they pass beneath the porte-cochere to the wide front entrance, cluttered now by the debris of a dozen ill-assorted children? Nor has she ever slipped down the North River on some ship bound for Europe without gazing upon the

old building, which once housed Marston, Cobb, and
Lassiter, and which still holds the room where Windswept
grew from a dream and a desire to a reality. When she
has seen it crowded there, squat and sooty and undistin-
guished among its cleaner, towering neighbours, she
becomes once more a spectator and listener at that ex-
traordinary conference which took place in James
Lassiter's office on January 4th, 1881.

2

When Ellen Marston arrived at the office, accompanied
by old Sarah, who was laden with wraps and frightened
out of her wits, she found in addition to her grandson
and James Lassiter a tall, long-legged man in ill-fitting
clothes, who carried in one big hand some rolls of paper,
and a short, almost square younger man, who stood by
the window drumming with short, almost square fingers
upon the sash. After she had greeted James Lassiter and
her grandson, stared at Jan, and assigned a far corner of
the room to Sarah, the man in the uncouth clothes was
introduced to her as Caleb Perkins.

"And who is he?" she asked in quick suspicion.

"He was engaged by Philip to build the house in
Maine," explained James Lassiter. "I sent for him."

"So matters have gone this far," she said, "without
consulting me. There is one Marston house already in
Maine, my own. There is no need of another. You are
only a child, John. What, may I ask, will you do with a
house?"

"I shall not always be young," said John Marston. "And I shall live in my house in the summer as my father planned."

"And who, may I ask, will live with you in such a god-forsaken place as that?"

"I shall," said Jan.

It was snowing outside in fine, drifting flakes, and Jan spoke from the window where he had been standing by himself, looking out upon the gray river with its ferry-boats and barges, tugs and steamships.

Ellen Marston stared again at him as he turned to look at her.

"You will live with him?" she asked. "And who might you be?"

"He is Jan Pisek," explained James Lassiter again. "He was a friend of Philip's."

"Pisek?" she said with distaste in every letter. "What kind of a name is that? I have never heard such a name in all my life."

"It is a Bohemian name," answered Jan. He came forward then and stood nearer her, his wide, gray eyes gazing calmly upon her distraught, angry face. "I come from Bohemia. Mr. Marston was always my friend. Now I am a friend to his son."

Ellen Marston turned from Jan's quiet gaze to James Lassiter, tapping her foot impatiently against the red carpet as she did so. Incredulity had for the moment swept the anger from her face.

"It's all a monstrous notion," she said. "It must be stopped at once. My grandson living in the wilderness of eastern Maine, miles from civilization, with a foreigner whom no one knows. It's absurd and outrageous. It's . . ."

"We all know Jan very well, Mrs. Marston," interrupted James Lassiter. "He was, as he says, a friend of your son. He has been in our employment here, and he has sailed with Philip for years. He is quite capable of looking after John. He has known him since John was five. In three or four years your grandson will need no looking after. John is far more dependable, I think, than you imagine."

"I have never seen the least sign of it," Ellen Marston said. "Should I not know him better than you or this Pisek man here?"

Her voice rose louder in the big, dim room which the snow was darkening. Jan took a match from his pocket, struck it, and lighted the gas jets on the wall.

"I'm frankly surprised at you, Mr. Lassiter," went on Ellen Marston, "for so much as considering such a mad scheme. I had thought you a man of more sense. I am the boy's grandmother and the only living member of his family. In that position I have rights. As his grandmother I forbid any further tampering with such nonsense."

"I'm afraid you can't forbid it," said James Lassiter. "It was your son's expressed wish that the house should be built. He bought the land and paid for it with this end in view. I have a letter from him to this effect written but a few days before his death. Moreover, we have his wish on the authority of three persons who heard him make it. If you do not choose to believe your grandson and Jan here, Mr. Perkins will tell you. He has brought

Philip's own plans which he made himself. He will be glad to show them to you. I asked him to come down to New York for that very purpose."

Ellen Marston stared at the big man sitting uncomfortably in the chair opposite her own, and as she stared, comprehension slowly took shape in her mind. But there were limits even to her gifts of speech.

"Am I right in thinking," she began, and then stopped, relying upon her face to complete what she dared not ask.

"You are quite right, ma'am," said Caleb Perkins quietly. "My son killed your son. He and I shall have that to remember all our lives. It is not an easy thing to have in one's mind. I am sorry. We both liked Mr. Marston. He was the best man we ever knew."

"Sorrow can't cure what's over and done with," said Ellen Marston. "But we don't have to add one tragedy to another, do we? And if a house has to be built, which it hasn't, why build it in a wilderness miles from decent people? It's that god-forsaken place that killed my son. I tell you once and for all that I won't countenance it!"

"If you saw the place, ma'am, I don't think you'd feel the way you do," said Caleb Perkins. "I don't know a finer place for a young man to live in."

"It's a beautiful place," said Jan from the window.

"Beauty!" cried Ellen Marston, her anger mounting. "What do *you* know about beauty? There's beauty enough in a thousand places. This country's full of beauty—there's more beauty than common sense, there's the pity!"

She turned to her grandson who sat next her.

"John," she said, "don't you have any respect for your

grandmother and what she thinks? I'm in charge of you now whatever the law may say. I'm your moral guardian. You're only a child. You can't disobey me like this. If the rest of these people haven't any sense, you and I have to have it for them. Don't you have any respect for me at all, I say, and for what I think is best for you?"

Jan always admired John Marston for what he said then, and if James Lassiter still harboured any misgivings concerning Philip Marston's wish, they vanished at that moment. He rose from his chair, a tall, thin boy in his black clothes, and stood before his grandmother.

"I have more respect for my father," he said. "He is buried there. I want to do as he wished. I should think you would want to do as he wished, too. Do you want to leave him there with us away off here? Before long I shall be a man with rights of my own. If we do not build the house now, we shall build it then."

His grandmother for the moment set aside the quiet certainty of his last words and leapt to answer his question.

"I have not the slightest intention of leaving him there," she said. "I have already taken steps to bring his body home to Gardiner. My lawyers will see to that. If he had to be buried like a heathen, he does not have to remain so."

"He was not buried like a heathen," put in Jan from his place by the window. "He was buried as he wanted to be buried. We know, we buried him."

"Will you please," cried Ellen Marston, "have the goodness to speak when you are spoken to? My lawyers will write you, Mr. Lassiter, and I beg you to pay decent attention to them. A mother surely has some rights over the body of her only son."

"But not the rights of a man himself," said James Lassiter. "I have the right to say where I wish to be buried, and so have you, and so had Philip. I think I must tell you once and for all that I shall oppose any attempt to remove his body from the place where he wished it to be."

"He was not himself, I tell you," she cried. "I knew my own son, didn't I? He would never have asked for such an insane thing had he known what he was doing."

"He knew quite well what he was doing," said John Marston then. He was standing by his grandmother's chair as he spoke, and he seemed to grow taller with every word. "And I'm sorry to hurt you, grandmother, but I don't think you knew him very well, even if he was your son. I think Jan and I knew him better than you did."

Ellen Marston grew red in the face then, distracted and ruffled like some angry goose, Jan said afterward, which had been driven against its will into a pen and kept there.

"I did not come here," she cried, "to be insulted by an upstart boy, who knows nothing of what is good for him. Or to be shoved aside by men half my age. And what about money, Mr. Lassiter? What about throwing away thousands which ought to be saved against this boy's future?"

"There is sufficient money," said James Lassiter. "You forget, I think, that that is my province."

"And you forget, I think, that I have asked you in every letter to inform me of my son's financial status. Why should I be kept in ignorance?"

"I shall be glad to inform you when things are in order," said James Lassiter. "At present you may rest secure that we are not jeopardizing John's future by building the house. Philip was not a rich man, as the saying goes, but he was well-to-do. There is not the slightest occasion for you to be anxious about money."

There was silence then in the big room. No one looked at Ellen Marston. Jan gazed out of the window at the snow, which was blotting out the shipping on the river. James Lassiter fumbled with the heavy silver paper-knife on his desk. Caleb Perkins sat awkwardly in his chair, his big hands folded about his rolls of paper. John Marston tried to keep his long legs from shaking and dug his hands into his jacket pockets for the same purpose. From her corner old Sarah snapped and unsnapped the hasp of her mistress's black bag until she was halted in her nervousness by an irritated glance from its owner.

At last Ellen Marston broke the silence, a new note in her voice.

"You are not yourself, John," she said. "One can't expect you to be yourself, I suppose, after all you've been through. You will come to Gardiner before you go back to school where we can talk things over quietly by ourselves. You must know that I want only what is best for you."

"I shall not come to Gardiner," announced John Marston. There was no defiance in his voice, only quiet, even courteous, decision.

His grandmother rose to her feet then and stared from one to another of them, astonishment battling with anger.

"Is insubordination then to be added to insult?" she cried. "Do you condone this, sir?"

James Lassiter rose to his feet also.

"I should not have condoned it an hour ago," he said,

"but I think now that I shall. I have this boy's happiness at stake. He will not be happy in Gardiner, and he has a home of his own in which to stay as well as my own in which he is always welcome."

Something in his quiet voice menaced the future as well as the present.

"A home of his own?" said Ellen Marston. "Do I understand, then, that you are mad enough to keep the New York house for a fourteen-year-old boy to lose himself in? He will get over this nonsense in short order unless he is aided and abetted in it, as I have every reason to suspect. As I wrote you, his holidays will be spent with me."

"There are no holidays for some time," said James Lassiter. "When they are near, it will be time enough to decide about them. As for the house here, we shall keep it for the present. I assure you John will be well looked after." He drew his watch from his pocket and looked at it. "There is a train for Boston leaving in an hour. I shall be glad to call a carriage for you. It's quite a drive to the station at this time of day, and the storm seems to be getting rather severe."

John Marston never quite remembered how his grandmother left James Lassiter's office. He did remember that Sarah smiled at him timidly as she turned to follow her mistress. He remembered suddenly, too, how kind she had been to him during his visits to Gardiner, and it was more for her sake than for his grandmother's that he opened the door for them to pass into the hall.

Jan said that Ellen Marston gathered her wraps about her and stalked from the room without so much as a word of farewell to any of them. She was so angry, he said, that

he looked to see the fire in her eyes come out of her nose
in flames like the fire-breathing bulls in the fable.

3

True to his resolve, John Marston did not go to Gardiner for the remainder of that school year. When he next
saw his grandmother, his visit was made under circumstances vastly different from those in New York. His relation with her during the winter and spring of 1881 was
confined on his part to infrequent, stilted notes telling of
his progress at school, and on hers to long and frequent
letters of irritating precept and example. Windswept was
never mentioned between them. Ellen Marston discharged
her duty and pampered her injured vanity by writing
often and at length to the Reverend Henry Augustus
Coit, Headmaster of St. Paul's, confiding to him her many
apprehensions concerning her grandson, whom, verbally
at least, she entrusted, even consigned, to the good doctor's vigilance and wisdom.

It was to the credit of the zealous, serious headmaster
that he did not attach too much importance to the anxieties and fears, even suspicions, which Ellen Marston at
regular intervals poured into his patient ears. As a matter of fact, he was at a loss to understand the old lady's
fears concerning the quiet, rather studious boy who had
been placed under his care. He had known Philip Marston, who at seventeen had spent a year at St. Paul's while
the school was in its earliest beginnings, a mere handful
of boys added to Dr. Coit's newly established home in
Concord in order to make a school. The headmaster's

unfailing memory of his earliest patrons warned him that the same admonitions had reached him from the same source concerning Philip Marston more than twenty years before. Parents, he often said wisely to himself, when, in his infrequent lighter moments, he allowed himself the freedom of personal annoyance, and not their sons, were the real problems of a headmaster.

Philip Marston had sent his son to St. Paul's because even from his own one year there he had been unable to forget Henry Augustus Coit. Not that he felt affection for the tall, often somber young headmaster in a white cravat and a long black coat. Affection was too trivial and quite too familiar a term to be descriptive of either the source or the result of that permanent, indelible impression which the headmaster of the new school in Concord had stamped upon him. Nor could he have defined the impression itself. When he thought about it afterward in Harvard or upon the high seas, as he often did, it beggared any attempt at definition. It was not wholly compounded of fear, although fear, even terror, had a part in its composition; nor of awe, although awe was an ingredient; nor of mere respect, although that was never absent. It reached for its being far back, beyond and behind the headmaster himself. It was born of some tremendous affirmation, with the possibility of which mankind had been endowed since its beginning, some faith, which, he vaguely knew, swept those whom it seized upon from the humdrum of existence into new and fervid life. Once possessed by it, one walked in lonely ways, consumed and nourished alike by the same glowing fire. It had its source far beyond creeds and doctrines, although it necessitated both for poor human explanation; and with both Dr. Coit was generously supplied from his evangelical, Bible-reading ancestors. And yet behind his passion for righteousness, his reliance upon the Word and the presence of God as the one thing necessary for the well-being of man in this world and for the assurance of his better being in the next, was something deeper and greater, some apprehension, mystical perhaps, of that Life which is within life, and yet which is so tangled and ineradicable, or so lost and out of sight, in the debris of daily existence.

Philip Marston, through his memory of his one year at St. Paul's, knew that its headmaster had unrelenting hold upon some Reality which no boy could understand and which few men would ever experience, save perhaps in fleeting glimpses, in all their later years. There it was, fiery and zealous, calm and serene, fundamental and unassailable, secure and everlasting. There it was, behind all his conservatism, his frequent tyranny, his probing irony, his stoicism, his almost fanatical purity, his passion for moral integrity, his persuasions, his exactions, his reserve, his dogmatic discipline, his aggressive insistence on duty. There it was, impossible of explanation, unrecognized perhaps even by him who possessed it, at one moment baffling and estranging parents, at the next, reassuring, even hypnotizing them.

Between such men and the rest of mankind there is a chasm never crossed, a gulf impossible of bridging. Yet from its farther edge a light bursts like some gigantic skyrocket blazing across a dark sky before it is again dissolved in darkness.

In John Marston's day Dr. Coit still wore his long black

coat, which no boy and no master had ever seen him without, still gave his Thursday evening talks in fervent, euphuistic English, still watched games from the edge of the playing-field, always interested, if a bit puzzled, still inscribed on the fly-leaves of Confirmation prayer-books or Greek New Testaments his name and the assurance of his friendship in his fine, formal hand, still exacted, and expected, from his boys their best and from most of them got it, because in failing him they were uneasily conscious of failing some greater demand than his own. In John's day the headmaster wore a beard, which he stroked in reverie or perplexity and pulled in fury; and between his fine brows were two deeply cut lines which in some odd way could add immeasurably to his look of pain, bewilderment, or reproach when some boy failed him in character or in construing. A magnificent teacher, he held even more firmly than other wise men of his day that the ancient languages were the irremovable basis of any education worth having.

But it was Windswept which supplemented, indeed complemented, John Marston's study of Greek and Latin in Dr. Coit's bare class-room at St. Paul's. It was the crashing tides of Windswept which made those barren, unharvested seas of Homer real and necessary to him; it was the winds there which swept the plains of Troy and filled the sails of the long Greek ships. Between his eyes and the hexameters on the page before him were familiar images, of which Dr. Coit, intent on syntax and prosody as well as poetry, was unaware, images which in the fraction of a second transformed the Aegean Sea into Frenchman's Bay, the Mediterranean into the open Atlantic

tumbling from Petit Manan to Fundy, the brown, sun-
baked slopes of Ithaca into the promontory where the
house at Windswept stood.

For by the time John Marston had left the dull, interminable parasangs of Xenophon for the wine-dark seas of
the *Odyssey*, the house at Windswept was on its way to
completion; and when, in his last years at St. Paul's, he
was hearing through the lines of the *Georgics* the hum
of Jan's bees in the clover and buttercups and yellow rattle of the field behind the barn there, the shingled walls
of both house and barn were beginning to weather in
wind and rain, sun and fog.

4

There were no years long or full enough to crowd from
John Marston's memory that summer of 1881 when he
helped to raise the four walls and the roof of his own
house. His memory always began with the prickling in
his legs and the odd emptiness in his stomach when he at
last in early June left Concord to meet Jan in New Haven
with *The Sea Hawk* in readiness. In Boston he was joined
by Julian Lassiter, James Lassiter's eldest son, who was
undistinguishing himself and his family at Harvard College and whose father, at the end of his wits and his
temper, had prescribed a summer at Windswept. Added
to the fifteen-year-old discomfort in the presence of a boy
four years his senior, there was nagging at John Marston
during the long six hours from Boston to New Haven, the
disquieting possibility that Julian might not like Windswept and that, disliking it, he would disrupt the neces-

sary order of their days in this first enthralling summer. There was another notion which had been in his mind ever since the building of the house had been assured, lying there, hopeful and comforting. In a new house, he had thought over and over again, in his room at school, in odd moments on the playground, in his walks by the stream, even in Chapel—in a new house one could take care that no harsh and bitter thoughts were lurking about; in the two houses he had known that had been impossible and quite beyond his control. He should always remember how as a little boy he had seen his mother, tall and lovely in a white gown, standing by the red velvet portieres, which separated the two big parlours of the house in New York, and staring at his father as he made ready to say goodbye before going to Europe or to some other place which seemed equally far away. Her face was still then, cold, careless, even cruel, not as it was when she bent to say goodnight to him. He remembered, too, the high, bitter voices he had overheard, sometimes at night, sometimes when he came upon his mother and father unawares; and he was unable to rid himself of the fancy that the words lingered there in the high rooms to disturb and puzzle him at his play. It had been the same in the house at Gardiner. But in a new house, he had thought, in which one began from the beginning, no such startling, sorry ghosts need be. Not that restlessness and dislike were the same as anger and disdain, cruelty and harshness; and yet if Julian did not positively like Windswept, even indifference would be hard to bear.

These fears tormented him as they sat together on the dirty red plush seats of the swaying coach. Neither he nor

Jan had welcomed James Lassiter's suggestion that Julian accompany them, yet neither had liked to refuse his request, remembering too well the stalwart part which James Lassiter had finally played in the realization of the house at Windswept. Julian was a handsome, well-built boy with a careless, haughty look, which increased John's discomfort. He tried to remember how Julian at his own age had been decent to him, a small boy, when their fathers had taken them on holiday jaunts together. But it was hard to recall Julian at fifteen in this young man in a light checked suit and gay tie, which, he told John, his club at Harvard had chosen in order to set its members apart from those less fortunate. John was still wearing his black clothes. He had been fearful of donning any others for his formal and terrifying goodbye to Dr. Coit. They accentuated even more the gulf between him and Julian, and he was painfully conscious of them.

Julian bought a magazine and pop-corn from the news-agent with an air which a mere school-boy could never assume, and in the intervals of his reading and munching strove to draw from John some definite information concerning this place of his unwilling exile.

"What's it like—this Windswept place?"

"It's hard to describe. It's—it's like itself."

"Oh, come off! That doesn't mean a thing."

"Well, in the first place, it's big and open without many trees, and the sea runs terribly high. There's always surf on the stillest days, and there's usually a wind."

"Cold, I'll bet. Maine's always cold. Any decent place to swim?"

"There's the anchorage. We could swim there, I'd think."

"What's the anchorage?"

"It's where we keep the ketch, out of the swells. It's quiet there with sand."

"Well, that sounds a bit more hopeful. What's the ketch like?"

"She's fine. She trims in most any wind, and she's good at catching whatever there is when there isn't any."

"Can we sail a lot?"

"Of course, why not? Only I expect we'll be busy on the house. Maybe you won't want to help, though, and if you don't, you needn't, you know."

"Oh, I shan't mind pounding a few nails. At least there won't be professors telling you you're no good. God! I'm sick of books and of frowsy old men. The trouble is those old moss-backs don't know a thing about life. They don't know anything except their musty old tomes. I suppose they're better at St. Paul's handling kids, but at Harvard they don't know beans about young men. Harvard's just a putrid sink with a lot of dead fish floating in it!"

John tried his utmost to think of something witty and disparaging to say about Dr. Coit and his other masters. He reviewed desperately all the injustices at St. Paul's which he could summon into his confused mind, all the overlong assignments, all the unfair, silly rules, the dull, interminable Sundays when no games were allowed and when one read pious books, if he read anything, the long hours at church. He strove to recall whispered conspiracies in the hall-ways, those empty threats of last term to throw wheezy Mr. Packard into the stream in retaliation for his insistence on poems written in Latin, those raw jokes played on dull old Walker, who in reality never got the point of the jokes at all. He longed to convert St. Paul's into a dark den of plotters, of outraged boys who hated school and books and masters. But, faced with this Harvard omniscience, all the stories he could tell seemed childish enough, and he succeeded only in looking red and feeling woefully inexperienced. It was almost a relief when Julian stormed on.

"Well, at least I'm not being tutored like last summer, saying *Sir* for weeks on end to some kind of pimply fool who can't serve a decent tennis ball and who carries a Vergil in his coat pocket. God! How I hated those *Georgics,* queen bees and grafting and all the rest of it! The *Aeneid* had some sense to it once you dug it out, but those silly effusions on the rustic life, those happy tillers of the soil! Excuse *me!* But there, I mustn't disillusion the young. I suppose you like the stuff yourself?"

John longed to say that he felt precisely the same as Julian, but even if he had tried to do so, his face would have belied him. His embarrassment was increasing every minute almost to the point of illness.

"I haven't reached Vergil yet," he said, "but some of the fellows at school say he's stiff enough. I—I can't say I like Cicero much."

"Cicero's pap to Vergil, food for babes. And anyhow he had some sand. Well, let's forget the dead languages. Out, out, brief candle! Tell us some more about Windswept. Miles from everywhere, isn't it?"

"Yes, but I don't think vou'll mind, really. There'll be lots to do."

"What, for instance? Be specific. I'm not the man for a wilderness."

"Well, there'll be the house first. It'll be fun to see it go up and to—to help. And I'm sure there'll be swimming. And there's *The Sea Hawk* and lots of fishing, and long walks, only maybe you don't like walking. And Jan means to set our own lobster traps. We can paint the buoys any colour we like so they'll be our own. And it's fun to haul them early in the morning."

"Jan's the Bohunk fellow. What's he like? My father said at Christmas time he was like a Maine boulder. He said he was as set in his ways as a balky old mule. I hope he doesn't get in *my* way."

John welcomed the anger which, mounting in him, put for the moment his embarrassment to rout.

"Jan's splendid," he said, turning in his seat to gaze for the first time straight at Julian. "And if you know what's good for you, you won't call him a Bohunk. He's the best man I know, Jan is. He's proud of coming from Bohemia, and he's as good an American as you or I. He was my father's friend, and he's my friend. If you don't like him, there's just something wrong with you, that's all. And if you don't treat him as you'd treat any—any other gentleman, you'll have me to reckon with, too!"

The sudden surprise in Julian's face banished its carelessness. He stared back at the younger boy beside him, seeing all at once beneath the honest anger the tears which he was striving to keep back. Julian felt a bit ashamed of himself. The kid had had a hard time, he remembered, losing his father and all. And, after all, you couldn't expect a mere school-boy, shut up in a prison, to get the right slant on books and professors. He would best change his line of talk before there was a flood of tears. And besides, he liked the kid for standing up for his friend. He even grew rather red, quite honestly, in his turn.

"I'm sorry," he said. "I didn't mean to be insulting toward Jan. I just don't know him, that's all. I'm sure we'll make out all right—I expect I'll have a ripping time —and I'll like straddling a roof in overalls for a change. Honest, I will. You don't need to worry about me. I'm not going to throw a monkey wrench into things. And it's darned nice of you to let me come along."

John felt immeasurably better then. Now that Latin and Greek were given a rest, the matter of Jan straightened out and understood, he could talk more easily about Windswept, how they would live in the cabin while the house was being built, how Caleb Perkins had already bought two cows for them, and how Jan planned to plough up some of the less rocky pasture land in the hollow near the cabin and make more field for grass and hay. By the time the Connecticut had widened its valley to near the blue waters of the Sound, he was able to look upon Julian less as an incumbrance than as a companion.

5

He was surprised to find Anton with Jan on *The Sea Hawk* in New Haven. He had not been prepared for him, but there he was, strong and quick and more than a bit quiet, hustling about with his usual efficiency, storing away provisions, seeing to the sails, looking at his watch from time to time, studying the wind, talking to no one. When John had escaped the curious Julian, who was inspecting the ketch, and had gone below to change from his black clothes to an old shirt and trousers, Jan followed him. Anton had not wanted to come, Jan said, but he had at last been persuaded to do so. There were things that he and Anton must talk about together, and in New York there had been neither time nor occasion. These things had to do with Anna's brother Ambroz, whom Jan did not like. Anton was going to marry Anna in September, and he seemed, Jan said with a rather tired shrug of his shoulders and an anxious clasping of his hands together, to be marrying Ambroz, too.

"Ambroz is not good for Anton," Jan said. "But Anton, he is blind. Maybe I can make Anton see about Ambroz while we go."

They got away at dawn under a good wind. By afternoon they had cleared the many craft of the Sound and were running free, wide of the coast, with filled sails. Now with everything shipshape Anton had no possible excuse for not talking with Jan. During the voyage to Windswept it seemed to John that they were always talking. Sitting aft and watching the sails while he and Julian lounged forward, smoking their old black pipes as *The Sea Hawk* lay at anchor in some harbour or cove at night, they talked in their own old language, shut away from John and Julian, the strange words sometimes rising above the shifting and easing of the sails, the creaking of gear under the wind, sometimes hushed in the stillness of the evening.

"Whatever are they saying all this time?" Julian asked.

"I don't know," said John Marston.

But he did, although he could not have explained to Julian even if he had wished to do so, because the things they were leaving unsaid were so much deeper than anything they were saying.

Nor did he himself understand it all fully. He was too young for that. And yet as he watched the two of them, crouching there below the filled mainsail, whispering on the deck at night, he remembered evenings in the Národní Budova, things his father had said, and Jan's stories of his past. And because of these memories he knew, although he could not put his knowledge into words, that Jan was striving to keep untouched and secure those old realities which he and Anton had known, the burden and the brightness of those old years in an old land. Jan strove harder than Anton because he was able to recognize more worth striving for. He was striving to keep alive in Anton the decencies of poverty and hard work and waiting, the desire to be true to old and simple faiths, the wish to remember in all the temptation to forget. Anton dealt in hours, Jan in centuries; Anton, with men, Jan, with mankind.

In Jan's mind a man dwelt by himself within himself, in an impregnable stronghold of old loyalties, within which stronghold he was the guardian of old gifts, the suffering and the sacrifice of countless others, long since gone but never lost, toil and privation, defeats and triumphs, fears and hopes. A man was thus the inheritor and the guardian alike of time, its guerdons and its punishments. Within him was the long past, the confusing present, the uncharted future. If this stronghold were stormed and overcome, a man was lost, set adrift, his identity scattered into fragments, the infinitesimal glow of life, for the tending of which he alone was responsible, absorbed into darkness.

Jan did not begrudge Anton the quick gains that Ambroz had promised; he did not resent Ambroz in his place as Anton's partner. What he feared was the loss of Anton himself, and more for Anton's sake than for his own. Ambroz was quick, shrewd, and hard. He would bring out these qualities in Anton, probe for them where they lay dark and menacing, lurking beneath the better things —the thought of home, its simplicities, its toil, its ingenuous faith in America and in Anton. Ambroz would make Anton forget.

Ambroz had always been waiting there since those first weeks five years before when Jan had gone with Philip Marston and John on *The Sea Hawk* and he had come to help Anton in Jan's absence. Waiting, watching with his small, sharp eyes like some snake with poison in its fangs and strength in its coils, ready to spring when the moment came, crawling into the shop through the winter, working with them on busy days, suggesting this and that. Ambroz knew ways of making money quicker. That, he said, would hasten the marriage of Anton and Anna, procure their farm for them, start them out on the sure road to prosperity and plenty. Why should they wait, he was always saying? Why should they hoard their savings in the bank when he knew men who could take those savings and multiply them many times in even a few weeks? The ocean was wide, he said, and Anton had his own way to make in the world. After all, he said, America was not the old country. It had its own ways by which one got ahead, and unless a man was stupid and a fool, he learned to use those ways.

He was careful not to say these things when Jan was there at his work. But they were there all the same, in his face and in his quick, sly ways. The worst of it was that they were creeping into Anton's face also, and in the two loyalties now tugging at Jan, his old loyalty to Anton, his new and necessary loyalty to John Marston and to Windswept, Jan was less able to cope with them, push them back out of sight behind the better things in Anton.

Once, three years before, Jan had seen Ambroz give the wrong change to a gentleman, who paid for his freshly repaired shoes with a ten dollar bill. There was a dollar short in the change which Ambroz gave the gentleman. Jan called Ambroz's attention to it sharply and set the matter right, apologizing as he did so. As he turned to go, the man had looked quickly at the three of them, at Ambroz pretending that it had been but a careless mistake, at Anton sulky and embarrassed, at Jan confused, angry, and apologetic.

"I've had this happen here once before," the man said. "You fellows better watch out. This country can get along without people like you. I'll go elsewhere for my work in the future."

There had been a scene in the shop after he had left and a worse scene between Jan and Anton in their room at night. Jan was for turning Ambroz out at once. It meant ruin to keep him there, Jan said, ruin to the shop and more lasting ruin to Anton. But he got nowhere with Anton, sitting there on the edge of their bed, sullen, drawn within himself, defensive, rebellious, studying his watch. Jan knew that Anna was waiting on some street corner and that he was no match against Anton's honest love for Anna.

Anna was good, though simple and unsuspecting. She kept house for Ambroz now that their mother, who had brought them to New York as children, was dead. Anna had the old country reverence and fear which women there gave to the men they cared for, and she would not dare to suspect Ambroz, to disobey him, or to leave him before she was married, in spite of her love for Anton.

Jan had been beaten then even as he was being beaten now as they sped northward in *The Sea Hawk*. John Marston recognized Jan's defeat in the slump of his shoulders, the nervous working of his hands, the pain in his eyes. And Jan was not one who would think he was well out of it all when Anton went back to New York and they were working on the house at Windswept. Jan was not made like that. He would cherish all the old memories which he and Anton had shared, keep a bewildered faith in Anton for the sake of the memories. Instead of resenting the suffering which Anton was causing him, he would love him more, having discovered, as people like Jan always do discover, that one never truly loves another until he has been made to suffer by that other.

Julian improved once he was out of his checked suit

and was helping to sail *The Sea Hawk*. The very fact that Jan and Anton were so much by themselves drew him and John Marston together. Julian shed his Harvard manner with his club tie; he was immeasurably more desirable in corduroy; and he even consented to say a good word or two, without too much patronage, for the *Odyssey*. John's fears of the possible ghosts of discontent within his new rooms swerved in their source from Julian to Anton.

But Anton did not stay long at Windswept. By the time he had spent two nights in the cabin, he asked Caleb Perkins for his horse to ride through the path to Heron Cove and on to catch the train back to New York. He had spent most of his time roaming about the open land, far from the promontory where the house was going up. He avoided Jan and, more than Jan, Philip Marston's grave on the top of the pasture slope. No one was sorry when he returned to Ambroz and Anna.

6

Of all the good things to which man may be the fortunate heir upon this earth, thought John Marston as he followed Caleb Perkins' directions that first summer, none is better than to help frame the walls and the roof of his own dwelling place. He had been amazed when, after skirting Mt. Desert and leaving Frenchman's Bay astern, they had at last swung westward again, to see upon the distant, bare headland the great joists and timbers already standing, fresh and yellow, above the sea. He had been unprepared for the leap inside him at the sight. That framework there, growing more distinct with every gust of the good southeast wind, took from him the last fear of returning, put to rout any dread of quickened sorrow. It put to rout, also, the loneliness and desolation of the long stretch of land, so dark and somber when he had left it in November, now green and sunswept with the approach of summer. Indeed, even this gaunt outline of a house seemed already to have conquered in its promises any threats which the land might once have seemed to make. Now awakened from its long loneliness, the place itself had become eager and alive, beneficent, filled with human expectations, mellowed and hospitable by the very presence of death within it.

Never did a house take form and shape so quickly. John and Julian, tugging with crowbars on the rocky beach below the headland to extricate the right stones for the great chimney, prophesied the curl of smoke from their first fire before August should be fully spent. Sitting astride the roof in the hot July sun, they laid the last of the shingles. It was good to sit up there in their drill aprons, drawing the nails from their pockets, driving them with sharp, quick blows of their hammers. No man could ever see more, hear more, or smell more from his roof-tree, John Marston thought. The long stretch of blue water; the sharp outlines of islands and distant hills; the long, even pounding of the surf, silence and sound, sound and silence; the crying of the gulls; the thin, clear whistle and rippling notes of the white-throats singing all day long; the smell of drenched seaweed and of dry, of wild strawberries ripe in the shaggy grass, of bayberry and juniper, of fresh wood, tarred paper, and pots of paint.

Some of Caleb Perkins' men began to raise the barn in August, and always others worked inside the house, laying the broad pine boards of the floor in the great living-room, which extended across the front, setting the panes of glass, sand-papering to a satiny smoothness the walls of cedar, leaving to weather as they would in the heat and smoke of future fires the great open beams of the ceiling. There was no staircase. Everything was on one level, the two long wings bending backward at right angles to the front, dining-room and kitchen in the east wing with three small bed-rooms beyond, three large bed-rooms in the west wing. The slack-twisted dowser had consorted well with whatever powers he called upon, for there was a never-ending supply of water already piped to the house.

Added to the fun of building was the excitement of new discovery, the daily increase in knowledge of the place itself. In late June and through July the three-mile stretch of land was blue with iris, blossoming so close to the water's edge that one looked down from the high bank upon spray-swept thousands, forming above on the land itself vivid patches of blue among the blueberry bushes, the alders, and juniper. Julian rather sheepishly drew from his belongings canvas, palette, and paints and made pictures of them among the red beach stones. After all, he said, one might as well handle a paint-brush now and then as well as a hammer. In August the goldenrod began to wave plumes of yellow along the path leading to the woods, and the tall fire-weed lent its brilliance among the tangles of raspberries. In August, too, the blueberries ripened, great clusters of them, which one could pull by handfuls and stuff in one's mouth. With the blueberries came the curlews in brown, marauding flocks, crying their shrill, quavering cries, settling on a patch of berries and cleaning it in a few minutes as clean as the picked bones of a fish. In August the highland cranberries ripened, millions upon millions of tiny round berries like drops of blood. It was fun to pick them upon the high, rough stretch before the house and to winnow them, a red stream in the wind. When they walked to the sea-wall, as they often did in the late afternoon to straighten the carpentry cramps from arms and legs, they were sure to see blue herons, ospreys circling above their nest in some tall, dead pine, and even an eagle now and then.

7

Jan was everywhere that summer. He worked from dawn until dark. It seemed as though he hoped by the frenzied activity of his body to set at rights the confusion in his mind. He ploughed the lower slopes of the pasture, holding the plough handles, the reins of Caleb Perkins' horse around his neck, his back straining, his feet stumbling over the tough, reluctant clods of earth. He wanted more grass for his cows and for the right yoke of oxen for which they were searching. He wanted more wild flowers for his bees. He laid stones for the wall, which was to connect the two wings of the house, and form the garden enclosure, which Philip Marston had planned. He dug clams in the sand of the anchorage beach. He gathered great hunks of driftwood and piled it in a huge, ungainly pile. He cooked the meals for John and Julian and Caleb Perkins, whose men shifted for themselves over a stove in the tent where they slept. He milked his cows in the small field, tethering each and sitting on his stool in the field grass, making the milk stream into his pail in straight white threads. He hewed from blocks of wood their new lobster buoys, planed them smooth, formed the tough, cylindrical stick at the top, inserted the iron anchor ring at the bottom to hold the trap rope. They were stout, splendid buoys. When he had finished a dozen of them, Julian painted them a bright yellow and when they had dried, printed *Windswept* upon them in fine, symmetrical letters. Then he cut each letter out with his pocket knife to the depth of a quarter of an inch and with black paint made the inscription stand out clear and unmistakable. The lobster buoys, making gay splotches of colour as they floated in the blue or green or gray water off the cove, gave them a sense of proprietorship over the sea as well as over the land.

Julian liked Jan. John Marston's threats on the train to New Haven had no need to be executed. Julian got into the habit, when he was not working on the house, of following Jan about, working at whatever Jan was doing. Jan seemed an odd lodestone for Julian, John thought, as from the peak of the roof he watched Julian helping Jan clear his new field of rocks. Perhaps the attraction lay in the fact that Jan knew precisely what had to be done and was doing it, methodically, bit by bit, carefully, exactly. Perhaps it was that Jan gave an odd kind of assurance to those who lacked it in themselves.

Once after a long day of particularly heavy work Jan fell asleep almost as soon as they had finished supper. The two boys were stretched out on the floor by the cabin fireplace. Jan was in his chair. A thunder storm had come up suddenly with a high wind, which drove the full tide crashing upon the ledges with vicious whirls of spray like a shower of stones.

Jan was a graceless figure as he slept, unmindful of the uproar outside. All the ugly, uncouth lines of face and feature, now that thought and purpose were for the moment lost in unconsciousness, came into being. His nose flattened with the widening of his nostrils, his cheeks sagged, his mouth relaxed and opened, the upper lip distorted and grotesque, the lower drooping in a crooked, unsightly curve. His large fists hung from his crossed arms, resting, one on either thigh, brown and coarse, the humps of the knuckles and the hollows between them making his hands look like ungainly loaves of brown, peasant bread. He had taken off his shoes, and his wide, clumsy feet with the outline of his big, awkward toes were flattened against the floor. He began to snore in horrid, repellent snorts like some flat-headed seal asleep in the sun on a rock above the tide. At his best he was like some symbol of squalid, dumb, thoughtless toil, of the toil which for centuries has earned bread only for more toil. At his worst he was like some satyr, some Caliban, deformed, inhuman, repulsive.

John would have laughed at him sitting there, at the sudden and grotesque change which made him all at once everything which he was not. He was surprised and not a little ashamed of himself when Julian said,

"Poor devil! Let's get him to bed. He's done in. Anyhow, I tell you, he's worth more than you and I put together."

8

In mid-August a week of impenetrable fog shut them in, and almost from one another. For against these massed battalions of shadowy hosts, moving in heavy silence from the open sea to beset the land, there was no resistance. Instead, after some singular manner of its own, the land seemed to yield itself willingly to the ghostly embraces of the fog and from their union to bring forth from itself all those dark and sinister aspects which the sun had put to rout. The total absence of the sky, the blotting out of space, made the vague outlines of earth all important simply because these outlines were the only things visible. To find oneself nearer the perilous edge of the high shore than one thought, to come suddenly upon an alder bush higher than the surrounding growth, to hear the sea pounding against the foot of a boulder when one could barely discern the top upon which one stood—these hitherto familiar things quickened one's heart-beat and lent to time and place a menacing quality of which all were conscious and before which each had his own peculiar misgiving.

On days of high wind the fog took shapes, gray shapes, green shapes, shapes of murky yellow, scudding above the land, trailing their frayed garments across the dripping juniper and bracken, sweeping on across the pasture slope to join the gray hosts mustered to receive them, slipping into the new house through the frame of one window and out through another. It was for all the world as though the place had become inhabited by ominous, stealthy phantoms, hidden before, now by fortuitous circumstance abroad to wreak their will.

The surrounding, engulfing silence deadened all sound; iron hammers smote like wooden mallets; saws lost their sharp and cheerful rasping and cut the damp wood with a subdued, asthmatic wheeze; the fire in the cabin hissed and spluttered, its smoke coiling up the chimney to join the gray clouds without; the bells of Jan's invisible cows in the meadow were muted and dulled; their occasional mournful bellow from the lost field held the stifled hoarseness of the fog horn, moaning all day and night from the great light, whose revolving flashes became only sickly glows when at intervals between the rolling banks of fog they were seen at all. From the roof of the house, where the ever-settling dampness had become water, great drops struck the stones of the new terrace with muffled, sullen plops. And always, in the clinging, opaque obscurity, the drumming of the surf reverberated minute by minute, sepulchral and hollow, grave and solemn, the undertones of an unseen ocean moving somewhere in the grayness beyond their sight.

Twilight was indistinguishable from dawn, and darkness came as no surprise. At night in the dripping tent and damp cabin voices were imperceptibly lowered as though the concealed world without were commanding concealment within. And when at last the retreating ghostly shapes allowed the sun again to appear in a sky which had been almost forgotten, one felt as though one had escaped from the stranglehold of death and knew for the first time the sweetness of returning life.

9

John Marston missed Daniel Perkins that first summer. His father, once his school was over, had sent him on a schooner carrying lumber from Machias to Boston. The captain was a friend of Caleb Perkins, and Dan's father had thought the boy would fare better in most ways if he were not at Windswept. John could see that Dan's father was worried about him. He had been silent and listless, unlike himself all winter, unwilling to play about as he had always done, shrinking from his friends. A summer quite away from home would be good for him, his father thought, and he was in the best of hands.

Although he did not doubt the wisdom of Caleb Perkins' decision, John kept thinking that Dan would feel immeasurably better about things could he have worked with him and Julian on the house. Dan would have seen as he was seeing every day how the very building of the house had taken from the place all the sadness it had known less than a year before. There was no longer the least shred of anything sinister about Windswept, if one excepted the days of fog, and they were soon forgotten. To become acquainted with it now, John thought, would have been better for Dan than to escape from it. Homesickness was a soil in which sorrows and self-reproach and confusion flourished. He would have liked to show Dan that the fulfillment of Philip Marston's wish had banished sorrow, and that it was wrong and dangerous to place upon oneself a reproach which did not belong there. In the intervals when he was not too busy to forget Dan, he discovered within himself lurking fears for him.

With all his anxiety for his son Caleb Perkins took pride in the now established work of his hands. He was like those diligent builders extolled in the Book of Wisdom, who trust in their labour, who are wise in their work, and who, because of their labour and their simplicity, maintain the state of the world. Like them he watched hourly the completion of his design, like them he was satisfied only with perfection, like them he laboured night and day, with his mind in the darkness, with his hands in the light. He was everywhere at once as the work progressed toward completion, striding from barn to house, from stone wall and chimney to the terrace, supervising, correcting, exacting. He allowed no one of his workmen to do the more delicate finishing of this and that. He alone must crown his own labour.

10

In late August, when the return to St. Paul's and to Harvard stirred uneasily in the minds of John and Julian, there came a day when one of the workmen, sent to fetch the mail from the village, brought back with him a telegram with the news of Ellen Marston's sudden death. John, standing in the sunny enclosure in his swimming-suit, waiting for Julian to run with him down the pasture slope and through the spruces toward the sandy anchorage, held the yellow paper in his hands, incredulous, annoyed. The news at that moment not only announced an unpleasant interruption, but also rudely intruded upon

him the sudden recognition of a portion of his world completely forgotten. He was frightened as he stood there to
realize that he felt nothing at all except inconvenience and
vexation. He grew red and uncomfortable before Julian,
who strove awkwardly to express sympathy and succeeded
in conveying nothing save disappointment that their swim
must perforce be abandoned.

Caleb Perkins took him that evening to the village and
the next day went with him on the train to Gardiner.
They remained for two nights in the great old house,
while he at one moment chafed at the decorous delay of
the funeral and at the next was swept by dread of the big,
echoing rooms with their harsh memories, which sprang
upon him from the chairs and tables and even from the
plates and cups from which they ate and drank. Worse
than the memories and the embarrassment which he felt
when his grandmother's friends called to give him their
condolence, was the deadness inside his body and his
mind. He tried to feel grief, and there was none, to summon up regret, and there was no regret, to feel sorry for
his conduct toward his grandmother in James Lassiter's
office, and there was no sorrow.

At intervals during the two days, out of a latent respect
for the presence of death in the house, he made himself
turn the black knob of the white folding-doors between
the two parlours and go into the one where his grandmother lay in her black coffin. The door always creaked
a little, and the noise never failed to startle him into sudden terror. Instead of looking at her lying there, he sat
uncomfortably upon the edge of a high-backed chair in
a corner of the room, twisting and untwisting his fingers,

picking nervously at the scab of a wound he had received while working on the house, staring now and then at a portrait of his grandfather above the white mantelpiece or looking at a picture of his grandfather's ship, the *Ellen Marston,* painted, as the star and crescent of a nearby lighthouse tower and as the mosques and minarets in the distance would suggest, in the Straits of the Bosphorus. He had never known his grandfather, but he thought he might have liked him, for he had a look of Philip Marston about his mouth and eyes. Could his grandfather have loved his grandmother, he wondered, or had he named his ship for her out of custom and a kind of ceremonious gallantry? Had there been harsh words in this house, too, suspicion and hatred between the long absences welcome to both?

The two days in Gardiner were clear and sharp with the prophecy of autumn. From the windows of his room he could see the masses of goldenrod on the unkempt hill sloping down to the river, the purple and white stars of the asters, the red of one maple branch, turned early from the green of the rest, and brilliant above the blue Kennebec. He longed to run down the hill to the water where the men worked among the logs, but the still face in the back parlour forbade alike such indecorous levity and such shuffling off of family responsibility.

Caleb Perkins felt no such demands. He spent his time during the day among the mills and lumber-yards, scrutinizing these products of the Kennebec region to see if they were superior to those of the Penobscot and the St. Croix. In the evening he played long games of dominoes with John in the big, still dining-room before they went upstairs to bed, their shoes echoing in the strange silence of the house.

In late morning and throughout the afternoon people called, elderly men and women, come not only to pay their respects to the dead but to take careful note of the living. This last fact was uncomfortably inside John Marston as he received his guests, ushered by old Sarah into the front parlour, speaking in low, seemly tones, scrutinizing him standing nervously by the center table, tall, sun-burned and healthy in his black clothes.

"Would you care to see my grandmother?" he always asked, as Sarah had told him to do, after the first formalities had been accomplished.

Since they always did care, he led them into the back parlour and, since there was no help for it, stood with them beside the coffin, while they gazed with a curiosity, which they honestly mistook for respect, upon the bold, strong features of the dead woman.

Death had not shrunken the features of Ellen Marston as it so often does, or placed upon her face either oblivion or peace. One expected her eyes to open, her mouth to speak, her hands to order her household. One knew that she was there against her will, that she was neither submissive nor resigned, but instead beaten and resentful. If he could only have seen less imperiousness on the high forehead and sharp, finely-modelled nose, if only the straight, firm mouth could have suggested acceptance and serenity instead of the power still to command and to hurt, if the white hands folded across the black silk dress could have added helplessness and futility to their stillness, John Marston, in spite of the memory of uneasy, fearful hours in that very room, could have felt sadness and sorrow instead of indifference, embarrassment and fear.

It was old Sarah, who, in the hours before the funeral on their last day in Gardiner, revealed to his perplexed mind wherein lay the only sadness of his grandmother's death. She had come to his room to go over with him the names of the persons whom he himself must thank for flowers or other kindnesses. He always remembered her there, old and tired in her black dress and white apron, her face swollen with tears.

"I'm glad you have your house, Master John," she said. "I wanted you should have it that day in New York, only who was I to speak up? No one has ever spoke up in this house except to his own hurt, but there have been those who have thought their own thoughts. It wasn't your house your grandmother was fighting or your father's grave away off down there. It was just being beaten she couldn't bear. I don't think she'd ever been beaten before that day. I was proud of you that day, Master John.

"I'm glad she never knew that death was coming after her. She'd have fought even death something awful. Only she had no time. I found her gone when I took her up her cup of tea that she always liked before her breakfast. I'll always mind how I looked at her and how I says to myself, 'Here's one fight you won't have to fight, Ellen Marston. Here's one fight that's been taken right out of your hands.' "

Young John Marston looked at the old woman. She had rolled the fresh folds of her white apron around her hands. It would be mussed and crumpled when she once let it go, he thought. Sarah must be nearly as old as his grandmother, perhaps even older. He knew that she had helped to care for his father when he was a little boy. He had been worried over her short future until his grandmother's lawyer had told him that she had been well provided for in Ellen Marston's will. Now as he watched her extricate one of her hands from her apron and raise her black-edged handkerchief to her eyes in order to dry the tears, which the story of his grandmother's death had seemingly evoked, his incredulity got the better of his embarrassment.

"Why do you cry so, Sarah?" he asked. "Were you really fond of my grandmother?"

The old woman stared back at him, amazement in her face. She did not answer him for so long that he grew frightened. Perhaps he should not have asked the question, he thought. Perhaps it was wrong for the young thus to intrude upon the years and experience of the old.

"How could you think I'd be fond of her?" she said at last, her voice dropping to a hoarse, angry whisper. "And I weigh my words, for there's death in this house, and it's bad luck, as all know, to speak ill of the dead before they're carried out. Only I speak out because I've had no chance to speak out, and there's not much time left for bad luck to get at me. I've lived here forty years with never a word to brace my heart, if you know what I mean. But I stayed on just so she couldn't beat me the way she's beaten everyone else, the old captain, and your father, and you when you was little, and all the others who have come and gone. She might have beaten me on the outside, but she never beat me inside. I kept my own thoughts where she couldn't get at them. 'Twas a game I played all these years with all the coming and the going, in the kitchen and the stable, but with me always here. You see, I had no folks, and so all I had was to play a game-like with her.

"And if you ask me why I cry so, I'll tell you the truth, come what may. I'm crying because there's nothing about her and all my years that's worth crying for. It seems as if there ought to be something to cry about after all these forty years. But there ain't. And so I'm crying because there ain't a thing I can find to cry about. It's a great grief, Master John, when there's no grief worth grieving for."

That afternoon when they followed Ellen Marston's body down the hill, Sarah still sobbed in the corner of the carriage. As they drove slowly on above the blue river in the wine-like air, John Marston suddenly understood anew what the old servant had meant, the sharpness of grief over the absence of grief, the poignancy of sorrow because there is no sorrow, the tragedy of being dumb to suffering when one longs to suffer and cannot.

Just before they entered the church, they passed some French Canadians loitering in curiosity on the sidewalks. The men removed their hats and caps as the hearse and carriages passed, after the custom of their old country, retained in their new. John Marston and Sarah were at that moment asking the same question of themselves, —whether Ellen Marston would have been incensed by their presumption or gratified by their subservience.

11

Jan stayed at Windswept that first winter after the house had been built and, thereafter, for all winters. He had not told John Marston of any such intention, nor, indeed, had he nurtured any such plan in his own mind. The three of them sailed back reluctantly enough in September, leaving Caleb Perkins to complete any finishing touches that were needed. But whatever yet remained to be done was not visible as they skirted the great point and swung westward. For there on the distant headland under the early autumn sky stood their house, its chimney rising straight and clear, the sun gleaming on its window-panes,—ready and waiting for many returns.

Jan saw Anton and Anna married the day after he reached New York. They were married in the Church of Saints Cyril and Method on East 4th Street. Ambroz acted as best man to Anton, standing with him in the chancel in a new blue suit with a red tie, drawing Anton's gold ring for Anna out of his breast pocket. Jan stood by himself in the front pew of the church while the priest read from his black book the Latin words which made Anton and Anna husband and wife. There were no other guests at the wedding. Anton and Anna made their vows in English instead of in the Czech language, which Anna did not understand. She would have liked to be married by the Polish priest, but Anton, with unusual firmness, had held out for the church which he and Jan had attended ever since they had come to New York. Jan felt grateful to Anton for this decision. He would have felt odd and out of place in the Polish church.

After the wedding was over, Ambroz, Anton, and Anna shook hands with Jan standing there in the front pew. They had found a flat near the shop where the three of them would live. After they had taken Anna to her new home, Anton and Ambroz would return to work. They had enlarged the shop during the summer in order to start an accessory business of hat cleaning and blocking. Anna, who had worked in a straw factory, knew about hats, and, once she had things running in the flat, she would help them part of every day. There was good money in blocking hats, Ambroz said, and a woman lent a nice tone to a shop.

They did not tell Jan about this as they shook hands with him after the wedding. Anton had already told him. Nor did they for a moment suggest that they did not expect Jan to be sitting in the shop on his stool in the far corner, cutting the tough leather for new soles, running the machine, for which he and Anton in their early days had with fear and hope laid down so many dirty bills. As a matter of fact, they did expect him there. They needed him for various reasons. One of these reasons was that he, like Anna, lent to the shop an atmosphere which Anton and Ambroz needed.

Jan stayed most of the day in the deserted church. It was quiet there. Now and then some tired people came and went, lighting a candle or two, dropping their pennies with a clink in the iron box for candle money, whispering their rosaries before one altar or another, cluttering about as they went from station to station of the cross.

In the late afternoon Jan went back to the room which he and Anton had shared for ten years and gathered together his things. It did not take him overlong. When he had given the surprised woman, who owned the house where they had lived, what she thought was fair and right, he went to the railroad station and sat among his belongings until at midnight a train left for Boston. By evening of that long day he was sixteen miles from Windswept, and Caleb Perkins, who had received a laboured telegram of his intentions, was waiting for him in his wagon.

He did not find the winter long or lonely. After the last work on the house and barn was done and his cows assured of comfortable quarters against the coming cold, Jan started to make a decent road out of the path that led to Heron Cove. There were fishermen at the Cove glad of a job when the fish were not running well and now that summer peddling among the coast settlements was over. They were good, strong men, and they worked well.

But no one worked so well as Jan there in the flaming October woods. He used every hour of the shortening days, cutting down trees, clearing out underbrush, removing stones, hauling gravel with the work-horse and blue dump-cart, which Caleb Perkins found for him. Next to building one's house there was no greater satisfaction to be had than to construct one's road to it.

He lived alone in the cabin once Caleb Perkins had returned to his work in the village and to Daniel, who was again at school. Before he set out for the new road in the morning and after he had left it in the late afternoon, he had plenty to do: his daily inspection of the house, his care of his cows, his daily chores for himself, his food, his water, his clothes, his bed, his fire. He was a good housekeeper. He kept his place at the table in the kitchen carefully set, his saucer and plate upside down on the clean, bare table, his cup upside down on the saucer. He spread his dish towels on a spruce bough to whiten and dry.

On the shelves above his wall-bed he placed his possessions: his wooden crucifix, which Father Urban had carved himself; his Missal and prayer-books; a picture of the old castle at Prague in the snow; photographs of Philip Marston and of John. On the highest shelf, half hidden from sight, he placed a tin box carefully locked, the key of which he carried in the breast pocket of his vest, transferring it whenever he changed his clothes and, for added safety, securing it with a safety-pin to the lining of the pocket. The box was filled with dry, brown soil from his father's field. When Jan should come to die, this box of earth would be placed beside him in his grave. It had been given him by his father when he had left Bohemia, after an old peasant notion that a man should never be completely separated from his native soil, however far he might wander.

Every Sunday morning Jan washed himself in the kitchen and put on clean clothes. Then he took his crucifix from the shelf at the foot of his bed and placed it on the table in the cabin living-room. He stood or knelt before it as he read the Mass from his book, reading aloud the Latin words as Father Urban had taught him to do, standing for the Gospel, genuflecting in the right places, making the sign of the cross. This was not what he would have wished, but it was the best he could manage under the circumstances.

He kept a quick eye to the weather, to which he daily grew more wise. He hoped that the deep snow would not fall until Christmas had passed, although he was ready for it with a stout pair of snowshoes, which he had made himself. If deep snow came, he might think it wise to dissuade John and Julian from coming for their holidays, and he quailed before the exercise of that wisdom. For the boys, once learning of his return, had sent hilarious, eager letters of their proposed plan to join him in spite of snow and cold.

Every Saturday afternoon in October he left work early and rode his horse to the village after his provisions. He liked coming home in the clear twilight, riding through the carpet of bright, fallen leaves, startling a deer now and then, hearing the drumming of the partridges and the high crying of the hawks, watching, as he came in the dusk through the last of the trees, for the companionable flash of the great light, seeing the long stretch of land lie in sharpened shadow under the round hunters' moon.

But as November drew on with its brief days, his isolation from the world of men and affairs became almost a passion with him. He ceased his weekly visits to the village and began to live by his own hands, to bake his own bread, to procure his own meat from woods and sea. He welcomed these renewed simplicities of his life as a child, the dependence upon the earth itself and upon himself as a part of it. He felt both young and old at once, young in the vigour of his body, old in the sense that he was among ageless, primeval things—the winds that tore over the headland at night, extinguishing his lantern as he groped his way in the darkness to the barn where his creatures stood, the pounding of the surf, the empty vastness of the ocean, the stars in the night sky.

Even his thoughts were primitive, having to do with the necessities of life, the battle for existence, the preparation for the winter. The line of dark trees to the north where the woods began, the expanse of the sea to the south, shut him away from the life among men lived beyond those horizons. When he sat by his fire at night, drowsy with the weariness of his body, he saw his father returning from his work in the fields, content to rest before his door until he should go to the heavy, unconscious sleep of those who toil. Whenever he passed Philip Marston's grave on the way to and from his work, he felt gratitude that in a new land he was thus receiving again and retaining the blessings and realities of an old. Sometimes he felt like the first man to receive life and inhabit the earth; sometimes he felt like the last man alive, his part to complete in dignity and in solitude the brief cycle of existence.

He wondered now and then why he did not continue to visualize the future, which the big house on the headland held within itself. He had been constantly thinking of it in New York and during the summer. He wondered, too, whence had fled his fears for Anton, where the heaviness about his heart had gone. He still worried about Anton in his mind, but the dull pain, which he had felt in the dim church and as he had sat among his belongings in the railroad station, had left his body. Surely these lurked still behind some curtain, now hiding one part of him from another, some curtain which would rise again and claim his time and strength. These were not dead, and yet for the moment they had not the life of the bread which he broke in his hands at his table or of the water which he poured over his bare neck and shoulders before he slept.

When in mid-December a two-days' blizzard, driving from the northeast, buried his new road beneath five feet of snow and enclosed his cabin almost to the eaves, he was surprised and a bit reproving of himself to discover that he welcomed rather than resented the wisdom of a solitary Christmas. Once the storm was over and Windswept was a vast, white, pathless waste behind and above a restless purple sea, he bound on his snowshoes and swung through the cold, up the high land, across its featureless summit, and on between the snow-laden trees of his obliterated road to Heron Cove and the village beyond, in order to send his carefully worded letter to John at Concord. He was honest enough in his fears, and he owed responsibility to John. But as he slung himself along over the hummocks and domes of the snow, half-blinded by the winter sun, he was monstrously content. He and his animals could dig themselves into this new, cold soil, they warmed by their own breath in the snug barn, he, beside his fire.

Caleb Perkins took him on his sledge part way back through the half-broken road to Heron Cove. When he left him four miles from home, his snowshoes strapped to his feet, the shadows of the trees were already dark and long across the snow. It was queer, Caleb Perkins thought, how one felt no fear for him as he turned into the path and was almost immediately lost among the trees. He was like some hibernating creature, who, looking for one restless hour upon the daylight, goes back to its cave for the long, still night.

Before Caleb Perkins saw him again, the hummocks of snow, wedged by the wind beneath the overhanging edge of the high shore, were sending swift streams of water to join the full spring tides.

12

It was James Lassiter's wife, Mary, who generously took upon herself the furnishing of the rooms at Windswept. It was she who had the idea of the big dining-room table, which Caleb Perkins, with the future in mind, made out of great lengths of smooth pine, the chairs to match; the wooden bedsteads and chests of drawers, painted a pale gray to tone with any colour which the sea outside the windows was destined to put on. She came to Windswept early that second summer when John Marston began his life as owner of a house and land, and after two weeks of study and imagination returned to New York to shop, with John and Julian at her elbow, for the few things which Caleb Perkins' saw, plane, and skill could not manage.

At first she had thought John Marston needlessly stubborn about what should, or should not, go into his house. This was at Christmas time when John had visited Julian

for the holidays forbidden them at Windswept by the
snow. Standing by the fire in the Lassiter parlour after
dinner, John had told his guardian politely but firmly his
wishes concerning the things in the house on West 28th
Street and the things in the house at Gardiner. With the
exception of a portrait of his father painted as a boy of
sixteen, which had hung in his room in New York, and
that of his grandfather from the back parlour of the
house in Gardiner, he wanted to keep nothing at all, he
said. He would like all the other things sold with the
houses themselves.

Mary Lassiter had stared at him standing there. She
had remembered him as a shy, small boy, brought sometimes with his father for Sunday evening supper, and she
was as unprepared for his quiet authority as for his added
height. He had left the parlour for his own room after
he had made his declaration. She could not know that he
had spent many hours at school framing his words and
mustering his courage.

"He's a queer boy," she said, when John had gone upstairs. "Hasn't he any feeling at all about family possessions?"

"It's possible he has too much feeling about them,"
said James Lassiter. "At all events I shan't press him."

"Leave him alone," said Julian. "It's his house. Leave
him alone, I say. I know him better than either of you."

"Maybe there's a dark secret behind it," said Eileen
Lassiter, who at fourteen was dressed for her first party.
"I think it's interesting."

"Don't be a dramatic nincompoop!" warned her
brother. "You're too grown up for your years. And if

you say a word to him about it, I'll not dance with you once during the holidays. Mark my words now."

But after Mary Lassiter had seen the house at Windswept, she was more ready to acknowledge the wisdom of John Marston's decision, whatever its source. This was clearly no house for antimacassars, marble-topped tables, what-nots, portieres, and black walnut chamber-sets, or even for heirlooms, regardless of their age and association. The house itself would have repudiated them all, been uncomfortable in their possession.

It was Mary Lassiter, too, together with Caleb Perkins' knowledge of the surrounding countryside, who had been responsible for the installation of Mrs. Haskell as the housekeeper at Windswept. Mrs. Haskell came that second summer to preside over the culinary destinies of the household. She remained for ten summers, until, after John Marston's marriage in 1891 and her own momentous decision to enter upon a new and more daring vocation, Jan brought Philomena from the old country to take her place. The verb, however, is inaccurate. No one could be found capable of taking Mrs. Haskell's place, at Windswept or elsewhere.

Mary Lassiter always said that she had purchased Mrs. Haskell at the awful price of her own comfort forever after. For no woman, she said, could live for even a brief fortnight under the same roof with Mrs. Haskell and ever again be even relatively satisfied with herself as a human being. She had driven many rough miles with Caleb Perkins from Cherryfield to Sullivan in search of Mrs. Haskell before, after a full week of calling at this back door and that, they had brought her home rejoicing.

"I've thought of these yellow chintz curtains for the living-room, Mrs. Haskell. They're cheerful, I think. Lace or muslin don't seem to go with this sort of house."

"I've never heard of 'em myself in a parlour. But it's no odds to me long as they'll wash."

"And I didn't buy many table-cloths. The table's so large and long, in the first place, and not the right shape for the usual cloths. Maybe you saw the mats Jan wove last winter from the dried grasses. I thought it might please him if you should use those on the table instead of a cloth. It will save so much washing."

"It'll be as you say, but I'm used to washin', an' nothin' looks neater to me than a clean white table-cloth with a bit o' starch to make it lay smooth."

"But the boys are careless. They'll make spots."

"My boys didn't. An' washin's nothin' to me. I'm here to work. Settin' still's the only way Satan'll ever get the upper hands o' me!"

"I got coloured spreads for the beds. The boys seemed to fancy them. They're something new, and people are using them for summer homes, I find."

"They'll wash, I spose?"

"Oh, I'm sure they will. The salesman said they were very practical. And I got plain blue china for every day."

"Well, blue's neat enough, but it'll show nicks more'n white or flowered. I don't know how 'tis, but nicks get on my mind somethin' awful. I can't abide things that ain't whole or what they ought to be, if you know what I mean."

Mary Lassiter knew precisely what Mrs. Haskell meant. In the two weeks she remained at Windswept, waiting for the furnishings to come from New York, she never once saw Mrs. Haskell deviate from her straight, but not too narrow path. Once the things were placed in the rooms, she knew they would remain unalterably there in spite of Mrs. Haskell's secret predilections, which would always be in bondage to her recognition of authority and to her hatred of change.

Mrs. Haskell did not like houses or people with too much *give* to them. She got used to what she had to get used to, and thereafter she stayed used to it. After the things had been placed to everyone's satisfaction, except her own, she surveyed each room to its minutest detail. There it was, she said to herself, for better or for worse, and there it would remain so long as she was in charge.

13

Mrs. Haskell had been born in 1830 on her father's ship off Cape Horn in what she was pleased to call, whenever she could be induced to talk about it, *a master gale o' wind.* The scene of her birth had been one of intolerable confusion: the mizzen mast had crashed and gone over the side; the careening decks were littered with rigging and wreckage; even her mother's bed was drenched with salt water. Only a brief acquaintance with Mrs. Haskell would inevitably suggest, to those familiar with her past, that she had been spared in order to spend her life in atoning for her untidy, topsy-turvy entrance into this world. She hated confusion and disarray of all kinds both in herself and in her surroundings; she adored with equal passion the straightening out of all manner of dis-

order; and behind her furious battles with the scant dust
and dirt of Windswept lay that moral integrity common
to Maine coast women of her day and generation and
by no means crumbled into ineffectiveness today. An untidy house suggested to her an untidy mind; careless
dishwashing resulted in, or might well spring from, careless or even loose behaviour outside one's kitchen as well
as within it. To skimp one's work which was clearly set
out for one to do was as dishonest as to cheat one's neighbour, indeed was a dark prophecy of that very act.

Mrs. Haskell was of necessity a religious woman. Without the knowledge that God Himself had created an
orderly world, life would have held no meaning for her.
Just as she found it well-nigh impossible to visualize an
earth without form and void, so she would have found
equally distasteful the chimerical notion of atoms hurling
themselves out of confusion into order with no supervision. She liked to read in her Bible the story of the neat
parceling out by God of His daily jobs for one full week,
of those mornings and evenings of each particular day,
none of which encroached seriously on any other. That
short week, in which the world was so systematically
framed with no loose ends, bore relation to the weeks
she had lived all her life, in her mother's house, in her
own, and now in this new, and, therefore, clean house
at Windswept. On Mondays she washed, on Tuesdays she
ironed, on Wednesdays she baked, on Thursdays she
cleaned, on Fridays she churned and mended, on Saturdays she caught up with herself and made ready for
Sunday. She could not understand how certain women
whom she knew, and suspected, could shift their days

about at will and thus distort and imperil the order of their weeks. If it rained on Monday, she washed notwithstanding, taking now great comfort in the assurance that the strong winds could not fail to dry her clothes sufficiently ror rolling up against the Tuesday ironing. Mrs. Haskell's road to Damascus was the path through the juniper and blueberries to her clothesline; her heavenly vision, the perennial shine on her pots and pans hanging from their rail along the wall, and she was not disobedient to it.

Captain Nathan Haskell, Mrs. Haskell's husband, had been lost at sea, leaving her at thirty with three sons to rear. The eldest was himself at sea, master of a steamship of the Savannah Line and living when ashore in that city. Mrs. Haskell had never seen his wife, who as a Southerner she secretly feared was slow at things and what she termed as *moderate*. Her two younger sons had gone West and taken up farms in Iowa. Since they had married there girls originally from Maine families, she felt safer about them. And yet her weekly letters to the three of them seemed to suffice. She was now in no position to receive visits from them, since her own home was closed, and she could never have borne even the fleeting notion of being an uneasy guest in their unfamiliar households.

To rural New England women of the last century this aversion to readjustment constituted one of their most typical and signal characteristics. In this they have been unlike many women reared elsewhere. Nor has this indigenous and intrinsic quality completely vanished today. It still accounts for elderly women living by choice alone in hill farmhouses and coast homes often far from neigh-

bours, or working, still contentedly, in the homes of
strangers, so long as they can have their way with things.
Deep within them is the terror of dependence, the re-
luctance to see things done differently, the fear of disappointment in the changed ways and thoughts of those
whom they have reared. Loneliness, in comparison to
disillusionment and to the necessity for coming to terms
with ways foreign to their natures, is as nothing. They
must live where they can preserve the order of their days
and end their lives without bewilderment or misgiving
where they began to live.

Mrs. Haskell hoped that the lives of her sons were as
much as possible like her own, and shrank from knowing
that they were because of the unspoken, unadmitted dread
that they, perhaps, were not. When she thought of her
past as she often did without rancour or regret, she was
given to remembering her mother more than even her
husband or the childhood of her children. She had loved
her mother with an affection more compounded of respect
and admiration than of itself, a composition which is
often the ground-work and sometimes the entirety of
loyalty between certain fine-minded persons of the same
family. Her mother had had a hard life, largely spent at
sea and often away even from her children. In her day
women of Maine seafaring families were not so likely to
accompany their husbands on foreign voyages as they not
infrequently did twenty or thirty years later. Nor had she
been the sort of woman to whom strange lands were more
of an adventure than a privation. She preferred the yellow boards of her kitchen floor to any one of the excite-
ments of a quarter deck, the most menial tasks of her

house to the long, monotonous hours of freedom aboard
ship. When at forty she came home for the ten years remaining to her, she spent the three hundred and sixty-five
days of each, not in remembering London and Calcutta
and Bombay, but in letting them slip completely from
her mind while she rose early in the morning and saw
to her neglected household.

Mrs. Haskell always liked to think of her mother's
death, which she accomplished, as she had always feared
she would never be permitted to accomplish, in her own
bed at home. She had been with her mother at the end,
a girl of eighteen, herself about to be married. The sick
woman had been unconscious for hours, slipping quietly
away with apparently no sense of the past or the present
and with no care for the future. But Mrs. Haskell always
liked to remember how, just before her mother left a
life, which through so many of its years had been inevitably not what she had wished it to be, she opened her eyes
and, pointing to a picture which hung on the wall opposite her bed, said in the clearest of voices:

"My dear, it's crooked. Straighten it for me."

Although Mrs. Haskell was by no means an imagina-
tive woman in the full sense of the word, she was able
to see what lay beyond and behind her mother's last
words, to understand that to go into a world of order
with any of her belongings in disorder or out of line
would have been to her not only insufferable but sinful.
When Mrs. Haskell sat in the afternoon in her immaculate kitchen, her sewing in her lap, she herself freshly
"cleaned up" and ready for whatever might happen, she
liked occasionally to recall her mother's death, and to feel

a neat pleasure in the knowledge that all her own belong,
ings also, within her and without, as well as all those of
others to whom she was responsible, were, in so far as she
could manage, in seemliness and order.

She loved her afternoons at Windswept. She had never
been one to whom "folks" were necessary. After she
had scrubbed her face and hands at the kitchen sink and
redone her hair, securing it in a neat coil at the back of
her head so that no lock could straggle from its rightful
position, she changed her morning calico for her afternoon gingham, her checked apron for a white, and made
ready to enjoy herself in the two hours which she allotted
for that purpose. Sometimes she sat in her rocking-chair
by the window that faced the sea, knitting or mending,
looking now and then in approbation about her spotless
kitchen and at the broad face of the clock, which ticked
away the orderly, inevitable minutes by which she lived.
She never sat in her bed-room during the day. Bed-rooms
in her code of behaviour were made for sleep and bore
no relation whatsoever to the activities of morning or of
afternoon.

On fair days in the berrying season she often put on
her white sunbonnet and went afield. She loved berrying.
Nothing elated her more than to bring home a clean
crock piled high with wild strawberries, meticulously
hulled as they were picked, or a basket laden with blueberries or cranberries with never a straw, a leaf, or an
unripe berry among them. She was often given to saying
that one could measure up a person accurately by looking
at the berries she had picked. She was used to the sea,
having never in her life been out of sight or sound of it,

and the wide land at Windswept was never lonely to her.

She was not a mothering woman in spite of her three sons, whom she had reared in the fear of God and of shiftlessness; and she never outwardly betrayed either sympathy or affection for the boy whose singular household she managed and whose clothes and well-being she had an eye to. Although she possessed to a strong degree the Maine coast wariness toward "foreigners," she liked and respected Jan, largely because his methodical ways were her own, and because he never forgot to wipe his feet on the door-mat before he brought his pails of milk into her kitchen.

John Marston, from the beginning of Mrs. Haskell's kindly despotism, grew to look upon the east wing of his house as a place secure from any manner of disaster. He liked to come into the kitchen on a hot July afternoon for the cold water, sweetened with molasses and sharpened with ginger, which she prepared for him and Jan, busy with their haying. He liked, as he read before his living-room fire on a windy, early autumn evening, to hear the ticking of her kitchen clock and to know that she was knitting busily beneath her lamp on socks for him. He liked the pot of oxalis swinging from a bracket before her kitchen window, the smell of fresh bread rising on the back of her stove, the strong, even strokes of the pump as she filled the tea-kettle at supper time. He liked to hear her singing at her work, *Jesus, Lover of My Soul* or *Shall We Gather at the River?* When he rammed the prong of a pitch-fork into his hand, he knew comfortably that she was there with the iodine bottle and sound advice. When he brought his friends home with him from St. Paul's and Harvard, he liked the knowledge that they would be stuffed with good food and that there would be no objection to the number of them thronging about the house. He liked the holly-hocks which Mrs. Haskell dug up from her own front yard and planted by the chimney in the enclosure between the stone wall and the back of the house. Jan liked them, too. They made him think of home. And when, late on autumn afternoons, just before he returned to school or college, he and Jan drove over the now completed road and came from the dark trees into the last glow of light, they both liked the clean, gleaming window-panes of Mrs. Haskell's kitchen and the curl of fresh smoke, just visible, of the fire which she had lighted against their return.

He was careful to warn his friends not to encroach against any of Mrs. Haskell's bulwarks. If they could manage to hang up their clothes night and morning, to put their shoes in their closets, it would help matters considerably. And on no account were they to give her any money upon their departure. They might thank her if they wished, but if the expression of their gratitude elicited no response, they must not, therefore, conclude that it had not been received with thanks.

Julian in his summers at Windswept, during Mrs. Haskell's early years there, was not always so wise.

"Here's five dollars, Mrs. Haskell. My friend, Dick Foster, asked me to give it to you."

"What for? Did I lend it to him? I don't recollect it."

"Of course not. It's just that he wanted to thank you for all the things you did for him while he was here."

"What things?"

"Why, cooking for him and doing his room and mending his coat for him."

"Well, it's my job, ain't it, to cook what's eaten in this house an' to mend what's torn? I earn what I earn an' there's an end to it."

"I'm sure he meant it kindly enough, Mrs. Haskell."

"I'm not sayin' but what he did. But his money ain't mine. Give it back to him for them that earn it or for them that's willin' to take it without earnin' it. I'm not one of 'em, that's all. And while we're talkin' man to man, Mr. Julian, I may say I don't like that young man over much."

"Now, come off, Mrs. Haskell. He's a fine chap. What have you got against him?"

"I'm not one to stick my nose in other folks' business, but since you brought the subject up like, he meeches round in a way I don't like. He don't seem to have no drive to him, no git up an' git. He slouches between the shoulders, an' he never picks up his leavin's. He don't put himself out for folks, don't have no respect for 'em, if you know what I mean. I don't think he's much good to you, Mr. Julian."

"Oh, come now, Mrs. Haskell. He's my room-mate. I guess I know him better than you do."

"That's likely, an' I'm glad of it. There's folks that hitch together an' folks that don't. He don't hitch with me, that's all. An' he don't make folks comfortable inside 'em."

"What folks?"

"Well, since you brought the subject up like, which I

shouldn't ha' done if you hadn't, I'll speak my mind about it, open and above board. He didn't put himself out none to make Mr. Perkins an' Dan'l comfortable inside 'em when they was here to supper. Mr. Perkins don't need to mind, but Dan'l's different. Dan'l was squirmin' about inside himself the whole evenin'. I felt sorry for him, an' Mr. John and Jan did, too. You don't gain nor give nothin' by takin' no account of other folks."

"Oh, well, John's a bit hipped about Daniel Perkins, and Jan is, too. Of course, one can understand that. Dick doesn't know about things. He meant nothing at all."

"Well, you can't go about this world meanin' nothin'. As I see it, you've got to mean somethin', an' the sooner, the better. If you don't mean somethin', but just go about meanin' nothin', it's hard for other folks to get the right slant on you. I've said my say. Take it or leave it."

14

John Marston always said that he owed his wife to Mrs. Haskell, indirectly if not directly. For after Mary Lassiter, her work at Windswept completed, had returned to New York, Mrs. Haskell still remained uncomfortably but firmly in her mind; and when she saw with re-opened eyes her daughter Eileen's room, she determined to turn her over for a season to Mrs. Haskell. The unsuspecting Eileen was thereupon dispatched to Windswept instead of to the Lassiter summer home at Tarrytown on the Hudson.

"Won't it look a bit queer to people," James Lassiter had said, "to send her off away up there with just the boys and Jan and that woman in the kitchen? What about Miss Thompson going along?"

"Nonsense," said Mary Lassiter. "She's gotten around Miss Thompson all winter. Just go upstairs and take one look at her room. I'm sick of living by the silly opinions of my friends. It'll be good for Julian to look after his sister for a change. Besides, they're all only children anyway. And, believe me, my dear, you don't know that woman in the kitchen!"

Eileen Lassiter and Mrs. Haskell got on famously after the first weeks of complete insurrection.

"Where's my red shawl, Mrs. Haskell?"

"Where it belongs, I spose."

"I left it on my bed this morning, and I can't find it anywhere."

"It don't belong on your bed. It's in your lower drawer."

"No, it isn't. I looked there."

"Yes, 'tis. It's got brown paper round it. It's moth time, an' if we once get moths in this house, we're done for."

"Is that what makes my bureau smell so? It positively stinks!"

"I don't like that word. It's unladylike. An' it ain't the truth anyway. A good, clean smell ain't what you say."

"Well, maybe you call it a good, clean smell. I don't. Whatever is it?"

"It's brown paper soaked in good, clean ammonia. That gets 'em. An' you're to wrap your shawl in it after you wear it."

"What a fuss over an old shawl! I've got others."

"I daresay you have. You've got far too many things for your own good. But that's not the point. Destruction's wrong and shiftless. An' it's not just your shawl. It's everyone's clothes we're lookin' after."

"Where are my walking shoes? Don't say in the closet where they belong, for I've looked there, and they aren't."

"Of course not. I'm not one to store dirt in a closet, I'm thankful to say. They're on the kitchen porch covered with mud. There's a boot-brush in the wooden box there that Jan made. When you get 'em cleaned, sweep the dirt off my porch. Or better still, clean 'em in the bushes where the wind'll take the dust."

"Why can't Jan clean them?"

"Because they ain't his shoes an' it ain't his job. If you ain't ever cleaned your own shoes before, now's as good a time as any to begin. An' while we're on this subject, there's an iron scraper outside the back door. It ain't put there to look at."

Mrs. Haskell had bed-rock convictions upon the decent sense of responsibility, which, barring actual illness, one should feel toward good food set before one on a clean plate. She had no patience with what she termed *flighty* and *finicky* notions about this preference and that. To pamper a healthy appetite by mere notional obstinacy, had never been condoned in her house, and she had no intention of allowing this new inmate of the household to dictate her larder or her oven.

"Is it lobster stew again today, Mrs. Haskell?"

"Yes, 'tis. What's the matter with it?"

"Nothing, of course, really. Only I don't just fancy it."

"It don't make you sick, does it?"

"No, of course not, nothing makes me sick. Only I like other things better. Lamb, for instance."

"Lamb's too high. They ain't begun to kill yet roundabout. Lamb means a trip to the village. Jan's busy, an' besides I don't take much stock in meat that comes by boat or train from God knows where an' tied up in dirty sackin'. The sea's at our door to live on. Lobster's a treat to most folks."

"I didn't say I didn't like it."

"Well, then, prove you do. You've picked at things ever since you come. When I see your plate good an' cleaned up once, I'll be ready to listen to your likin's."

"Don't you like some things better than others, Mrs. Haskell?"

"No, I can't say as how I do. I don't claim I haven't got my leanin's same as most folks, but I was brought up to eat what was set before me, thank the good Lord 'twas set, and ask no questions. Fussin' makes bad savin's. It pays poor."

"I'll really try to eat everything today, Mrs. Haskell, if you'll only press my muslin dress for me. It got frightfully mussed in the trunk."

"No, I can't say as how I will. First, I ain't the bargainin' sort, an' second, it ain't good for you. I'll press for the men folks. It ain't their work. I'll get the irons nice an' hot an' start you off right, but it's high time you learned to press for yourself."

After half a summer of such bickerings, with the odds weighted against her, Eileen Lassiter's defenses fell. She was clearly no match for Mrs. Haskell. And once she had succumbed, life at Windswept was immeasurably smoother for all concerned. Moreover, Eileen really liked Mrs. Haskell. She tacitly respected her for sticking to her "views," however irritating they sometimes were; and although she would never have confided in Mrs. Haskell certain of the fears and bewilderments of sixteen, the things that were secretly troubling her seemed always ironed out or, at least for the time being, put to rout in Mrs. Haskell's presence.

Years afterward when young Philip Marston and Ann were cleaning their plates and searching after the bottoms of their bowls at the same pine table, they always thought that to finish what was set before them was to *haskell* it.

"Haskell your plate, Philip," his mother always said. "You can't see the new puppies in the barn until you do."

"Ann, you haven't haskelled your milk yet. I'm waiting."

So natural a part of their vocabulary did this verb become, so free from humour or from any reference in their minds to a single personality, whom they had never known, that young Philip Marston, at St. Paul's like his father and grandfather, used it on paper to his later discomfiture.

"I'm a bit puzzled over some of your words in this essay, Marston. *Haskell,* for instance. There's no such word that *I* can find. You say here, 'When we had haskelled the boat.' I'm not a sailor. Is it perhaps a nautical term, not in the dictionary?"

Young Philip grew red with embarrassment.

"No, sir, I'm afraid not. I'm afraid it's just a word in

our family. I didn't think. I'm sorry. You see, sir, it means, well, it means to tidy up. *Haskell* means to clean something, to clean up anything at all."

15

Daniel Perkins did not grow in grace, or in graciousness as he grew older. In Mrs. Haskell's homely phrase he continued to *squirm about in his insides* whenever he came to Windswept. He did not come often, and it took hours of urging from John Marston to get him there at all for any length of time.

He adored John Marston, following him about at his heels like some thin, rangy red setter; but he disliked John's friends who came and went, partly because they were John's friends, partly because they represented to him another world, a world which, though a part of John Marston also, never seemed intrusive or disquieting to Dan when he was alone with John.

In those few weeks, scattered throughout the summer, there could not have been a better companion than Dan. Alone with John, except for infrequent lapses, he broke down his defenses, forgot his stubborn, almost sullen pride, cast aside his ungraciousness and the crude manners, which, to John's discomfort, he always seemed to keep in reserve, ready to assume them when he had been induced to come to Windswept while others were there also.

Added to his honest liking of Dan, John Marston felt a sense of responsibility toward him. He knew that far beneath Dan's taciturn, resentful ways lay a deeper, almost morbid resentment of himself. He understood that not all the new security of Windswept, the contentment there, the knowledge that out of sadness and tragedy had come strength and confidence, the flower of safety from the nettle of danger, could completely dislodge that resentment, that sense of guilt, from where it lay, dark and sinister, in Dan's mind, making him upon occasion crude, even cruel, suspicious, quick to take offense.

Sometimes in nights of high wind or on days of fog John's fear for Dan had an element of foreboding in it. Sometimes he thought it might be better for Dan if he did not come to Windswept at all. And yet he felt even more strongly the confidence that with patience and understanding, and, above all, with time as his ally, he could at length make things straight and right once more with Dan. In this hope Jan and Mrs. Haskell with their common sense and wisdom lent him their support.

Mrs. Haskell understood Dan. Beginning with the close of her first summer at Windswept she had decided to go to the village to keep house for Dan and his father. She would vastly have preferred a return to her own home; but she was not one to nurture such a preference when she saw a need placed fairly and squarely in her path. Dan was a different boy once Mrs. Haskell had straightened out his father's home and got it running as all decent households should run. He felt the same confidence of which Eileen Lassiter had become aware in the kitchen at Windswept. When he came home from school on winter afternoons, Mrs. Haskell was there with supper in warm, comfortable preparation. There was nothing between him and Mrs. Haskell which was hidden, as there had come to be between him and his father.

Sometimes during the first two winters Dan spent some days with Jan in the cabin. Windswept buried in snow with all its evidences of the past covered and blotted out was a safer place than Windswept in the summer. Jan, like Mrs. Haskell, seemed able to manage Dan, mostly because, like her, he kept nothing in his own mind which could leap to touch something in Dan's. Mrs. Haskell and Jan had the advantage over John Marston in that they had known fears sooner than he had known them. One more fear, added to those with which their lives had so generously provided them and which they had learned to handle, did not assume the major proportion which John's fear for Dan was constantly assuming. By not fussing over Dan they did well by him.

But with the coming of summer Dan took a strange, dark journey backward into a place which no one of them could reach. Mrs. Haskell saw him slipping back there when a letter from John in late spring announced the date of his coming home. Dan grew moody and restless then. He left home after supper, rowing his boat down the small tide river and out beyond the village harbour toward the open sea, or roaming by himself through the woods. He grew sullen about doing his chores, became silent or rude at the table. Not all Mrs. Haskell's matter-of-fact cheerfulness could quiet his father's anxiety concerning him.

"He's at a bad age, Mr. Perkins," Mrs. Haskell would say. "I know. I've had sons. The old tarnation gets 'em around sixteen. 'Tisn't just what you think 'tis. A good part of it's plain natural to man. Give him rope and let him haul on his own sheet. He's got to trim his own boat, if you know what I mean. We can't do nothin' but set where we be, with his knowin' all the time that we be where we're settin'."

Before Dan had gone the whole way back into the dark room in his mind, John always begged him to come for a week to Windswept. John thought that once he had him there to himself he could stop Dan's journey back, start him out on another safer road. But with all his hopes and plans he never quite managed to do it.

Things went well at first. There was the winter to talk about, what each had done, the weather at Windswept, how Jan had made out. There were the old places to re-visit, new things to see: the cove, the sea-wall, the pond, the new calves in the barn, Jan's first sheep, his bees, the diving float he had made and secured beyond the ledges of the anchorage. Dan was a prime companion during these days. But once they were over and the last half of the week lowered menacingly before them, it was not so easy. For beyond the week itself stretched other weeks which, John knew, tormented Dan with imaginings of what took place at Windswept when he refused to be present. If he could only once be induced to stay on and to see for himself that nothing at all took place which could hurt him in any way, these specters would lose their shapes, dissolve into healthful nothingness.

"I wish you'd stay on, Dan, for another week longer. Your father says you can as well as not. We're going to build a skiff to fool around in up the anchorage bay here. You'd be a great help at that. We thought maybe you'd do the drawings for her, measure her up decent for us."

"Who's we? Julian, I spose."

"Well, yes. And another friend of mine, Dick King. He's a fine fellow, you'd like him, and he wants to know you."

Dan looked away with quick suspicion. They were skipping stones across the calm water of the anchorage, Dan curving his long, thin shoulders, his bare right leg bent behind him, his right elbow crooked to make the underhand throw which never failed to skip the stones as John could never skip them.

"What's he want to know me for?"

"Why, because I've told him lots of things about you."

"What things?"

"Why—why just the things you do tell about the friends you like."

"Oh."

"Won't you stay on? Please do, Dan."

"No, I can't. I don't like it here when there's other folks around. I don't take to them, and they don't take to me. So what's the point?"

"Julian wants you, too. He's got a gift for you."

"He can keep it. I don't want none o' his gifts. I don't like him."

"Why not, Dan? He likes you."

"Don't tell me that lie."

"It's not a lie. Why don't you like Julian?"

"He's stuck on himself. I don't like forrard fellows like that."

"That's not fair, Dan. Really, it isn't. You're hard on Julian. He's not a bit stuck up, really. I thought so myself at first, but now I know I was all wrong. Julian's all right, really. He likes you heaps, and he wants to be friends."

"I don't need no friends."

"That's foolish. Everyone needs friends."

"I don't, leastwise not your high-toned kind. I'll make out by myself."

"Eileen will be sorry, too."

"Oh, she's comin', is she? Seems like she's always stickin' around lately."

"Don't you like Eileen either?"

"She ain't so bad, p'raps. But she hasn't no use for a country fellow like me."

"Yes, she has. She thinks you're fine. She said so just last winter."

"D'ye see her in the winter, too, same as in the summer?"

"Sometimes. When I go to New York, I do, and she said that very thing to me."

"Well, she won't think so if I stay on. I can't make out when there's company. I like bein' with you and Jan. Seems like there's always high-toned folks hangin' round. I don't take to 'em, that's all."

"I'm not high-toned."

"No, you ain't with me. I'll have to say that for you. But how'm I to know what you're like with them?"

John Marston never knew how to meet these reproaches of Dan's, especially since he knew that Dan himself was ashamed once he had made them. After the first few days of a visit from Dan, John always felt as though he were skating on thin ice with him, hearing warning cracks, sheering away from danger spots. He was forever trying to avoid a break in the ice, knowing that Dan, even more than he, was bound to pay for it inside himself. When the break came and they floundered about together, John tried desperately to get them both back to safety.

Afterwards Dan always tried on his part to make up for it in some shy way that cost him as much as the break had done. That was the two-fold trouble, John thought, Dan paying at both ends.

"Here's somethin' for you."

"What is it, Dan?"

"It's that old French coin my father found in that wreckage at the cove when I was little."

"I can't take it, Dan, really I can't. Thanks just as much."

"Why not? It don't mean nothin' to me."

"Yes, it does. You showed it to me when we first came here."

"Well, what of it?"

"You've carried it in your pocket all this time."

"Well, what if I have?"

"I can't take it. It's old and valuable, and it's yours."

"All right, then. Have it your own way if you're so high an' mighty. Catch me tryin' to give you somethin' again!"

"Oh, I didn't mean it that way, Dan. It's—it's awfully generous of you."

" 'Tain't generous. What do I want of that old thing? 'Tain't no use to me."

"Well, thanks anyway. I'll like having it. I'll carry it for good luck."

Dan laughed then, a queer laugh, which he had acquired with the inches he put on year by year. It was the kind of laugh that made one uncomfortable because of all the things within it that made it what it was. It had sneers in it, recklessness and scorn, and, if one listened carefully, there was pain behind it. When Dan laughed as he was laughing now, all the old wounds, which one thought were at last healed, opened again.

"I've brought you a heap of good luck, ain't I now?" he said.

16

When John Marston in later years tried to discover to his own satisfaction the day and the hour when he first fell in love with Eileen Lassiter, he always failed. There had been no such tidy, easily located revelation. He finally came to the conclusion that he had been in love with her from the beginning and that, contrary to the way such knowledge usually manifests itself, he had known it all along with no need of that lesser recognition which seems the necessary crowning of lesser matters.

There had been from the start none of that obstruction which disapproval of behaviour often builds between association and companionship. No one in his senses could have approved of Eileen's conduct during her early weeks at Windswept. She was stubborn, irritating, given to fits of noisy temper, overbearing, recalcitrant, impertinent. John Marston saw all these things with his eyes, heard them with his ears, was momentarily confused and embarrassed by them in some upper chamber of his mind; yet five minutes later he was completely untouched by them. He could rescue Mrs. Haskell from some hot argument in her kitchen, and utterly forget the embarrassing occasion for the rescue when he and Eileen had started to walk to the sea-wall.

This miracle of transformation from acute embarrassment to complete oblivion never failed to surprise him whenever he stopped to think about it as, indeed, he rarely did. For he was a boy who hated upheavals of all kinds, was troubled by violent arguments at school and later at college, disliked to see anyone at all discomfited or hurt. As he grew older he became almost ashamed at the seeming lack within himself of convictions, of all those points of view and principles which loomed so large in the thoughts and talk of his friends. He could never seem to whip himself into an attitude in which the things which so concerned them, questions of politics, of religion and ethics, the theory of this thinker and of that, could be made to count for so much as they clearly ought to count. He worried about himself as he was growing up, sometimes felt positive alarm lest he should fail to take upon himself this burden of men and affairs, which all intelligent men everywhere were clearly destined to take in an imperfect world. And yet he worried more over the validity of a singular perception, which grew yearly within him and from which he never managed entirely to free himself: the perception, which was itself a conviction, that all arguments and theories, however frenziedly adhered to, were but fragmentary, unstable realities compared to those unspoken conversations of the mind and spirit which a man could hold only with himself.

Perhaps it was this perception, only imperfectly realized in his early years at Windswept, but even then vaguely tantalizing him, which kept him both from rec-

ognizing in Eileen Lassiter those qualities recognized by
others of the household and from outward reproach of
her. For when they were together, even at sixteen during
that second summer, he was always forgetting those whirlwinds of domestic confusion, those lapses in seemly behaviour, those occasional outbursts of belligerency, which
were upsetting all but himself. Once well beyond Mrs.
Haskell's kitchen, he was always surprised to realize that
he had failed to remember the cause of the angry tears,
now dried on Eileen's face. Had he remembered, he might
have reproved her with good reason and with excellent
effect, but he never did. And as the whirlwinds lessened,
he might have shared the relief of Jan and Mrs. Haskell
and Julian, had he ever been more than outwardly conscious that relief was welcome and necessary.

From the beginning he had always felt completely secure with Eileen, not with that sense of homely, physical
security with which Mrs. Haskell provided him, not even
with the mental and emotional safety which he felt with
Jan, but with a kind of subconscious, almost psychical,
security which baffled definition. When, once out of Mrs.
Haskell's range of vision, Eileen bound her skirts and
longer petticoats about her waist with the length of tape
which she had hidden in her pocket for the purpose, and
ran down the long pasture slope, he felt as he ran with
her that he was racing not with her but with the wind itself. When she lay sobbing in the hay-loft over a dead
puppy, stillborn among a healthy litter of four others, he
felt no impulse to comfort her, because the understanding
of her pain was so much bigger than the pain itself that
mere comfort would have been extraneous, out-of-place,

and unwelcome. When she sat by the fireplace at night, her brown hands clasping her knees, her white or sprigged muslin dress pulled up so that her slender feet in their white stockings and black slippers could easily swing back and forth, he forgot his momentary anxiety over Mrs. Haskell's upbraiding of such an unladylike position, should she see it through the open kitchen door, in the very vitality that cracked and sparkled like the fire itself.

The fireplace at Windswept must have been built with a mysterious view to Eileen herself, he often thought, even although at the time of its framing she had hardly been known and her presence there not even remotely envisaged. Unlike any other fireplace which he had seen, the hearth had been built a foot and a half below the level of the living-room floor and surrounded on its three sides by a shelf of stone, completing the floor itself. On the great rung at one side which held the fire-irons, Jan had hung the rush mats he had woven from the dried marsh grasses. In the evening, instead of sitting in the chairs, one seized one's mat and sat upon the stone shelf, his feet upon the hearth, the fire before him, not too close for comfort, not too far for pleasure.

Eileen always chose to place her mat upon the angle at the left, in spite of the possible danger of Mrs. Haskell's vision from the kitchen. John Marston placed his mat at the right, in the corner beyond the opposite angle. From here he could watch Eileen, the waving of her slippered feet, the swaying back and forth of her back as she clasped her brown hands about her knees and rocked herself to and fro, the firelight in shadow on her face. He became fascinated as he watched her, not by her dark gray eyes below her black brows, not by the usually untidy fair hair, which had a way of escaping from the band of ribbon worn about her head, but by the life which in some odd way burned and blazed within her. Even after long years, when she still waved her slippered feet, although her hair was tidier and her hands less brown, he always thought she was the most alive thing he knew. If one could only catch that life there, he thought, one could know the deep, unapprehended secret of life itself and need seek no longer.

It was doubtless this perception of the life within her which made John Marston at the outset of things oblivious to lesser matters, her untidiness, her quick bursts of fury, her sudden tears of sympathy or of pain. For her prodigal vitality ignited his own lesser measure, quickening him both to his surroundings and to himself. Because of this quickening there was from the beginning a spiritual affinity, which made possible between them those very unspoken conversations usually held only by us with ourselves. His mind spoke with hers; his desires met hers, unexpressed; his fears registered not only themselves but her own.

17

This last was true particularly in the matter of Dan. From her first uneasy summer at Windswept Eileen had understood Dan. Her swift, arrow-like discernment had pierced through his churlishness and suspicion to the fear and the pain which gave them the semblance of reality. By the same intuition she knew them for what they were, seemings only, and because she could not bear to see this double suffering, she set to work to give to Dan the confidence which, in curing the pain, would correct its ungracious expression. Impatient by nature, she was never impatient with Dan, and although he was rarely spoken of between her and John Marston, she knew that they worked together with the same understanding and the same purpose. Whenever Dan had weathered a day or two without a sullen withdrawal into himself, she and John shared the same sense of triumph, mingled with the same dread.

"Don't let him slip back," John Marston could hear her mind saying to his own. "We've got him this far. Don't let's let him go."

Dan's manner with her was different from that which he assumed when he was with John and Julian or even by himself with John. Once she had overcome his initial diffidence and suspicion, he became co-operative, even friendly. His speech invariably changed in her presence. He clipped his words less, became more careful of his grammar, lapsed less into his coast vernacular. When the three or four of them were together, this matter of speech was clearly embarrassing to him, yet he rarely failed her.

She had a way of deferring to him, of setting his knowledge and experience above those of John or of Julian.

"There's a bird's nest over by the sea-wall, Dan. John and Julian think they know what it is, but they don't any more than I do. You'll know."

"I wish you'd take me out in the boat, Dan. I'm not getting anywhere with my rowing. John and Julian haven't a bit of patience."

"I've lost that drawing, Dan, that you made of the house. Couldn't you make me another? I want it for my room in New York."

Sometimes in her room at night she evolved situations by means of which Dan might be brought farther along his road toward confidence and assurance, made up conversations in which she would say this and that and to which Dan might be subtly led to respond as he ought. Like all intrinsically dramatic persons she was not wholly altruistic in her designs, liking to see herself as the author of his destiny, yet at the same time genuine in her eager interest and pity. Four years younger than Julian she was years his senior in her skillful avoidance of awkward predicaments in which Dan was likely to be the loser through Julian's carelessness or stupidity. Whenever she could manage it, in Dan's infrequent visits during her first summer at Windswept, she saw to it that Dan and Julian were seldom brought together.

18

During the third summer at Windswept, when Dan was sixteen, John Marston's anxiety for him took a new turn. That summer Dan had stayed on after his initial week was up, induced, John well knew, by Eileen's presence there rather than by his own. Eileen had prevailed even over the threatened advent of Julian early in July. So long as no others of John's friends were coming, Dan quite clearly preferred to weather Julian than to be deprived of Eileen.

John feared lest another hurt was in store for Dan. He

knew what was all too likely to be the price of Eileen's labours in Dan's behalf. This slow release of three years' agony and self-reproach, this building up of confidence and self-respect, would never be content merely with itself. In place of one pain there was bound to be another.

As June gave place to July and the coming of Julian, John saw the pain waiting to make itself known to Dan, disguised now as hope, now as care for Eileen lest she walk too far or row too long or get out too much beyond her depth while they were swimming at the anchorage. He saw it in Dan's new care for his appearance, his better hair-cut, his more careful speech. Dan had grown into a good-looking boy. His freckles had merged into a becoming tan, his red hair, now that it was brushed properly, had an attraction of its own, his blue eyes had lost their sullen heaviness, his mouth now rarely looked contemptuous and scornful. And yet John knew that Dan had not come far enough along his new road to be able to meet and conquer that new pain waiting for him, all unsuspected, concealed by Eileen's friendliness and understanding.

Whenever the familiar smouldering look came now into Dan's eyes, John knew that it sprang, not from the old fear, but from jealousy of him. Dan now could cope with Julian better than with John. This in itself was a new pain, a forerunner of greater suffering. When the others came and Dan had gone home, John would be there with Eileen. John had the winter to his advantage with letters to and from New York, which Dan would never dare to write. John belonged to Eileen's world as Dan could never belong save in these few intoxicating days which frightened him with their new comfort and happiness.

John would have talked with Eileen about this new, terrifying aspect of Dan had he not been sure that she was aware of it as well as he. Moreover, there was after all nothing to be gained by talking of it. In all fairness to Eileen John had to grant that she sought no favours from Dan. She was merely herself, kind and friendly because she was sorry for him, less flattered by his admiration than pleased by her power over him to become what she had set out to make him become. Not that flattery was entirely absent from the picture, John admitted. To persons like Eileen flattery would always be an element in all that she did, even the awkward, fumbling, ill-expressed flattery of Dan.

Mrs. Haskell was not so sparing in her words as John.

"I don't like the way things are blowin' around here, Miss Eileen."

"What things?"

"Don't put on that innocent look. You know as well as I do. I don't like the way you take with Dan'l. It ain't good for him."

"What way do I take? I'm just kind to him, that's all."

"There's a powerful lot o' danger sneakin' round when one's just bein' kind. He's gettin' to set too much store by you and your ways."

"Nonsense, Mrs. Haskell. He just likes me, that's all."

"That ain't all. If it was, I wouldn't be talkin'. You'll get him to broodin' the way he used to do. Broodin's broodin' no matter what it's about. One sort's bad's 'tother."

"You're always fussing at me, Mrs. Haskell. Dan's been lots nicer since he's come to see that I think he's a fine boy. You can't say he hasn't."

"I'm not tryin' to say nothin'. What I'm sayin', I'm sayin'. S'pose he has been nicer? That's for now. There's a future comin'. That's what's pesterin' me. He'll go off home an' others'll come, an' he'll set an' brood. I know. I've seen him. Broodin' ain't good for Dan'l. You ain't his kind, an' he'll have to find out that you ain't."

Eileen was halted in her argument by the simple fact that Mrs. Haskell spoke the truth. She was too quick not to have seen that truth earlier, too kind not to have been vaguely troubled by it.

"Well, suppose you're right. What can I do about it now?"

"You couldn't go off home, could you?"

"No, I couldn't. The very idea! That's—that's fantastic, Mrs. Haskell."

"Maybe 'tis, maybe 'tain't. But you don't need to say Dan this an' Dan that the way you do. You don't need to keep askin' him to show you things an' take you places, or to run round like a wild thing with him a-prancin' at your heels. No good'll come of it. You mark my words!"

"I'm just trying to make him see he's just like the others. I—I'm sorry for him, really I am, Mrs. Haskell. I wouldn't do any harm to him for anything."

"I ain't a-questionin' your motives nor your meanin'. You're a lot nicer girl'n you was last summer, I'll say that for you. You may turn into somethin' likely after all. What's pesterin' me's what's comin'? I'm just warnin' you to mend your ways."

After her conversation with Mrs. Haskell, Eileen honestly tried to mend her ways, sitting for dull hours in her room on the pretext of letters to write, sewing on a hated traycloth for her mother. But her absence from their doings only brought a new suspicion into Dan's mind to torture him in place of the old from which he had suffered.

"Why didn't you come sailin' with us this mornin'? You said you would."

They were sitting by the fireplace the evening before Julian's arrival. Jan had called John to help him with one of the cows who was sick, and Eileen and Dan were by themselves.

"I couldn't, really, Dan. I—I wasn't feeling awfully well."

"That's just an excuse. Don't tell *me*. You didn't want to come."

"Yes, I did, really."

"Why didn't you then?"

"I told you. I didn't feel well."

"Well, you ate your dinner all right an' your supper, too, an' you helped John bring the cows in. That don't look like bein' sick to me."

He rose from his seat by the fire and began fumbling with the pieces of a puzzle spread out on the table. Eileen, embarrassed as she watched him, saw that his big, awkward hands were trembling. She thought of ways of escape, but no reasonable one offered itself.

"I know. You needn't lie to me. John took me out in the boat so I needn't be in your way. Besides he don't like me bein' along of you."

"Oh, Dan, what nonsense! Don't be so silly!"

"I'm not silly. I'm not blind either. I haven't been so welcome round here the last few days. What have I done to make you so stand-offish all of a sudden?"

"Dan, please. Don't spoil things like that."

"It's you that's spoilin' 'em, not me. Why don't you tell me what I've done?"

"You haven't done a thing, of course. It's just that I've had things to do inside."

"Seems queer you haven't had 'em to do before. Seems queer you got so offish all of a sudden."

He sat down again by the fireplace, stretching his long legs out before him, gripping the edge of the stone shelf with his hands. Eileen had the horrible thought that he was striving to keep from crying. Not knowing what to do, she rose from her seat and put her hand upon his shoulder. He drew away from her abruptly.

"You don't need to be so nice all of a sudden," he said, his voice breaking in spite of him. "I can get along without any of your pretendin'. It's John you like better'n me. He's got better ways than I got. I'm not high-toned like you an' him. Why don't you say you're sick o' me an' my hangin' round? You don't have to worry none about me. I can get along without any o' you. I'll be clearin' out soon, I will."

It was John who mercifully put an end to this conversation. He came through the door just as Eileen was at the end of her resources. She never forgot the look of mingled misery and hatred on Dan's face as he made room for John by the fire.

"Clover's not going to calve tonight after all, I guess,"

John said. "Jan thinks now she'll go till tomorrow. He's putting her back in the field."

He stopped suddenly, looking from one to the other. The expression on Dan's face, which he had not noticed on entering, had changed to one of acute embarrassment and disapproval. John all at once realized that he had forsaken propriety for excitement. After all, one did not speak of such things in the presence of girls. His sense of companionship with Eileen, so conscious that it was unconscious, had for the moment banished from his mind the realization that she was a girl and, therefore, unaccustomed to frankness on such matters. He grew embarrassed in his turn and felt relieved when Dan took his disapproval out-of-doors. He felt more relieved that Eileen showed no confusion whatever. As a matter of fact, she had suddenly found herself with other things to think about.

19

Jan would have been more aware of the suffering lying in wait for Dan had he not, during that summer of 1883, had matters of his own to cause him pain. In May after his long, quiet winter at Windswept he had received a letter from Anna Karel. He had left his new potato field early one afternoon to drive into the village to post a letter to John. He had been feeling particularly good as he drove over his road, noting how the gravel he had spread upon it had absorbed the spring mud, seeing the frail white blossoms of the wild pear foaming among the dark firs and spruces, feeling the warmth of the sun upon his neck, listening to the song-sparrows and the hermit thrushes.

"This morning," he had written to John, "I swept January and February clean out of the house."

It sounded good, he thought, as he drove along, looked good on the white page in its black letters. There were ways and ways of saying things, he thought. John would smile at the way he had said that. It would stay in John's mind much longer than if he had merely said,

"I swept the house this morning."

He was surprised when the postmaster handed him a letter. This day was Thursday. There would be no letter from John. John's fortnightly letters always came on Tuesdays, written on Sundays when there were no games or studying allowed and when, therefore, John had less to do. Julian never wrote letters, nor, to Jan's sorrow, did Anton. This letter was in a crumpled envelope, addressed in an awkward, unfamiliar writing, which sprawled unevenly across the square bit of dirty paper. It looked, Jan thought, as he stood there fingering it, as though it had been carried about in someone's hands for a long time before it had been posted.

When he had opened and read Anna Karel's letter, Jan stood for so long in the corner of the post-office that the postmaster asked him finally through his little window if he wanted anything.

"No," said Jan then, coming to himself. "No, thank you."

Then he got into his wagon and drove home with the letter in his pocket. Every now and then as he drove along, he reached his hand into his pocket to be sure the letter was there, that he had not dreamed it all. The letter was always still there. He did not read it again until he had driven his cows in from the pasture, milked them, cared for his oxen and horses, set his barn to rights. He would have his supper later, he thought, when he had once got things straight in his mind.

Making sure once more that the letter was actually there in his pocket, he walked in the spring twilight up the pasture slope to the house. He would feel less lonely there, he thought. Perhaps he would even open the big front door facing the sea. With the door open he might be able to hold the impression that John or Julian might be inside, waiting to speak to him. Perhaps he might even hear Mrs. Haskell bustling about in the kitchen.

But the loneliness increased once he had opened the door and sat down upon the step. In all his confusion and grief he was surprised. He was never lonely. He had not been lonely since that night nearly two years before when he had sat among his belongings in the railroad station, waiting for the midnight train. When he turned and looked into the house, the loneliness increased again. Now it was a leaden weight within him. There was a ball of red wool on the table near the fireplace, left over from the scarf Eileen had knit for him the summer before. He had scolded her, he remembered, for running in his first standing crop of new, good hay, and she had knit the scarf for him as a proof of penitence. He had found the red ball in a corner of the room that morning when he had swept out January and February. Since it bothered him there, apart from the hands to which balls of wool always belonged, he closed the door again and sat looking out upon the sea.

It was a windless twilight. The empty sea was unbelievably calm. Even its sound against the rocks, which some invisible strength, propelling, withdrawing, made even on the stillest of days, was hushed, a frail breaking of water, its drowsy spreading of itself among the stones, its stealthy retreat, a pause, a slow return. The rough grasses beyond the terrace, the shaggy growths of bayberry and juniper, sweet fern and bracken, were still. No wind rumpled their new, young green, already conquering the languid browns of autumn and winter. The gulls circled lazily above the quiet water, their raucous, hungry cries silenced.

He must read his letter at once, Jan thought, or the light would fail. He drew it from his pocket and from its soiled envelope.

"Dear Jan," it said. "Praised be Jesus Christ."

Jan was shocked by the pious words as he had not been shocked in the post-office, not knowing then that God could hardly be praised for the content of Anna's letter. He could see Anna penning the words, impelled by old custom to begin her letter after the manner of her old country.

Dear Jan:

Praised be Jesus Christ. I write to tell you about Anton. This letter that I write is a very hard letter to write. Anton is not here. Ambroz is not here, too. No one knows where Ambroz has gone for he has run away, very far, I think. He went away at night, two days before the men came to the shop to get Anton. Anton signed a name which was not his name to a piece of paper. I do not know why he did it, but I think it was because he could write names better than

Ambroz could write them. Some men came to get Anton out of the shop and took him away. I was there and I cried, but it was all no good. I could not do nothing at all for Anton. The men took him away. Then they had what they call a trial. Mr. Lassiter tried hard, but he could not do nothing more than I. Now for ten years Anton must stay in a prison. Tomorrow I go from the flat to live in a place Mr. Lassiter has found for me to live in. He will have me clean his firm for him so that I can earn money. All of Anton's money is now gone. I am glad now the baby did not get born. It is better.

I know you will be sorry like me, Jan, for you was Anton's old friend. I hope Ambroz will never come back. He did a wrong thing, too, Mr. Lassiter says, but what good will it do to catch Ambroz, too? It will make more sadness to make all the sadness more.

I should like to see you, Jan. You was always a good man and Anton's friend.

Anna Karel

I shall not write the sadness back home to Anton's father and mother. For what good could that make, Jan?

By the time the spring darkness had fallen, Jan knew Anna's letter by heart. It was strange, he thought, as the stars came slowly out and the air grew cold, how one could never get oneself quite ready for sadness. One could know for months and years that sadness must come, and yet one was never ready for it when it came. All the good food a man could eat could not prepare his heart against its sickness. All the good thoughts one could think could not save one's mind from the pain which the very act of unasked-for living made sure and certain. Even all the prayers one could say, in the woods, at his work, in the

Holy Presence of God Himself, could not frame a wall so high and strong that suffering could not crawl above it.

After Jan had sat upon the door-step for a long time, he went behind the great empty house and across the high land beyond it to the barn. His animals there rattled their chains in their stalls and clumped about in surprise as he entered at such an unwonted hour. He climbed the ladder to the hayloft and stretched himself out above them on the hay. The birds were beginning to sing and the gulls to cry in the chill, pale dawn before he slept.

He remembered before he slept those times when he had slept in the hay before. They had been when Kaspar was born, and again when Rudolph was born, and yet again when Olga was born, and his father had slept in the boys' bed. His mother on those few nights of her life had had a bed to herself.

20

The morning after he had received Anna's letter, Jan had driven his three cows before him through the road to Heron Cove. A fisherman there would care for them during the few days of his absence. One of the cows, who was to have her first calf early in the summer, needed attention and, Jan thought, company; the others must be milked. The oxen and the horses could shift for themselves in the pasture.

After he had left the cows, he walked on to the village. It was easier to walk than to ride or to drive. The action of his legs made the tumult in his mind less noisy and hard to bear. He had not been able to tell the Perkins household, with whom he ate his dinner, what was taking him to New York. He told them instead how well things were faring at Windswept, how close the summer was, and how tall Dan had grown.

Once he reached New York, he had gone straight to Marston, Cobb, and Lassiter. When James Lassiter saw him standing in the door of his office, silent and steady in his ill-fitting city clothes, he felt ashamed of the fear which had postponed his own letter to Jan about Anton. There was nothing that could be done, James Lassiter had said. Ambroz and Anton had been at their underhanded dealings for too long. Even before the forgery had been proved beyond a doubt, a dozen lesser crimes had sprung to light. James Lassiter had thought at first of sending for Jan in order that he might say what he could for Anton at Anton's trial. But, knowing Jan, he had decided against it. After all, there was nothing which an honest man could say. The law was not impressed by the good behaviour of one's youth in a far-off country. It was a man's doings in the land of his adoption with which the law had to deal.

As a matter of fact, Anton had had little enough to say for himself, James Lassiter said. He had been like a man in a dream, incoherent, mixed up in his mind, not seeming to know what it was all about. He had been the despair of the counsel with which James Lassiter had provided him, convicting himself at every turn by his evasions, his contradictory answers to questions, his stupidity. Jan could have done nothing for Anton had he been there, and to be quite frank, since Jan wanted to know the facts as they were, Anton had been quite clear in his mind about not wanting Jan to see him. Moreover, Anton had said to James Lassiter, who had seen him just before they took him away, that he did not want to see Jan ever again.

"Tell Jan," Anton had said, "that it is all as he many times said to me. Tell Jan that I am dead to him, always dead to Jan Pisek."

As he listened to James Lassiter, Jan stood by the window looking out upon the river with his back to the room, just as he had stood, James Lassiter remembered, that January morning when the fate of Windswept had been at stake. Anton was not dead to Jan in those minutes while he listened. He was alive in the past of twelve years before. He was a boy of seventeen, lying in the grass beneath a lime tree filled with fragrance and the drowsy, even hum of bees. He was saying:

"In America, Jan, we will work hard and become rich. Don't be a priest, Jan. Priests are poor men even though they sometimes eat well. We will work in America ten, maybe fifteen years. Then we will come back home. We will put new thatch on our fathers' houses, and everyone will stare at us when they see we have money in our pockets."

"Well, you will want to see Anna," James Lassiter had said when he finished his story. "She is scrubbing somewhere in the building, but she cries more than she scrubs."

Jan found Anna on her knees, crying, as James Lassiter had said, over her mops and pail. When she saw Jan coming across the damp floor, picking his way among the drier spots, she rose from her knees and backed into a corner, holding a great piece of brown soap in her red,

water-wrinkled hands. The rims of her eyes were red and
swollen; her feet in their black felt slippers looked weary
and hopeless. Jan took her to a restaurant across the street
and bought her dinner for her. She could not talk at
all as she ate the beef stew and dumplings from her plate.

Jan had to do all the talking. Instead of asking Anna
questions, which she clearly could not answer, Jan told
Anna what she was to do. Even in a prison, he told Anna,
a man could read letters and sometimes even write them.
They were read, of course, by some of the officers there,
but what did that matter? Since Jan could not write to
Anton, Anna was to write to him. She was to say to
Anton: "Jan says he is still your friend." Then when she
went to see Anton on the days she was allowed to see him,
she was to explain to him how he should still write to his
parents, saying to them that he was well and hard at work,
too hard at work to write often, but well as he hoped
they were well. Anna was to wait there while Anton wrote
his letter and then she was to mail it in New York, putting in it the money that Jan would send her. Anna must
not mind if the officer standing there should read Anton's
letter. That was only the way they had to do.

Jan said this over and over so that Anna would get it
straight and right in her mind. It was well, he told Anna,
that Anton had written home but seldom in the years he
had been in America. Between times Anna could write
herself, saying in her turn that Anton was well but so
busy at his work that Anna must write for him.

When Jan had once started for home, he sat in his
corner by the window and stared out at the fleeting countryside. The lilacs were out here, hanging in full plumes

of blossom, although they were hardly budded in Maine. The apple orchards on the Connecticut hills were pink and white, their petals drifting down through the bright air. In time he might have a few trees of his own on the bare summit just before the woods began. They would get all-day sun there to give them strength against the wind. Or, perhaps, it might be wiser to yield a corner of the new field to them where they would be sheltered more. There were no trees like apple trees to give a man a sense of home. They linked the past with the present and the future.

The present, Jan thought, what was it but a meeting of the past with the future? The present was made of both. It was made of what the past had done to one and of what one would do with the future. The present without the past and the future could not be borne. It was the reality of the past and the hope of the future which made the present possible for a man to bear. So then, if this were so, what would a man do if there were no future before him, if all days were but present days since they were without change, without mystery, and, therefore, without hope? Even one's yesterdays could not continue to stir and move in a man's mind unless there were a future for those yesterdays to make.

21

Julian's arrival at Windswept precipitated a crisis. Julian had a way of stupidly precipitating crises so far as Dan was concerned, although in all fairness to him it must be admitted that the crises usually arose, ironically enough, out of Julian's initial attempts to be friendly.

Daniel Perkins was in no mood to weather a crisis. He had spent the morning roaming by himself about the shore, well out of sight of the house, nursing a two-fold grievance: his unfinished conversation with Eileen, which John had interrupted, and his outraged sense of decency, which John's casual reference to the cow's condition had engendered. His father would come for him that evening, and he was heartily glad of it.

And yet the grievance which had torn him from Eileen and John, who had begged him to sail with them, was more than a momentary attack of frustration and anger. It went far deeper than that. It was merely one of the many ignitions of the fire which was always smouldering within him, now quenched in an hour of self-confidence, now burning with slow torture for hours on end.

He hated them all, he said to himself, as he lay stretched out in the blueberries above the high shore: Julian with his stuck-up air and his pretensions of friendship; Eileen, whose kindness toward him had been only a sham and who was already tired of him; John, whom he wished he had never seen. He hated the house, which had been born out of his suffering, and, more than the house, the fascination which it held for him in spite of his hatred of it, making him unable to sail away and leave it for the summer as his father had wished. He hated the way people still looked at him in the village. He hated himself and the memories which still made him wake at night, crying out in the hated darkness. He hated the useless struggles he had made to speak out of a grammar book so that they might like him better. He hated the rude things which had clutched at him for action and for utterance until they had had their way, and the self-loathing they had caused him after they had been done and said. Most of all he hated the weeks ahead when he could not know what they were all doing in his absence, the fear and suspicion, jealousy and anger, which would rack his body and his mind.

He hated those new and wicked thoughts which had suddenly come to torture him at night, those stirrings within his body, that desire to use it in a way that must be wrong. He hated a queer, new-born imagination within him, which had suddenly come upon him unawares, forever suggesting the evil in things heretofore taken for granted, forever seeing in the most ordinary appearances shapes and forms never recognized before. He hated the sudden, fierce protection he had all at once found within himself for Eileen Lassiter, lest she should see things and hear things which only men and boys should see and hear. And he hated and feared the awful thought that her recent refusal to be with him had risen because, through some uncanny means of discovery, she had learned of the wrong things in his mind, and feared him.

He hated to go home more even than he hated to stay. He was afraid of himself at home. There was a girl in the village whom men talked about on the street, in the store and post-office. Her name was Molly Carlton. She had meant nothing to him until now, for although he had known in his mind that men spoke slightingly of her, he had not known in his body. Just before he had come to

Windswept, he had met her one day when he was walking by himself in the woods.

"Hello, Dan," she had said. "You're growing up to be some good, aren't you? Well, what do you know about that?"

That was all she said, but although he had gone on his way with only a brief response to her greeting, he could not get her out of his head. Ever since he had come to Windswept, he had found himself wondering whether he would see her again, what she might say, what he might say, what might come of those things that they might say. Three years ago, before all these many things had happened, he could think whatever thoughts he liked, go into his mind, find whatever thoughts he wanted, and think them. But now thoughts sprang upon him all unbidden, clutched him, would not let him go. He could not fight these new thoughts, because now he had no other good old thoughts to take their place.

When he got home, he might go to the Banks on a fishing schooner. They were going every now and then, and some man was sure to give him a berth. If he went away, he would at least not run into Molly again. There was hard work on a fishing-schooner, once one began to fish. It was better than sitting on a deck piled with lumber for Boston, coming back in ballast, with nothing to do for hours except to draw pictures and be laughed at by the other men for drawing them. But if he went either to the Banks or to Boston, he would miss Mrs. Haskell, whom Jan drove in every now and again to clean up and cook for them. And missing Mrs. Haskell would mean that he could know nothing at all of what was happening at Windswept, who was there, what John and Eileen were doing.

He was like the horses, he thought, who trod on a thresher, going on and on, but never getting anywhere at all. Or like those on the merry-go-round at the fair in September, which went round and round, always coming back to the same place in the circle. There was no road for him that led straight away from things, any more than there was for the horses on the thresher or on the merry-go-round. If he went away in the fall to the academy in the next village, as his father and Mrs. Haskell wanted him to do, the road there would suddenly curve about and come back, once someone would say, or think,

"There's the boy who killed a man three years ago. You don't mean you haven't heard about it?"

He did not want to go back to dinner, but between going back now or facing them all later when his father should come and he must get his things and say goodbye, going back now was easier. He would try to cover things up inside him so they could not be seen, make one last, mighty effort to be what Eileen liked in spite of her treatment of him.

"Hello, Julian."

"Hello, Dan. Glad to see you. Gosh! How you have shot up! John's a dumpling compared with you."

"John and I missed you, Dan. Wherever have you been? We made a poor come-about without you to help. I thought sure we were going over one minute."

"That so?"

"Whatever have you been doing with yourself, Dan?"

"Been huntin' for a fish-hawk's nest over at the sea-wall."

"Did you find it?"

"Sure. I climbed an old dead tree there. There's four birds in it."

"Show it to us after dinner, will you, Dan?"

"Well, maybe."

22

After dinner they went out across the terrace to the edge of the headland. The tide was coming, and there was a strong wind. The horizon beyond the open sea was dull and indistinct, and there was a chill in the air.

"There's fog outside," said Julian. "Gosh! Wouldn't you know I'd bring on a fog mull?"

Julian brought worse things than a fog mull, Dan thought, staring across the open water, not looking at Julian in his city clothes. A fog mull was nothing to what Julian always brought.

"You kids wait here," Julian said. "I want to get into my old togs before we go to see the hawk's nest. I've got a present for you, Dan. I'll go fetch it. You all wait here for me."

Dan felt the hot fire surge from somewhere inside him up into his head and face. He felt himself burning there in the high, damp wind. He did not want Julian's presents, bought with the pocket money he himself never had, bought only because Julian felt sorry for him. He shivered in the wind in spite of the fire burning him. He felt his control leaving him, joining the wind. He felt as

though he might cry before them all. His throat was tight-
ening. There was something heaving inside him, coming
higher and higher.

The screen door of the house slammed shut. Julian was
coming across the terrace in his dirty old flannels, a box
in his hand. He was undoing the box as he came. When
he reached them standing there, he held a hunting-knife
in his hand, new and shining, the blade long and stout
and sharp, the handle black and strong. On the handle
were the letters D. P. in silver.

"Gosh!" said John. "What a beauty! You aren't hand-
ing them around, are you?"

"Look, Dan," said Eileen. "It's even got your initials
on it!"

Dan turned and faced them all. His eyes were alight
with anger. His hands were shaking.

"Thanks," he said, his voice trembling. "I don't want
it. I don't go huntin'. John can have it."

Eileen stared at him. She saw the anger mounting in
Julian, the embarrassment of John. She must say something, she thought.

"You can't be impolite like that, Dan," she said. "Julian had it marked especially for you. It's not John's, it's
yours."

Dan's eyes blazed at her. Now that the moment had
come for her to choose allegiance, she had given it to
Julian and to John. His voice screamed in the high wind.

"I tell you I don't want his stinkin' old presents. He
can't do nothin' for me. None of you can do nothin' for
me. An' don't you go correctin' me an' my manners.

Don't you go lordin' yourself over me. I'll be impolite if I choose. Let him take his old knife and go to hell with it!"

Julian had the ill sense to laugh then. There was something comic to him in the three of them standing there, put to rout by the crazy antics of a rude country boy. After all, to laugh was better than to lose one's head over nothing.

"Oh, well," he said. "Excuse my fatal error. I'm sorry I didn't keep my change. I might have known a bumpkin like you couldn't appreciate a knife like this."

He laughed again and turned to go to the house, carelessly twirling the knife in his hand as he did so, its blade gleaming in the sun. As he turned, Dan sprang forward, his strong, bony shoulders rippling inside his shirt, the fingers of his hands ready to seize and to hold. But Eileen was quicker than he.

"Dan!" she screamed. "Leave him alone. He's not worth your touching him. Julian, you damn fool!"

Dan stood still, amazement battling with anger. Eileen had struck her brother a ringing blow across his cheek. Her hair had fallen from its knot; the neck of her dress had become undone; her face was crimson. John stared at her, too, half-unwilling admiration slowly conquering him. She was like some primitive creature standing there, her breath sounding in her nostrils, her eyes distended, the wind blowing her loosened hair about her face and shoulders. How did such things end? John Marston thought. Would they always stand there, like statues frozen in fury? He must do something, he thought. They

could not always stand there while shame and embarrassment slowly took the place of rage. Unwittingly he
made the wisest move he could have made.

"Come, Julian," he said.

He and Julian walked away then along the path, down
the high shore, leaving Dan and Eileen together. Dan
gazed out to sea, his back to Eileen. Anger had left him,
like a mill race tumbling into quiet water, its spray and
foam absorbed into stillness. His face and hands were
wet with sweat, though the air was cold and damp, his
shoulders and chest streamed with it inside his shirt. He
felt suddenly free from himself. Even Julian's insult had
gone, blown away on the wind. He did not speak to
Eileen. He was conscious that behind him she was fastening her hair again into its knot, retying the ribbon
around her head, straightening her dress. After what
seemed a long time, she said:

"Let's go to the meadow, Dan, and see if the calf has
come."

He walked beside her to the meadow like one in a
trance, or like one hypnotized, not knowing what he
does, obeying commands, careful for nothing. He knew
without consciously realizing it that his pain had gone,
that he had for the moment no memory of the past, no
care for the present, no fear for the future. Eileen took
his hand as they walked beyond the house, beyond the
barn, across the pasture, the wind whipping them, down
the slope toward the field surrounded by Jan's neat fence
of criss-crossed logs. They did not speak as they went.
When they reached the fence, he sprang over it and
helped her across the stile that Jan had made of flat

stones, like the stiles in his old country. The part of the field reserved for mowing was white and yellow with daisies and buttercups. The field for grazing was just beyond, across another stile.

When they reached this stile and he was about to help her over it, Dan's breath stopped in his throat. Just below and at one side of the stile was a clump of wild cherry trees, which Jan had left for shade for his cows. From this clump of trees there came strange sounds, a sound of a heavy body plunging about in the undergrowth, a sound of heavy, stertorous breathing, of moans of animal pain. Eileen mounted the stile quickly, Dan stumbling after her. From its top they could see below into the trees.

Clover was there, her cream-coloured sides heaving in great ridges, her neck taut, her eyes bulging as she gave quick birth to her calf. The calf was half in the world already, half within its mother. Another of Jan's cows, old and experienced in such matters, grazed unconcernedly at the other end of the field.

Dan came to his senses then, grew purple with embarrassment.

"You mustn't stay here," he said. "Let's go back. It's no place for a girl here."

"Nonsense," said Eileen. "I'm not a child, Dan. I want to see what happens. Let's sit here and watch."

She crouched down upon the flat rock of the stile. He stood beside her, trying to recall his humiliation for her sake the evening before, wondering where it had gone. For with her matter-of-fact, casual words, her calm way of sitting there beside him, her chin in her hands, her eyes upon the straining, suffering creature below them, every

act of abhorrence for these untidy acts of nature, every
vestige of that seemingly evil curiosity, which he had in
the past months associated with the physical acts of ac-
complishing blood and breath in one's kind, vanished.
That sudden, purifying wholeness, which her anger for
his sake had given him on the headland, came again to
him here. He was no longer afraid of his body or of its
temptations, understanding through this very act of birth
that the necessary process of engendering life itself was
neither repellent nor evil, but, in its natural course,
simple, plain, and inevitable.

When the calf was at last standing unsteadily on its
long, tottery legs, he was surprised that he could laugh so
easily with Eileen—at the way it gazed about the field, apparently in mute wonder at what the earth afforded, at its
submission to its mother's frenzied cleaning of it, at its
early frantic efforts for food. When he saw Julian and
John approaching, he was more surprised that he felt not
the slightest embarrassment at meeting Julian again.

"Clover's got a heifer," he heard himself calling excitedly to them. "Where's Jan? He'll be pleased."

"A heifer!" cried John, racing ahead of Julian to the
stile. "My word! What a beauty! I wonder just when it
came."

"Ten minutes ago," said Eileen. "You missed it. Dan
and I saw it all."

"You did!"

"Well, I'm blessed!" said Julian.

Then he suddenly remembered what this present excitement had completely swept from his mind. He put
out his hand to Dan. He said:

"I was no end of a stupid ass, Dan, a damn fool, just as Eileen said. I didn't mean a word of it. I'm awfully sorry, really I am."

"That's all right," said Dan, shaking hands with Julian, looking straight at him to the amazement of Eileen and John. "I'm sorry I was rude. 'Twas nice of you to bring me the knife. Thanks. I've never had one, and I'll like using it."

"I forgot," said Julian, hurrying to change the subject. "We saw your father in the village. He's too busy on some job to come for you tonight. He'll be out tomorrow."

"All right," said Dan. "That's good."

"That's fine, Dan!" said Eileen and John.

23

That evening they sat by the fire, the four of them on the broad stone shelf. The fog was blowing in from the sea in great, gray clouds, racing above the land, shutting in the house. The darkness had fallen early. It was cold. At supper, while they had eaten hot, steaming bowls of Mrs. Haskell's clam chowder, they had watched the sea fade from sight, blotted out by a moving, opaque wall, the headland disappear as though it were not, the outlines of the land eastward slowly enveloped by the white, scudding mist.

The fire was doubly welcome on such a night. Jan brought in armfuls of spruce kindlings, dry from a long winter under cover. These would combat any degree of dampness which might settle in the chimney. He brought in, too, great hunks of driftwood from his pile in the cellar of the barn, silvery gray in colour, in shape everything imaginable: arched pieces from the groins of forgotten ships; smooth lengths of discarded logs from overladen schooners, porous and light from days of sea water and years of sun on the beach; old lobster buoys drifted from their moorings in storms long since past; great awkward chunks of unrecognizable timber with brown bolts of iron encrusted with rust and salt, and trailing bits of dried seaweed and kelp.

"These will burn fine," he said. "I've been saving these against a fog like this."

He sat with them smoking his pipe, suffused by a glow of comfort he had not felt in weeks. The calf was bedded down with its mother on clean straw in the barn, he said, warm and snug.

"It's a fine calf," said Jan. "We'll raise it, John."

Dan looked at Eileen. She had on a pale blue dress that he liked. The firelight played on her face, brought out flickering lights from her hair. Dan felt comfortable and at home in spite of an odd feeling of sickness now and then, which made his head swim and his stomach shake inside him. Perhaps he should not have eaten his second bowl of chowder, he thought, but they had all been hungry and merry at the table. Even Julian's talk of his commencement doings at Harvard had not seemed strange and outlandish to Dan. He had laughed with the others, joked with Julian.

Now when Julian and John were whispering a bit on their side of the fireplace, he did not feel suspicious or left out. He watched the fire, looking shyly now and then at Eileen. He was sorry for the first time in two years that his father was coming for him.

"We've got some news for you, Dan," Julian was saying. "I finally got your father to say that we could tell you instead of him. John didn't think we ought at first, but now he does."

"It's fine news, Dan," said John.

"News?" asked Dan. "What do you mean, news?"

"Well," said Julian, savouring his words, enjoying his excitement, "my father's been writing to your father about you. My father wants you to come to New York. He saw those ship drawings that you made last summer. He says you've got the makings of a first-class draftsman. He says you might even be a big ship-designer some day. He'd like you to come to New York right away now and work in his firm with a man he has there, who likes your drawings, too. There's a school you can go to in the evenings, my father says, that teaches draftsmanship. Your father's awfully pleased. He got the letter yesterday from my father and was at the train to see me."

Dan was speechless, looking from one to another. His head suddenly felt lighter; his stomach again turned over inside him. A stampede of thoughts assailed him. All the things he had feared rushed through his head and out again into bewildering space: the long, idle hours at home, suspicious and fearful about them all at Windswept; his plans to escape, to the Banks, to Boston with the lumber; Molly Carlton with the queer look in her eyes; his father's ill-concealed anxiety about him; the threatened academy with those who somehow would

know about him, and its unfamiliar studies, Latin and
chemistry, and all the rest. Were these then to have no
being? Was he then to escape them all? He looked again
at Julian and John, at Eileen and Jan. They were all
looking at him, waiting for him to speak.

"Me?" he stammered at last. "Me in New York drawing things?"

"Of course," cried John. "It's a splendid chance, Dan.
We've been talking about it all the afternoon, Julian and
I. We've been saving it till tonight."

"My mother'll look after you, Dan," said Eileen, her
eyes shining at him. "My father says so in the letter,
doesn't he, Julian? And I'll show you around New York
in the holidays. You'll make good, Dan. I always said so,
didn't I, John?"

"Of course," said John. "We've all said so, Dan."

"There's a fine chance in New York for a boy like you,
Dan," said Jan from his chair. "I came to New York
from the old country when I was just your age."

Dan had never felt as he felt then. He was intolerably
well in his mind, intolerably sick in his body. He grew
white there by the fire, dizzy in his head. Things swam
before his eyes, the walls, Eileen's blue dress. His legs
grew suddenly weak under him. He ought to run away
from them all, he thought, out into the cool dampness of
the fog, but he somehow lacked the strength.

"When shall I go?" he managed to ask.

"The sooner, the better," Julian said. His words seemed
to come from a great distance, although Dan strove with
all his might to catch and hold them. "The sooner, the
better, my father says. Next week, your father thought,

Monday maybe. Why, Dan, what's the matter? Gosh!
You're sick! Give us a hand, here, Jan."

For Dan had all at once slumped forward, fairly fallen
into the midst of them. He *was* sick. To his shame and
humiliation he retched there before them all, lost his
supper on the hearth, disgraced himself completely, he
thought, while the room tottered and swayed and for a
moment he lost sight of everything in a ghastly faintness.

He thought he would never get over the mortification
of it, but once Jan and Julian had gotten him to his bed
between the clean sheets which Mrs. Haskell spread on it,
he somehow felt quite different. He felt tired and clean
both inside his body and his mind. He stretched out his
legs between the smooth sheets; he heard the roar of the
surf which the wind was hurling against the headland
and the long shoreline beyond. The air coming through
his window was damp and cool; the light from the fire in
the living-room lay in warm, moving shadow on his wall.
He heard their lowered anxious voices, concerned about
him, glad for his incomprehensible, healing future. He
fell asleep then, waking later for the hot, salty gruel
which Mrs. Haskell fed him herself from a spoon while
Eileen looked on from the foot of his bed.

Eileen left a candle burning in his room when she and
the others went to bed. She placed it on a table in the
corner, well out of the draft from the window. It burned
with a clear, steady flame, lighting up the pleasant darkness. He had never had a candle burning in his room before. It added to this singular contentment and freedom
which he felt. He tried hard to stay awake in order not to
miss an instant of this new life which was surrounding

him, blotting out the past, making the future bounteous and secure; but in spite of his striving, the warmth and well-being of his body conquered him and he fell asleep.

Sometime in the night he woke suddenly with the quiet opening of his door. Eileen crept into his room in a red dressing-gown over her white nightdress. He could not believe it for a moment, but there she was, her yellow hair braided down her back. He could just make out her features in the candlelight.

She came close to his bed, bent above him.

"Are you really all right, Dan?" she whispered. "I was so worried about you I couldn't go to sleep. I just wanted to be sure you were all right and didn't want anything."

"I'm fine, Eileen," he whispered back, astonishment and pleasure making his voice tremble. "I'm all right, really. 'Twas nice of you to come. I'm so sorry I was sick that way before you all."

"Nonsense! What does that matter? That doesn't matter at all so long as you're all right."

"I'm all right really. Thanks for coming, Eileen."

"Goodnight, then," she said. "If you're all right tomorrow and the fog lifts, we'll go to see the fish-hawk's nest, shall we?"

"There isn't any nest," said Dan, "but we'll go all the same."

Eileen understood at once about there not being any nest. She laughed there by his bed. He laughed, too, in this delightful sense of conspiracy between them. He could see her features more clearly now, the dark arch of her brows beneath her fair hair, her straight, imperious nose, her parted mouth and white, even teeth. She shivered a little in the damp, cold air.

"You'll get a cold, Eileen," he whispered. "You mustn't stay any longer. Thanks for coming."

"Goodnight, then," she said again. "It's wonderful about New York and your future. I always knew that something big would find you out, Dan."

She turned to go, then stopped suddenly and, bending over him, kissed him on his cheek. He lay there as she went quickly, silently away, unable to move of his own will, although his body was trembling with surprise and happiness. He heard the door closed gently, her footsteps steal across the living-room, lost in the silence as she went toward her own room in the farther wing of the house.

Now no drowsiness enfolded him. He lay awake for hours, trying to remember just how Eileen's lips had felt against his face, wrapped close in an ecstasy he had never known, in a freedom he had never believed possible for him. He heard the moaning of the fog-horn from the great light, the faint cry of some night bird, the crashing of the surf. He heard the slow, sure ticking of the great clock in the living-room, muted yet audible through his closed door. He watched the candle on the table grow paler, flicker in a pale blue flame, die away in the darkness. He saw the first dull, leaden approaches of the foggy dawn creeping in through the windows of his room.

When the light grew stronger and he realized that a new and different day had come, he suddenly discovered that he was hungry, hungrier than he had ever been in his whole life, literally starving to death.

24

Mrs. Haskell was an early riser. Five o'clock each morning saw her scrubbed and dressed, ready for the day. She liked to put her kitchen to rights before she got things running for her seven o'clock breakfast. Mrs. Haskell always assumed that, although she left her kitchen at rights when she went to bed, the very passage of time during the night did things to it which made necessary her putting it to rights again in the morning.

This morning she was up a bit earlier than usual. In the first place, she did not like this fog. It made her jumpy with its clinging dampness, its blotting out of familiar, reassuring objects. Fogs made rooms messy. It was well to get a good fire started early in a fog. In the second place, she had conceived the idea of flap-jacks sometime in the night watches, and she liked to allow her batter to set a bit on the back of her stove under a clean piece of butter muslin. This hardly influenced the batter, but it made a deal of difference to Mrs. Haskell's mind. Dan'l could not eat flap-jacks, to be sure, after his unprecedented upset of the night before, but she would poach an egg for him.

When she opened her bedroom door and came into her kitchen, she was startled half out of her wits to see her patient gnawing a bit of hard-tack in her rocking-chair and looking better than she had ever seen him.

"Lord bless my soul, Dan'l! Where on earth did you drop from?"

"I'm hungry, Mrs. Haskell," said Dan. "I'm hollow in my insides. I'm hungrier'n I've ever been in my whole life. Can I have a doughnut?"

"No, you can't. Doughnuts'll set risky on your stomach after that performance o' yours last night. You fair scared me half out o' my senses. You can have a piece o' bread with a smatterin' o' butter. What on earth are you aimin' to do at this hour with this fog thick as a blanket o' wool? You ain't haulin' traps, are you?"

"No, of course not. You can't see more'n a foot ahead o' you. I'm just takin' a walk."

He did not tell Mrs. Haskell where he was walking or why. Yesterday in his solitary roaming about the shore he had spied some wild roses blooming in a tangle of raspberries close to the edge of the high shore. As he had lain awake waiting for the dawn, he had planned to get them for Eileen, have them at her plate for breakfast. Yesterday he would not have ventured to do such a thing, but today was different from yesterday. Today he would not for an instant mind John's or Julian's eyes when they should see the wild roses at Eileen's place at the table.

"It's a queer mornin' for a walk, seems to me."

Dan ate his bread in hungry gulps, planning as he did so just how he should break his news to Mrs. Haskell. He decided to be as casual as he could, thereby increasing her surprise.

"I don't suppose you'll be spreadin' much more bread for me, Mrs. Haskell."

Mrs. Haskell looked up sharply from the batter she was mixing in her yellow bowl.

"So you've come to your senses after all, have you? Made up your mind to go to the academy after all? Well, I'm right glad of it. Your father'll be easier in his mind.

You've caused him a heap o' worryin' one way an' another, Dan'l."

"Well, he won't have to worry about me any more, Mrs. Haskell. Only I'm not goin' to any academy."

"What do you mean you ain't goin'?"

"I mean just that, that I ain't goin'. My plans have changed all of a sudden."

"Don't keep me jumpin' round in my mind any longer. It's hard enough to breathe this mornin' anyways without your pesterin'. What plans might you have, I'd like to know, that I'm foreign to?"

Dan was enjoying himself immensely. Things were working out better than he could have planned. He cut another slice of bread and buttered it slowly for himself. Now the time had come.

"I'm leavin' for New York in a few days, Mrs. Haskell," he said. "I've got a full-sized job there waitin' for me."

Mrs. Haskell banged the yellow bowl, which she was holding in the stout circle of her left arm, on the kitchen table. She stared at him, her big spoon uplifted in her hand. Even in her amazement she could not remember when she had ever seen him look like this before, his red hair neatly brushed, a clean shirt on, his blue eyes shining.

"Have you plumb lost your wits, Dan'l Perkins?" she said at last. "Why don't you tell me you're huntin' gold in California an' done with it? Why don't you tell me you're ropin' wild steers in them far western states? Whatever do you mean, a job waitin' for you in New York?"

Dan smiled at her as he ate his bread and butter. He

repeated his words slowly, emphasizing each one to make
it last longer.

"I'm leavin' for New York in a few days," he said. "It's
true. If you don't believe me, ask John or Julian, or even
my father. They'll tell you it's true. I'm goin' to New
York to learn to be a draftsman with Julian's father and
at night school. Julian's father likes my drawin's. He's
goin' to teach me himself, him and another man. I might
even be a big ship-designer some day. I'm goin' soon,
maybe as soon as day after tomorrow. I expect there's
great things ahead o' me if I just make good. I'm goin' to
do my best to make good, Mrs. Haskell."

He did not know why, but his voice broke a little on
his last words. Perhaps it was because Mrs. Haskell had
suddenly raised her clean checked apron to her face. He
had never seen Mrs. Haskell's apron an inch out of its
wonted place before, and the sight startled him. He left
the rest of his slice of bread on the shelf and ran out-of-
doors into the fog.

The fog was thick as blazes. He had never seen worse
fog. You had to pick your way along the path which your
feet had to feel since your eyes could not see it. You had
to keep your ears pricked for familiar sounds, much as
the fog deadened them. You had to judge how near you
were to the edge of the high shore by the feeling of the
wet air on your face. When you got dangerously close, the
air felt different, for then you were just above the sea, on
the very brink of things.

But he knew precisely where the wild roses were. Before you got to the cove, the shore rose again almost as
high as the headland itself. It rose in just one sharp sum-

mit and then sank as suddenly, the land dropping
downward in a steep incline to the great rocks and boulders of the cove itself. You would know when you were
getting there in spite of the fog, for your feet all at once
went up and up. The tangle of the raspberries against
your legs would show you, too, and the crashing of the
sea against the boulders, louder and stronger here than
even at the headland itself.

The roses were at the very top of the sharp rise of land.
Once he got there he was sure he could make them out,
even in this blasted fog. If there were no other way, he
could grope about on his knees until his hands felt them.
You could never mistake wild roses, once you had
touched them.

25

"Flap-jacks!" cried Eileen when Mrs. Haskell came
into the dining-room with a laden platter. "That's awfully nice of you, Mrs. Haskell. Where's Dan?"

"Dan'l was up betimes," said Mrs. Haskell. "He went
for a walk in spite o' me. Dan'l's fair beside himself this
mornin'. He's so full up with this New York idea that
he's jumpin' round inside himself. I declare it's kind o'
your father, Mr. Julian, an' I daresay you had a hand in
it yourself."

Julian had rarely been in Mrs. Haskell's good graces,
and he enjoyed the new experience.

"I can't say I did much, Mrs. Haskell, except to show
him Dan's drawings. But I'm glad for Dan."

"It'll fair be the makin' o' Dan'l. He's laid heavy on

me an' his father for a long time now. He's a good boy, Dan'l is, though hard to make out now and then."

"Flap-jacks, Mrs. Haskell!" cried John. "That's ripping! I've been to see the calf. It's coming on fine. Where's Dan? Is he all right?"

"I'm just sayin' as how he went for a walk, Mr. John. He was carryin' his news so high 'n' mighty I couldn't do nothin' with him. I've seen Dan'l for goin' on a year now, summer'n' winter, but I never see him so happy in his mind about himself. It fair does me good to see him like this."

The fog lay heavy above the land, deadening their voices as they went along the shore path calling for Dan. Mrs. Haskell let the beds go while she stared out of her kitchen window into its dark, leaden grayness. Jan forgot the calf and went with the three of them, shouting and calling—to the anchorage, where they found the dory still moored after Julian had swum out to make sure, to the woods, north and east, the trees dripping dampness, to the cove where the rising tide swirled and crashed in the high wind. They joined hands there on the path above the high shore, unable to make out anything in the gray obscurity, hearing no answering shout when they stood still and listened. There was no silence like the silence of fog, Jan thought, muffled, stifled, mute, dead.

At noon they stood in the barn door and watched Jan drive away into the gray indistinctness toward the village to fetch Dan's father. Eileen sobbed at dinner, tears falling into her plate. John and Julian on either side of her stared at each other.

At three o'clock without warning, with no slow piercing of a heretofore vanquished sun, the gray pall lifted, left the land. Its massed dun hosts were swept high in the air by a swift change in the wind, then blown out to sea between the blue sky above and the wet green earth beneath. The sudden sunlight seemed miraculous, flooding the dripping land, gleaming in the beads of moisture thick on alder and blueberry, glittering in the frail meshes of thousands of spiders' webs strung across the spaces between the spines of juniper. Now their voices rang clear, now their eyes could see, now their ears could hear Dan's answering shouts.

They found him, Julian, Eileen, and John, when the air was quite clear and bright, when there was no longer the least sign of fog. He lay between two great boulders just below the high, sharp summit above the cove. He had fallen straight as a plummet from the edge of the summit to the nearer boulder. He lay with his head in a clump of sea lavender, its tiny, fragile, drenched flowers catching the sun. His face was so still and calm, happy even, that they thought he could have felt no terror at his instant drop into nothingness. They found some scattered wild roses near him, which they rescued from the tide.

Ann Marston has one of these today, pressed in an old book belonging to her mother. She has never quite gotten to the point of destroying it.

THE POSSESSION

1891–1907

1

Windswept in 1891 showed few signs of change. The three-mile stretch of land was still unkempt and shaggy, ancient and inviolable. The dark woods to the north had receded a little, driven back from their former supremacy by the sharp blows of Jan's axe in the late fall. Among the stumps too recalcitrant for his plough and oxen, his sheep grazed. The sea to the south and east was as changeful and changeless as is the sea everywhere.

The house in ten years had weathered to a pale gray, a pleasanter colour each year, they all thought. Jan kept the shutters painted a fresh, deep green as they needed it, after wintry onslaughts of wind and storm. His clumps of firs and spruces at each corner had grown taller with every year in spite of the wind, although that had taken its toll in the bent and crooked angles of their dark branches.

Jan still spent his winters at Windswept, still saw Orion starting his march in the cold hours of early dusk, completing it in the late dawn. Jan liked the strength and simplicity of the winter, the earth stripped even of its rough finery of the summer, the bare, undecorated, hard bones of it ringing against his feet as he went about his work. He liked helping his ewes to give birth to their young in the early spring, now and then carrying a limp,

long-legged lamb in his arms to spend a warm night by his
cabin fire. He liked to pour the broad white streams of
the milk which he and his creatures could not use into
great, tight cans and haul them in his cart over his road
to the fishermen's children at Heron Cove.

"He's a good feller, that Bohunk man," the fishermen
said, mending their nets around the corner of some shack
out of the wind, splicing the ravelled spaces of their
trawls, pulling on their clay pipes. "He's a queer one,
livin' alone way out there, but he's got better points 'n
most, no matter where he hails from."

The fishermen's wives always had hot coffee for Jan
when he brought the milk; they had doughnuts or a piece
of pie to go with his coffee. They liked him sitting in
their kitchens, drinking his coffee. Their children always
greeted him with noisy shouts.

Jan liked best of all to be where he was. No hour was
dull for him. Each day was new. Here his life slowly returned to its old continuity which his years in New York
had broken, spanned those years, stretching across them
the broken strands of the past, knitting these securely to
the stout threads of the present. Now warp and woof
could once more be woven into an invincible fabric, old
days, old years, new hours, new sights and sounds, old
and new thoughts. Thus he daily prepared himself, all
unconscious that he was doing so, for that magical presence, which is about us everywhere, not quite out of
sight, not quite out of hearing, but too often lost, unheard and unseen, in the tumult of the world and the
engulfing onrush of egoism. That old, eternal presence,
which listens to no arguments, reveals itself to no stran-

gers, Jan was rediscovering daily by himself in the poetry
and prose of mere circumstance. Time had been too
quick in New York, he said often to himself. How time
in New York had seized one, bruised and hurt, never left
one alone a minute! Here time was slow and gracious,
unobtrusive, courteous even, a companion rather than a
master.

Jan never quite knew why he did not go back to the
old country for Philomena, why he sent her the money to
come by herself instead of fetching her as he had planned
for years to do. When he tried to think it out clearly, he
never succeeded in discovering the exact reason, hiding
somewhere in the very bottom of his mind, eluding him
whenever he tried to go into his mind and seize it. There
were many reasons, of course, but none of these more
tangible reasons was the actual one.

Anton was one reason. Anton was still in prison. When
Anna wrote to Jan, as she did at long intervals, she said
that the prison had made Anton a different man. She said
that Anton was slow and quiet now, in his body and in
his mind, and that he would make no plans for himself
against that good day soon when he should come away
from the prison. Anna had made the plans for him.

Anna was now with a Polish farmer whom she knew,
in Massachusetts, working in the onion fields, cultivating
the tobacco in the Connecticut valley, where, she told
Jan, it was so hot in the summer that the tobacco grew
fine. Anna was happier here than in New York. When
Anton was free, Anna said, she would bring him to the
Polish family where she lived. There was always room
for one more, Anna said, and the Polish farmer for whom

she worked had no bad thoughts about men who had
been in prison. Nor did this farmer dislike the Czechs as
some Polish people did. Anna liked speaking her own old
language, she told Jan. Jan must excuse her bad English,
she said.

In the continuous, closely woven fabric which was now
Jan's life, there was a strand that was Anton. For since
Anton belonged to Jan's past, he had had his share in
drawing the broken threads together even as he had had
his share in rupturing them. And yet, after the strands
were knitted together with Anton's help, Anton went
back into the past. Jan knew Anton in the past and loved
him there. If Jan went back to the old country, Anton
would be there, in the past and yet in the present, under
the lime trees, at the altar in the church, at his father's
door with his family in the twilight. Jan could not picture himself going to the old country and saying to Anton's mother, who still lived:

"Yes, *matko,* Anton is well. He has done fine in New
York. He sends this money by me to you since he cannot
now leave his work."

Nor did Jan find it any easier to picture himself in his
own father's house, now, since his mother's death three
years before, presided over by his sister Olga and her husband, Krištof. He remembered Olga as a little girl with
yellow hair in plaits. To see Olga now and Krištof, whom
he had never known, would be to talk to strangers, who
might not on their part take to him after all these many
years. Unless one lived with time, Jan thought, worked
with it, learned its ways as one could only do alone with it,

it might do strange, cruel things to one. It had to be watched and guarded, this time, if one were to keep on good terms with it. He did not like to think of his father eating Olga's food, sleeping in his mother's bed alone. But was he sure that he would have words to say to his father or even that they could sit at peace before the door at nightfall without speaking? Would it not be better, perhaps hurt less, to stretch one's hands across the wide miles of ocean, laden with money to make the life there easier for them all, to send one's thoughts and prayers to heal hearts which one might unwittingly break by one's very presence among them?

All these, however, although they looked like good reasons and undoubtedly were, were not the real reason lying out of sight in the bottom of his mind. Jan had become aware of this real reason at the time of his mother's death, although he lacked then as now the power to define it satisfactorily, even to himself. When Philomena had written to him that their mother was dead, Jan had read her words as the statement of a fact, which to his surprise held, in itself, no meaning for him. The words in Philomena's letter meant only that their mother had ceased to breathe, that the framework of bones and flesh, which had held her life and the lives of her children within itself, had weeks before been laid within the soil of the old country. Already, thought Jan, his mother's body was becoming that soil. For him there was no meaning in Philomena's words, because his mother's life had so made his mind by means of his memory that her death could not make that life to cease.

His memories of his mother were not memories in the ordinary sense of the word, because they had been translated into pain and pleasure, wisdom and understanding, sometimes at once, sometimes in later months and years. Her stifled cries at the birth of her children had become, even in his boyhood, the awful cost of life not only to those who gave it, but to those who must pay a debt they had never promised. Her suckling of them, even as she worked about her cottage, had become the food which those, weary with labour, give to those who must labour in their turn. Her long hours in the field with a child strapped to her back had become the symbol of the never-ending struggle against hunger and cold, which is the heritage of the children of men. Her care of them in sickness had become the triumphant renewal of life from the threat of death. Her falling to sleep in the midst of them all at the end of the day had become the wise provision of nature for those who serve her long and well. Thus she had, all unconsciously, provided food for his mind as well as for his body, placed therein long and warm thoughts, made him inviolable against time and chance.

After he had read Philomena's letter three years before, Jan had known he should not go back for her because of a fear which he found within himself. It was a fear which somehow had something to do with the danger of memory, stirred and re-clothed, with the intrusion of half-forgotten present sights and sounds upon their own past gifts, still warm and ripe in one's mind. But just what that fear was, how one put it into words, he had never been quite able to discover.

2

In 1891 John Marston brought Eileen Lassiter to Windswept as his wife. He had wanted to bring her there long before, but she had not been ready to come. There were things at Windswept, Eileen said, which she must get straight in her mind, sort them out, learn to look at them in the right, safe way, before she came back to live with them.

John had come back year by year. Some years he had not thought he wanted to come back, but when the time came for coming or for not coming, he had discovered that he wanted to come more than he wanted to stay away. He had come during his four years at Harvard College, and back across the ocean during his three years in Germany, where he had studied in Heidelberg below the red and green hills of the quiet Neckar. Jan and he, with Julian Lassiter and others of his friends, had spent the long summers together. There were roots at Windswept, growing deeper and more tenacious each year like the roots of the juniper, and of the windblown firs and spruces at the four corners of the house. He could not pull up those roots, disentangle them from among other pursuits and pleasures, which, given a chance, might make other roots elsewhere. But he could never seem to give these others their chance.

The roots at Windswept had dictated his choice of a profession. At twenty-two, when he had finished at Harvard, he had sold out his interest in Marston, Cobb, and Lassiter, not without thought and a measure of regret, for there were roots there also. But the interests of his

father's firm were no more his than they had, in reality,
been his father's. He had no gifts for that mathematical
knowledge and precision which was the daily food and
drink of Marston, Cobb, and Lassiter, for the great com-
partments of black and white drawings which the engineers there conned, watching from the dusty windows
the sure passage of one of their steamships making her
way up the muddy river. His fare lay in the food of other
books than those of engineering. He would utilize his
growing knowledge of languages by translating certain of
those books, in which these languages concealed their
thought, into his own. This could be done at Windswept
as well as anywhere else, with a few of the winter months
spent in the libraries of New York or elsewhere.

During these years in which he had been making up
his mind, or rather in discovering that it was made up
already without any help from him, he had waited for
Eileen Lassiter. This waiting had not always been easy.
Sometimes it had entailed pursuit. He had followed her
to California where she had gone for two winters to be
with Julian, who had been entrusted by his father to
watch over the destinies of a new Marston, Cobb, and
Lassiter, now established in San Francisco.

"What a place that California must be!" Mrs. Haskell
had said, when he had returned home and told her of
the days of endless sun which Julian and Eileen were
enjoying. "Changes o' weather are meat an' drink an'
vittles to me, Mr. John, an' I maintain they are good for
folks. Life's made up o' changes, bad 'n' good. I couldn't
abide that California for an hour."

During his years at Heidelberg he had pursued Eileen

to Switzerland, where she was studying embroidery and the French language in a select school for young ladies in Lausanne. They had sat by the ruins of Chillon and discussed the pros and the cons of early marriage. They had watched at sunset that miraculous pink glow on the white summits of the Alps and talked of those things at Windswept which only made deeper roots for John, but which were not yet satisfactorily straightened out in Eileen's mind. He had spent his holidays with her at Davos in the snow and at St. Juan-les-Pins on the Mediterranean, admirably chaperoned by a certain Miss Boyden from her school, who had certain of Mrs. Haskell's virtues without a trace of Mrs. Haskell's peculiar and inimitable charm. And during all these years he had spent many torturing, sleepless nights over rival claimants, who had fully as much to offer Eileen as he, if not more, and who, in more than one instance, seemed perilously near the privilege.

In the winter of 1890 after Mary Lassiter's sad and sudden death, when John had come back from Germany and was tying up certain loose ends in Cambridge, he had sat with Eileen for hours on end in New York. Eileen saw herself in these months the willing sacrifice to her father, her single future devoted to his welfare. Against this bit of improvised drama, James Lassiter, once he had been informed of it, was again John Marston's ally. He was quite able to look after himself, he said, and vastly preferred to do so; and if Eileen were not completely stupid, as he was beginning to suspect, she would prove she was not by coming to her senses in short order.

"For God's sake," said James Lassiter, "let's have an end of this nonsense. My sole objection to John is the

way he's waited around all these years. He needs a bit of
that early Roman technique in those books of his that he
prefers to my own, the kind that worked well with the
Sabine women."

"There's really no need of being vulgar, father," said
Eileen.

3

Windswept, in fact, witnessed a double romance in
1891. For Mrs. Haskell, after eight years of that careful
deliberation not uncommon to rural New England court-
ships, and as many years of winter companionship with
Caleb Perkins, decided at long last to merge the remainder of her life with his own under only slightly different
circumstances.

"He's a good man," she said to John and Eileen Marston, when she told them of her belated decision, "an'
Fate's hit him harder'n most. I spose we'll make out as
well as most folks, at that."

The young Marstons had not the slightest doubt of
Mrs. Haskell's assumption as they drove the eight miles
home together after the simple wedding in Caleb Perkins' sitting-room. In a few days the new bride and
groom would move, bag and baggage, to Eastport where,
Mrs. Haskell said, a tidy lot of building was going up,
and start a new home there. Mrs. Haskell liked the
thought of a new home, since it could be furnished, or-
ganized, and run by her own genius. A new home could
better blot out old memories, start out folks afresh, give a
new spurt to them.

"Folks say," said Mrs. Haskell, "that you can't begin

life over again at sixty or thereabouts, but I've never been one to hearken overmuch to what just folks say. Seems though I've been startin' a new life, so to speak, all my days. So long's the life's your own an' not your children's, you can do what you will with it. One more new life ain't goin' to put me out a mite."

In Mrs. Haskell's homely words, John Marston thought, there had always lurked a wisdom of which she was unaware. It was just this power to start a new life at every turn which made life what it might become and so rarely was. Mrs. Haskell, he thought, was one of the ageless among the enforced dwellers on this earth. Her stout percale and gingham skirts might have swept the asphodel and thyme of Grecian hillsides, the lilies of Judean fields. If they had been put upon her, she might have played the parts of Hecuba or Antigone or of Judith, the widow of Manasses, and comported herself as well as they had done down the long reaches of the world. He was glad that she had ordered the affairs of his household for ten summers, sorry that his children must be deprived of her. With all her obvious gifts and graces, Philomena, now in the kitchen at Windswept, would never be Mrs. Haskell.

4

Philomena Pisek, whose odd name had been mysteriously salvaged from a civilization foreign to Bohemia, was assuredly not Mrs. Haskell, but she was herself, and she grew on one the longer she stayed at Windswept. She was much taller than Jan, less thickly set, resembling him

only in her wide gray eyes, placed like his between wide,
rather flat cheek-bones. She was quiet in her ways like
Jan, although quicker than he about her work. She
worked from dawn until dark. She was never through
with her work because she could not conceive of one who
worked ever being through with it.

In the afternoon when her baking was done and her
kitchen in order (an order that would have passed with
merit even the scrutiny of Mrs. Haskell) she undid the
white kerchief, which she wore about her head in the
house, put on a brighter one of red or blue or green, took
off her slippers of black felt, and started barefoot for the
fields or for Jan's garden, which grew in extent year by
year.

"Why do you work this hot afternoon, Philomena?"
Eileen Marston was always saying. "Jan can manage, I'm
sure."

Philomena was patient with her mistress, if puzzled by
her lack of understanding.

"I always work," she said simply. "In my country I
work. Here I work. What do I do then if I not work?"

"You could mend, I should think, or knit. You could
sit down then."

"Why do I sit down? There is after supper to sit down.
To mend there is the long night by the good lamplight,
and there are the days when rain comes. But you like me
to knit or sew, and I knit or sew. For me it is to do what
you like for me to do."

"Heavens, no! Go to the field if you like, of course.
Only I don't want you to be tired."

Philomena always gazed at Eileen Marston then as

though her mistress had come from another world, as, indeed, she had.

"Me tired in this good country where there is to eat too much and a bed, soft, to myself? I am tired never."

After one of these conversations Eileen never failed to watch Philomena start for Jan's field or garden on her long, bare feet. They were amazingly slender feet even after years of walking and standing on them. They were not peasant feet at all, Eileen thought.

"However her feet have stayed as they are in those awful slippers she wears, I can't see," she said.

Philomena walked out of her kitchen door and through the blueberries and juniper as though she were treading on the most carefully tended lawn. She had a spring to her walk. It was not the walk of the labourers Eileen had seen in Europe, trudging to or from their work. Philomena walked as though she, like some tree, were an emanation from the earth, as though she felt the rhythm of it beneath her feet. She was not bent from all her years of toil. At thirty-six she was straight as any girl, her hips supple, her legs long and lithe.

When she got to the garden, which Jan began to leave to her care, she sank upon her knees among the long rows of vegetables, moving slowly on beneath the hot sun as she weeded. She cultivated the smaller vegetables with a hand fork, stirring up the soil with it, crumbling the soil in her hands. She belonged there on the earth as a man could never belong, her knees upon it, her bare toes digging into it, the kerchief on her head a bright, slowly moving spot of colour among the greens of beets and carrots, peas and onions.

Jan had had his secret fears when he had set out for New York to fetch Philomena and bring her to Windswept. Perhaps time had been cruel in his long absence, time in Bohemia, time in New York, even the good time at Windswept. Perhaps space had done its work as well, those long miles of water and of land, those high wide skies of home, those closer skies here above the sea. But time and space had been kind, he discovered, conquered by his own and Philomena's eager years of waiting.

Jan was touched by the care she had taken to carry out all his tactful instructions to the last detail. She wore a hat, for instance, the first hat she had ever owned, so that she might feel less odd and out of place in New York. Although pure chance had purchased the hat, it might have been far worse than it actually was. Her belongings were in a neat trunk, and she had on a decent dress and coat. When she had once greeted Jan in their old language, tears streaming down her face, as she did so, she began to surprise him by speaking in English. The priest had got her a book, she said, and a man who had returned from America on a visit had helped her to pronounce the strange words. After she had once arrived at Windswept, she and Jan returned to their old language. To Jan the speaking of his own tongue after years of absence from its nourishment was like the completion of some half-finished meal when one is hungry for the rest of it. He was proud, however, of the English which Philomena must speak at Windswept.

To Jan, Philomena completed the now unbroken fabric of his life. She was the past, which before her coming had been dependent upon the gifts of memory; she was the present, homely and secure; she was the good future, which that past and present made possible. One was aware of that closely-knitted fabric when Jan and Philomena worked together in the fields or sat together in the evening when their work was done. They always sat upon the ground, crouched together there, their hands clasping their knees, among the rough growths just outside Philomena's kitchen door. Sometimes Jan smoked his pipe, sometimes he scanned the sky and sea without his pipe. Philomena sat beside him, her clasped hands rolled in her shawl or her apron. They often sat there in spring or in summer until far into the night, silent, resting, watching the stars. They did not often talk. The things they had to say were, after all, mostly incommunicable, after the manner of past things well understood.

Their familiar presence never grew quite familiar to John and Eileen Marston when, upon returning from their walk, they saw them there, dark forms in the spring twilight, indistinct shapes in the summer darkness.

"Whenever I see them sitting there," said John, " I always have to shake myself to believe that this is just Maine after all. It might be—well, Troy or Argos or some ancient island off somewhere, centuries ago."

"It isn't just Maine, darling. That's the trouble with it. It's never been just Maine. If I'd been sure it was just Maine, I wouldn't have waited so long to come back to it. It's a terrible place to live up to, John, even with Mrs. Haskell in Eastport."

"Well, Philomena isn't Mrs. Haskell."

"No, she isn't. Sometimes I wish she were. You always knew what Mrs. Haskell said and did was just that and nothing more. Whatever Philomena says and does has a queer, old meaning trailing back behind it, way out of sight somewhere."

"I don't know. I always thought Mrs. Haskell was a kind of ageless being myself."

"I suppose she was, perhaps, but the difference is she didn't once know it. Philomena knows it all the time, even if she doesn't understand it. She can't once separate herself from all those eerie centuries behind her. She makes me nervous sometimes. Mrs. Haskell only made me mad."

"I guess you're right at that," said John.

5

When young Philip Marston came in the summer of 1892, it was Philomena who officiated at his birth, with the holy assistance of the blessed Saints Cyril and Methodius. For Philomena never recovered from her joy that this heir to the Marston name and to Windswept first saw the light on the day sacred to the patron Saints of Bohemia. This fact was clearly not a coincidence, for young Philip's advent had been scheduled and prepared for late July. When, therefore, he came on July seventh and at an hour when, with due allowance for the difference in time, the earliest masses were being sung throughout the old country in veneration of these ancient, holy men, Philomena was convinced that the last gulf separating her new home from her old had been triumphantly bridged.

Eileen Marston's fears had been at least partially put to rout when she saw the calm, imperturbable way in which

Philomena went about things. What if the nurse could not get there, said Philomena. She had never so much as heard of a nurse before on such occasions. And the doctor? What if Jan did not rouse that doctor from his good sleep and bring him over that dark road before this baby came? What difference could it possibly make, asked Philomena. Had she not made—how many babies come and in how many ways, but all safe and well at last.

There was Ántonia, the wife of Jakob, the cobbler, a woman too full of years, a half a century at least, said Philomena, ten years after childbearing was Ántonia and stricken with fever at the time. Yet Philomena, quite unaided, for Jakob was shaking in the thicket beyond the cottage, had brought a fine boy into Jakob's cottage. There was Teresa, whose pains came upon her at midday in a field of early rye with no time to do anything at all but to get her flat on the ground at the edge of the field out of the sun. And the back coming first instead of the head! What a time, said Philomena, and she all alone except for Teresa's twelve-year-old! But they managed, using some field tools as they were needed, well washed in the stream they were, and that baby Olga now, said Philomena, had presented twins to her husband Ludvik just before Philomena left the old country. There was that poor girl Yulka Petrasek, gone but fifteen years, she was, who had no father to her child at all and who had cried for six months day and night.

"A bad sign that," said Philomena. "You, Mrs. Marston, so still and happy in your head and heart all through your time. A good sign that."

And yet Yulka, when her pains came and Philomena

ran to her sad mother's house, was delivered through Philomena's hands of a boy with his head wrapped up in a holy mist, and, though fatherless still, he was bringing great joy to his mother's heart by serving at the altar and perhaps, who knows, becoming one good day a priest. As for Kaspar and Olga, what would they have done without Philomena, barely twelve, to help their mother through it all?

Philomena talked more that night than she had ever talked before or than she was ever to talk afterward. Eileen Marston, following her directions, did not recognize Philomena in this eager, reliable woman now suddenly grown to full stature in this requirement of all her powers. Philomena talked to divert her mistress, to relieve her from anxiety; she talked to show herself the equal, if not the master, of any not too benign spirits who might be lurking about; she talked to give strength and confidence to this father, who was behaving after a manner strange to her, shaking at times worse even than Jakob in the thicket and with less reason; she talked to prove to herself that birth in this new country was precisely the same as in the old, inevitable, simple, nothing to fret about. And yet Philomena knew that at birth Death was close, out of sight and yet there, waiting to note the strength of the living, ready to spring if that strength faltered. She would tell that listening Death, she said to herself, how many times she, Philomena Pisek, had outwitted Him.

If a woman were not quite a *honza*, had strong arms and a quick head, she knew what to do, continued Philomena, fastening long sheets to Eileen Marston's bed-posts, for her to pull upon, heating numberless kettles of hot water on her kitchen stove, getting her scissors and thread, her soap and ointments ready. And since the night was fine and still with stars, just as on the night when the Lord Himself came, what was there to fear? A high wind now, which was bad for one's breath and one's mind, or a clinging fog, which was worse for both, might put a different face on matters. But on such a night, said Philomena, going to the door now and then and looking at the stars, there were few, if any, evil spirits abroad, as there sometimes were with a high wind, no matter what the priest might say. All was going well, said Philomena, making Eileen Marston rise from her bed and pull on her sheets standing, and, after all, pain came in one way or another throughout one's life, if not in one's body, then in one's mind. "No pain, no life," she said, so what was the use of the master looking white and frightened and wearing out that good and costly carpet by his walking to and fro upon it? The one thing that sat wrong in her mind, thought Philomena to herself, was that the pains might come too quick and fast so that the child, by being born before midnight, might be deprived of the special care of Saints Cyril and Methodius.

Young Philip Marston escaped that plight by coming hastily and head first into his mother's bed at exactly one o'clock on Bohemia's festival day.

"In the city of Prague the bells ring," Eileen Marston heard Philomena saying, when she had gathered together her scattered senses after that last intolerable spasm of unrelieved pain. "In all the churches in the old country, in the great and in the little, the bells now ring."

"Hold your son," said Philomena to John Marston, after her brisk slap had brought forth the baby's first cry, and she had busied herself for a quick minute with her scissors and thread. "I see to his mother. Then we wash him, a fine boy."

She made the sign of the cross over the filthy, squirming child before she wrapped him in a blanket and delivered him to his father.

"It is well, as I said. Do babies in America come not like babies in the old country? They come the same—only not so quick maybe, and with more pain, and in better beds. But all is now well."

When he came a half hour later, the doctor was less impressed with Saints Cyril and Methodius and all their inevitable gifts and graces than with Philomena. And Jan, although he shared Philomena's joy in young Philip's birth-date, felt his pleasure even deeper within him. Philomena's imagination was like a shooting star, falling quick and blazing from darkness into darkness. Jan's was like that slow, steady march of Orion across the sky from winter dusk to dawn.

Philomena never relinquished her initial hold on young Philip Marston. He was hers, in a way that his sister, born a year later, never was. The doctor had been present at Ann Marston's quick and easy advent, and Philomena had no course but to obey reluctantly his terse commands.

But Philip's nurture from the start was in Philomena's hands, aided by those blessed saints, of whom Philip learned from her when he was old enough to learn anything. Philip learned all manner of amazing matters from

Philomena, with which, by the time he was nine, he was astonishing his mother.

"Philip, it's time for your Bible lesson. First question: Who was Judas Iscariot?"

"That's easy! I know. He was a German."

"Philip! Whatever do you mean?"

"Ask Philomena, mother, if you don't believe me."

"Judas Iscariot, dear, was a traitor. He betrayed his Master."

"Yes, of course. I know that. Judas Iscariot betrayed the Lord God, and he did it because he was the worst German that ever lived."

6

When it came to Anton, Philomena was a solace to Jan. No one at home, Philomena said, when she had once learned about Anton, so much as suspected that Anton was not still in New York, polishing and repairing shoes so well that he could send those generous sums of money to his mother and father. Who would suspect, said Philomena, when the money came so steadily?

Philomena grieved for Anton, but she was not without hope for him. Now that he was back on the good soil, she said, he would after a time forget his years in the prison. The sun and the rain would heal the scars of those years and make atonement for Anton's sin less hard for him. And it could not be so long an atonement, since Ambroz, wherever he was, must share in the larger part of the sin.

But with all Philomena's comfort and assurance Jan was not calm in his mind about Anton. It would be hard for Anton, if not impossible, to bridge those long years in the prison, hard to knit up those dark threads with the brighter ones of the past of his boyhood, to join them with the difficult present and the inescapable future. The fact that he was not sure of Anton's present and future troubled Jan. If he could only once see where Anton was, once look upon the place where Anton worked with the Polish people, he might feel happier about him. He would not try to see Anton. That would be wrong in the face of Anton's wish. But now that Anton could no longer be kept in the safe past, now that he was actually in a new present, Jan would feel immeasurably better if he could look once upon the place where Anton was.

This desire, which Jan could not put out of his mind, led him to take a journey after his haying was done in late July in 1895. He went to Boston by train, thence by another train farther west toward the towns and villages in the hot Connecticut valley, where already the Polish people were coming in great numbers to startle the indigenous New Englanders by their thrift and willing penury. It was not an easy journey to the village which Anna had named and to which he had sent his letters to her. It necessitated a stage-coach once he had left the second train, and after the stage-coach, which set him down before a white church on a broad village green, a long walk.

"I want the farm of Peter Osinski," Jan had said in his slow, polite way to the village postmaster.

Peter Osinski's farm lay three miles west, the postmaster told Jan. It was a farm, he said, that was dead and no good four or five years back, but Peter Osinski had made it come to life with his wife and children and God knew

who else on their knees all day upon it. Peter Osinski was
a good man, he said, in spite of his outlandish tongue and
his perpetual smell of onions. He did his share for the
poor, and he was a kind neighbour. If Jan followed the
dusty road for three miles, then took a path through the
fields which lay by the river, then went up a rise of land,
he would come to a new fence. Beyond this fence was
Peter Osinski's farm.

Jan took off his coat as he walked along the road. The
dust lay in uneven mounds on either side of the wheel-
tracks and around the imprints of horses' hoofs. It rose in
smokelike curls at the steady tread of Jan's feet; it pow-
dered his trousers to the knees of them; his boots were
coated white with it.

There were nice flowers among the rough, roadside
growth, thought Jan, tall lilies, some yellow, three or four
on a stalk, some red, upright and mostly single. After a
shower they would be fresh and lovely. So would the
orange daisies with jet black centers, the purple vetch,
the sweet clover.

It was hot, this Connecticut valley, hotter than the old
country in the most fervent of summers, hotter even than
New York. The sky was a hard, burnished blue with a
shine like the shine on metal. The sun was so bright in
this hard sky that it was almost white, white with its own
heat, Jan thought. There was not the slightest breath,
even whisper, of wind. Jan felt the sweat running down
his back, soaking his clean shirt, which soon became filthy
from the dust. His collar was wilted, creased and rumpled about his neck. He took a clean handkerchief from
his pocket and tucked it within his collar like a bib.

When the road rose as it sometimes did into ridges and hills, Jan could see the country stretching left and right. Beyond the dust-covered roadsides the fields looked green and fertile. There were fields of tobacco standing straight and tall, fragrant and spicy in the heat. Every now and then the fields were broken by the long tobacco barns, red or brown, sometimes standing in a long row, sometimes alone. They were beautiful barns, Jan thought, long like the country, hospitable, friendly.

There was the smell of onions as well as of tobacco. This was a fragrant country, Jan thought, even if it was hot. There was no wind as at Windswept to blow the fragrance away. It filled the air like the heat. The onion fields were dotted with women busy with harvest. They were on their knees as in the old country, moving slowly, the sun hot on their kerchiefed heads, pulling up more and more onions, cutting the tops, leaving piles of onions behind them, reddish yellow, shining in the heat. This was Anna's life then, thought Jan, and not a bad life at that, for it could not always be hot like this.

A cart was rumbling toward him, almost out of sight in the brown clouds of dust. The particles of dust caught the sun so that the cart and horses were surrounded by a light-filled cloud like that which led the children of Israel. Jan drew away from the road as the cart drew nearer, turned his back and looked off across the fields. When the cart had passed, he saw that it was piled high with onions, round and golden in the hot sunlight. This might well be Anton's life, he thought. Anton in the old country had had a good way with horses. He would like driving the onions to market.

It was a relief to turn off the main road to the less dusty path through the fields, a great blessing to come upon the river, broad and deep and swift. There were trees growing there, willows and maples. Jan stretched full length on a small beach of sand and put his face in the cool water. It might not be good for one to drink, this river, but he would chance it. He washed his hands and face, took off his shirt, his shoes and socks, washed the grime from his chest, his feet. When he had rested there out of the sun, he put on his things again and climbed the field to the fence to which the postmaster had directed him.

He stood leaning on one of the fence-posts a long time. He saw no one, and he could quickly go back to the river should he see anyone coming, lose himself in the trees and bushes there. Peter Osinski had a fine, big farm. Just beyond the fence was a hay field already cut. Beyond the hay field there were fields of tobacco and, on the right, acres of onions. There were women working in the onions, kneeling there, their figures blurred by the distance and the shimmering heat.

Peter Osinski's house was big and white, not so big as Windswept, but far bigger than peasants' cottages in the old country. It had two barns, one old and red, one new and yellow. Jan could make out the forms of several men about; some were getting into a cart, others seemed busy about the barns. The house faced the river and must get a breeze on hot nights. Beyond the river there were high hills, a long range of hills, their summits in a wavy line. They were pale, silvery blue now in the heat, but in the winter when the snow lay on them or in the autumn when they blazed with colour, they would be good to look at, give a man courage just to see them standing there, always the same, yet always different.

Jan saw the cart by Peter Osinski's barn move away in the opposite direction. Apparently the entrance to the farm lay beyond the fields which he was looking upon. That was good, he thought, that was safe. Now he did not have to hurry. Now he could imagine Anton in all the seasons he would know in this Connecticut valley.

The spring here must be good, fresh and green without any heat. Once the snow went, how pleasant the trees would be, budding by the river! The wild cherries there were plentiful, he had noticed, and the plums. They would be white above the freed, high water. This valley had apple trees, too, here and there on knolls and hills, sizable orchards they were, to be filled with blossoms and the hum of bees like the lime trees in the old country. The onions would prick the fresh, damp soil in the spring, tiny spear points of promise. This must be a fine country for birds of all sorts.

In the autumn when the harvest was in and a man had time to look about him, what colour there must be, the New Jerusalem itself, Jan thought. At Windswept, except for the reds and russets of the blueberries, the colour flamed only here and there where the spruces, firs, and pines in the woods gave way to an occasional birch or maple. But with fewer evergreen trees on the hills this Connecticut valley must be brave with colour, and the air without this heat clear and fine like old wine. In October that range of hills would be nearer, almost upon one, rising above the blue river, strong and close.

There would be plenty of snow here in winter, white

miles of it. What care must be taken of horses and cattle in these great barns against the bitter cold? In the sharp air of December and January how the smoke would rise from all these farm houses which he could see. For a man who liked neighbours better than Jan did, it would be pleasant to watch from one's home the curls of smoke from other chimneys, to see at night the lamplight of other windows across the snow-covered fields, to think of one's neighbours beneath their lamps.

Best of all, Jan thought, the strength of the good past would be here without one's ever having to search for it. For here in this Connecticut valley the fields were like the fields at home, larger a bit, but yet fields with soil and crops and women on their knees. There were hills, too, not high, to be sure, like the mountains of the old country, but yet hills, rising above one into the blue distance. Here the language of the old country was spoken, not one's own identical language, of course, but nevertheless a language which meant age and labour, pain and hope. Here one sat at one's door in the evening with many children about; here one ate the fruits of one's own toil; here one still felt the long past, and might even, with the help and prayers of one's friends, knit that past once more to the present and to the future.

7

In those long, quiet years at Windswept, between the birth of his children and their leaving home for school in the early years of the new century, John Marston, looking up from his books upon the sea beyond his windows, thought often among others of Dr. Samuel Johnson. Between the lettered and the unlettered man, the dishevelled old doctor had written, there is as much difference as between the living and the dead. This was true, thought John, because of the simple yet almost awful fact that life without conscious associations is not life but death. It was the very absence of these quickening and healing associations that made so many dead among the living.

Dr. Johnson did not much exaggerate, John Marston thought, and yet it was not alone the associations afforded by books which insured the immortality of one's mind, made life a matter of daily re-birth. To Jan, for example, the honey from his bees did not suggest Hybla or Hymettus; the empty miles of sea were not in his mind like those unharvested seas of Homer, as they had been in John's so many years ago at school; his plough and his trees were not the ploughs and the trees of Vergil. Yet Jan was a lettered man, too, in his way, a poet, his books, the perception of the centuries behind his daily labour, his bees, the bees in the lime trees of his boyhood, his cows, all unwittingly the cows of Homer, of whom he had never heard, "with their trailing feet and shambling gait." Jan, like the poet, created by forever bringing together the incommunicable heritage of the past and the actuality of the present, the old and the new, forever transmuting the outward and visible into the inward and spiritual.

And the reason that Jan and others like him were able to perform this simple miracle, upon which the success or the failure of one's life hung, was that in his childhood he had somehow become aware of the essence and reality of life itself without thought to any of its fruits. In poverty he had found wealth; in simplicity, splendour; in labour, patience and wisdom.

Not that many men were like Jan, John Marston thought. To most, poverty and hardship, the struggle for breath and being, obscured rather than illumined the breaking of bread, the flight of a swallow. Yet upon men and women like Jan life depended for its very apprehension, its release from tumult and confusion, its freedom from the bondage of possessions, its pain and laughter, grief and gayety.

This long, slow process of building one's mind and spirit was what was meant by education, of which so many men were talking now that the old century was giving place to a new. Yet these men were absorbed, as he gathered from the newspapers and magazines, more with ways and means than with ends, misinterpreting this end of which they wrote as something to be attained rather than as something implicit in the means. The end should be discovered, he thought, in the very process itself. For did not the end lie in the beginning rather than in the fruit of some problematical future?

Education was the constant, often unconscious, rescue within oneself of life from death, beginning long before one was aware of it in the associations made possible through the places in which one found oneself, through the persons one knew, and, as Dr. Johnson had well said, through the books one read and loved. And among all these sources of life, John Marston, sitting among his books at Windswept, was inclined to think that the very accident of place loomed largest, either with its gifts or its denials.

There had been no denials at Windswept, or at least none that he could call substantial or important. Through the long succession of days there from April to November, and sometimes even through the winter months, there had been for years enacted a drama which too few men and women looked upon as drama at all—the drama of the constantly recurring familiar, always sudden and revealing if one stopped to grasp it. The dawn of new days; the changes of weather; the coming on of frost and cold; the waxing and waning of life in the barn and pastures; the often unapprehended change in the children until, upon some unprepared for occasion, new words or new thoughts, new expressions on their faces, made it suddenly apparent; the infrequent coming and going of friends who thought the life at Windswept less poor than rich; the increasing knowledge of the birds who flew over the sea, nesting among the rocks or in bare trees, those gulls and cormorants and herons of Vergil, winging landward when they became aware of the "certain tokens and warnings" of Nature; the falling to sleep at night in the sound of the surf; storms and fogs with their long hours of reading together; hot days of harvest, clear evenings of stars; the simple eating together of food grown by their own hands in their own fields; their very isolation from what was falsely called the larger world of men and of affairs.

This was drama, these acts and scenes of daily existence, these small tragedies and comedies of woods and fields, this pageantry of the seasons, these overtures of the sea, reflections, recollections, slow or quick understanding through long association of the meaning hidden within the familiar. He could not ask more or better for himself or for his children.

The day was coming, nor was it far off, if he read the signs of the times aright, when, at least in America, it would be difficult to put down roots in any one place, roots sufficiently strong and deep to hold one against the fluctuations already apparent in the changing face of things. A man's roots mattered, he thought, his identification with a given place which might well serve as an anchor to windward against the storms of time and chance. Old Heraclitus was doubtless right, speaking as a philosopher, in the swift passing of all things, in the remaining of nothing. And yet to descend from the metaphysical to the substantial and tangible, a man's possible wealth clearly consisted in his power of recovery, of salvage, while today gave way to tomorrow. For this salvage, in a world now concerning itself with the acquisition of material possessions and with the delivery of man from labour by the discoveries of science, roots were daily becoming not only more necessary but more hard to procure.

Was science, then, seen in its new application to the means of life and living, certain to deliver men from hardships? Might it not be a tyrant as well as a saviour, reviving old evils, trampling ruthlessly on the good promises latent in its beginnings? Might it not exact a heavy payment in return for its releases, its mis-named freedoms? Under a smiling mask of civilization might it not destroy simplicity, darken men's minds, harden men's hearts, becoming less the friend than the remorseless enemy of mankind? Was the dream which sometimes beset him by day as well as by night nonsensical and absurd—that terrifying dream of vast conflicts, of blood and cruelty and chaos, brought upon the world by this very mechanical skill, this power of invention, which promised so much to men and women, but which held lurking within itself dangers which few were foreseeing?

It was to fortify themselves against such monstrous possibilities that he wanted roots for his children, put far down in old, sturdy soil, the soil, first of all, of some actual place, benevolent, even sacred to those who had gone before them, the soil also of discovered realities and values. And if, as the increasing numbers of modern sophists were contending, that which we call the Unknown must forever be the Unknowable, if the anguish of the prophets is meaningless and the strivings of the wise but idle dreams, if the longer reaches of faith must be rejected as fancy, then from out the resulting calamity man, in order to live at all with himself, must build his own faith merely in order to keep faith with himself. And for this building, John Marston felt sure, no entirely new world could suffice.

On one of these many days of thoughts provoked by his books, he had taken from its shelf his old *Anabasis*, which he had studied at St. Paul's with Dr. Coit, now seven years dead but yet living. He had been wondering whether it would be wise to start young Philip at ten off on his Greek and Latin before he should follow his father and grandfather to school. Turning the pages, which had seemed to him, he remembered, dull for the most part, he came upon an incident in the fourth book,

which, if he had read it at fourteen, had apparently
missed its mark.

It was the story, told with an imagination and understanding which he had not somehow before attributed to
Xenophon, at least in the *Anabasis,* of a mountain tribes-
man, who had guided the Greeks through unfamiliar and
hostile regions, thick with foes, telling them that if he
did not in five days bring them to the sea, he would gladly
accept death at their hands. He did as he had promised,
leading them at last to the top of a mountain from which
they saw with tears in their eyes, with great shouting and
embracing of one another, the blue waters of the Euxine.
The man was a barbarian, hating his own enemies more
than he loved the Greeks, but he had done his work well.

In reward for his sacrifice and his labour the Greek
soldiers had laden him with presents, a horse, a silver
cup, rings, money, valuable possessions to carry back with
him on his return home, a journey fraught with perils
both to himself and his gifts. At nightfall he turned from
the Greek camp where there was light and companionship and started back alone through the country of his
foes, bearing those gifts which, if safely brought homeward, would make of his life something better than before.

The Greek language, John Marston thought, held
within itself a suggestion to which English never could
attain. And yet even the translation was beautiful in its
enforced simplicity.

"When evening came," Xenophon had written, ἐπεὶ
ἑσπέρα ἐγένετο, "he took his leave of us and went his way,
by night, alone."

8

Young Philip and Ann Marston so hated the infrequent winter months which they spent in Boston or in New York with their parents that, as time went on, they were left behind with Jan and Philomena at Windswept. There was never anything to do in cities, at least anything which they liked; they hated the schools in which they were entered for even a three months' sojourn. After Christmas when their father and mother left, following frenzied days of packing, which, they early gathered, their mother loved and their father with great good nature endured, their three months of mingled isolation and companionship began.

The road from Windswept to Heron Cove was now rarely impossible even in the heaviest snow, so well did Jan keep it broken with his sledge and yoke of black oxen. It was fun to break the road in the cold and the brilliant sunlight on the untrodden whiteness. The oxen wallowed and laboured, sometimes standing waist deep with great clouds of warm breath coming from their nostrils, while Jan and Philip plunged ahead of them to attack with their shovels an especially high drift. The air was so still that the snapping of a bough echoed like a pistol shot and the whine of the sledge runners like the continuous high cry of some invisible creature lost somewhere in the surrounding black ranks of the trees.

They loved dashing from their icy bed-rooms on bitter mornings to dress by the great fire in the living-room, which Jan had going well before Philomena called them. The dogs were there, the red setter, Captain Kidd, and the spaniel, Billy Bones, delirious over seeing them for the thousandth time, upsetting things in their madness. They saw the sun rise over the gray or purple sea beyond the white reaches of the silent, buried land. They ate their breakfast in the dining-room at the great pine table, proud of being there by themselves with no supervision, stuffing themselves with Philomena's hot porridge and Jan's fresh eggs and sausage.

After breakfast, except on the worst days, they sat astride Philip's pony, whom Jan had named for good King Wenceslas, since he had been a Christmas gift, and rode through the woods to the school at Heron Cove. When it was very cold and their legs felt suddenly numb and stiff through their thick red leggings, they jumped off into the snow and ran until the ache had given place to a warm tingling. In fall and spring they carried their dinner in baskets, which Jan had made for them from sweet grasses, their initials P.M. and A.M. woven in colour on the covers, Philip's in red, Ann's in blue. They had good sandwiches and milk inside, and Philomena's *kolache,* thick with raisins in the centers. In the winter they ate their dinner at one of the fishermen's cottages at the oil-cloth covered table in the fisherman's kitchen with the children of the family, soda biscuits and sizzling salt mackerel, which made them thirsty, and thick cups of hot coffee, which they were never allowed at home.

Dinner in the fisherman's cottage was an event, for the school-teacher, whoever he or she was, ate with them. The teacher of the Heron Cove school changed from term to term with astonishing rapidity and great excitement. The same one rarely weathered a full year, even with the considerable vacations. Most of the teachers were boys or girls from some Maine college, working their way there by staying out to teach for a term. The Heron Cove community was not too desirable a place, its cottages perched there on the rocky ledges above the sea like so many gray and white gulls ready for flight, their few rooms cold and cheerless, the school-house itself little better than a shack, with the heat of the air-tight stove escaping through the cracks in its old shingles. Still a teacher was usually found at the last moment, and the school rarely closed.

Philip and Ann shared the excitement of the thin, sharp-eyed Heron Cove children over whom Fate would send to be their teacher. There was one memorable year when a young man from Bowdoin College stayed for three terms of eight weeks each. His name was Cyril Cobb, like the names of their grandfather's firm in New York and of Philip's patron saint, whom Philomena could never let him forget. He was nineteen and a wonderful teacher and friend. He did not seem to mind at all his rickety cot in the loft under the roof of one of the cottages, ate hugely, and sometimes even washed the dishes for his tired landlady. When any of the Heron Cove boys did well in their lessons, he jumped over the teacher's desk in one leap of his long legs, and was altogether such a surprise and pleasure that they all missed him intolerably when he returned to Bowdoin College.

In the autumn term he stayed for a fortnight at Wind-swept, walking back and forth the four miles through the woods morning and night with Philip and Ann, for until the snow came they rarely used King Wenceslas. What walks those were through the still, sunshot woods in the

early morning and late afternoon when sometimes the
light had almost faded from the sky before they were
home! Cyril Cobb knew all about animals, birds, and
trees. Nothing escaped his eyes or ears. He liked to sing
or to recite lines of poetry as they swung along, Ann and
Philip singing with him. If they did not know all the
hymns or old songs, Cyril was delighted to teach them.
"Ancient of Days," they sang, or "When You and I Were
Young, Maggie," or "Believe Me If All Those Endearing
Young Charms." Captain Kidd and Billy Bones bounded
through the woods, behind or before, for Cyril did not at
all mind their coming to school, too.

Cyril and their father and mother talked late at night
sitting on the stone shelf of the fireplace, after they had
been made, reluctantly, to go to bed. But before they
went, they had heard all about Cyril's home in northern
Maine, where the farms stretched in acres upon acres
of potatoes, and of his plans to go to Harvard College
after he had finished Bowdoin and someday to be a pro-
fessor himself. Sometimes before they went to sleep, they
heard Cyril and their father and mother singing together.
It was a pleasant sound, echoing above the breaking of the
surf.

Philomena loved Cyril, first for his name and then for
himself. She cooked special things for him, mended his
shirts and socks, and even knit new socks for him out of
thick gray wool. She and Jan loved having him come into
the kitchen at night and ask them about Bohemia, learning Czech words for things and laughing when his tongue
could not quite manage the strange words. They would
all have been glad to have him with them for all the

terms, but he said it was not in the bond, much as he
would like to stay.

When Philip helped him to carry his things back to
the fisherman's cottage where he stayed, the fisherman's
wife looked sharply at him, seemed a bit out of humour.

"You'll likely be farin' slim now, Mr. Cobb," she said,
"after your long visit with folks better off an' more to
your likin', p'raps."

Cyril had laughed then and actually put his arm
around her shoulders as she stood bent over her wash-
tubs.

"Avaunt such idle fancies, woman!" he cried. " 'Love
alters not with its brief hours or weeks.' Here, let me turn
your wringer for you!"

Not any other teacher was like Cyril Cobb, and yet
with all who came and went Philip and Ann loved the
school at Heron Cove, its windows looking out upon the
rocky harbour, the way it stood slightly askew upon a
ledge above the cottages. They liked the boys and girls
at Heron Cove with their quick, weatherwise eyes, their
skill in handling boats, their wild, free ways. They had
good manners, too, whenever they thought them inescapable; they were generous and decent to one another.
Sometimes on Saturdays they came over the road to
Windswept, the horde of all fifteen of them, for an hilarious party with John and Eileen Marston, or with Jan
and Philomena when the children's parents were away,
saying *please* and *thank you* and minding their table
manners. They always set out for home well before darkness fell, because for some odd reason they did not like

the blackness of the woods and, even less, the thick trees
in moonlight.

9

Jan and Philomena were always at their best when they
had the Marston children to themselves during the
months when their father and mother were in the city.
Although they had their meals together in the kitchen,
they sat in the evening by the fire with Philip and Ann.
How snug and warm it was there with the snow lying
still and cold without or sometimes beating before the
wind against the windows! On nights of storm when the
surf crashed before the tide and the great gusts shook
the very beams and rafters of the house, Jan always said:

"God keep all souls at sea this night!"

"Amen!" said Philomena.

"Amen!" said the children, obeying Philomena's eyes.

Philomena was an unaccountable creature. One never
knew how Philomena would be from night to night. In
this very fact lay a great excitement. Sometimes she was
sad, knitting in her chair, withdrawn into herself, saying
nothing at all. On such nights they played checkers with
Jan by the table beneath the lamp, glancing now and
then at Philomena, hoping for a sudden change in her
sadness, although one rarely came. But there was sure to
come a night when Philomena acted like a mad thing.

She always prefaced such madness by joking with Jan,
calling him *tatinek,* which in Czech meant daddy, little
father.

"Come, *tatinek!*" she would cry. "A dance for me, for us all!"

She would dress herself then in her Bohemian clothes, her red bodice, her embroidered full white skirts, her kerchief edged with little jingling bells. She made Jan play his mouth organ.

"Quicker! quicker!" she would cry, seizing the children, spinning and whirling them about the room, until they fell exhausted by laughter and dizziness. The dogs yelped with excitement; the bells on Philomena's kerchief jingled; Jan beat time with his foot as he played and played; the surf crashed without. What a din it all was!

"We will this good evening end with a story," said Philomena, coming from the kitchen with a great pitcher of milk, *kolache,* and cups for all. "*Tatinek* will speak the story because my breath, it has joined the wind. It has gone to the sea. It helps now to blow the ships!"

Jan had stories without end. Sometimes they were of Windswept itself, its beginnings, sad and joyous. Philip and Ann could not remember when they had not known every word of these stories, of their grandfather, their father as a boy, their mother and how she had once run through a crop of Jan's good standing hay in years when every blade was precious. Sometimes they were of Bohemia, with him and Philomena there, of the bad ox Krok and the devil within his skin, and of some beautiful but wicked maidens called Jezinkas, who tore out people's eyes and placed them in a cavern until a brave peasant boy outwitted the Jezinkas and returned the stolen eyes to their grateful owners.

Philip could never get out of his mind the picture of that dark cavern, full of glowing eyes, blue eyes, brown and black and green eyes, still alive, staring into the blackness. When the clever boy outwitted the Jezinkas and took the eyes back to their blind owners, they were more often the wrong eyes than the right ones.

"These are not my eyes," an old man would say with horrible distinctness, when he had once fitted the pair of eyes, which the boy had brought, into his empty sockets. "With these eyes I see nothing but owls."

Or again, "I see nothing but wolves."

Or yet again, "I see nothing but pike."

But at last after the three failures:

"Praise be to God! Now I see the good, green world again!"

There was one story about a monstrous white snake in the telling of which Jan was at his best. Even their father liked to hear Jan tell that story. When he told it on winter nights of storm and wind, they drew together by the fire, prickling with terror, sure to dream of it at night, but, nevertheless, unable not to ask for it.

"This is a good story," Jan always said, just as though it were new and unheard, "so listen well, Philip and Ann. This is a story my father and mother told me whenever we saw a snake in the woods or fields. 'Snake', my mother and father said to that snake, 'you are the Devil who has again beaten the good God.'

"Now why my mother and father said that to that snake is because of this good story. Many hundreds of years ago there was a place in the old country suddenly very full of snakes These snakes they crept into the church and startled the priest at Mass, crawling slowly across his big book, raising their heads, looking into that priest's eyes. They crawled into the dairies and coiled themselves around the big cheeses and the little pats of butter. They crawled into the beds of the peasants in their cottages. When those peasants put down their tired feet—well, think what their toes met in those beds! There was not even at supper quiet, because these hungry snakes made their way into the big bowls of soup and into the children's mugs of milk. How big and frightened those children's eyes grew when they saw in their mugs those lizards, green and blue!

"And worse than all these many snakes, small and big, was one monster white snake, so big that he could coil around a great cow, three times, four times, five times, like ropes around a big bag of grain, and crush that cow's bones into a jelly. This snake looked like a great white mist rolling over the land or like a racing white waterfall, so fast did he come across the green fields in the spring and the summer.

"The poor peasants did not know how to help themselves from this monster white snake. They made processions, carrying the cross and the holy bread; but as they walked, they heard a great hiss through the air, making them drop even the holy vessels and run for their homes. They went to holy towns to pray to the good God; but when they came back, they found their cows and their sheep still again crushed to a jelly, lying in the fields, covered with flies, torn by the birds.

"And now," said Jan, "this good story grows better or does it grow worse? Who can tell?

"Well, one day a strange, unknown man came to this sad place with a pipe in his pocket made out of bone, and on his pipe he played tunes that made ears to tingle with their magic. This stranger said to the people: 'I will rid you of your snakes, great and small, if you can tell me truly that you have seen no great white snake here in these green fields and woods.'

"The people were so frightened and so glad to get those snakes from their cottages and from their fields, from their dairies and their beds and their churches, that they forgot the command of the good God, that a man should never speak a lie.

" 'Good stranger,' they cried then. 'We have seen no white snake,' they cried.

" 'Very good,' said the stranger. 'Very good, indeed, my friends,' said that unknown man with the bone pipe.

"Then he made to be built a great pile of good, dry wood around a tall fir tree with all the peasants bringing their fagots which they had saved for the cold winter, and when the stranger had climbed above the pile to the very top of that tall fir tree, he told them to set the great pile of wood on fire and then to run quickly to one side.

"When that fire had risen high on all sides of that tall fir tree, this strange man blew on his bone pipe so long and so hard that a tingling was in all ears. Then quickly there came crawling all manner of snakes, even lizards and salamanders, so thick that they mixed with one another like macaroni hot in the pot or like tangled coils of rope. They came and they came, those snakes, crawling and hissing and creeping from all corners. And my mother used to say that one foolish *honza*, who was standing there with his mouth wide open, felt his hat rise from his head where a snake had been asleep under it. They came and they came, and at last all these snakes sprang into that great fire, and they died there with hisses and sizzles like frying bits of meat. And all the devils inside their skins, they died also.

"That was, indeed, a good thing, a very good thing, indeed; but all was not yet past and gone. For at once in all the frying and the sizzling a more mighty hiss was heard in the air, and a great white mist was seen creeping over the tops of the trees in the distant woods, coming nearer and nearer over the green fields. Then the people trembled with fear, and that unknown man in that tall fir tree cried,

" 'There is now no help for me. I have heard the hiss of the great white snake. Why did you tell me a lie?' he cried. 'For me you can now do nothing, but hear the wish of a dying man, and do not forget to give food to the poor every year of your lives to atone for your sin.'

"When this unknown man had said these sad words, the white mist became the great white snake, winding its way with a great noise like a furious waterfall, over the tops of the trees, over the fields, raising itself up, coiling and uncoiling until at last it reached the man in the fir tree, still blowing on his pipe. Up against the fir tree it raised its white coils. It surrounded the stranger and threw him into that hot fire. But when the stranger's body fell into the fire, the flames rose so high and red and hot that that white snake, which had done so much harm to the sheep and the cattle, died in that fire with the stranger.

"So that great tribe of snakes was perished, dead and gone they were, with all the evil spirits inside their ugly skins, and the peasants could now pasture their sheep and their cows without fear; and the priest could now say Mass without the devil to torment him, crawling across his book; and the good butter and cheese could now rest on the shelves of the dairies; and the children need now no longer fear lizards blue and green in their mugs of milk; and the people could put their tired legs now down in their beds without trembling.

"But the people said to one another, 'This good deed came about by a bad deed. The Devil dwells in a lie,' they said. 'We must atone for that lie,' they said.

"So every year from that long ago day to this very day the people once a year in that place in my old country give bread to the poor.

"But I never see a snake now," Jan finished, knocking out his dead pipe on the tall black andirons, "that I do not say to him, 'Snake! You are the Devil who has again beaten the good God.' "

10

When Philip Marston was ten and Ann nine, the chapel at Windswept was built. Its building took an entire summer with everyone working upon it. They placed it half a mile beyond the cabin, a few feet back from the ledge sloping down to the sandy beach of the anchorage. There was a fine place for it there among the mosses and bracken, with firs and pines so close to its small east window that one looked straight into their sunlit branches when one sat inside.

They built it of stone with a peaked wooden porch after the model of a small roadside church, which John Marston remembered having seen and liked on walks in Cornwall years before. When the Heron Cove fishermen got over their initial surprise at the idea of it, they were glad to exchange their precarious fishing for a steady summer job of hauling and fitting stones together; and a mason from the village proved an artist at his work, as Maine coast artisans often do.

By mid-September, when the birches and maples in the woods behind it were turning yellow and red, it was completed, ready to be dedicated on Advent Sunday. It had a square, squat tower with an old bronze bell in it, which Philip Marston liked to ring on Sunday mornings, going early there, pulling on the bell-rope, hearing the deep, full, resonant tones resound across the quiet bay of the anchorage. It was small inside, only large enough for fifty people on the benches which Jan had made; but beyond the benches there was an open space near the entrance, for more people should they ever come, and in the west wall just beyond the door a fireplace had been built for heating in the winter months.

Young Philip Marston grew to look upon this chapel at Windswept as his especial possession. The care of it from the beginning had been given over to him, the sweeping and dusting, the fetching of wood for the fire, the gathering of flowers or greens on Saturday afternoons for the altar. He took turns with his father in reading the service to which the people at Heron Cove often came, the children scrubbed and brushed, curious and quiet.

By the turn of the century a church of Jan and Philomena's old faith had been built thirteen miles away. They
drove there on Sunday morning, sitting straight and a
bit solemn in the wagon in their best clothes. This journey on Sundays did much for Jan and Philomena, con-
necting still more closely their new country with their
old.

But it was on weekdays rather than on Sundays that the
chapel at Windswept seemed especially Philip Marston's
own. He liked the walk to it through the path beyond
the cabin, the sudden coming out upon the ledge to the
door which always stood open in good weather, the light
which fell through the small, leaden-paned windows, the
stillness which lay over everything. He liked seeing it
there at the close of an afternoon of sailing, its tower
just visible as he swung into the anchorage bay. He liked
looking up from mooring the ketch or the sloop, seeing
the way the late sun lay full upon it, conscious of it there
behind him, companionable and homelike, as he rowed
ashore in the dory and stepped upon the ledge below it.

Here before the chapel door the tide rose and ebbed
quietly with no sound of surf, an almost imperceptible
flooding of the red ledges, a noiseless receding down the
narrow beach. The boats swung at anchor a few feet from
the shore, obeying the tide, their ropes sometimes tapping or slapping the masts as they caught the remnants
of the wind, which even on blustery days rarely reached
this protected inlet. Philip liked to sit on the top step
of the porch, watching the shadow of the clouds at full
tide, the gulls drowsing on the olive green seaweed when

the rocks were bared at dead low water, a heron standing motionless above his clear shape in some shallow pool. One could sit for hours here on summer days when the sun was warm.

The chapel early became associated in his mind and memory with days of grief as well as of pleasure. When Cyril Cobb went away from the Heron Cove school not to return and left behind him a yawning, empty place in Philip's life, he could come here, unashamed of the tears which he could not have shed at home, no matter how much they had liked Cyril, too. When he had pained his father by some unexpected, uncalled-for rudeness to his mother, he ran here to frame the apology which, no matter how he had wanted to make it, refused to be made at the moment. When the spaniel, Billy Bones, had at last forfeited his life because he could never be taught to keep away from porcupines, Philip ran desperately here, stopping his ears so that he might not hear, even in the distance, Jan's merciful pistol shot.

On that warm July evening the fireflies were lighting the fir branches with tiny sparks of light, and when he went inside the chapel to escape them, there they were in the green trees behind the altar window, like so many tiny, flickering candle-flames. He never forgot them, how they gleamed and glowed on his way home in the dark, becoming thereafter to him always associated with sudden heart-break.

There were other griefs also, not tangible, perhaps, or even reasonable, yet filled with strange and difficult pain. The overwhelming sadness when the iris faded, giving up its blue above the water's edge, turning brown and yellow among the juniper; the sadness latent in the marsh grasses by the pond, swept on a dull day by the wind from over the sea-wall; the sadness of a certain kind of rain, not the comforting, ringing, heavy rain at night, not the turbulent rain of thunderstorms or of the fierce equinoctial gales, but those days of gentle, almost diffident rain, ill at ease, apologetic, falling in tiny beads and slanting silver threads from a close gray sky. Such a day one could bear better in the chapel porch than by the fireplace at home or in the barn with Jan.

On sharp autumn and early winter afternoons when there was no school, he built a fire in the chapel and stretched out before it with his book. The chapel was a prime place for reading. When he looked up from his page in the stillness, broken only by the crackling of the fire, a branch snapping in the woods, the sudden movement of the dog at his feet, the call of a bird or the crying of the gulls, he saw the still or stirring green branches of the trees just outside the window above the little altar.

From the beginning of his devotion to the place there had been mingled with his love of it a kind of pleasurable awe, from which in later years at school and college he never entirely freed himself, an undefined, yet recognized, sense, on the one hand, of the homeliness and naturalness of sacred places and objects, and, on the other, of the spiritual counterparts of those things which are to most children, and, indeed, to most persons of every age, the merely familiar. Here within the walls of the chapel outward and inward things met, merged, were woven together, lost their separation one from the other.

Familiar things took upon themselves here a permanence never understood elsewhere. Here there was a constant substitution of the lasting and typical for the momentary and actual, extending even to physical things, the light of the sea and sky always in one's eyes, the touch of the dog's nose always in one's hand. Here on weekdays in his old play clothes with his dog beside him and his book in his hand, the thoughts which on Sundays sometimes embarrassed him in the presence of others seemed natural and at home. Here the people in his books grew to fuller stature. The words of stories and of poems which he loved had a way of repeating themselves over again in his mind, trailing their meaning and association, haunting him after he had closed the door in the twilight and set out for home through the gathering darkness.

He held, in fact, almost a jealous sense of ownership, only grudgingly allowing his sister to bring her book along with him, never feeling completely himself or at home while she was there. And when at fourteen he went away to school, he was forever returning to it in his mind rather than in his memory, instinctively seeing things as they could be seen only there, finding himself tied securely in numberless ways to those comprehensions and discoveries possible only there for him.

In the storms and the cold of winter, whenever he thought of home, seeing one by one the places there, the sea-wall was always gaunt and bare, swept by the ringing surf, deserted and menacing; the long stretch of land held death more than life in its icy grasp; the woods, darkly blotted out by the driving snow, were often lonely and desolate, frightening even. For away from all these it was difficult to remember them in the old friendly way. Even in the house itself, he often thought, a fight went on day by day against the winter, a struggle unappreciated in his childhood, recalled now with gratitude, but yet, with all its compensations, a struggle.

The chapel alone was a place of light and warmth, the pale blue light of the snow itself, the remembered warmth of the fire there and of Sunday and week-day thoughts, the glowing warmth of the coming to life of things heretofore dead, because unperceived. Throughout the winter it gathered up and held within itself against the coming of the spring all the meanings of things now hidden by the snow. And together with these meanings it held that of the snow itself, falling in white crystal disks above the gray, almost invisible sea.

Once, Jan had written him, in a monstrous December gale, which had left no portion of the land or sea untouched, which had swept even into the anchorage bay and dashed the chapel with spray, he had heard from the barn where he had been milking his cows, the tones of the chapel bell, swung suddenly by a crazy gust of the wind, sounding deep and resonant through the storm.

Philip Marston at school thought again and again of Jan's letter. He liked it the best of any of the letters which Jan wrote to him about things at Windswept.

11

Eileen Marston was never able to discover to her own satisfaction just how she felt about Windswept. That she loved it enough to live with it nine months of each year, not only in contentment but in excitement, was certain. That her detestation of it by January of each year amounted almost to a panic, was equally certain.

As a matter of fact, she was rarely able to discover precisely how she felt about anything except her husband and her children, and this feeling needed no discovery or analysis. Feelings, points of view, about less tangible matters were constantly eluding her. Her very physical and emotional vitality made thought in itself inactive, put out its lesser flame. Her mind was the "quick forge" of Shakespeare rather than his "working house." Her powers of fancy were rampant. Added to the excitement which she was able to extract from the events of every day was the excitement she was forever creating from those events which might have happened but did not. She took pleasure not only in what her children were, but in what they were not, save in her imagination; not only in what conceivably would happen to them, but in what in all probability would never happen to them. She had retained her quick, intuitive understanding of her husband, sensing the intrinsic nature of what went on in his mind although she rarely followed his thinking, not because of lack of intelligence or even of interest, but because her imagination dealt with other matters. If she had a regret, it was that she had not married him five years earlier than she did.

At forty she had the body of a girl of eighteen, her own at that age. When her husband watched her at night, swinging her feet by the fire, her hair as fair as it had been when she had sat there with Dan and Julian and him, he felt again, as he had so often done, that time did not so much alter things at Windswept as it deepened them. As though the abundant life within her refused to be vanquished and put out when its day should come, it had given itself through her, at least in its outward appearance, to her children. Both looked like her rather than like their father in features and colouring, though neither, John Marston thought, sometimes with regret, sometimes without, had her wasteful prodigality of nature.

Like so many of the moods and humours which were so constantly seizing her, this sudden yearly hatred of Windswept, sweeping over her when she least expected it, puzzled and, in a sense, displeased her. She would never explain it on the ground of recurring custom.

"I can't see why we left at all," she always said, when in early or late spring they came back from New York or California or a suddenly conceived voyage to Europe. "There's no place in the world like this. Now next year we stay right here. Promise me you won't pay any attention to my nonsense."

John Marston always promised with the same good nature with which he packed his bags on some cold January day when he saw the unmistakable signs of revolt. He would have liked to stay on at Windswept, playing with his children in the snow, watching the weather with Jan, enjoying that uncontrollable and fearful, yet pleasurable excitement which continued bitter cold holds within itself, or which a three days' blizzard often engenders. But the cost of staying was greater than the cost of going and far less easily paid.

His chief compensation for three months away lay in

the admiration which other men accorded to his wife. Even more than the pleasure he took in her own excitement, the dramas she was always conceiving about the persons whom they met in New York, in Europe, on steamships and trains, he enjoyed the effect which she made on others, taking an almost ecstatic delight in her beauty and charm, in the way men's eyes followed her when she swept into dinner in one place or another, when she walked along a hundred different streets. He liked, too, the having her to himself without the children, largely because she took such almost jealous delight in being by herself with him.

When Philip and Ann were thirteen and twelve and their leaving home for school was but a year away, Eileen in a supreme act of self-sacrifice conceived the notion of taking both for the winter to Europe.

"We've got to give them something besides Jan and Philomena, that horrible school-house, and this desolation," she had said on one of her days of revolt. "If we don't, heaven knows what will happen to them when they go away to school."

The experiment proved the most dismal of failures. Philip was moody, homesick, and irritable, baffling his father, who had seen in Philip's equable nature and sensitive response to things as happy a future for his son as Fate can grudgingly accord her creatures. Now and then as he sat that winter over some manuscripts in the Bodleian or the British Museum, John Marston was tempted, in spite of himself, to question these tenacious roots of Windswept. Ann, her tired mother said at night, was a complete and total loss.

"I'm really worried about Ann. Do come out of that stupid book, John, long enough to listen. There's nothing in Europe that's made a dent on her so far. In Paris all she wanted to do was to buy presents for those wretched children at Heron Cove. And now she's begun all over again in London. She wants now to take them presents from every country. This morning she hardly looked at the changing of the Guards. She doesn't like pictures, she doesn't like cathedrals, she isn't even interested in a new coat I wanted to buy her."

"Oh, well, she'll wake up in time."

"I doubt it. It seems to me she grows less awake every year."

"She's facing a bad age. Were you such a model at twelve, my dear?"

"I was a loathsome brat at twelve. I was completely intolerable, flying into tantrums every other minute, a vile child. I had less than no right to exist. But at least I was alive."

"I've not the slightest doubt of that."

"I'd really welcome a tantrum once in a while. Or a case of sulks like Philip's. I honestly can't remember when I've seen her touched by anything except those dead birds she found last summer. She cried for hours then, but it's the last sign I've seen of any emotion whatever. I'm at my wit's end. It's lucky she's pretty. If she wasn't, I'd be even more tempted to slay her."

"She looks so much like you when I first saw you that it's startling. You had on a blue dress and were going to your first party."

"Well, maybe if she ever goes to enough parties, she

may improve, but I'm not so sure. She seems completely lifeless to me. I can't imagine where she gets such passiveness."

"Surely not from you, my dear. By the simple process of elimination, she must get it from me."

"Don't be silly. Well, I've learned my lesson. Next winter they'll both stay at home."

"Oh, there's going to be a next winter, is there?"

"I'm afraid so. I've got to have some recompense for this nightmare. We might go to California next winter to see if Julian and Lucy have managed any better with their offspring."

"I doubt it. How's Philip been today?"

"He's equally unbearable. He got a letter from Jan this morning. I could have murdered that Cook's man when he handed it out. Philip wouldn't budge till he'd read it twice over. That miserable dog has had puppies again, and Philip actually wants to cable Jan not to drown a one. He's in a perfect fit for fear some are dead already. He was half crying all day, and wouldn't take an interest even in the Tower."

"Well, let him cable. I don't like drowning puppies myself."

"John, you're incorrigible. There are at least eight dogs on the place already."

"Well, there's room enough. I'm sorry, dear. I'll let my work go tomorrow and take them off your hands. I'll take them to the wax-works. Mrs. Jarley ought to wake them up."

"Darling, Mrs. Jarley's Dickens, isn't she? You mean Madame Tussaud."

"So I do. Well, that ought to wake them up all the same. I used to love those things when I was their age and my father took me."

"So did I, but I doubt if they do. I'm completely discouraged about them."

"Don't worry so. They're only homesick. After all, you know, Windswept's an exciting place in the winter."

"I'm actually beginning to think it may be. And, John, if you could shop for Heron Cove it would be a help. I did think I might forget Heron Cove for a time, and even Windswept, but I've given up."

"Well, they're hard places to forget," said John Marston.

Some time in the middle of the night Eileen remembered her chief piece of information.

"You'll be glad to know," she said to her drowsy husband, "that the one place your children really want to see is Bohemia."

"I don't blame them a bit," said their father.

"Only Philip says he wouldn't go a step without Jan, even if you'd take him."

12

Among the occasional and unexpected rewards of his work as a translator John Marston counted as chief some letters which he received now and then from a certain Mother Superior of a French convent on the Hudson, Le Couvent de Sainte-Croix. His unknown correspondent signed herself in a strong, lively hand, Mère Radegonde, when she wrote him in French. When she wrote in English, which she used with equal facility, her name was Radegund, Mother Superior.

John Marston was surprised and captivated by Mother Radegund's handwriting. It entirely lacked the painstaking, unoriginal character of the few examples of convent script which he had seen from time to time in surreptitious glances over the shoulders of nuns, working occasionally in this library and that. He had heretofore taken for granted the notion that, once a woman dedicated herself solely to God, her handwriting, as well as her clothing, was skillfully designed to conceal any possibly troublesome personality which she might possess.

He was interested, too, in his correspondent's name, at first only vaguely known to him, and spent some fascinating hours in discovering more about its source. The Lady Radegund, he learned, had been a Thuringian princess of the sixth century, captured by the murderer of her father and married, while still but a child, in Soissons to a Frankish king. Although she lived with him in his palace near Soissons, her husband rightly complained that she lived rather like a nun than like a queen, spending her days in prayer and fasting and in holy works of charity, which, John Marston concluded, must have been not only rare but welcome in those monstrously confused times of the well-named Dark Ages. When her life with her Frankish husband became unbearable, she fled the Court at Soissons and at length founded at Poitiers, through the generosity of that very discarded husband, her order of the Holy Cross.

Here at Poitiers, John Marston read with ever-increasing pleasure, this ancient Radegund, for whom his new friend was named, administered her new order with vigilance and devotion, to say nothing of astounding energy. Since she never asked another to do what she had not first done herself, she was not above household drudgery. She stoked the fires, she swept the rooms, she bore away refuse from the kitchen, she drew water from the well. While her nuns were still asleep, she cleaned the Community's shoes, prepared the food, cooked it, washed the plates, scrubbed the kitchen. In her solitary Lent she wore iron chains about her body, so tightly drawn that the flesh stood out around. If ever the tired nun who read aloud by her bedside in her infrequent hours of rest stopped for so much as a moment to draw her breath, she would cry instantly, "Why do you stop? Go on with your reading!"

And yet with all her engrossing tasks, she found time to form and to cultivate the friendship of her chaplain, one Fortunatus, whose sonorous Latin hymns were familiar to John Marston, but whose association with the Lady Radegund had, before this new discovery, been unknown to him.

Fortunatus had himself written of Radegund's piety. A little mouse, he said, who had ventured near her needlework, fell dead at its first impious nibble! *Est et in rebus minimis magna gloria Creatoris,* her chaplain had commented. But all the chaplain's revelations of his friend were not pious ones, just as all his poems were not sonorous Latin hymns. He wrote poem after poem to thank Mother Radegund and the Lady Abbess Agnes for delightful presents for his table, raspberries, butter and milk, blancmange.

"White eggs and black grapes!" he wrote. "I hope there will not be war in my stomach. You bade me have two eggs for my supper. I had four really. I shall get fatter than ever. Pray that I do not sin through indulgence of appetite."

In the long forty days of Lent, while his friend was in solitary retreat, he wrote: "The light of mine eyes has disappeared. The days are sunless. Nothing I see matters now. May these hours of Lent hurry swiftly on their way!"

And again: "Best of mothers, we beg you, the Abbess Agnes and I, to relieve the anxiety of your two children by drinking a little wine. 'Tis but what Paul imposed on Timothy!"

A discovery such as this, John Marston thought, was but one of the constant delights of years spent largely with books. And especially if such discoveries could be made among perfect surroundings, what more ought a man to desire of life? The scholar, he thought, placing himself for the moment humbly among the elect, was, as some essayist had said, like the Angel of the Resurrection, gathering from the four corners of the earth what else were but dead things and infusing them with life. The thought of this small oasis of peace and at least relative security in a turbulent century had given him, he wrote Mother Radegund in her convent on the Hudson, many hours of pleasure. Long before he actually met this namesake of the holy Radegund, he made a special journey one winter from Paris to Poitiers to visit Sainte Radegonde's Church and to send Mother Radegund from there some pictures, which he thought might interest and please her.

But it was her letters themselves which at last prompted his visit to her convent, a visit which, in its momentous consequences, was to add other pages, dark and light, to this story of Windswept. Mother Radegund, he thought, must be totally unlike his perhaps false impressions of women who gave their lives to God. He often re-read her letters. In her strong, full hand she had first written him:

I am yielding to a desire which I cannot set aside. I must thank you for your translations of Villon, which fell yesterday into my hands by the graciousness of a friend and, shall we boldly say, by the special Grace of God. I have always loved that scurrilous rascal who knew my beloved Provence, both for his poems and for his miserable, charming self. I often find myself when I should be attending to far holier matters, reciting:

> La royne Blanche comme lis
> Qui chantoit à voix de seraine;
> Berte au grant pié, Bietris, Alis;
> Haremburgis qui tint le Maine.

And familiar as they are but always new to me, the words:

> Où sont elles, vierge souvraine?
> Mais où sont les neiges d'antan?

Holy Church may well have abjured him; he deserved ill at Her hands; but he has more than once kept me to Her vows!

To introduce myself, I am the Superior of a French convent in —— on the Hudson. A French woman, I have since a

child loved English, and have for many years now seized upon
translations from my own language into yours, seeking but
rarely finding what you have given me, a most excellent
rendering of the French both in language and in spirit.

Accept my deepest thanks, dear Sir, and believe me

Yours in Christ,

+Radegund, Superior

P.S. Do you by chance know the essay on Villon by R.L.S.
in his *Familiar Studies?* It fills me with rage. Contrary to his
usual mercy and humour, he becomes here a moralist, almost
allying himself (though falsely, I must believe) with those
many misled souls, who by the conscious pursuit cf virtue
succeed only in becoming tiresome!

When John Marston published his translation of certain poems of Paul Verlaine, he sent Mother Radegund
a copy, not without hesitation. Yet if she loved the vaga-
bond, François Villon, she might conceivably, he thought,
possess charity, even affection, toward this modern vaga-
bond and ne'er-do-well, who, with all his undeniable
brutishness, was as undeniably a poet. Mother Radegund
was not in the least horrified by Verlaine, and she was
extremely grateful to John Marston. She wrote:

I presume I might quiet any uneasy conscience I might
possess in my enjoyment of Verlaine by the recognition of
his re-conversion, however mad, to Catholicism. But I must
confess that my admiration and enthusiasm over his verse
has little to do with that somewhat bizarre occurrence, much
as it unquestionably contributed to his poetry. In spite of my
liking for the religious poems I like even more those in
which his power of combining cadence and association is at
its best—*Après Trois Ans,* for instance. And may I say that
you have admirably managed to convey here that *esprit et*

delicatesse so difficult for English to capture in a prescribed verse form.

I often wonder what poor Verlaine has now in his existence, assuming, of course that his hysterical return to faith was sincere, to make up for the Quartier Latin, the filth of his home, and Eugénie with her little, and doubtless dirty, market basket. I pray for him—in gratitude!

John Marston now and again came to Mother Radegund's aid.

I wonder, my good friend, she wrote, how you would welcome a bold and intrusive suggestion. In these degenerate days when Latin, even in the cloister, is often misunderstood and usually mispronounced, I am at a loss for a really lively English rendering of the oldest and most familiar hymns of the Church. We sing some of them, of course, in the original, but half the time I am convinced that my Sisters, as well as my girls, do not fully know what they are singing. Why not try some renderings for us? Saint Hilary's hymn for Pentecost, for instance, *Beata nobis gaudia*, or Saint Joseph's hymn for the 19th of March. The Office Book, of course, gives English translations of these, but wouldn't you give us yours? And also of that magnificent song of the pilgrims thronging to Rome:

O Roma nobilis, orbis et domina?

I love to think of that unknown singer. Why not give him his long-delayed due by a translation better than the dull and lame things heretofore accorded him even by the most learned? I am in your debt already. I shall be more so, *in saecula saeculorum,* if you will do this for me. Of course, if you also fail, you may take comfort in the fact that conventual secrets are not divulged, and really you can hardly do worse than your predecessors.

After several years of such delightful exchange of letters, John Marston accepted Mother Radegund's repeated invitations to call upon her. It was a cold December day when, before his return homeward from some Christmas shopping in New York, he stepped from the train at the station on the Hudson and walked toward Le Couvent de Sainte-Croix. He felt some misgivings and not a little embarrassment as he traversed the mile or more between the station and the convent in the sharp air. He was unused to religious houses. They seemed alien to him, even those which sheltered girls at school; and he was experiencing at the same time that fear which is likely to clutch at all of us when a long-cherished expectation is about to be demolished or fulfilled.

He could see, as he ascended the high road which led to the heights above the river, the gray towers of the convent. Rising above the trees, their conical shape and tapering wooden spires suggested the towers of the many châteaux about Tours and Blois, out of place as they were in this American setting and wanting the quiet streams and rolling green fields and hills of the Loire valley. He hoped that the resemblance was some slight comfort to Mother Radegund, exiled now from France for many years. She had never suggested her age in her letters. Would she be old or middle-aged, he wondered? She could not still be young.

The snow had come early that year and lay deep over the lawns and gardens of the houses which he passed. More had begun to fall as he drew near the entrance to the convent; and some girls in red capes and hoods over their black convent dresses gave him courage. Moreover, they were speaking English, and not too decorously at that, as they hauled their very corporeal sleds up a steep incline in the convent grounds. One slight, dark-eyed girl of fifteen, perhaps, and very pretty, left the group and came forward to meet him as he entered the drive.

"Can I do anything for you, sir?" she asked, a French accent unmistakable in her careful English. "Did you wish to see anyone?"

John Marston always remembered her standing there, the snow white on her red cape and hood, her brown eyes looking at him, both she and he so mercifully unconscious of the manner in which their lives were later to be united by life and by death.

"Perhaps you will tell me," he said, "at which entrance I should ask for Mother Radegund. I have come to see her. She is expecting me, I think."

"Oh, you are Mr. Marston then," said the girl, smiling up at him from beneath her red hood. He saw then that her eyes were almost black rather than brown and that her nose had an excited little twitch at the nostrils, not unbecoming, he thought. "You are the gentleman who put into English our Latin hymns for us. Mother Radegund is expecting you. She told us you were to come to see her. We liked the hymns very much, indeed, far better than in the French translations, except for one line which Mother took the liberty to change. And they go much better when we sing them in Latin now that the American girls understand them better. The Latin here is not so well understood as it is in France when French girls study it."

John Marston marvelled at the self-possession of this

child, who was leading him up the long drive to the door. She could not be over fifteen, he thought, contrasting her with the shy awkwardness of his own daughter in a similar situation. She seemed so little embarrassed by what must be at least a somewhat novel circumstance in such surroundings that he resolved to question her further.

"I'm interested," he said, "in the line which Mother Radegund changed. Which one was it, do you remember?"

"Oh, just one in the Pilgrims' Hymn. I've a bad memory or I'd know. Mother says I never remember anything unless it pleases me to do so. It was Sister Agnes, who teaches religion, who wanted the change. She's very holy and very dull. We all have to—what do you say?—humour her a bit. But don't trouble yourself at all, sir, about it. It's—it's quite unimportant."

He looked at her again, more amazed than ever. She had a mobile red mouth in a rather pale face and white even teeth. They were drawing near the door.

"You're French, I take it," he said.

"Yes, sir, from Aix-en-Provence. But I've been here four years—four long years—ever since I was eleven."

He smiled at the careful note of sadness, which she obviously wanted him to appreciate.

"And why did you come away off here to school when the Latin is so much better in France?"

"It's quite too long a story to tell so quickly. You see, I'm Mother Radegund's niece."

"Oh! And your name?"

"My name is Adrienne Chartier," she said.

She preceded him up the long flight of steps and rang the bell.

"The portress today is Sister Agnes," she whispered, as the black shadow of a nun fell across one of the long panes of glass at the sides of the doorway. "You'll easily see what I mean by dull and holy."

The door opened. A slight, rather somber nun stood in the entrance. Adrienne made only the faintest suspicion of a curtsey.

"This gentleman is Mr. John Marston, Sister," she said. "He is here to see Mother Radegund."

She turned and faced John Marston, her black eyes conveying a glance of quick discernment.

"Goodbye, sir, and thank you," she said.

"Thank *you*," said John Marston.

He was still surprised and amused as the dull and holy Sister Agnes led him down a long and spotless corridor into a small reception room. Apparently the duties of portress enjoined silence, he thought, or perhaps Sister Agnes still smarted over the ill-advised line in his translation. At all events, except for her formal and polite acknowledgment of the child's introduction, she did not venture further conversation. When she had ushered him into the room, she stood a bit aside and bowed sedately.

"Pray be seated, sir. Mother will be here directly."

John Marston felt precisely like a school-boy as he waited in the quiet room. He quite forgot Adrienne Chartier and the sudden interest he had felt in her. He had not suffered such nervousness, he thought, since those old occasions at St. Paul's when he had waited in Dr. Coit's study in answer to a mysterious summons from the headmaster, fearful lest he had failed in some way to come up to the good doctor's expectations. Now that he was here, he wished devoutly that he had not come. It would have been far wiser to have guarded his rare pleasure in Mother Radegund's letters instead of thus recklessly chancing its ruin.

He could not imagine the author of those letters in a room like this. It was clean and bare except for the walls. The uncomfortable, straight, uninteresting chairs were placed as if for an equally uncomfortable conference, two against each wall, standing straight and stiff. A fern on an ugly wooden table stood in the exact center of the one window.

The walls engrossed his anxious attention. They were painted with religious pictures, garish, startling, badly done: Saint Christopher bearing the Lord across a turbid river, on one wall; on the other, a fore-shortened angel holding a crucifix before the eyes of a dying martyr torn by lions. Even the lions seemed impressed, he thought, gazing, subdued, upon their grisly accomplishment. He could not imagine the author of those letters in such a room, and he again devoutly wished he had let well enough alone.

He rose awkwardly to his feet as he heard a door at the far end of the corridor open and close, the quick, steady tramp of feet, the clicking of a swinging rosary. A tall, blue-eyed woman came into the room and took his hand with a warm, firm clasp. He had not expected such blue eyes in a French face, he thought confusedly, nor such height, nor, after Sister Agnes, such ease and friendliness.

"Well, Mr. John Marston," said Mother Radegund, after she had looked at him for what seemed an extra-long minute, "this is dangerous business, isn't it? I've been thinking all day of a wise saying of Plautus, which I read years ago. 'We lose what is certain while we pursue uncertainties.' And there's that old French proverb which you doubtless know: *La chandelle qui va devant vaut mieux que celle qui va derrière.** Still, I don't think I'm going to be sorry."

The room with its hideous walls faded from John Marston's sight.

"I'm sure I'm not," he said.

"Well, the first thing is to get out of this place," Mother Radegund said. "I often wonder how we keep any patrons at all when we receive them in a room like this. I'm having a hot cup of tea brought to my own study for you. That, after some time, not to say casuistry, I've been able to make presentable."

He followed her down the long, clean corridor and through another equally spotless to a room which looked out upon a courtyard with walks and trees.

"This is nice," she said, "in spring and summer, and even in the snow. Your snow is the thing I like best in America. I never tire of it."

Mother Radegund's study was a bare room, too, but it was comfortable and in good taste. There were a few good pictures on the plain, light walls; the inevitable crucifix was delicately carved in wood and unpainted; on one side of the room books reached the ceiling. There was a coal fire burning in a small grate below a black

* The candle which goes before is better than that which comes after.

marble mantel, and two comfortable chairs were drawn
up before it. Mother Radegund motioned him to take
one of these. She took the other, busying herself with
the re-arrangement of a tea service on a small table between them covered with a white cloth.

He watched her hands below the long black sleeves
of her habit. They were white and strong, long and quick,
not an artist's hands, he thought, and yet the hands of
one who recognized the meaning and the associations
of touch. She handled objects as though they had relationship with her rather than as though they were merely
things to be seized and moved about. The nails of her
fingers were well-shaped and cared for.

"You are much younger than I thought you were,"
she said.

"I'm not what you'd call young, I'm afraid. I've just
celebrated my fortieth birthday."

"I have six more years to my discredit. And I had pic-
tured a man not so tall as you and with graying hair perhaps. And surely without so much an air of the country.
Without your clothes being what they are, you might
even be a farmer, or shall we say, a countryman. The
word has nicer connotations, and I like its ancient usage.
Still I gathered from your letters and your address that
you lived in the country. I've never seen Maine. I've always wanted to."

"You must," he said.

As they talked on easily about Windswept, the life
there, his work, his family, her own past and present, he
kept thinking how beautiful a woman's face could be
without the softening effect of hair about it or without

the forehead visible. Smooth bands of white starched linen covered her forehead and the sides of her face; her broad pleated guimpe below her chin encircled her shoulders; her full black habit fell to her feet in their broad black shoes, a scapular covering the line of the waist. Still even these garments could not hide her tall, fine figure or obscure the clear texture of her skin, white like Adrienne's. She had a strong, straight nose, rather bold for beauty, he thought, but her extraordinarily blue eyes, long rather than full, her finely arched dark brows, and her sensitive, though rather full mouth, were entirely satisfying. Just above the bridge of her nose between her brows was a straight deep line, almost a cleft, and oddly whiter than the rest of her face. It lent expression and attractiveness. He was glad that he had come.

"You don't look French," he said, "either in face or in figure. I wasn't prepared for such tallness or for such blue eyes."

She laughed.

"I've Irish ancestors," she said, "though so far away as to be almost out of mind. And actually, though I adore Provence and spent my childhood there, my family came from Brittany. My grandfather was a Breton fisherman. We come from simple stock, Mr. Marston."

After a few minutes a knock came at the door, and a nun entered with a tea-tray. She was an improvement on Sister Agnes, he thought, bustling, capable, good-humoured.

"This is Sister Sainte Geneviève," Mother Radegund said. "She teaches mathematics to unwilling minds. Sister, this is Mr. John Marston, who translated our Latin hymns for us."

"I'm sure it was most kind of you, sir," said Sister Sainte Geneviève.

"Draw the shades, please, Sister," Mother Radegund said. "I always like this snug, shut-in feeling in a winter dusk. Sister Hélène, I see, has made you some hot *croissants*. Now just how will you have your tea?"

"You're not having any with me?" he asked when she had served him to his liking. "That's hardly fair. Are the Provençal people not tea-drinkers then?"

"We do not eat with guests," she said. "It is a rule some potentate has placed upon us, or perhaps some Higher Authority has thought it wise. It really doesn't matter. I've learned that when there's no good reason to be found in a rule, one is vastly more comfortable if one stops searching for it."

The tea was hot and good, the buttered *croissants* delicious. She filled his cup three times as they talked. He had rarely felt more at home.

"The smell of tea," she said, "always brings back my Breton grandmother to me. I used to visit her each summer when I was a child. She always made it hot and strong over a peat fire. I used to carry the smell of peat back home with me to Provence. She dried my wet clothes by it after I had been playing in the rain. She lived on the coast near the little town of St. Gildas de Rhuis. My grandfather was one of Loti's Iceland fishermen. He was lost on a voyage there when I was twelve."

"Smells have a way of staying with one," he said, somehow knowing that the smell of the tea and peat rather than her grandfather's death was uppermost in her mind at that moment, "more even than colours or sounds."

"That's right. They do. Still there are colours that stay, only I think not by themselves. They have to be associated in some way with light or with dark to really remain. I remember once when I was ten or so, I was in a hayfield near St. Gildas on a hot July day. I had been scrambling down some high rocks to see a shrine to St. Gildas, placed there in a cleft in the cliffs just above the sea. I remember how cold and dark it seemed down there out of the sun, and how I disliked staying to say even a few of the prayers I should have said. I clambered up the rocks as quickly as I could and found myself suddenly in a warm hayfield flooded with sun. There was a convent near, and some nuns in bright blue habits were gathering in the hay, pitching it upon a rack drawn by white oxen. I don't know why a scene like that should have so impressed a child, but I have never forgotten how I stood at the cliff's edge in the sun and watched those nuns. They and the field were so flooded with light that ever since then all strong, clear sunlight, wherever I have seen it, has been the sunlight in that noonday field. All the light since the world began seemed concentrated there in that one field, and even as a child I think I felt that. Only, of course, we can never quite know what we felt then and what we've felt since, looking back. Maybe just the undefined realization was there, waiting to be defined years afterward."

She had a beautiful voice, he thought, low, even a bit husky, but musical with a rhythmic rise and fall. Peculiarly enough, there was little trace of foreign accent. As he listened, he thought how odd and yet how pleasant it was that they were not talking of books as he had expected they would.

"I often wonder," she said, as though reading his own thoughts, "if many people ever realize what just a thing like that sunlight in that field can do to a child's life. I sometimes get frightened at the way time is beginning to seize us these days, even in convents. When I read of big dams being built to harness more power and of all these new motor cars, whenever I turn on all these electric switches, I wonder if some day all this control of power isn't going to turn on us and control us to our own hurt. But your children must be safe in that place with the lovely name. I'm sure places are more important to a child even than books, old, well-weathered places full of associations. Without the olive trees of Provence, for example, I could never have loved poetry."

"And probably without poetry you could not remember the olive trees as you do."

"Perhaps. It's comforting to have no quarrel with one's life at middle age, isn't it?"

It was five o'clock before he realized it. A bell rang somewhere, and he heard girls' voices outside as they apparently hurried indoors.

"I'm afraid I've stayed too long," he said. "It's been so pleasant I haven't thought of time."

"There's no hurry. That's the bell for Benediction. Things won't collapse completely if I'm a bit late. Now you've found that convents aren't so different from other nice places, you'll come again, I hope."

He promised.

"Before I go, I must ask you about a black-eyed French

child who showed me in. I never saw such self-possession in a girl of that age or such good manners."

"Oh, Adrienne, of course."

"She's your niece, she told me."

"Yes, my youngest brother's child. Her parents died within a few months of each other, and she came to me four years ago."

"She said so. 'Four long years,' she said." He smiled.

"They've been extremely happy years, as a matter of fact," said Mother Radegund. "It's like Adrienne to see them as miserable, upon occasion. Adrienne has a way of shaping Destiny, of getting precisely what she wants, sometimes in one way, sometimes in another, and not always laudable ways at that. But some day I'm afraid Destiny will hit back."

"Well, she's an extremely attractive child. My own daughter, who isn't so much younger, could never have risen to such a situation with such *savoir faire*."

"Adrienne loves situations. For that matter, she was quite aware of your coming and had probably been watching the gate with her speeches all prepared. She's a nice child, but I have my uneasy moments about her. She's doubtless furious at this moment that her prayers prevent her from seeing you to the gate."

"I'm rather sorry, myself."

"I'm not at all sorry," Mother Radegund said.

13

Ann Marston was neither a dull nor an insensitive child, but for some inexplicable reason she developed far more slowly than her brother Philip. She lacked his early quick response to things and happenings. Unlike his imagination, her own failed to discover associations in familiar objects and pastimes. Rather she took things for granted, the comfort and security of her home, the long, free miles of land and sea, the boundless physical activity, which made her so drowsy at night that she fell asleep, much to Philip's disgust, even in the most exciting chapters of the books they read aloud before bed-time. She adored her brother, who, for the most part, merely tolerated her companionship, preferring to be by himself.

"I've hunted two hours for you, Philip. You're mean to run off like this. I thought we were hauling the traps with Jan. You said you would."

"I didn't want to haul traps."

"Well, it's mean anyway to break your promise."

"I'm not hindering you, am I? Go on and haul them."

"They're hauled already, stupid. It was no fun just by myself with Jan. What are you doing anyway away off down here by yourself?"

"Leave me alone. I'm thinking."

"What are you thinking about?"

"Don't be such a nuisance, Ann. You're always bothering me."

"Well, what *are* you thinking about?"

"I'm just thinking. I can think if I want to, can't I?"

"Well, you've got to think about something, haven't you?"

"Oh, well, I'm thinking about how the French ships came past the cove here three hundred years ago this very September."

"What French ships?"

"Ann, you were right there at breakfast when father told us. You never hear anything!"

"Yes, I do, too. I was thinking about hauling the traps. You said you would. It was mean of you."

"I don't have to haul traps if I don't want to. If I'd rather think than haul traps, I can think, can't I?"

"What's the use of sitting here just thinking about some old French ships? We're going on a picnic to the sea-wall. Mother's making sandwiches with Philomena."

"Well, why don't you go back and help?"

"I did offer to. Mother said I needn't. She said to come and find you."

"It's not time for a picnic yet. I'm going to stay right here till it's time."

"All right, cross patch. I'll stay here, too."

She sat down beside him on a huge flat rock above the full tide of the cove. It was a clear September day with a high wind and surf. The sea was deep blue, ridged with white, rolling on toward a distant, luminous horizon. Ann did not like quarrels, and she always felt uncomfortably in the wrong whenever she quarrelled with Philip.

"What about the French ships?" she said after some uneasy moments.

"You don't care anything about them. You never so much as heard at breakfast. You never hear anything that matters."

"Don't be so mean, Philip. I do hear things."

"No, you don't, and you're always bothering me."

"I won't bother you if you'll just tell me. I want to know, really. What about them?"

"Oh, well, you'll only forget if I tell you. I'm always telling you things and you forgetting them. They came right past here three hundred years ago. Champlain was there. He was the geographer of the expedition."

"What expedition?"

"Why, the one the French ships took. They were exploring all the coast here. Father told us this morning. They went right past here. They went to Mt. Desert and way up to the Penobscot River."

"What did they look like?"

"Oh, big, high ships like frigates. They must have seen this cove and the place where our house is."

"Well, what are you thinking about them?"

"Oh, just how they looked, silly, and what the sailors must have thought, and the things they said."

"How do you know what they said?"

"Don't be so stupid! I don't, but I like to make it up."

"Oh, well! What's a geographer, Philip?"

"Someone who makes maps and keeps journals. That's what Champlain did, and he gave names to the islands and the points of land."

"Well, that must have been fun. Maybe it was a nice day like this."

"Maybe it was."

"Did Windswept look like it does now three hundred years ago?"

"Probably it did."

"Did the French name Windswept, too?"

Philip's exasperation was increasing to explosive heat.

"Ann, there's something wrong with your head. You

get stupider and stupider! How many times, I'd like to know, have you heard about grandfather's naming Windswept when father was not much older than me? Sometimes I think you haven't any brains at all. You're just the limit, Ann!"

"Of course, I know. I just forgot for a moment, that's all. Don't you ever forget things? You *are* mean, Philip."

"Well, who wouldn't be mean with such a stupid?"

"Well, anyway, I'm glad the French didn't stay and take it, else we'd never have had it. What are you going to do after you get through thinking, Philip—before the picnic, I mean?"

"I'm not going to get through, so you'd better run along home."

"I shan't. Are you just thinking about the ships, Philip?"

Philip sighed and hitched away from his sister on the great rock.

"Not just. I'm thinking about drawing a map for father for his birthday. Maybe I'll put in the French ships in colours, and try to find the names that Champlain gave to things. There are some maps somewhere that I mean to find, but I'm not going to copy them. I'm going to make my own."

"You always have nicer ideas than I do, Philip. I'll give you a whole half-dollar from my pocket money if you'll only tell me what I can give father."

"Ask mother."

"I did, but she said I'd have to think up something by myself. I just can't think up a thing."

"That's what I told you, didn't I? You can't ever think up things."

"Don't be so hateful! I can, too. Only father's so hard to think up things for. Let's hunt stones, Philip."

"What for? I'm busy."

"You can't be busy just thinking."

"I am, I tell you."

"Well, I've got an idea for mother. I'm going to find a little round stone with a pretty colour, purple maybe. Jan said if I did, he'd polish it with a tool he has and make it a pretty shape, and then we'd send it away and have it set in a ring for mother."

"Then it's not your idea at all. It's Jan's. I told you you never had ideas of your own. You just can't make plans by yourself."

Ann's eyes suddenly filled with tears, and Philip as suddenly felt sorry. He did not like to see anyone or anything in pain. He felt mean, too, as well as sorry, and forgot the French ships.

"Why don't you find two stones then and have one set for father in a stick-pin for his ties? He'd like that."

Ann wiped away her tears with the skirt of her gingham dress.

"Will you help me, then?" she asked.

"Oh, sure," said Philip, "I suppose so. Only we'd better wait till after the picnic when the tide's out. There'll be more good stones at the sea-wall anyway."

"And I'll give you the half-dollar just the same, Philip, because it really was your idea and not mine, wasn't it?"

"Oh, well, you'd probably have thought of it after a long time. I don't want your old half-dollar. I wouldn't think of taking it."

Ann Marston was a more active child than her brother,

busy, always doing things, yet she lacked the dramatic instinct of her mother. What she did was fascinating in itself and for itself. Her absorbing occupations changed year by year. At ten she was a naturalist, keeping frogs' eggs in jars, tearing among the blueberries and juniper with a butterfly net, sticking over-killed beetles and moths on pins, her room messy beyond description. At eleven she was a farmer, helping Jan with the milking, living in overalls in the barn, smelling of grain and manure at the table. At twelve she was a chemist, working avidly with a small set of tubes and bottles which her father bought for her, filling the house with ghastly odors, burning her hands. She went through all phases of the collecting stage. She did not love to read as Philip did, disliking to sit still with a book, no matter how exciting. On rainy days, when reading was a last resort, she took her book to the hay-loft since Philip rarely welcomed her in the chapel. When she read on good days, as she rarely did, she lay flat on her stomach at the very edge of the headland above the sea, half out of sight in the rough grass. Her father, looking from his study window, knew that she was there by the waving of her brown, bare legs in the air. She wriggled her toes as she read, as though she could not bear to be completely still.

She possessed tenacious and absorbing loyalties, deep and solid rather than quick and sensitive, to her friends at Heron Cove, the fishermen, their wives and children, who liked her better than they liked her brother. She could enter into the lives of people as Philip never could do. Unkindness or injustice at school or at play angered rather than pained her. She adored her father and mother,

Jan, Philomena, Philip, not so much for *what* they were, about which she rarely thought, as for the simple fact *that* they were, that they made her world and could be depended upon to keep it secure. She loved her possessions for the same simple reason. Toward the animals at Windswept, the dogs, the horses, and cows, she felt an affection almost like their own for her, simple, basic, unapprehended in any significance it might possess. When tragedy befell any of her pets, she wept bitterly, her grief not like Philip's, which had within it a sense of the pathos of animal suffering and death, but rather the grief of loss, of separation from what she had been long used to and could not do without.

At twelve, when her mother had been concerned over her unresponsiveness in Europe, she was not so much unresponsive as completely lost, since she was absent from the tangible, customary places and objects which made her life. She loved Windswept because it was hers, its air, the spring of its soil beneath her bare feet, all its familiar things. She did not feel, as Philip did long before he was twelve, its age or its isolation, its prose or its poetry. That it belonged to her and that she was miserable away from it completed her understanding of it. She was a noisy child rather than quiet, slamming doors, upsetting things in a whirlwind of activity. Her hands were rarely clean; she had no interest in her clothes; and her room was an untidy depository of animal, vegetable, and mineral life and death.

At thirteen to her father she was like some strong, well-made basket, heaped with an assortment of good things, well-wrapped, waiting to be discovered, seen and touched,

sorted out, valued. Or like a well-laid fire, waiting only
to be kindled to give out its heat and light. An apprehension of familiar things, their associations and meanings,
would not for her, he thought, be the means of discovery.
That would come later, and as an end rather than as a
means. For her to apprehend the capital she had amassed
for living, to learn how to draw upon it, it would require
some sudden, unfamiliar experience, some surprise, springing upon her unaware. When the time and the means of
discovery came, he was not sure but that she would handle matters better than Philip, with more courage and
with less pain.

14

On another clear September morning in the year 1907
Ann Marston was standing just at the turn of the road
where it first entered the woods on its way to Heron Cove.
She had been waiting there for hours, she thought. It was
fully two hours before that she had said to Jan when he
took the cows to pasture,

"Tell Adrienne I'm here. I'm not coming down to the
house to say goodbye."

Jan had stared at her. Jan had annoying moments, she
thought, when he stared at one, his eyes seeing things
which people did not want him to see. She was sure that
Jan had seen the marks of tears about her eyes although
she had dashed water on her face at the spring before she
ran to tell him.

"All right," he had said, looking and looking at her.
"Shall I tell the others, too?"

"I don't care," she said, trying to make her voice sound as it should. "I'm not coming, that's all."

She had had her breakfast early in the kitchen, even before Jan had come in for his. Philomena had found her there over her bread and milk.

"What do we do here so early?" asked Philomena. "Do we eat two breakfasts then?"

She had not answered Philomena at all, standing by the window, her back to the kitchen, gulping down her bread and milk.

"Do we eat two breakfasts then?" Philomena had persisted stupidly.

"No, I don't," she had said rudely. "I'm not coming in to breakfast. Don't ask questions, Philomena!"

"This morning we have no good manners," said Philomena, as she would never have said to Philip. "We step from our bed from the wrong side."

"Oh, shut up, Philomena!" she had cried. "Leave me alone! You're always picking on me!"

Philomena had almost dropped the bacon griddle in her excitement. She had doubtless told Jan, and his knowledge of her rudeness had made him stare the more when she told him what to say to Adrienne.

She could not say goodbye to Adrienne before them all. Not one of them felt as she felt about Adrienne's going. Philip did not like Adrienne. She could see that, stupid as Philip thought she was. Philip was polite to Adrienne, treating her always with the new manners he had brought home from his year at school, helping her into the boat, helping her out, seating her at the table. But he did not like her. Sometimes he grew red when she came into the

room, and he never wanted to go on walks with her by
himself.

"Let's walk to the sea-wall, Philip. I want to see the
osprey's nest."

"All right, but Ann has to come. She found it. I'm not
sure where it is."

"Hasn't Ann lessons at ten? It's almost that now."

"No, I haven't lessons, Adrienne. Father's too busy this
morning. I have them this afternoon. I can come."

Philip had never before been so decent to her as during
this summer. That was one of the good things Adrienne
had brought. Still she would have been happier if Philip
had liked Adrienne, if she had not been constantly aware
that he did not. She loved Adrienne so completely that
she was jealous for Adrienne's hold on the affections of
others.

Once when she had been lying in the grass pretending
to read but really trying to think up some new thing to do
which Adrienne might like, she had heard Philip and
Adrienne talking on the terrace. It was odd how, when
one loved another, one seized upon all means, wrong or
right, of knowing all about another. Instead of trying not
to hear what Philip and Adrienne were saying, she had
tried with all her might to catch every word, angry at the
wind which took some words away.

"Do you know, Philip, I believe you're scared of me."

"How absurd!" (She had never heard Philip use that
word before.) "Why should I be scared of you?"

"I'm not concerned just now with why. That's another
question. But you are, aren't you?"

"I certainly am not."

"Well, if you're not, why don't you ever take me places just by ourselves? Why didn't you take me to the chapel when I asked last evening?"

"Because I didn't want to, that's why."

Adrienne laughed then, a silvery, mocking laugh which Ann caught in spite of the wind. A sudden gust took the next words, and then she heard Philip say:

"What do you know about French boys? You left France when you were eleven. What chance do you have in a convent to know about boys?"

"Don't worry, Mr. Know-it-all. I wasn't quite a baby at eleven, and I've read books."

"Oh, you have, have you?"

"Yes, I have. But you needn't worry. I don't want anything of you. I don't like you either. Just remember that, will you, Mr. Wiseman?"

It was odd about Philip's rudeness to Adrienne. In his rudeness to Adrienne there was a different quality than there was in his rudeness to Ann, a quality which Ann did not like. It was almost as though Philip were insulting Adrienne. After the strange conversation on the terrace Adrienne stopped asking Philip to do things for her or to take her places, which was good for Ann, since during this last month of Adrienne's stay, she had had Adrienne mostly to herself.

Nor did Ann think that her mother really liked Adrienne, much as she commended Adrienne's manners to Ann and the neatness of Adrienne's appearance. Ann almost hated her mother for not liking Adrienne, for looking at Adrienne as she sometimes did with an air of puzzled suspicion, for saying, when Adrienne had politely ventured an opinion opposite to her mother's:

"My dear child, you're not quite sixteen, you know."

Ann had seen her mother's dislike of Adrienne come boldly out into unmistakable assurance upon the occasion when Ann had begged again to go to Adrienne's convent school with her instead of to the one already chosen.

"I'd be so much less lonely, mother, with Adrienne. You don't want me to be lonely, do you?"

"We're all lonely sometimes, Ann. It doesn't hurt any of us to be lonely once in a while."

"But, Mother, you've never given really good reasons. It's a good school, father says. Father knows Mother Radegund. She's wonderful, he says."

"I've no doubt of that at all. But neither your father nor I think it's wise for you to go to a convent school."

"Why not wise?"

"We have our reasons, Ann. In the first place, it's a Catholic school, and we're not Catholics."

"What difference does that make? Adrienne's a Catholic."

"Adrienne's a French girl. Many French people are Catholics. We're not French people."

"Jan and Philomena are Catholics. What's wrong in Catholics?"

"Nothing at all. It's simply that you are not used to that way of thinking."

"Well, couldn't I get used to it?"

"Very likely, but we do not think now it would be the best thing for you."

"Why not?"

"Ann, I'm tired of talking. I don't want the subject brought up again. You must do as we think best for you. Now remember, this is settled, once and for all."

Ann had burst into angry tears then. It was odd how tears had always seemed about to come during this summer just past for many reasons stranger than this one.

"You don't like Adrienne, mother. That's the reason."

"I do like her very much, in many ways."

"Why do you say *in many ways,* just like that?"

"Because in many ways I think Adrienne is too old for her years."

"That's just because you don't know her the way I do. Adrienne's my very best friend. I hope I'll be just like her when I'm sixteen."

"You're not sixteen yet. Run now and pick the blueberries Philomena wants for supper. Let Adrienne help you."

"Adrienne doesn't like to pick blueberries. It's stupid, picking blueberries."

"Stupid or not, they're to be picked. And you may tell Adrienne that the matter of school is settled, once and for all."

Jan and Philomena did not like Adrienne. One morning two weeks ago Philomena had found a book hidden under Adrienne's mattress, when she was turning out Adrienne's room. Philomena had brought the book to her mother, distastefully, holding it up with two fingers. Ann had been in her mother's room at the time.

"For a child this is a bad book," Philomena had said. "My poor English, it can read enough to know that these stories, they are bad."

Her mother had taken the book from Philomena and sent Ann from the room. That afternoon her father had talked with Adrienne for a long time in his study. When Adrienne had come out at last and asked Ann to go for a walk with her, there had been the marks of tears in her eyes.

"Your father is the best man in all the world," Adrienne had said, lying in the grass on the high bank above the cove. "I shall love him always. If I had not lost my father when I was little, I should be a far better girl than I am."

Ann had struggled to free her words, aching with sorrow for Adrienne, loving her as she had loved no one else in all her life, longing to comfort her.

"You're good, Adrienne. You're the best girl I ever knew. Don't cry, Adrienne! I can't bear to see you cry."

The clear afternoon light had suddenly seemed cruel in its loveliness. Ann had never seen it in that way before. She could have died for Adrienne at that moment.

"No, I'm not good. But if I had a father like yours, I would be good. It's hard to have no father and mother, to be brought up by stupid nuns."

"Are all nuns stupid, Adrienne? Is Mother Radegund stupid, too?"

"No, of course not. She's nice. But nuns are different from us. They've never been in love or married, so they don't know some things."

"Don't nuns ever get married, Adrienne?"

"Of course not, dear. They give their lives to God. They just love Him. You're such a child, Ann, a precious, darling child!"

Adrienne then had thrown her arm around Ann, hold-

ing her close. They were all alone above the sea. Ann had
thought then that she would have liked to stay forever,
right there with Adrienne. She could not go to sleep that
night for thinking of it.

Only her father liked Adrienne. With all the puzzled
way in which he sometimes looked at her, he liked Adrienne. Sometimes he had spent a whole hour in his study
with Adrienne, hearing her read Latin, telling her how
well she did.

"That's splendid, Adrienne!" he said. "If you can learn
to read Latin as well as that, Ann," he said to Ann, who
was listening, consumed with pride of Adrienne, "I'll be
proud of you."

Often he had gone for a long walk with just the two
of them, swinging his stick, they hurrying to keep up
with him, showing them this water bird and that, talking
of interesting things. She was proud of the way Adrienne
talked with her father, saying things as Ann could never
say them, acting as grown up as Ann's mother. Once
when the wind was brisk and the air cold after a shower,
Adrienne wore her red cape with its hood.

"Well," her father had said, "you look just as you did
when I first saw you."

"Yes, I remembered," Adrienne said. "That's why I
put it on."

And yet with all her father's kindness to Adrienne, he
refused to correct Philip for his rudeness, would not make
Philip play with Adrienne.

"Father, I'm sorry to disturb you, and perhaps I oughtn't
to tell you."

"What is it, Ann?"

"Philip's awfully rude to Adrienne, father. Haven't you noticed it?"

"I can't say I have exactly, Ann."

"Well, he is, father, especially when you're not about. It hurts Adrienne's feelings awfully."

"I'm sorry for that. I can't believe Philip means to be rude.

"Won't you speak to him, father, please? I don't like Adrienne to be hurt."

"I'm afraid it's Philip's problem, Ann. Isn't it perhaps possible that Adrienne is rude to Philip, too?"

"No, she really isn't, at least at first. She likes Philip very, very much. She told me so."

"Well, I guess we'll have to let Philip and Adrienne work it out in their own way, Ann."

And now Adrienne was going away after the most wonderful two months of Ann's whole life. She was going back to the convent, to those nuns who did not understand her at all and who often made her most unhappy. She was a bird with a broken wing there, wanting to fly but kept from flying. Had Ann been able to return with her, it would have been different in the convent. Ann's father would come once in a while to see them, and perhaps Philip, to take them out to see things, to eat good food, go to the theatre. With Ann there, Adrienne had said, she would have had a real friend to sustain her. The other girls there did not understand Adrienne. They were provincial, Adrienne said, knowing nothing, stupid cows and sheep. As for the nuns, what did they know about life as it was? They were worse than cows and sheep, muttering prayers, lifting their eyes like so many hens around a pool of stagnant water.

Adrienne was going. There would be no more nights like last night; the moon full and round, like a great, ripe fruit in the sky, like the oranges in Provence, Adrienne had said. The land had been flooded with moonlight, the sea still, a sheet of silver. Because Adrienne was going and Philip thought he must be polite on her last evening, the three of them had sat on the edge of the headland in the moonlight. Adrienne had looked so beautiful, in her red cape, the hood thrown back, over her white dress. Adrienne had said wonderful things there as they looked at the stars.

"You should see the stars in Provence," Adrienne had said. "They burn in the dark blue sky. They do not glitter like these cold northern stars. Provence is warm and gay, like the stars, and the people are warm and gay, too. This is beautiful, yes, but it is cold."

Philip did not say a word on the headland, sitting there, chewing bits of grass, looking out to sea. Ann could not speak for her heart was breaking. Adrienne did all the talking.

"Some day I shall go back to Provence, to my own country and my own language, which is beautiful like France. You should learn French, Philip. You have a nice voice for it."

Philip said nothing. Ann hated him for his rude silence.

"Aren't you going to learn French, Philip?"

"No," said Philip. "No, I'm not."

Her father and mother sat on the terrace in silly chairs,

silent, not saying a word, at least that they could hear from the edge of the headland. They were old, thought Ann. What did they care about such a night as this?"

"Children," her father called at ten o'clock. "It's bedtime. Come along."

Ann rebelled at the word. She would never be a child again, she thought.

Now from her place among the trees Ann could see Jan before the stone wall with the wagon. They were all gathered there to say goodbye to Adrienne. Someone was putting Adrienne's bags in the back of the wagon. That was Jan. Someone was helping Adrienne into the wagon. That must be Philip. She hoped he was being friendly at this moment of Adrienne's departure.

They had gone inside the house. The wagon was coming across the high summit of the land, along the road before the barn, nearer and nearer. Jan was driving, Adrienne was in the back seat, not sitting with Jan as Ann always did. She was glad that Adrienne was sitting by herself in the back seat. When they reached the turn of the road, Ann would climb in there with Adrienne, drive to Heron Cove, walk back by herself. Jan in the front seat with the horses' hoofs sounding on the road and the rattle of the wagon could not hear whatever she might be able to say to Adrienne, could not see the gift she had for her.

"Well, that's over," Eileen Marston said. "I don't know when I've ever spent such a trying summer. And the worst of it is I can't really put my finger on an actual reason. She's such a model child in so many ways."

"Did you say *child?*" asked John Marston.

"Well, I guess that's the reason. And still even that's not clear. There are so many things I can't get at behind those inscrutable black eyes of hers, things I somehow don't like and still don't know why. Ann's broken-hearted, poor dear."

"I'm sorry. But maybe in the long run it won't be bad for Ann. I'm sorry I put you through it, dear. It was a foolish impulse, I suppose, but I was attracted to the child, and I did want to do something nice for Mother Radegund. She couldn't take Adrienne to France. She said she didn't want that particular kind of excitement for her, and I can see now what she meant. After all it was my stupidity. I asked her to come."

"Well, never mind. You steered things marvellously. I feel now as though I could really begin to live. I've felt all summer like a chief of police."

"Where's Philip?"

"I don't know, but wherever he is, he's happier than he's been for weeks. Adrienne's been trying all summer to discover things in Philip that he isn't half aware of himself. Philip's been like those poor mortals pursued by harpies in the schoolbooks. What a vacation!"

"Well, shall we take a walk and forget it? Ann won't be fit to speak to for hours. We'd better let her be."

"No, I think I'll stay put. She may come back sooner than we think. I'm sewing name tapes on her clothes, hundreds of them. That's a good, normal occupation. Here's Philip."

Philip came into the house, whistling, slamming the door, calling to the dogs.

"I think you and I need a swim, Philip. How about it?"

"Fine, father."

They went out together, down the long path. The tide was high.

"Some morning!" said Philip.

A year at school had done good things to Philip, his father thought. He was tall and strong, filled out, a good-looking boy with his heavy, fair hair, his tanned face, and his mother's eyes. He was safe, his father thought. You did not have to worry much about Philip.

"What's for today?" said Philip. "We ought not to let this one go without something really good, father."

"We might sail down the coast to Cliff Island," John Marston said. "There couldn't be a better wind, and it's apt to swing late this afternoon and bring us clipping home. We might have a clam-bake down there, and we ought to see some interesting birds around those cliffs just now. And, Philip, I think we might be sort of especially decent to Ann. She's not feeling so good right now."

"Sure," said Philip. "I know. Ann's worth three of Adrienne, if you ask me."

"You've got a good head, Philip," said his father.

The wagon did not make half the noise it ought, Ann thought, but there was one good thing about Jan. He did not tell things to Philomena the way she told things to him. Jan was decent that way.

The trees were already turning in the woods, red, yellow, and orange among the dark spruces. They somehow made Ann's tears, which she had been striving to keep back, come again. If it had only rained, she thought, then things could be borne better than in this light and warmth. Adrienne held Ann's hand when she saw that she was crying, put her arm about her. At last Ann succumbed completely and sobbed against Adrienne's blue coat.

"You mustn't cry, dear," Adrienne whispered behind Jan's broad back. "I'll always love you, you know. You're the best of all my friends, even in France. Perhaps your father will ask me again, and he'll bring you to see me in the convent. You mustn't cry."

They were nearing Heron Cove. Her mother had been cruel to say she could drive only a piece with Adrienne. She drew a box from the pocket of her dress.

"These are for you," she said to Adrienne, whispering between her sobs. "They're the best of all my things. They're to keep always to remember me by."

Adrienne drew the string of pearls from the box. She had loved the pearls once she had seen them among Ann's things at Windswept. Ann's father had given them to her. They had been her grandmother's. They were rare pearls, he said, and sometime Ann would appreciate them more. Ann was glad to see even through her tears how Adrienne still loved the pearls, handling them with her long, lovely fingers, her black eyes shining with pleasure.

"But you mustn't give them to me," she whispered. "Your father mightn't like it, you know."

"He'll not know," Ann whispered back. "He'll never think to ask. I want you to have them. Can you wear pearls in a convent, Adrienne?"

"I'll tell you what," Adrienne said. "I'll wear them at night when I'm all alone. I'll put them on when I'm all undressed, in my nightgown. Then I'll surely dream of

you, Ann. And once I'm in the train, I'll put them on.
It's a long way to the convent, so I can enjoy them on the
way and think of you."

"It's here you're to get down, Ann," said Jan bluntly,
stopping the horses. "Your mother said to set you down
here."

How she hated Jan for his stupid, commanding words,
his turning around to look at her and Adrienne, clinging
to each other, both crying! She would never like Jan
again.

She could hardly see the road for her tears once she was
standing there above the harbour at Heron Cove with the
gulls swooping in the sunlight, dim shadows before her
eyes. The wagon driving away was a great black blur. She
could hardly make out Adrienne's wet waving handkerchief.

She ran back along the road through the woods. She
could not now take the chance of seeing any of her old
friends at Heron Cove. She ran on and on, still sobbing,
until at last she came to a tiny foot-path, which led away
from the road toward a marshy place that she knew.

She flung herself face downward under some trees at
the edge of the little marsh. She could lie there undisturbed, have her cry out, get ready to meet all her hard,
untouched family at dinner time, prepare for the cold,
reserved manner with which she would greet them all.

When she at last rose to walk the four miles homeward,
she saw at the edge of the marsh one last iris, flowering
late among the thick, oval seed-pods of the lavish summer
growth, blue against the green marsh grass. She stared at
it, her heart aching within her.

How Adrienne had loved the iris, the thousands of them colouring the long stretch of land, blue against the blue or gray of the sea! Adrienne would never call them blue flags.

"The flower of France!" Adrienne had said. "It makes my heart break, Ann. The fleur de lis of my own country!"

She picked the iris, careless of her wet shoes and stockings. She would place it in Adrienne's room, go and look at it there. It would break her own heart more than it would comfort her, but it was Adrienne's flower. Perhaps it had blossomed for Adrienne, late like this, when all the iris had gone.

It must not be left in the loneliness of this marsh, beyond these dark trees.

THE POSSESSION

1918–1939

1

JOHN MARSTON was waiting at the small village station for the late afternoon train. It was a still, spring afternoon in May, 1918. It would have been nice for Eileen to have come from New York to Boston by boat, he thought, thence to Rockland and along the coast east. When he was a boy and had sailed *The Sea Hawk* up from New Haven, how he had loved that coast, Fox Island thoroughfare, Owl's Head, Penobscot Bay, the islands of Eggemoggin, Frenchman's Bay, all the coves and islands, all the small, inconsequential, lovely harbours.

But it was hard to arrange such a trip on the days one wanted, now that the small coastwise steamers were every year being taken off their old familiar courses, the *J. T. Morse*, the *Goldenrod*, the *Catherine*, the *Pemaquid*, and all the others which he knew so well and which suggested such pleasant things. Within a few years there would be hardly one left, he thought.

That smell, made of dirt and steam, salt water and oil, sardines and coal smoke, would go, never to come back. There would be no more fascinated children leaning over the deck railings, watching the roustabouts with their two-wheeled iron barrows, trundling the multifarious cargo up the slippery gangway of this village wharf and

that, dumping it with thumps and bangs, giving a yell
as they slid skillfully down the smooth, oily planks and
into the hold again, one hand on their barrows, the other
waving in the clear or foggy air. His grandchildren would
never smell that smell, hear those yells or watch some
bronzed deck-hand standing with a coiled rope in his
hand, ready for the signal, throwing the rope across
twenty feet of water to another acrobat on the pier, leaning idly against the wharf-post sucking on his empty pipe,
waiting carelessly to catch the noose of the rope when it
swung through the air. These were gone or quickly
going. This was what was called progress.

He could have met Eileen at the dilapidated steam-
boat wharf a few miles east just as well as at the station.
Now that they had the automobile, a few miles more or
less did not matter. Jan had rebelled at first against learning to drive the automobile, but even Jan had yielded as
everyone else was yielding. Now he drove over the improved road to Heron Cove and through his own wood-
road, bumpy, of course, but quite passable, like an old,
experienced hand.

"I don't like it," said Jan. "I don't like it at all. But
what is one to do?"

That was it, thought John Marston. What was one to
do but to keep one's head and continue to hold fast to
what still remained one's bread of life?

The train must be late, or else his watch was fast.
Everything was fast nowadays. No, the train was not
late, the ticket agent said from his window. It was just
on time. He walked back and forth across the dirty plat-

form. Why must stations be so ugly, he thought? Why couldn't they be painted a nice red instead of this dingy gray, or built of brick the way country stations in England were built? Why couldn't these Village Improvement Societies, which were springing up like mushrooms, or these new garden clubs plant a few trees and some flowers around somewhere so that arrivals and departures could be more joyous, less depressing? This concentrated ugliness by the side of the road when everything about was springing into new life was inexcusable.

Maybe his grandchildren, when they were half his age, would travel neither by boat nor by train but by air, when they were not whizzing over the roads at forty or fifty miles an hour. Much as he distrusted the way life was madly shaping itself, he would like to live thirty years longer to see what would happen to Europe and America, what men might be able to make happen for good or for evil when this frightful war was over. How he had dreaded this war, seen it coming year by year, blacker on every new horizon! How he had dreamed of it, awake and sleeping!

He did not know why he seemed to be living in the past and with the future when the present was so much with him at the moment, why he was thinking of potential grandchildren when none was in sight. Perhaps it was because of the letters he had received from France this morning. He really should have waited for Eileen's return to read them, but he had been quite unable to do so. She would not mind. Eileen never minded things like that.

He was as impatient at fifty-two as any youngster, he thought. That was because of Eileen. She had managed, without trying at all, to keep him excited and impatient through all these many years. If this blasted train ever came, she would alight from it, eager as a girl herself, in a new hat probably, the price of which she would never tell him. He should have gone with her, he thought, not let her go off alone to see some doctor by herself. But she had been so insistent upon going alone that he had given in as he always gave in. Still, twenty-seven years of giving in had been all right, he thought. He had never regretted one instance of giving in.

"Hello, Mr. Marston," said the baggage-man, trundling his truck at last along the platform. "Pretty day, ain't it?"

"Fine. I understand the fish are running well."

"Prime. Not so good for years. These fishermen are all stowing away a pretty bit o' cash. One from over Heron Cove way made five hundred dollars this last week selling straight from the weirs. Business is good with an army to feed. Trouble is, none of 'em won't keep their earnin's. It'll burn in their pockets till it's spent. They'll buy cheap liquor or even an automobile. I shouldn't wonder a mite if some of 'em'll be on the town next winter with it all blown in. Here she comes. Stand back a bit, sir. You're too close in."

Eileen did have a new hat, rakish, perched on her fair hair, becoming all the same.

"You're looking fine," he said when he had kissed her, encircling her with his arm, leading her across the dirty platform. "How's your father?"

"Splendid. Ribald as ever upon occasion, but really great fun. At eighty he's planning a fishing trip to Oxbow."

"Fine. We'll leave the bags there. Jan's in the village getting the car fixed. There's always something wrong with the thing. He'll be back. Let's sit down on this bench here. I can't wait to read you the children's letters. Two came this morning. Great news! You'd never guess."

He spread his handkerchief on the dirty boards for Eileen to sit upon. She had on a new suit, too, a pale gray, fetching, if a bit light for May. Eileen was always ahead of things.

She seemed a bit abstracted, he thought, even not so keen over the letters as she usually was. Perhaps New York was still with her. Perhaps that doctor—

"What did he say, the doctor?" he asked, drawing Philip's letter from its envelope.

"I'm fit as fit, darling. Don't worry about that."

"Honestly?"

"Of course. I'll tell you all about it later. What does Philip say?"

"Listen to this."

You'd never guess in 1,000,000 years who's here with me. Cyril Cobb. Can you beat it? He came up last week with his men. He's a first, one ahead of me, and looking swell. He got over with the first lot and has seen a good deal of action, been decorated. in fact, though he told me not to blat it around, just like Cyril. We're hoping for a leave together, get to Paris, and have a whale of a time. He's seen Ann no end. They were right near where she and Adrienne are now.

"The censor's blotted that out."

"How annoying," said Eileen. "What possible difference can it make to that censor where my children are!"

I don't want to be spreading false tidings, but I think
there's something up between Cyril and Ann. He looked so
fussed that I kidded him a bit, and then he looked more
foolish. I'm all for it. What could be better? He's eight years
older than she, but I think that's all to the good, only why
he hasn't been snapped up before beats me. When I asked
him, he said, "Too busy." Cyril's just the same as years ago
at home. We're quartered in the same village, and we've
managed to talk for hours, all about Heron Cove and the
weeks he stayed with us. He says it was one of the nicest
things that ever happened to him. He left a good job at Yale
to enlist, but that's like Cyril. He'll get a captaincy before
long, everyone says. Believe me, it's made no end of difference to me to have him about. We talk about Windswept
until I can actually hear the surf at the cove and see Schoodic
on one of those days so clear that you can almost make out
the spruces.

I hope Philomena got the cards I sent her. Tell her for
me that there's an old church not far from here named, oddly
enough, for the first of our patron saints. Tell her I went in
a while ago and said a prayer to him for her and me.

About three miles back of us there's a road off the main
tracks with plane trees on both sides that make an avenue
actually a mile long. They're just budding out now. In spite
of all this unholy mess around here they're budding just the
same, and there's not one of them hurt yet. They're wonderful with their trunks all gold and silver. I mean to see the
moon through them some night. The shadows ought to be
lovely.

"Isn't that just like Philip," said Eileen, "to look at

plane trees in the moonlight in the midst of a war? Save
the rest, darling. How marvellous about Cyril if it's
true! What does Ann say?"

"Well, knowing Ann, you know she's not giving herself away."

He drew Ann's letter from its thin blue envelope.

I'm not far from Beauvais in what was once a nice little
village near a stream where the ducks still float about. They
needed a nurse here and chose Adrienne, and I came along
as they wanted a couple of volunteers and the unit could
spare us. We're all very fit, so don't worry. This is better than
my four years of college, even better than teaching. I'll never
be sorry I'm having this.

You'd never know Adrienne here. Or perhaps you would,
for she hasn't completely changed some of her old ways. But
she's really wonderful. She's a superb nurse, and all the
soldiers fall for her, of course, sick or well. Just now there's
one called Raoul Vallon, a French captain, who hangs about
all the time he can get. I'm not exactly keen about him, and
I don't think she is really, but he's very persistent. He's a
young French intellectual with supercilious ways, rather ad-
vanced, and entirely dashing. We've had a run-in or two. He
calls me *la Puritaine*. Adrienne says there's too much Windswept in me, and perhaps there is, but I'm not sorry.

It's really fun to be with Adrienne. I've lost my childish
ardour for her, but I'm still fond of her. She's completely
fearless and she's terribly kind. She really doesn't think about
herself as she used to years ago, and she works night and day.
She's still entrancing to look at, and that means a lot in this
grim place. She's more fatalistic than any soldier, just shrugs
her shoulders the way she used to, and says, "I just move on
with things. What will be, will be."

Cyril Cobb's been about. Imagine that. He's Lieutenant
Cobb now and going higher, I expect. He's as nice as he used

to be and quite handsome. We've had fun talking about Windswept for hours on end. Adrienne fell for him, much to Raoul's fury, but he didn't respond, and, of course, he hasn't the dash of Raoul. I don't like Raoul much, between ourselves.

I wish you could see the children here. A lot have gone long ago, but still some are left, and some families have even returned, at least what is left of them. The other day I came upon two little girls playing house in the shelter of a half-ruined wall. They had marked off their rooms with broken bricks and had named them all, *la cuisine, la salle à manger.* I wish I could fill them all up with Philomena's *kolache* at home.

I'm dying to see Philip. He's got a leave coming, and we've some plans for Paris before things start moving faster, as everyone suspects they will. We're quite far back now. Anyhow, don't worry.

Adrienne and I were talking about the pearls the other night, about what she calls my "passion" and her "concupiscence". We laughed and laughed, but with all the laughing I'll never quite forget my broken heart. I like to remember how I felt at the time even if I'll never feel that way again about anyone. It still makes me love Adrienne and foolishly want to protect her from herself. What a traitor Jan was! Give him my love and Philomena, too. And thanks forevermore for Windswept and you.

"That's like Ann," said John Marston, "all about everyone else except herself, and not too long a letter at that. I only hope Philip's right about Cyril. Well, I'm glad they came today. I don't like the papers much these days. Where's Jan, I wonder? He oughtn't to be so long as this. I wish I'd never bought that blasted thing."

He looked at his wife sitting beside him on the deserted

station platform. It was getting toward supper time, and the air was growing sharp. Some peepers began to shrill from a little pond in the field across the single track.

"You're tired," he said. "Did that doctor really tell you the truth?"

"He certainly did, pressed down and running over. Well, I never thought I'd make a romantic announcement in a place like this, but I can't wait for a better. Sit tight, darling. We're going to have a baby."

"A what!" cried John Marston. He got up and stood in front of her, staring. "Are you out of your senses or is he?"

She laughed. The last light from the sun shone full in her eyes. They were blue rather than gray, he thought, dark blue. He was unsurprised at the change, in the face of what she was saying.

"Neither of us," she said. "He was quite sane, and I've come to be. I wanted to telegraph you, and then I thought you'd die of shock and leave the baby fatherless. Besides I didn't know how to word the telegram so as not to have the whole county talking. I was completely floored when he told me. I said, 'I can't have a baby. I'm fifty-one!' 'A woman in Texas had one at fifty-seven last week,' he said, 'and both doing well.' 'That sounds like Texas,' I said. Well, it's evidently true, dear."

John Marston sat down again.

"I know I'm not acting well," he said, "but I still don't believe it. I can't say I'm delighted, can I, when I'm merely flabbergasted and scared to death?"

"There's not the slightest reason to be scared, the doctor said. He said I had the insides of thirty-five, a rather vulgar compliment, but reassuring. He said age didn't make any difference if you kept young inside you."

"Well, that's something. Didn't you have the least suspicion?"

"Not a shade. I may as well confess now that I thought I had something inside me, but I meant to have it outside before you knew a thing."

He still stared at her, incredulous.

"He's coming in five months, dear, the baby, I mean. Imagine our being so stupid!"

"So you've got him all sexed, have you?" he asked, trying to stifle his apprehension. She looked so young sitting there, one leg crossed over the other, her foot swinging in the air.

"Yes, and named."

"Good Lord! You *have* been busy. What's his name?"

"Roderick, just Roderick Marston."

"*Roderick!* What a name! Whatever for?"

"Completely for nothing and no one. It just slipped into my head on the way to the house from the doctor's office. It came so surely and quickly that I haven't been able to think of a rival. Don't you like it?"

"No, I can't say I do. It sounds rather warlike to me. All the Rodericks I've ever read of have been heroes in one way or another. But I guess if you can manage a baby at fifty-one, you can name him what you like."

"There's no St. Roderick, is there?"

"Not that I know of. No, I don't think even Philomena can rouse up a St. Roderick."

"Well, that's a relief."

"Did you tell your father?"

"Heavens, no! I couldn't face that. Father's always secretly thought me a complete ass ever since I took so long in deciding to marry you. He still talks about it."

"He's a short-sighted man. Still we owe him a lot."

"We surely do. John, don't let's tell the children. Let's have him safely here before they know a thing."

"It'll leak out somehow."

"No, it won't. You could have a dozen babies at Windswept and no one the wiser. Before they get home, he'll be here and maybe running around."

"I'm afraid that's all too true," said John Marston.

2

Philip and Ann Marston were sitting with Cyril Cobb at a table covered with a red and white checked cloth outside a small restaurant in the Quartier Latin. It was a fine evening in June, the last night of a three days' leave. The air was quiet except for the intermittent sound of bells from here and there over the city, above them all at intervals the deep, solemn tones of the old bell of Notre Dame, holding within its echoing resonance the age and the learning of medieval Paris, ancient griefs, forgotten hopes, caught up centuries ago and held to be given forth in sound for all who, listening, understood. The inevitable fishermen sat on the stone walls above the Seine, holding their long poles, catching nothing. Soldiers clattered along the pavement, English, French, Colonial, American, singly or in pairs, some with girls hanging to their arms, some in noisy, curious groups, all suggesting a respite from the business at hand. The sun was going down, catching the tips of the fishermen's poles, flooding the gray walks and walls, bringing the square towers of Notre Dame nearer.

They had had their dinner, a good one in spite of rationing, and were sitting over their coffee and wine.

Ann said: "I wonder if Heloise heard those bells while she waited for Abelard in Fulbert's house. I don't know why I like French bells so much. You can't call them joyous."

"If she didn't hear these, she heard others like them," Cyril Cobb said. "When this filthy mess is over, let's come back to Paris, Ann. I like this part of it. Anyone can have the rest. I was here ten years ago, worked my way across on a cattle boat. God, how sick I was, and how those beasts smelled! I used to lie in my bunk at night, longing to die, wondering why I'd been such a fool to come. But after I'd come here and spent one night roaming around these old streets in June, I'd have slept in the straw with the cattle in order to come again. Only then I never dreamed I'd be fighting for France, to preserve the memories of these same old streets. I like to think of all the students here centuries ago, milling around, starving and stealing, singing their bawdy songs, making a nuisance of themselves, going to hear Abelard talk at seven in the morning. I want to lean for once, just as long as ever I like, over that wall there and watch the river in the sun. It's funny. That's about all I want to do, really. If I can do that when we come back, Ann, I think I'll know better than I do now just why I fought for France."

In a tiny walled garden next the restaurant a bush had blossomed. It had a hanging yellow flower, in panicles, catching the light, and a sweet, penetrating smell.

"What's that flower, Cyril?"

"I haven't the faintest idea."

"I'll always remember the smell," Ann said.

Philip was scanning a newspaper, which someone upon leaving had thrown down on the table nearest theirs.

"Any news we don't know about?" Cyril asked, filling Ann's glass, lighting a cigarette.

"I wish I were a scientist," Philip said.

"Whatever do you mean, dear?"

"Then I'd know whether the tide serves at different times in different places."

"The tide? What has that to do with news?"

"It says here that the tide serves at Havre at eight this evening. If it's the same tide, it's high now at home. There's not likely to be fog in June."

"High tide at Heron Cove," Cyril said. "Three o'clock there. My old love, Mrs. Orren Leighton, probably has her dinner dishes done by now and is helping Orren with the trawls. I wouldn't mind a bit sleeping in her loft tonight and teaching the brats tomorrow. I sent her a postcard this morning of some barges on the Seine. Fourteen years ago! All my charges are grown up by now."

"There are plenty more," said Ann. "There are always children at Heron Cove. You were so good to her, dear. She adored you. I believe I fell in love with you then and didn't know it. I didn't know much at that age."

"That's right. You didn't," Philip said.

"Mother's back from New York by now. I'll bet she had a good time. I wish we could send things home safely. I saw a hat this morning that mother would die for."

The sunlight had gone. A soft haze lay over the river. Darkness was falling. Some of the fishermen had left the wall, were winding up their lines. The bells were still.

"How's Adrienne?" asked Philip.

"Flourishing. She's getting a bit beyond her depth with a French captain named Raoul, I'm afraid. She sent her love to you."

"Thanks. Adrienne was always more than a bit beyond her depth."

"I know. Don't be hard, Philip. We're most of us a bit beyond our depth these days."

"That's true. I'm not hard. I'm way beyond my own."

"Well, on we go," Cyril said, "to the great tragedy or the great triumph. The next few weeks are going to get us places, or I miss my guess. When the next few weeks are over, things will be looking up, or I miss my guess completely."

"See that first star over Notre Dame," said Philip.

"Wish on it!"

"I have."

"Now you mustn't look at it until another comes, or you'll not get your wish."

"That's very likely, whether I look or not."

"There's an old Frenchman near us," Ann said, "who looks in every now and then to ask about America. He's not more than fifty or so, about father's age, but he looks twenty years older. He's lost his two sons, one at the Marne and the other in the Argonne. He asks me the oddest things,—whether it is true that we eat raw fish and meat in America and whether the Indians are really red. He came in a few nights ago, just after supper. You know how the sunset lasts here in places where the fields are so flat. There was a wonderful sunset last week when he came in, a sort of afterglow of pink and that apple green, which we get so often in November at Windswept, lingering on for almost an hour. He said to me: 'Mademoiselle, is it true that you have no twilight in your country?' "

No twilight? thought Philip. Those long June twilights at Windswept over the new green land. The tide high there at night, flooding the rocky shores, touching the budding iris, filling the cove. The hermit thrushes calling from the woods; the gulls circling with the light on their wings; the song-sparrows trilling from the tops of the spruces by the house.

No twilight? he thought. Jan letting out the cows into the meadow, their breath sweet among the opening buttercups and daisies in the cool damp air. Philomena sitting just beyond her kitchen door, waiting for the first gleam of the great light, thinking of him. At the anchorage the bay filled with still, golden water, the boats swinging at their moorings, the chapel door open, waiting for him to come along the shore path with the dogs. The last pale shadows circling about in the depths of the water; the ropes slapping a bit in the light capricious wind; the smell of the ferns, sharp and new, in the cool salt air. The first star trembling out, with glow enough left in the sky for one to see its long shadow, a wavering pencil of light piercing the water.

He, a boy on the chapel steps, wondering over the sorrow and yet the comfort of the fading sky, over something immense and vast that he could not grasp. The cry of a loon in the stillness, breaking the silence into quivering fragments, which, if he could piece them together, hearing them now again at this table in Paris, in this alien darkness, would tell him what he longed to know before it was too late of this beautiful, yet strange and bitter miracle called life.

No twilight at home?

"Well," Cyril was saying, "I suppose we'd better pull up stakes. *Monsieur le propriétaire* is wondering, I think, whether we're spending the night with him. We've got to get some sleep, Philip, against tomorrow."

"I'll join you later," Philip said. "I'll stroll about a bit. You and Ann will want some time to yourselves."

"Just a minute, dear. I want to talk with Philip."

Cyril went on down the little street. Philip and Ann stood together. The stars were out now. The night had a soft quality about it, blue rather than black. The few street lamps were dim.

"Goodbye, old darling," Ann said. "Saints Cyril and Methodius protect you! You're pleased about me and Cyril?"

"Monstrously! It's the best thing I know to come out of all this mess."

"We've thought madly of being married right away. We don't know the ropes here, of course, or even whether we could, but Cyril thinks so. There's a lot of marrying going on. But we've decided not to. I couldn't quite face it without Windswept, and Cyril feels that way, too, only, of course, one never knows."

"One never knows anything really, just now," said Philip.

"Well, we're both glad we're waiting."

"I'm rather glad, too."

"Keep an eye on Cyril, will you? He's got a rotten cold."

"Sure, I will."

"And, Philip, I think no end of you, you know."

"Same here," said Philip.

"I've been thinking about that day years ago at the cove, you've probably forgotten, when you were thinking about the French ships, and I was such a nuisance. You were always thinking about nice things, and I always bothering you. I've taken such a long time to grow up to you, Philip, and I'm still a long way off."

"You're nothing of the sort!"

"And, Philip—"

"What?"

"I hope someday I'll have a son who will be just like you, thinking of the French ships at Windswept, and all the rest of it."

"Good Lord, my dear," Philip said, "don't wish that on the poor kid!"

3

Mother Radegund was returning to Le Couvent de Sainte-Croix after four months away. She had been in the South, in New Orleans, visiting some convents there and in other places along the Gulf. An attack of pneumonia the preceding winter had sapped not a little of her vigorous strength, and the doctor had advised a change of climate during the trying months of March and April. Mother Radegund had gone, protesting. But the doctor, who for many years had watched over the therapeutic destinies of her nuns and her girls, was more than a match for her, and she knew it. She hated the sacrificing of his respect more than she hated the means taken to preserve it.

Mother Radegund disliked visiting. She disliked also the deferential air which nuns in other convents always bestowed upon her, fluttering about, bringing her this and that, rising at her approach. Fortunately a relapse in April, although it had annoyingly prolonged her stay, had sent her to a hospital where she could order her door closed and watch some red-bud trees in full flower beyond her window.

Red-buds were the most entrancing trees in the world, she thought, bursting like spray into that brilliant purple foam, or was it rose, or was it pink, or was it really red?— catching the light, startling the imagination into quick action, filled with life, in fact, the very colour of life. Alice Meynell had said in one of her recent essays that the colour of life was not red; red was the colour of life violated, betrayed; the colour of life, she had said, was the colour of the body. Mother Radegund was skeptical. She did not care much for the colour of the body, at least for that of the human face, especially now that it was becoming so disguised by art as well as by nature. She wondered if the red-bud grew in England, in London about which Mrs. Meynell had written so much.—Mother Radegund had not seen England. She meant to before she died if she could possibly manage it: the smoke and fog of London, the cliffs of Tintagel, Grasmere, and in noisy Soho the grave of Hazlitt, whose English she so admired.—To her, lying for so many pleasant days in the hospital, the red-bud had seemed the very colour and essence of life. She had hoped more than once that poor Judas Iscariot in Hell had been granted a few minutes' respite from his torment by knowing that such a lovely thing had been named for him.

Now it was June and she was hurrying home, sitting in the train, counting off the miles. What red earth these southern states had, copper, rust, whatever colour was it? She had it! It was almost precisely the colour of strong, well-brewed tea, poured from an earthen pot into a cup in the late afternoon sunlight streaming through a western window. And when the light fell upon it in a certain way, it was almost the colour of certain hills in Provence. Only it needed the blue of the Mediterranean to set it off rather than the green of these flat fields.

How oddly one's fellow travellers looked at one, she thought. Most people either shunned religious dress, looking upon it with ill-concealed suspicion, or else they were frankly curious. Then there were those whose faces held awe in them as though a nun were a holy person, not just, as in this instance, a very impatient woman, who could not concentrate on the reading of her Office. She would like to draw a good old thriller from her luggage and lose herself in it, now that she had exhausted these swamps and scrub pine and red earth; but she could not risk the disastrous effect it might have on that admirable woman in the seat opposite, who looked upon her with such reverence and longed to be of service to her.

Her old friend, John Marston, had sent her two Wilkie Collins while she was in the hospital.

"Old chestnuts as they are," he had written, "this new vogue for thrillers can't touch them. I'm hoping that with all your English reading you've missed *The Woman in White.*"

As a matter of fact, she had missed it. She was on her second reading now, and, were it not for that helpful creature opposite, she could go on with it. She had read so late in her berth the night before that the porter had been anxious.

"I was afeard you was sick, ma'am," he had said that morning, "but I didn't feel in me to disturb you. I'm a religious man myself. I likes my quiet times with de good Lord."

"Thanks," she had said. "No, I wasn't sick."

She had a good deal to be thankful for, even without *The Woman in White,* she thought, staring piously at *The Day Hours* for the benefit of the woman opposite. What if two nuns from home had come for her as they had threatened to do? What if two from New Orleans had come with her as Mother Augustine there had ventured to insist upon? These railroad rates for religious, or even in some instances free transportation, could be a bane as well as a blessing! Either arrangement would have been intolerable.

"But, Mother, you can't go all that way alone," Mother Augustine had said. "It's contrary to all custom as you must be aware."

"I adore setting custom aside," she told Mother Augustine, an efficient Superior with rather too much dark hair on her upper lip. "I'm fifty-eight and in a habit. Whatever harm can come to me? And you don't expect me to flee the cloister, do you?"

She was devoutly thankful, too, to be alive. The thought of death as she lay so ill last winter had been more irritating than it was solemn. Now that the war was at last over, with all its frightful toll, she wanted to live to see a better, more generous world. She wanted to watch this great, rich country of her adoption line itself up with Europe, lend its vitality and wealth to those older lands, weary with age and war. She refused to believe, in spite of the discouraging things she was every day reading, that America would refuse to join this new League, which President Wilson's splendid mind and spirit had conceived. She would have been furious if Death had beaten her before her hopes had been justified, her faith confirmed.

She wanted to see John Marston again, and now she could. It had been a year now since she had seen him, just before the death of his son in Belleau Wood and of that other fine young man whom his daughter was to have married. Most of her prayers during this past year had been for John and Eileen Marston, for Ann, and for those two boys lying there in her own land so far from home, under those alien skies. She had rejoiced in the safe arrival of young Roderick Marston.

"There is no possible excuse for giving him such a mad name," John Marston had written her, "but my wife is set on it."

Mother Radegund, sometimes secretly, sometimes daringly in the open, adored things that had no possible excuse for being. She liked Roderick as a name.

"The only way to beat Death," she had written John Marston, "is by more life."

She was devoutly thankful also for Adrienne's new outlook on things. A year in France, hard at work for others, had remade Adrienne. And being with that wholesome Marston child had wrought wonders. She had hardly been able to readjust herself to this new niece of hers when Adrienne had returned in December and begun to teach at Le Couvent de Sainte-Croix. She had never in her wildest moments expected Adrienne to come back, at least to the convent. When she had written that she wanted to come back, that the convent was more her home than any other place in the world, Mother Radegund had been so startled that she was guilty of abstractions during Mass for days on end.

She was almost more startled at Adrienne herself, so much older, so much more composed, so singularly dependable, beautiful as ever, more lovely now that her face held thought and, at times, a sadness, even an odd apprehension. Adrienne had been indispensable during Mother Radegund's illness; the doctor could not have managed without her, he said, always there, quite selfless, and a marvellous nurse. Her devotion had been touching in its tirelessness. All the irritation which each had caused the other during the past fifteen years had vanished. Mother Radegund was glad to think that now she and Adrienne were companions rather than Superior and student, aunt and niece. Not that her reservations concerning Adrienne had completely vanished, but they had at least been pushed into a far background.

Well, the Scriptures were, after all, unassailable, thought Mother Radegund. *Cast thy bread upon the running waters: for after a long time thou shalt find it again. Running waters* was a good phrase for Adrienne! *Give and it shall be given to you: good measure and pressed down and shaken together and running over shall they give into your bosom.* All her anxious labours for Adrienne, greater in mind always than in body, were at last proving themselves not wasted.

Sister Sainte Geneviève had written that Adrienne was a splendid teacher, exacting, patient, and so alive that the children loved her classes. And to Sister's surprise she was devout in the chapel, up early every morning for Mass, going there many times a day, an example to all. Sister Agnes was so entirely converted that she was mad enough to suggest an actual vocation.

"Nonsense!" said Mother Radegund to herself in the hot and dirty train. "Let's not lose our heads completely."

That good woman opposite was getting hungry. She had washed her hands, now she was powdering her nose —queer that even somber, over-large women like that carried these compacts about—soon she would depart for the dining-car.

"Can't I see that you get something to eat?" she asked
Mother Radegund, eyeing the *Hours,* staring at the long,
heavy rosary on Mother Radegund's lap.

"Thank you. I'm not hungry."

She had gone, praise be to God! What a problem
human relationships were! How trying human kindness
at times! How frightfully tiresome the uninteresting
enthusiasms of others! What an entrancing gift complete
neglect could be! Now for Wilkie Collins and a half hour
at least of utter delight.

It was long past supper time on the next day when
Mother Radegund's train pulled into the Pennsylvania
Station. One of the patrons of the convent, who was
always ready to atone for the presence of his troublesome
twins at school there, met her with his car, two excited
nuns in tow. It was nine o'clock when they turned into
the convent gate. Mother Radegund was tired. She would
have some toast and hot tea brought to her study, she
said, and would go to bed early. No, she did not need any
help, and any news there might be could wait until
morning.

"Where's Adrienne?" she asked Sister Hélène, who was
solicitously bustling about, divesting her of her long
black cape, placing a pillow in her chair, bringing in the
tray. "I'll hang up my own things, Sister."

"Adrienne's so sorry, Mother. She's not feeling well
and went to bed early. She arranged the roses for you
herself. Such a change, Mother, in that child! You'd
never think! Each day she grows more helpful and un-
selfish. She's becoming the idol of the place.

"But I really think she should see a doctor, and at once. I've been waiting for this moment to tell you. This terrible war has exhausted her. All the gruesome things that poor child has seen are right there on her face at times. She's been so nervous lately and shaking with cold. Imagine that, Mother, in this heat, always cold, she says. For weeks she's worn her long red cape about, the one she had years ago as a child. I've not seen her without that cape for weeks, and white as a winding-sheet. Today at dinner, Sister Agnes said, her hands shook so that she quite dropped her cup, spilling her tea. I'm glad you're back to take affairs into your own hands. She refuses to listen to the others of us."

Mother Radegund listened to Sister Hélène with ebbing interest, not to say patience. Extreme garrulousness and a kind of perennial philanthropy were apt to become not only the stopping-place, the dead end, for many women, in convents and out, but actually the objects of their pursuit in the difficult conduct of life.

"I'll see her in the morning," she said to Sister Hélène. "I'm really not up to Adrienne tonight."

Sister Hélène looked aggrieved, Mother Radegund thought. So Adrienne had captivated her also? Well, it was just as well not to be surprised at life. Mother Radegund in these last sad and puzzling years had learned not to be surprised at anything.

She dismissed Sister Hélène and drank her hot tea, three full cups of it, eating her toast slowly. It was a warm night, but after the heat of New Orleans and that stifling train, this early heat was nothing. All her life she had loved returns, those early childhood returns from Brittany, from its gray mists and pale sunlight to the clear skies and rich, ripe light of Provence; those rare returns home to France, her father's house sold to someone else, her sisters curious and eager; returns even from short journeys, shopping in New York for the convent, going to Philadelphia on business. Just hanging up one's clothes in one's closet, moving one's own chair a bit nearer one's own fire, seeing one's own trees through one's own window frames—all these held their own peculiar and quite incommunicable excitement.

When she had eaten the last bit of toast and drained the tea-pot and hot water jug, she opened the door into her bedroom. There was a grand surprise for her there, actually a lamp at the head of her bed. What could be more thrilling? And why in the world had she not had it through all these years? Now she would not have to lie at the foot of her bed during her stolen hours of reading in order to get the full benefit of the overhead light. This *was* a welcome home, and what an indulgence!

Her linen sheets, they were an indulgence also, very likely a wicked one. She had but one pair, kept in her lower drawer, used only on special occasions. Sister Hélène had spread them on her bed, wisely thinking this return home a special occasion. Mother Radegund's grand-mother had woven the sheets herself, years ago in Brittany, before she was married. When her grand-daughter was about to start for America, she had given them to her as a parting gift, in defiance of the rule which forbade religious unnecessary possessions. Linen sheets! Mother Radegund had thought—she was only Sister Radegund then—what intemperance, what epicureanism, almost voluptuousness! One should mortify one's flesh, not luxuriate in linen sheets. If she were like holier souls, St. Martin of Tours, for example, she would cast them from her, give them to the poor. When she had taken them to Mother St. André, her Superior in France, for permission to keep them, to carry them with her to America, Mother St. André had said:

"No scrip for one's journey, no shoes for one's feet, but nothing said about linen sheets. I think probably you can weather them, my dear."

How many rich, wise women she had known, Mother Radegund thought, in what the outside world might call a circumscribed life! And, indeed, odd as it was, the seven cardinal virtues had proved themselves, for her at last, far more easily attainable between cool, clean, smooth linen sheets—prudence and faith, charity and hope, yes, even humility, obedience, and chastity.

Once she had scrubbed away the dirt of the train, put on clean night clothes, said her night prayers, begging Heaven to be charitable in that she had not gone to the dark chapel for them, she stretched out her tired legs and feet between her linen sheets. The courtyard outside was quiet; the syringas were sweet in the cooler night air. Soon these hordes of children would be going to their homes. The halls and walks would be still, if hot. She could work in the garden a bit, say her Office there occasionally between her weeding, do some of the reading which always got so ahead of her during the busy year. There would be rainy days. What a blessing a rainy day was! Rain in torrents, rain in sheets, slashing against the windows. How good to look up from one's book or from one's neglected darning upon the rain!

It had begun to lighten outside, blue flashes, revealing the white of the syringas, the rustling green of the court-yard trees. She liked to go to sleep in thunder, slowly sinking into unconsciousness, the rumble of the thunder sounding farther and farther away. Thunder in Provence, echoing among the purple hills, the gray, dusty leaves of the olives still before a storm, waiting for the rain, a peasant with his donkey climbing homeward on the pale brown road. . . .

"Mother, you'll have to come at once!"

It must be hours later. There was no thunder, but the rain was falling in sheets, almost white rain in the gray light of dawn. She sat up in bed.

Sister Hélène was there, white, shaking with fright, in her black habit and veil, without her guimpe, dis-traught—completely off her head, Mother Radegund thought with sudden anger. Sister Hélène switched on the light. In the doorway stood two young nuns, cowering with fear, pale, standing together there as in a picture, a painting entitled *Two Nuns in Terror,* hanging in a gallery.

"Whatever is it?" said Mother Radegund, still angry at being discovered in her night clothes, ugly, incomplete, unpresentable without her habit. Where were manners, she thought? This bursting into one's room without the decent formality of a knock was intolerable.

"It's Adrienne," Sister Hélène said. "Be quiet, Sisters! Hurry, Mother!"

One of the young nuns came forward, stood at the foot of Mother Radegund's bed, her eyes distended, her breath in gasps. The other young nun closed the door.

"It's a baby, Mother! Adrienne's having a baby in her room, alone!"

Mother Radegund for the first time in her long life lost command of her own senses. She got out of bed, bore down in her nightgown upon the terrified nuns.

"Go to your rooms!" she cried, then, remembering, completed her orders in a hoarse whisper. "What do you mean? Are you all quite mad? Where do you think you are? This is a convent!"

"The baby's almost here," the nun at the door said. "We're not mad, I tell you. It's almost here, I say."

Mother Radegund got into her habit. Sister Hélène held it over her head. The young nuns tried to help, fumbling with her veil, sticking the long pin into her head, one of them sobbing with fright. Mother Radegund herself was shaking, but with all her frenzy she was thankful for the awful beating of the rain, the rushing of the wind. She altered her quick commands.

"Whatever has happened, keep what heads you've got! Stop that snivelling, Sister Angela. Cécile, stop that shaking. Turn on the hall light, Sister Hélène. Don't make a sound! This is a convent, I tell you. My God! What have we all done to deserve this?"

"Shall we call the nurse, Mother?"

"Call no one. Keep your mouths shut! This is a convent, I tell you. Go on! Don't make a sound!"

The two young nuns fled down the long corridor, Sister Hélène and Mother Radegund after them. Queer,

what things come into one's head, thought Mother Radegund, when one's world is tumbling into bits. With
their veils and their wide skirts floating about them as
they ran, Sisters Angela and Cécile looked like nothing
so much as two black waterfowl flying low, close together,
over some long river.

They reached Adrienne's room. How long had it been,
thought Mother Radegund. Five minutes? Ten? When
they got there, Mother Radegund, still half convinced
that the young nuns were mad, saw that they were not.
The baby had come. It was alive, Mother Radegund saw,
beginning to scream weakly, a little girl. It's so tiny, she
thought. She had never seen so tiny and helpless a thing.
It can't live, she thought.

Adrienne was white as chalk, as white as those awkward rounds of chalk that they used to use for the black-
boards in France, before chalk came in smooth sticks,
packed tightly in a wooden box, round disks of white,
packed closely together, smooth.

"There are things in my bottom drawer," Adrienne
said. Her voice sounded small and far away. Then she
covered her white face with her long white hands, lying
there, saying nothing while they worked frenziedly and
the rain fell in sheets.

"Call the doctor from the lower floor, Angela, from
the telephone in my study. Tell him to hurry. Tell him
nothing else. Carry the child to my room, Hélène. Wrap
it in this, no, not that way—like this. Keep it warm. Don't
try to wash it. Get the medicine chest from my room,
Cécile, then wait in the hall. If you hear anyone, send

them to their rooms at once. Don't let anyone in here. If you do, you'll repent of it forevermore."

Mother Radegund stood in Adrienne's room. It was light enough outside now to see without the lamp. She snapped it off, feeling safer in the sure light of morning. She did not speak to Adrienne; but when she had put clean sheets on her bed, moving her skillfully and gently in order to spread the sheets, when she had put a clean nightgown on her, she put her hand upon Adrienne's hands, not trying to move them from her face. She felt in those moments engulfing pity for Adrienne, for all the tragic, inexplicable sorrow of life, its hate, its love, its irony. She felt, too, a kind of fierce admiration for the frantic, silent endurance of pain which this room had known. Adrienne had rapped upon Sister Angela's and Sister Cécile's walls next her own when her terror quite overcame her. But only a few minutes before. Beyond that, they said, there had been no sound, and they had both been awake in the storm so that they would have heard had she cried out.

Somewhere Mother Radegund had read of certain unrepentant souls in Hell, who, having loved and misused life, hurling it away, scorning its threats and persuasions, now paid their debts in torment, but in silence. She had ever since felt respect for them.

She asked no questions of Adrienne, and Adrienne did not speak. Questions now which might probe into past moments of temptation and tenderness, of defiance of life, seemed only a cruel and barren literalness. She wondered why she was not more frightened standing there, waiting, her hand on Adrienne's cold fingers. For all she knew she was in the presence of death as well as of life, but both facts at this moment seemed quite beyond her grasp. She was praying as she stood there, not that sin might be spared its bitter fruits, not that life might be quickened and restored, but that all humanity might learn to pity itself and thus to understand, might some day want above all else to bind up the broken-hearted, to proclaim deliverance to those that were captive, to open the prisons to those that were bound.

Bound by what? thought Mother Radegund as she prayed, the familiar, lovely words in her mind. Captive in what prison-houses? Bound by what chains? Not alone of the body, although those chains were stout and strong, working for good as well as for evil, for life as well as for death. The prison-houses of the soul, she thought— these held the strongest, most unrelenting chains. Not the chains of sense, she thought, not of those quick, intuitive promptings, which made one sometimes love unwisely and perhaps pay its price, which leagued minds and hearts together in quick and beautiful response, which leaped in sudden, miraculous moments to a knowledge of God Himself. Not these, but rather the chains of misbegotten thought, of reason, of custom, even of education, the cruel chains which so often guarded one against a broken heart, fortified one against unhappiness, against the torture of the soul, which alone promised life. It is the happy people of the world who are hard, she thought. If I could, she thought, I would have all my children know of this, understand it, weep for it. It is hardness, she thought, which is the unforgivable sin. It is the chains of hardness which make captives of us all. It is from these that we must be freed in order that our hearts may break. The unbroken hearts in the world, these build the prison-houses of the soul.

It was for more broken hearts that Mother Radegund was asking God.

De profundis clamavi ad te, Domine. Domine, exaudi vocem meam.

Out of the depths have I cried unto Thee, O Lord. Lord, hear my voice.

Just before the doctor came, Mother Radegund felt Adrienne's hands, upon which she had placed her own, slipping from her face. Her eyes were closed. She was still sleeping when Sister Angela led the doctor into the room.

Wise men do not talk, thought Mother Radegund, as women, even wise women, sometimes do. There was nothing on the doctor's face that suggested that this was a singular occurrence for a convent. After he had done all the customary things, he sat by Adrienne's bed, watching her, his hand on hers. The rain had stopped. The early sun was shining through the clouds.

Mother Radegund replied to his unasked questions.

"I know nothing about this," she said, "nothing at all. I don't know who the father is. I don't think I want to know. If I had been here, if you hadn't made me go away, I could have perhaps helped this poor child. I didn't once guess how she was suffering in her soul. I thought I was beyond surprises, but I guess I'm not—at least about myself."

"Didn't anyone know? My God, these nuns are women, aren't they?"

He looked at Sister Hélène, cowering in the corner.

"I thought they were, but maybe I'd have been as blind, too. I don't know. Just at this moment I'm judging no one. Just at this moment I know nothing at all."

"Where's the child?" he said.

"In my room downstairs."

"I'll take a look at it. There's nothing more I can do here at the moment."

"Take the doctor downstairs, Sister," said Mother Radegund.

It was nearly five o'clock, she saw. The nuns rose at five. Soon she would hear in the corridors the dulled tread of feet, the clicking of rosaries, the stir of heavy skirts.

She looked at Adrienne. Her dark lashes against her white cheeks were quivering slightly. Mother Radegund bent above her, took her unresponsive hand.

"It's all right, my child," she said. "Don't worry. We'll make it come out all right."

There was no sign that Adrienne heard.

The doctor came back.

"The child's all right," he said. "Premature, but sound enough, a nice child. I've put Sister Hélène with it in my car. I've got a place for it for the present. We'll talk of the future later."

"I can never thank you."

"Don't try."

"I hate concealment like this, as though we were in the midst of crime. I don't mind the nuns knowing, it would

do them good, but there are all these children. We can't
explain to them or to their parents."

"Of course not."

"They love Adrienne. I want them always to think
kindly of her."

He looked at her. He wondered why such women ever
went into convents. And still perhaps it was just as well
that this one had.

"There's nothing more I can do. I'll take Sister down
town now and come back directly, but it may be over
here before I can get back. Give her this if she stirs, but
I don't think she will. The girl's killed herself with fear
and mistreatment, and she hadn't enough strength anyhow to start a thing like this, at least at such a time. This
war's got a lot to answer for! Why the child is alive, God
only knows.

"You've covered up traces of everything here. You'll
want to call the priest, I suppose. There'll be nothing
else. Nothing hard to see, I mean. She'll just sleep away.
You're used to death?"

"Yes," said Mother Radegund. "Death, and life."

4

Mother Radegund is right, thought John Marston, the
only way to beat Death is by more life, whether the death
of the body or the death of the spirit.

He looked from his study window out upon the sea.
It was a windless June morning, warm for the season, at
least in Maine. The sea held scarcely a ripple, stretching
blue and still. The outline of Cadillac was like a clean

line of deep blue ink. One could almost discern the
uneven outlines of the spruces on the hat-like point of
Schoodic. There was hardly a trace of white about the
islands.

Jan was rowing the dory in quick, long strokes down
along the shore line to haul the lobster traps. Young
Roderick Marston was standing excitedly in the stern in
a blue cotton suit, white gulls, avid after discarded bait,
circling about his yellow head. He looked taller than
five, nearing six, as he stood there, straight, watching the
gulls.

"Do you see that child?" Eileen asked, coming in
through the open door, alarm in her face. "Really, dear,
he could at least be made to sit down. Philomena's standing by the kitchen window, perfectly crazy."

"He's all right. Jan's watching him. We mustn't act
like aged parents, darling."

"He hasn't his sweater on. It's cold out there."

"I don't believe so. I've never seen a warmer morning
for this time of year."

"Suppose anything should happen to Jan? You forget
that Jan's not young any more."

"I don't suppose he is, at that. Good Lord, can Jan be
nearing seventy? Well, anyhow, dear, he isn't going to
collapse while he's hauling those few traps. Give Philomena something to do. Tell her my bed has a bump in
it. The mattress needs turning. Send her out to pick some
iris for Ann's room."

When people had children at fifty and over, he thought,
once Eileen had gone, they had to watch their step in
order to give a child a fair deal. Were it not for Jan, he

thought, and Ann, who was returning tonight for the
summer, young Roderick would have no show at all
under his mother's anxiety and Philomena's constantly
recurring moments of panic. It was best for all concerned
that Jan was ageless, entering into the child's life, yet
treating him always as a kind of dwarfed contemporary.

They were coming back now, he saw. Jan had not col-
lapsed. He was allowing Roderick, sitting beside him, to
pull an oar, patient with his splashings, keeping the dory
on her way by his own quick shiftings. They would
doubtless not see Roderick till dinner-time. Once they
were in and had brought the lobsters to Philomena's
kitchen door, they would hustle for the barn or the garden. There was always something to do in either place.
Now that Philomena, in spite of her robust denials, had
rheumatic knees, Jan cared for the garden.

Young Roderick was out of doors with Jan from morning till night, brown as bracken in November, growing
tall by the month rather than by the year. He looked so
much like Philip at his age that his father, who could
never succumb to the imperceptible undertow of time,
was constantly startled. Was Philip dead? Was he himself fifty-eight? What had become of the years, bounteous, gracious, in this place at least, keeping one steady in
a world which disappointed, even alarmed one?

Was one steady because kindly circumstances had en-
abled one to escape the so-called life of the world—a nega-
tive accomplishment, then? Or was one steady because,
through these same kindly circumstances, one had amassed
sufficient resources of mind and body to be invulnerable
against the beatings of the world? These were questions

which could not be answered, save perhaps by the psychologists who interested, yet puzzled him. Perhaps Plato had answered them just as well in those words about setting one's own house in order. And yet how much credit did one deserve who had never in his life been conscious of any active and actual setting in order of his own mind and soul?

Even death with all its heartbreak had not meant disorder, or even, strange as it seemed, the cruel shattering of one's hopes. It had not meant resentment, or that almost as bitter effect of death, resignation. Six years ago that morning they had heard of Philip's death. He had seen the reality of it in Jan's eyes, bringing him and Jan more closely together, when Jan had come to fetch young Roderick to haul the traps. It was in Eileen's face and Philomena's, as it would be in Ann's when she reached home this evening, hurrying so as not wholly to miss that day with them. What had it meant then, he wondered, trying again to put into tangible thought what death had meant.

Pain, then, first of all. There was no mistaking pain, no sublimation for its strangling hold. There it was, gnawing at one's body, filling one's eyes, actual physical pain at one's throat, in one's heart. Pain, which time could not entirely heal, the quick stabs of it surprising one, after the first almost intolerable weeks, by its recurrence in moments of association and memory, growing more bearable, yet still there. And outlasting the pain, inundating it in quick healing floods, moments and hours of tenderness for those who suffered the same agony, Eileen, Jan, Philomena, Ann, and finally, beyond them, for all everywhere who knew pain. There was gratitude also in this suffering, the almost instinctive gratitude that one could know grief, grief complete and inevitable, welcome almost in that it knew no torture of remorse, no confusion of self-reproach, no absence of its very self.

He thought suddenly of old Sarah, dead now these many years, standing in his room in his grandmother's house, twisting her hands in her apron. "It's a great grief, Master John, when there's no grief worth grieving for."

This grief, which death had granted, was simple in the old classical sense of simplicity. It was a gift bestowed by life, forever incomplete without the dignity of suffering. Life was thus enriched by grief, making possible a newness of days by the very quickening which its own gift had given it. What was it that old Hecuba had said, lying desolate in the dust of Troy, about her tears promising immortality to ruined Ilion?

He had forgotten the passage, at least in Euripides' words. He reached for the book on his shelves and, turning, saw Jan in the doorway with the same reality in his eyes.

"Heather's got four pups, fine ones. She chose the buffalo robe in the old sleigh. I'm afraid Rod saw it all. It was happening just when we got back from hauling the traps, and I couldn't pull him away. Eileen won't like it much, I don't think."

"What? The pups or Rod's seeing? That's all right, Jan. It's good for him."

"Philomena will think it's bad. She'll be upset. Philomena gets upset more than she used to, don't you think?"

"I'm afraid she does. But don't worry. She'll get over it."

"Can I take Rod to the village with me?"

"I don't see why not. Ask his mother."

"He'll make an awful fuss if we don't keep all the pups."

"I suppose so. Well, we're used to keeping pups, Jan."

"Yes," said Jan.

John Marston watched him as he went out. The years had done well by Jan, or rather Jan by the years. His heavy gray hair now almost matched his eyes. There was no perceptible narrowing or weakening of his broad, square shoulders. His hands were not the hands of a man of seventy.

From his desk he could hear Eileen's voice.

"If you're going to take him, Jan, get his red sweater from the hall closet. And whatever you do, don't buy him any licorice. He was sick last time."

It was odd what stability lurked in such simple words and acts, he thought. *Sweater, licorice,* a daily drive to the village, eight miles over an old, still bumpy wood road. It put an end to abstractions. The day was fine. He would fetch Eileen, see the new pups, and take a walk with a few of the other dogs. There might still be surf running on the rocks of the point where the tide was stronger. Yesterday on the tail of a northeast storm it was superb, running beneath a sunny mist, a sea of green and silver, swelling in sleek rollers, dashing against the boulders, spending itself in clouds of spindrift and white masses of churning foam. Roderick, standing too close with him and Jan, had been dashed with it, soaked to the skin, to Philomena's panic. He smiled as he remembered her face when they had come home, and she was rubbing Rod down in the kitchen, he and Jan looking on, culprits beneath her accusing eyes.

It was just as well that Ann was coming home. Ann took over Roderick once she had arrived, quieting her mother's anxieties, ridiculing Philomena's fears. He had been casting about in his mind for some days in search of the best way for him and Ann to ensure the school at Heron Cove for young Roderick in the autumn. What he had been unable to accomplish thus far with Eileen might be managed with Ann's cooperation and influence. He did not much like this consolidation of schools, which was every year gaining headway in the state, this transportation of children from the rural districts into the towns and larger villages. It was just another of those increasing sacrifices of drama and humour to efficiency and dullness, which this age of progress was constantly effecting. He wondered if the indubitable gain compensated in real measure for the more indubitable loss. So long as the Heron Cove school maintained its doubtful status as an institution of learning, together with its ways and means of purveying the kind of democracy he believed in, he would like young Roderick to partake of its blessings. A four-mile walk for a stout youngster could not be without its assets, and for bad weather a successor to King Wenceslas was already in the barn. He relied upon Ann's grateful memory of the Heron Cove school to further his design.

Rod adored Ann, sitting next her at the table, forsaking Jan to follow her about, swimming with her at the anchorage, crawling into her bed in the morning. Rod could belong to Ann, he thought, as well as to him and Eileen, and perhaps with more justification. Queer that none of his children in face or feature bore any resemblance to the Marstons, Lassiters all of them, as old James Lassiter had proudly said when he paid a long-deferred visit to them last December and went home to die in February, at eighty-six.

"Strange you haven't managed to put your mark on one of them, John," the old man had said. "But, there! Eileen's always had the upper hand of you!"

It was true that the children in face and feature, hair and eyes, looked like Eileen rather than like him. Perhaps that theory, which he had read somewhere, that the more vital of the parents dictated the appearance of the children, had some truth to it. And yet, although they were the colour of Eileen's, there had been unmistakable in Philip's eyes, just as there was in Roderick's, a look of his father. The blue eyes of his father were always looking at him out of the gray eyes of his sons. It had been a kind of daily return of his father through many years to this place which he had loved and made, and he was grateful for it.

5

Roderick ran to meet them down the high shore as they returned from their walk, breathless, stumbling in the path as he reached them, falling headlong in the juniper.

"Darling! Whatever is the matter? Can't you ever walk?"

"Jan's gone away! I came to tell you."

"Jan gone! Wherever has he gone to?"

"Philomena's crying, and Jan's gone, I tell you."

"What do you mean, Roderick? Pull yourself together and tuck in your blouse. Now tell us."

"Anton's dead!"

"Anton!" said Eileen Marston. "Anton who?"

"You know, father. He used to shine shoes in New York with Jan, long before I was born, long before Philip and Ann were born. Jan told me all about him coming home. He was Jan's best friend. You know, mother, he was the boy who went to Prague with Jan when the wicked man tried to sell the bad ox. He's dead, I tell you. Jan found a letter in the post-office. We had to hurry home so Philomena could pack Jan's things, and he could go back to get on the train. Philomena cried and cried, and said things to Jan that I couldn't understand. But Jan went all the same. It's really true, father. Ask Philomena if you don't believe me. Anton was your friend, too, Jan says, and my grandfather's friend. Why haven't you told me about Anton?"

"I really don't know, Roderick," said John Marston. He had hardly thought of Anton Karel through these many years. At first, after Anton's imprisonment, he had hesitated to uncover grief in Jan. Then once more Anton had come into his thoughts, when Jan had returned from seeing Anton's Connecticut valley—could it be twenty-eight years before? Jan had told John Marston of Anton's new home, and then, in his curious, quiet way, had seemingly closed the matter of Anton against all but himself. Still, John Marston thought, he had failed Jan in not recognizing, even in silence, a part of Jan's life lying deep within him.

As the years had slipped past, Anton had slipped out of sight among them. Now as he stood in the path listening to Roderick, accepting his reproach, Anton was alive again, fingering his dirty cap in the old drawing-room on West 28th Street, shining shoes in the shop on 12th Street, snapping his cloth with pride in his work, sitting with his father and him in the Národní Budova, breaking Jan's heart on *The Sea Hawk* while he and Julian wondered at the Czech words sounding on and on. He had not really forgotten Anton; he had been there, behind all the things of the present and of the nearer past, now summoned from the longer past by Roderick's question. It was like Jan to go back to see Anton dead among the Polish people, when he had been forbidden to see him alive.

"I should have told you, Roderick," he said. "Anton was good to me when I was a boy your age and older. I'm sorry he is dead."

Philomena was more remonstrant concerning Jan's mad decision than sad over Anton's death. She had, in fact, no room for sadness over Anton, whom she had not seen for more than fifty years. Today her thoughts were with Philip, whom her ancient saints had deserted in his hour of bitter need. Philomena had never been reconciled to Philip's death. All the prayers that she had said had not mended her heart.

"Jan is not now young," said Philomena. "Why should he now go so many miles to see a dead man, who would not see Jan while he yet lived? I said to Jan, 'How much

better, Jan,' I said, 'to pray for Anton, to spend our
money for Masses for him and not for the train for you.
What good will it now do,' I said, 'to go that long way to
see Anton, who cannot now speak to you?' All my words
were like the wind, blown away out of sight. Jan said,
'Anton was my friend in the old country and in New
York, and in all these many years I have yet been his
friend. So I go to see my old friend, Anton, before these
Polish people put him away in the earth.' If you had been
here, Mr. Marston, you could have said to stay, and then
Jan would not have gone."

"I should not have told Jan to stay, Philomena," John
Marston said.

"But it was so long ago, not even a few years ago as
Jan would have one think, but many, many years. And
on this day, too, which is sad for us all, to make us all
more sad. It is not kind of Jan. Jan, he remembers always
too much."

That was true, thought John Marston. Jan had always
remembered, but not too much. The past to Jan had
never passed from sight. It was not to him as to most men
like dark water flowing unseen beneath cold, white ice.
It was instead a bright stream, carrying the years in its
course, but lighted always by the warm sun of memory.
He recalled now how even as a boy he had recognized
that Jan remembered while Anton forgot.

"It is good to remember, Philomena," he said.

"Jan is not unkind," Roderick said, staring at Philomena, disapproval in his round eyes. "You must not say
such things, Philomena. And it is not a sad day. It's a
nice day. Ann is coming home tonight, and Heather has

four new puppies in the barn. Jan and I saw them all get born, one, two, three, four! They were born quick as scat, and Heather started licking them."

"Run to your room and wash for dinner, Roderick! Really, John!"

Philomena looked after Roderick's retreating figure and then at her amazed mistress.

"Jan is not just unkind," she said. "He is as well the most stupid of *honzas!*"

6

In twenty-eight years, thought Jan, sitting in the swaying bus, even this Connecticut valley had changed itself. It was now more cultivated. The rough roadsides which he had seen on his long hot walk had disappeared. Now the fields extended almost to the very edge of the highway, which was not dusty any longer, but paved, black and firm. There were more tobacco sheds standing about on the green fields, their slatted sides open to the sun and wind. Every now and then Jan saw what looked like a shimmering lake set down on the fields. These were those tents of stretched white netting, of which he had heard and under which the larger-leaved tobacco grew, safer here from wind, yet still catching the sunlight.

When the bus drew near one of these tents, he could see the young tobacco plants spreading in circles of small fans upon the brown soil. He saw, too, the figures of men working among them. It must be hot in there on this warm June day. If Peter Osinski had continued to be the ambitious farmer he was twenty-eight years before, he

doubtless had such a tent over some of his own tobacco;
and if that were true, then Anton had doubtless worked
within it, his shadowy figure seen by those who passed
along the road. These people who now went along the
roads in so many motor cars, seeing the country, would
say to one another:

"Look at that man working inside that netting. My!
It must be hot in there!"

That was all they would have known about Anton, seeing his stooped, indistinct figure, his busy hands, but not
seeing his mind or his heart.

Through all these many years Anna Karel had written
Jan now and again about Anton, not long letters, sometimes only a post-card with a picture on it of some church
or of the city hall of the nearby town. She had usually
written in response to letters from Jan, brief letters asking only how Anton was and saying at the close:

"If Anton should die before me, you will write to me,
please, Anna, for I shall want to come to his burial."

He had never shared Anna's letters with anyone, not
even with Philomena, taking them from the post-office
himself, reading them there, as he had read Anna's first
letter so many years ago, jealously guarding them, not
because he was unwilling to share their contents, but because he feared that the sharing with those who remembered less might in some way injure the identity of Anton
so carefully tended within him.

The bus hurtled on. Jan felt uncomfortable and a bit
out of place in his black suit, his stiff collar, and his well-
polished shoes. His bag was on the floor, a good footstool
for his somewhat short legs. He would have liked to take

off his hat so that the air from the open window might cool his head, but a sense of decorum prevented him. He had taken another train from Boston at dawn, after spending most of the night in the station there, and then this bus in place of the stagecoach which he had taken so many years before. He had sent Anna a telegram, saying that he was coming and that he hoped they could wait for him. The bus driver had told him that he passed close to Peter Osinski's farm so that there was no danger of his missing his destination. The driver was familiar with Peter Osinski's name on his mail-box. He knew the place, he said. Jan need not worry in the least.

What had these many years done to Anton, Jan wondered. Anna's letters had not told him much: Anton was well, or Anton was working hard, or Anton was better after a long sickness with his head. But Anna had kept her promise to Jan. For that he was grateful. He had feared all these years lest Anna might fail to keep her promise, might not tell Jan, when the time came, that Anton was dead.

"It's the next house," said the bus driver, turning in his seat, his voice sounding above the clanking of his loose gear-shift, the drone of his engine. "Don't worry. I'll set you down all right."

Jan had sat all the way just behind the bus driver so that he might not miss Peter Osinski's farm. Twenty-eight years was a long time in which to remember places, especially with a changing countryside to confuse one and with coming by a paved road to a different entrance, not leaning over a fence by the river as he had done before.

"Here we are," said the bus driver.

"Thank you very much," said Jan.

There were a number of people about Peter Osinski's farm-house, which stood back from the road about thirty feet. Jan saw that there were some women on the porch, some men in the barnyard. He felt nervous. His heart beat fast within him, and his hand shook on the handle of his bag. It was three o'clock in the afternoon. He noticed as he stood there that the shades in the front room were drawn over the windows.

He looked for Anna among the three women on the porch, sitting in rocking-chairs, rocking to and fro. The rocking-chairs, thought Jan, did not belong to women from the old country. How should he know Anna, he wondered, after exactly forty years? He stood in the gravel path leading to the house, looking at the three women on the porch.

It seemed a long time, though it was not, before one of the women left the others and came down the steps. This then was Anna. Anna was now a large woman, stout, almost bursting from the front of her black and white checked dress, which was partly covered by a white apron. Her feet were not now in black felt slippers, but in patent leather shoes with straps to them. Her hair, Jan saw, was nearly white, parted in the middle with waves over her ears. Anna did not now look like a woman from the old country, thought Jan, not like Philomena, but Anna now lived in this Connecticut valley, near large towns where people kept up to date.

"Is this then Jan?" asked Anna.

She took Jan by the hand which he freed for her, setting down his bag on the ground. He saw now that Anna was crying, not for Anton, he thought, so much as for the long years, their burdens, their old memories.

Anna led Jan to the porch. When he took off his hat to greet the other women there, he saw Anna looking at his head, his graying hair.

"This is Stasia, Peter Osinski's wife," Anna said. "This is Rozia, her sister."

Jan acknowledged the introductions.

"How do you do?" he said.

Stasia and Rozia were large women like Anna, or at least not small. They had dark eyes and high cheek bones. They looked well-kept like Anna, in black shoes like hers, although they did not have waves in their still dark hair. Jan wondered if they still worked in the onion fields as he had seen those women working years before. Perhaps it was only that they were not working today because Anton was dead. They looked like Polish women, not like Bohemian women. There was a difference, he thought. He wondered if Anton had noticed the difference through all these years.

But Stasia Osinski and Rozia were kind and hospitable.

"You will be hungry then," said Stasia, speaking English with more of an accent than his own, or Anna's, or even Philomena's. "Rozia will make ready the coffee."

"You will wish to speak with your old friend, Jan, Anna," Rozia said.

Rozia was quicker than Stasia, Jan saw, seeing her glance quickly at Stasia, who then rose and followed her into the house.

Jan and Anna then sat in silence for what again seemed a long time, Anna crying a little. From the door that led beyond the hall-way to the kitchen they could hear Rozia and Stasia moving about, rattling some dishes, whispering in Polish. There were some flowers blossoming in the strip of garden below the porch railing, bleeding-hearts, pansies, a late iris or two. The house was a good-sized house, painted white. The bit of lawn in front was carefully mowed.

Jan noted all these things because he could not quite think how to begin to talk with Anna. He found it hard to look straight at Anna, sitting there in her rocking-chair, fumbling with her handkerchief, blowing her nose. A rocking-chair somehow made a barrier between him and Anna. At last he said:

"Thank you for keeping your promise to me, Anna."

"I have meant to keep my promise, Jan, for all these years," Anna said.

After that things were not so hard.

"Was Anton then sick for long?" asked Jan. His words sounded too polite and formal, he thought.

Anton was not sick at all, Anna said, not what you could call sick. He had died sitting on the step, at the back door, after a day in the fields. Felix, Peter Osinski's son, had found him there when he had come in from the milking. "You're in my way, Anton," Felix had said, and then, would you ever think, Anna said, Felix had seen that Anton was dead.

"There are many things I did not tell to you, Jan," said Anna, talking more willingly now that Rozia had brought coffee in heavy white cups, coffee and some sandwiches with meat in them. I did not tell you because you would feel bad, and what would be the use? But you would not have felt bad had you seen Anton, Jan. Anton went back to be a child again, six, or was it seven years after he left the prison.

"He was kind and good all the time, not angry and excited as he sometimes used to be in the old days in New York. You remember, Jan? But he was a child all the same. Once when we said to him, 'Will you go to the circus, Anton?,' he clapped his hands like a little boy. I was glad when he went back to be a child again because he was happy then as he was not happy when he first came from the prison. He was pleased when we brought him candy from the town or even at Christmas a little toy dog.

"And Anton could always work hard like a man even if he was a child. Every day he worked, and at night after supper when we all sat outside or in, he looked at picture-books and smiled. He would show us the pictures. He would say, 'See this man up in a flying-machine. See this cow with her calf.'

"And always he lived back in the old country, Jan, talking to himself. Sometimes he talked with you, Jan. He said, 'Let's fly kites today, Jan.' Or, 'Let's roll hoops.' And once he said, 'Let's go to Prague with old Jonas, Jan.' Whenever he talked that way with you, Jan, I wrote down the things he said in a little book so I should not forget to tell you just what he said."

Anna cried for some minutes while Jan sat in silence. Then she said:

"You will like to see Peter and his sons. Peter is a good man. He was always kind to Anton. Now he grows older like us all, but his sons are strong, and they know how to farm good. Felix and Josef are his sons. They have both been to a college."

She led Jan down the porch steps and around the house toward the barns. The old red barn, which Jan remembered having seen from the fence by the river, had given place now to a new one. There were two good barns and several sheds, in one of which was an automobile and in another a truck. Jan could see how the land behind the barns sloped gently down toward the river, toward the fence where he had stood on that hot July day. Peter Osinski had a good farm, he thought.

Anna was right. Peter was a good man. He greeted Jan kindly, shaking him by the hand. He was a rather tall man, at least compared to Jan, wiry, not stooped at all, nor gray, nor much lined in his face. He had restless dark eyes, quick, intent on things. Jan could tell that Peter Osinski did not like the notion of growing old, of yielding his work to his tall sons.

"You must see my sons," he said, when he had moved his arms about to show Jan the extent of his acres, his onions, his tobacco, his orchard. "There they are. They work at that automobile. It is all automobiles now in this country. My sons are American fellows. They are not Polish, no. Felix, Josef, come here."

Jan could not tell whether Peter Osinski regretted that his sons were Americans or whether he was glad that they were. Felix and Josef were Americans, as their father had said. They did not look too different from John or Julian when they were young, or from Philip before he went away to France, in spite of their farm clothes, which they wore with a jaunty air.

"They have been to a college," their father said, "to the State College. They learn good farming at that college. I send them. I pay their bills."

Felix and Josef were embarrassed by their father's pride, Jan thought. They greeted him pleasantly enough, yet without their father's interest. They were tall, good-looking young men, somewhere in the early twenties.

"They are my next crop," Peter said. "They come when I am already growing old. My first sons and daughters, they marry men and women, but Polish, too. Then they go away."

Throughout all this hour and longer Jan had been thinking of Anton. It seemed strange in the midst of this life and activity to think of Anton, dead in the room with the drawn shades, Anton a man again, returned to manhood now that he was dead. But he was grateful to Peter Osinski for being kind to Anton.

"By and by," Peter said, when Anna was about to lead Jan back to the house, "I walk you about my fields, Jan. After supper we do this while the women work."

Anna took Jan back to the house through a long shed which led to the kitchen. When they were nearly through the shed, which held wood stacked neatly in piles, tools, and odds and ends of other things, she pointed to a shelf just outside the door to the kitchen. On the shelf was a shoe-cleaning kit, which Jan recognized as belonging years ago to Anton. There on the half circle of its stout wooden handle was the name ANTON KAREL, carved by Jan himself when he and Anton, with the help of Philip Marston, had begun their business in New York. Jan started, sharply and with pain, as he saw it there, so many miles

from New York, so many years from the shop on 12th
Street, so many heart-breaks from their old life.

Anna was saying, "I got it myself, Jan. What do you
think! I kept it ten years for Anton. When the men came
to close the shop and to take the things, I was there, waiting. I said 'Can I have this? It's only a little thing. It
can't cost much. I will pay,' I said. But one of the men
said, 'Let her have it. What do we want of that old kit?'
So I have kept it, Jan, and after Anton went back to be a
child again, he liked to shine all our shoes. You remember, Jan, how well Anton shined the shoes, always?"

"Yes, Anna," said Jan, "I remember."

*Anton, the shoes you shine, they are not for this earth.
They are for Heaven, before the throne of God.*

After supper Peter Osinski took Jan for a walk around
his fields. Jan felt more comfortable with Peter than with
Anna. Peter could not uncover the things in Jan's mind
which the presence of Anna uncovered. He could ask
Peter about Anton as he could not ask Anna.

"Anton," said Peter to Jan, "he never forget the old
country. When he lose his thoughts like, then he go back
to the old country. Always he is there. Anton was a happy
man when once he lose his thoughts. He would say like
my grandfather said when I was a boy in Poland, 'The
apple trees, they grow not well if one not love them.' Last
summer the hail, it hurt my tobacco, and Anton, he said,
'We must not speak wicked words about that hail, Peter,
or bad luck will come.'

"The day before yesterday," Peter confessed to Jan,
"I come out to the barns, and I tell my animals that
Anton is dead. I do that like we did it in the old country,

in Poland. In Bohemia, too?" Jan nodded. "But I do not tell what I did to Felix and my son Josef. They do not know the ways of the old country. They do not like to talk about Polish things."

He looked at Jan then. They had completed half their round of the fields and were enjoying a quiet pipe by the river in exactly the spot, Jan saw, that he had rested and washed himself years before. There were things in Peter's eyes, Jan saw, which could not be spoken because there were no words for them. Jan saw them lying there and knew them because of their earlier companions within himself. They were born, he knew, of the tug of the old world, of the tired backs and shoulders of many generations at toil, of tragedy in new American homes, the old beaten daily by the new, of fear lest this old should fade away from sight, even from the eyes of those about to die when they themselves were old.

"I like this country," Peter was saying, knocking out his pipe as a signal that they must be soon going on. "It is good. It is better for a man than the old. I never, since I came, want to go back. But a man must not forget his old country. To forget good things does bad things to a man. Anton, he always remember all good things."

Jan felt warm within his heart at Peter Osinski's words. They had suddenly opened doors, once darkly closed within him, now opened to the light. The thought that Anton had returned in his mind to the old country, that he had learned to remember good things there, was the one possible knowledge of Anton which made all things as they should be. This was the answer to Jan's prayers of many years. Anton had not then forgotten old faiths, old loyalties. They had been within him through all this long time, not quite out of sight or hearing, waiting there within Anton's mind until he should discover his need of them.

He was grateful, too, to Peter that it was he and not Anna who took him into the front room to see Anton. When they skirted the house and heard the women still in the kitchen, Peter led the way through the front door and into the front room. He stood with Jan by Anton's coffin, tacitly understanding that Jan welcomed his presence there.

Anna had placed some flowers about the coffin, wild flowers, some from the garden, daisies and buttercups, bleeding-hearts, pansies. They were on little tables at the foot and head, in glass jars of water. She had placed some candles among the flowers, at Anton's head and feet. Their light in the darkened room made Anton's face pale and indistinct until Peter raised one of the shades so that Jan could see him more clearly. Jan did not know whether he would actually have known Anton. His hair was very white, and his features had the quiet, expressionless look of a sleeping child.

Jan and Peter knelt for a few minutes beside the coffin, saying prayers for Anton.

"God speed Anton's soul to Himself!" said Peter in Polish.

"Amen!" said Jan.

While they stood again beside the coffin looking at Anton, remembering him, Jan took a small package from his pocket, wrapped in a clean white handkerchief. He did not think he could have done this before Anna, but with Peter it became suddenly easy.

"This is earth from Bohemia," Jan said, "from my father's field. I should like to place it beneath Anton's head."

"Good, Jan. We will do so," said Peter.

In the evening they all sat outside by the kitchen door. Peter did not like to sit on the porch so near the road.

"I like to sit where I see my fields," he said.

It was a clear, soft evening. Jan heard a whip-poor-will sounding from somewhere its three plaintive notes across the fields. The women knitted. He and Peter smoked their pipes. Felix and Josef had gone away somewhere in the automobile.

When it began to grow dark, Peter said:

"We do not leave Anton alone in the dark. The women, they sit there until twelve o'clock comes. Then I sit there."

"You sleep tonight, Peter," Jan said. "At midnight I will sit there."

"Good," said Peter. "If you wish it so, Jan, it shall be so."

After Peter had gone gratefully to bed, Jan sat by himself. The moon was so clear that it dimmed the smaller stars. The smell of Peter's gardens and dampening fields was fresh and good. The outline of the hills was distinct. He could not see the river, but he felt its steady flowing behind the clumps of trees which the moonlight made visible. This was a pleasant land, he thought. He should always like to remember it like this.

He felt no trace of sadness within him, but rather a

secure and comforting completion of one long, deep part of his life, beginning almost before he could remember, now ending in peace. When he went back home, he thought, there would never again be so much as a moment of uneasiness about Anton. He could go about his work, knowing that all was well, not through Anton's death, but through his return in his mind to those things long ago which had meant life for them both.

At midnight Anna came to the door.

"It is twelve o'clock, Jan," she said. "Have you been to sleep then?"

"All right, Anna," said Jan. "No, I have not been to sleep."

Jan went into the sitting-room where Anton lay. He opened the window before which the coffin stood and sat in a chair facing the window. Anna had placed fresh candles at Anton's head and feet. They cast shadows on the walls, adding to the shadows which the moon cast.

Jan looked out of the window toward a little ridge of land, which rose beyond the road in the field opposite. He remembered how he had learned years back at home that Death likes to linger on ridges and about hedges. He remembered, too, the saying that when a man has died, his body is not really dead. Until it has begun to return to earth, it may waken at certain moments, moments unknown to them that watch beside it. Was Anton even then perhaps awake, thought Jan, winning a last pleasure from this Connecticut valley where he had worked, and perhaps also from the thought of an old friend watching beside him?

Stasia's clock in the kitchen struck two. The time came as a surprise to Jan. He had not realized he had been two hours with Anton. Anna's candles were burning low. He must light from them two others in the box which she had left.

He stood beside Anton, once the fresh candles were glowing, and looked at him. They had dressed him well. He had on a good gray suit, a good black tie, tied carefully and well. The white line of his shirt sleeves showed below the cuffs of his suit, stiff with starch, clean and fine. The fingers of Anton's hands were longer than Jan's fingers. It was hard now to think of them caked with soil, brown with earth. Because they had been longer than Jan's fingers, Anton had been more deft and quick at shining shoes than Jan.

The thought made Jan pause in his mind as he stood there. An uneasiness began to assail him. He had suddenly thought of Anton's shoes, of those now upon his feet, out of sight below the cover of the coffin. Had they been brushed and polished as Anton would have wished, Anton who had himself been an artist at shining shoes?

He went to his chair and sat down again, but the worry in his mind gave him no rest. The moon was out of sight, but the reflection of its light over the still land lighted the room. Once or twice Jan moved toward the coffin and then sat down again. Stasia's clock struck three. It would be dawn soon, Jan thought, and Anna would come to take his place.

Unable longer to bear his fear, he walked firmly to the coffin and drew back the lid so that he could see Anton's shoes. He stood there gazing at Anton's feet in the light of the candles and the moon. Then, unsatisfied, he went to the wall beside the door and switched on the electric light, hanging from the ceiling in the center of the room. The shoes might look well to Peter and Stasia, Rozia and Anna, thought Jan, but never to Anton. They were good; they were fine; but they were not perfect. Surely, good as they were, they were not the work of an artist like Anton.

Jan left Anton then and tiptoed through the silent kitchen to the shed beyond, where Anton's old kit lay on the shelf beside the door. He found the kitchen light and secured the kit. From a rack in the kitchen he took one of Stasia's towels and returned to the sitting-room.

Then he lifted Anton's heavy feet and spread the towel beneath them. He polished Anton's shoes just as Anton himself would have done, first one and then the other, the right shoe, the left shoe, rubbing in the polish, once, twice, brushing again and again.

When he had finished, he took the kit to the shed and the towel to the kitchen before he should once more cover Anton's feet.

A bird had begun to sing and the sky to lighten when he came back to the sitting-room. The song took Jan back to the days when he and Anton had flown kites with Father Urban, running over the fields.

"It is not enough to be kind to the birds," Father Urban had said to them, "to feed them in the snow, to spare their nests in the spring. We must listen to them. They also praise our Lord Jesus."

Jan stood listening to the bird and looking at Anton's shoes before he turned off the light. The shoes shone now almost as well as Anton could have made them shine.

They would be shining when the day broke and when the day wore to its close. They would be shining for days to come, long after Anton had ceased to wake on this earth.

He heard upstairs the sound of someone getting up. He replaced the lid of the coffin and went back to his chair. Now many birds were singing, and the sky was growing brighter. The day would be fine, he thought. How good to have a fine day for Anton!

7

Ann Marston sat beside Mother Radegund at the long table at Windswept, looking at Adrienne Chartier's child. She answered Mother Radegund's questions, attended to her needs, all the time thinking:

"I am not really here. I am back in France, living over again that long, yet brief, year, and more, in Picardy, in those old, ruined villages, Canizy, Hombleux, Esmery-Hallon. I am on those brown plains, walking by those still canals, watching those long twilights, the setting of the evening star. An hour and more it took for the evening star to set beyond those wide, flat plains."

She kept looking at Adrienne's child, trying, as she had tried all through supper, to discover any trace of Adrienne. There was none that she could see, unless it were in Julie's slender body and in her hands, delicate and mature for the hands of a child only ten years old. How could Adrienne have given her daughter so little of herself, she wondered, remembering the way in which Adrienne had always placed her indelible mark on things and people.

She was back in France again, seeing Adrienne at night

with her long fingers clasping a brown hot water jug, shivering in the bitter cold, hearing Adrienne say: "I wonder why we are here, what all this means. I wonder how we are going to pay for all this one day." She was back in France, seeing Adrienne come back late at night from walking somewhere with Raoul Vallon, her black hair untidy, her shoulders shrugging under her old red cape, laughing, saying: "I just move along with things. What will be, will be."

She heard her father saying, in response to Mother Radegund's question about the storm which was shaking the house:

"No, I don't remember in forty-seven Septembers such an equinoctial gale as this." And then to the little girl who sat beside him:

"But don't worry, Julie. The wind won't blow us away. We're always snug and warm at Windswept. You'll see."

Roderick was talking now. He was saying:

"There'll be fine surf tomorrow at the cove, won't there, father? I'll show you the surf, Julie."

What had Raoul Vallon really looked like? It was hard to remember how he had looked because his features had always meant less than the expression of them, the way he had used them. He had had blue eyes, she was sure of that, having wondered at such very blue eyes in so French a face and among so many brown ones. But they had been light blue eyes, long eyes, she remembered, rather cold and inscrutable with scorn in them. They were not the rounder deep blue eyes of Adrienne's little girl. His hair had been dark, straight and smooth, shining with some sort of concoction, brushed back from his rather low forehead. This child's hair was brown, a light brown, and her forehead, Ann felt sure, was high, if one could only see it beneath that ugly convent hair-cut, bangs in front, the rest straight over her ears and around her neck.

Her mother was saying behind the driving of the rain against the windows:

"No, this may well blow itself out tonight. Philomena says that Jan thinks the wind is shifting a bit. We have all manner of weather here, Mother Radegund. That's a part of the fascination of the place."

Who were those other French boys whom Adrienne was always befriending? Pierre, Vincent, Alain, that frail boy called Michel, who, oddly enough, had come from Mont St. Michel, had been a guide at the Abbey there, was homesick for the sea and those wide miles of white sand. Michel had adored Adrienne, but she had accorded him only a tolerant pity. She tried to recall all their faces and could not. Michel had been killed at Soissons in late May, two weeks before Cyril and Philip in Belleau Wood. She remembered how his pale, now forgotten face had haunted her, still there in her mind, when she had met Philip and Cyril in Paris.

Roderick was saying:

"How long are you going to stay at Windswept, Julie?"

"I don't know," the child answered. She seemed a shy little thing, with no trace of her mother's early self-possession. But, of course, one could not tell much about her in that black convent dress buttoned so sedately over her flat little chest.

"Julie's going to stay a long time, we hope, Roderick,"

John Marston was saying. "We hope she'll be so happy
here that she'll want to stay with us."

"That's fine," Roderick said. "That's good, Julie."

When supper was over and they all went into the living-
room, the wind showed no sign of lessening. It shook the
house, it held voice as well as force, wailing, high and
shrill.

"It makes me think of storms in Brittany when I was
a child," said Mother Radegund. "I remember how I lay
in bed praying for the fishing-boats."

"There have been storm signals out for some days,"
John Marston said. "We're always looking for something
like this in September."

He looked at Mother Radegund standing by the fire,
tall, pale, in her black habit and white face bands. He was
thinking how one was always saying casual things when
behind them, deep within one, lay things one could never
say, partly because one did not know exactly what they
were. There are moments in human experience, he was
thinking, when life seems suddenly to concentrate itself,
bringing together in a kind of nucleus of itself, all its po-
tentialities and powers, all its gifts and graces, all its
knowledge and wisdom. At such moments and hours of
intermission, he thought, before the half-apprehended
flow of conscious and unconscious experience resumes its
baffling course, one is aware of a truce with time, which
for the moment has been overtaken and captured, seen,
even partially understood. This is one of those moments,
he thought. This is one of those hours.

How old is Mother Radegund, he thought. "I have six years more to my discredit," he heard her saying, moving some tea-cups about upon a tray. She is sixty-eight then, he thought. It is not possible, but it is true. And she is ill. She has not told me so in her letters, nor will she tell me now because of the foolish embarrassment which such comments make even between friends. One does not speak of approaching death for fear of giving discomfort to others, putting them on the spot, so to speak. One cannot say simply, "I am going to die," because all the long, unsuccessful conduct of life, its conventions, amenities, manners, withdrawals, forevermore prevents as simple a recognition and acceptance by another who hears that inevitable truth.

"Won't you sit down?" he asked. "I'm sure you're tired."

"If you don't mind, I'll stand a bit longer," she said. "I love this room. I want to get every detail of it in my mind before I leave tomorrow."

How black and austere Mother Radegund's shadow is on the wall, thought Ann Marston, stretching almost to the rafters, swaying in the firelight. This house has known many odd things, she thought, things which one does not expect on a point of land in Maine—that Siamese boy, whom Philip brought home once from Harvard, that Barbados negro, swimming ashore from a wreck on the Castle Rocks, scrambling up the headland and scaring them all in the dead of night when she was a child—but it had not known just this before.

She thought, as she watched Mother Radegund's shadow on the wall, of those odd, quickened moments which one

always remembers, those objects which somehow catch
and hold emotions through the years, more real and tangible than the emotions themselves: that yellow bush in
Paris ten years ago, its smell in the cool night air; that one
blue iris in the marsh, holding her broken heart; those
two fat, brown earthenware tea-pots, which Madame
Morand had saved from the Germans in Canizy, looking
for all the world like two fat, happy old men, talking gen-
ially together; and now this shadow on the wall, which
I shall never forget, she thought.

Roderick and Julie were sitting together on the stone
shelf around the hearth, toasting marshmallows on long
sticks.

"Not so close, Julie," Roderick was saying. "That only
makes them smoky and burns them up. This is the way.
. . . Will you have a toasted marshmallow, Mother Radegund?"

"Thank you, Roderick," Mother Radegund said, taking the hot sticky mess in her long white fingers. "This
is good. I'll have two, please, or perhaps even three."

"Once the child is out of that horrible black dress,"
Eileen Marston was saying to herself, "she'll not look
so shy and frightened. In a blue dress, the colour of her
eyes, with her legs bare in white socks, and a round comb
—yes, a comb will look far more individual than a ribbon—to hold back her hair and show her forehead, she'll
be a different child. I don't mind a bit having her here,
especially now I've seen Mother Radegund. Queer how
some people make you think you've wasted your life and
still make you not mind thinking it! She'll be good for

Roderick, and if anything happens, there's always Ann to fall back on. I've always wanted another daughter. Am I sixty-one? I don't believe it for a moment!"

Jan came through the door with an armful of wood. Jan's seventy-three, thought Eileen. I don't believe that, either.

"Good evening," said Jan to Mother Radegund, pausing a moment with his wood to bow to her. "I hope you like Windswept in spite of this storm I gave you."

"I do," she said. "I like it mightily."

"There's a new calf in the barn," Jan said to Julie. "Rod will have to show it to you in the morning. It's a fine calf, isn't it, Rod?"

"It sure is," Roderick said. "No, Julie, not that way— this! We're toasting these for you, Jan."

"There seems always to be a new calf," Eileen said. "I thought spring and early summer were the times for calves, Jan."

"There's likely to be more in the spring, that's true. But it's no rule, hard and fast. Clover's always been a surprising cow."

"Is this one Clover, too?" Eileen asked. "John, just why must we always have a Clover?"

"I don't know," John Marston said.

"I named her," Roderick said. "Didn't I, Jan? Was I six when I named her, Jan? Clover's a nice name, isn't it, Julie?"

"Yes," said Julie.

"You children would never think what else I have in the barn tonight," said Jan, patiently eating the blackened marshmallows, which Julie offered him with a sudden smile. (What a nice smile she has, thought Ann Marston.)

"Never in the world would you guess, so I'll tell you. I have two sea gulls in that barn. The wind blew them into the barn while I was milking. Right out of the storm they came into the light. And there they have stayed. I gave them some corn, and there they are, standing in a corner, full of corn, half asleep."

"Gosh!" cried Roderick. "Sea gulls in a barn! Let's go to see them, Ann. Julie, let's go to see them."

"Darling, it's such a terrible night, and Julie isn't used to wind like this."

"It won't hurt her," Mother Radegund said. "What a thrill, Julie!"

"It's not raining any more," Jan said, "and the wind's coming round. It'll be fair tomorrow."

"Come on then, children," said Ann. "Get your sweater, Roddy. I'll get a coat for you, Julie."

"You won't mind my saying goodnight, will you, Mother Radegund?" Eileen Marston said. "The doctor's some crazy notion about my going to bed early, and I know you and John want to talk. Ann will see that you have everything you need, and you and I will have our talk in the morning." She turned to go, then came to Mother Radegund. "I've wanted for years to have you here."

"I've wanted to come for years, my dear," Mother Radegund said.

"Jan's right. The wind is swinging in," said John Marston coming in from the terrace where he had been making his nightly inspection of the weather. "Sit here where you'll be comfortable."

"I've a longing to sit right here," said Mother Radegund. She sat down on the stone shelf above the hearth, in the angle at the left, in Eileen's familiar place. "I've never seen a fireplace like this. I'll like to think of Julie sitting here with Roderick."

He took his old familiar place in the opposite angle. He was waiting for her to talk to him. There is nothing I can say now, he thought, which will not in some way be an intrusion. There is too much that is real in this room tonight, he thought, to risk a shattering of it.

After a few minutes she said:

"You're the one person among all those whom I know, in the world or out of it, who can understand why I've done what I have done in this matter, why I've left so many things undone. You can understand it because you're not complex, thank God. This world would be so much less a puzzle to us all if people could just be simple, look at things as they are and then let them alone, not go ferreting about to discover only misery. If you weren't as you are, I couldn't leave this earth without being tangled up in doubts and all kinds of upbraidings of myself. But since you are as you are, I can leave it without a bit of fuss. You're like the centurion in the Bible. I've always liked that man."

So it had come, this simple announcement which he had thought could not be made or received simply. Still he was surprised that he did not feel confusion in the face of it, did not try in the least either to deprecate or to deny it.

"I don't like to think of your leaving this world," he said.

"Nor do I. As a matter of fact, I don't like it at all, mostly because there's no certainty that the next one will give me what I particularly want. I'll probably be horribly disciplined in the next world, and I deserve it. I've been hanging on to all the things I'm going to miss ever since I knew, two months ago, trying to beat time. I've had an interesting race at that.

"There's *Great Expectations,* for instance. I've always saved it because I couldn't bear to have Dickens cease to be an entirely fresh surprise. It's an odd one to save. Most people read it straight away once they get the Dickens madness on them, but I saved it. I read it two weeks ago —Mr. Pumblechook, and Wopsle with his Shakespeare, and Wemmick and the drawbridge—what a thrill! And Villon over again in my French and your English, and as many others of my best beloved as I could manage. I'm still at it!"

"Well, I owe Villon a lot myself. It's nice to be able to discharge a small bit of the debt by having Julie here."

"Anyone but you would think I was mad by asking you to have her here. Of course, that's why I asked. Sometimes I fool myself by pretending I'm a very apostolic Christian, but I'm afraid I have all the annoyances with few of the virtues, looking for a cloak after I've calmly taken a coat, and all the rest of it. When I was a child, there was a man in the hills near us who used every year to give away all his wine and olives to his poorer neighbours, and then expect us in the town to feed him through the winter. Once when he came begging to our door and my father questioned him as to his odd manner of life, he said,

'To make better Christians of you all.' "

"I should say you'd given away a good bit of wine yourself."

"I'm not so sure, and besides you don't need renovating. . . . Well, to get down to things as they are. I want to tell you while I can all there is to tell. To get ways and means out of the way first, there's money for school and college. Adrienne had some from her father which I've never touched. It's been carefully tended, and there's more than enough."

"If there weren't, you know that wouldn't matter."

"Yes, I know. But there are limits even to my presumption. I'm leaving papers with you here. You'll understand them far better than I do. They're all in order. And now for the rest. I hope you won't think me quite a fool, but I've learned nothing about the child, and what is more, I've never really tried to learn."

"I think you've been extremely wise."

"Thank you. I've been waiting for that. You remember I sent for Ann just after Adrienne died and asked her what she knew. She doesn't actually know a thing as you are aware, and she's too sane and honest to overwork assumptions. If it were Raoul Vallon, as looks probable, he was killed, as you know, a week before the Armistice. So if we had ever wanted to open that door, which I doubt, it was closed again before we had a chance.

"So I've tried to open no doors. Even if there'd been any to open, I'm not sure I should have tried. I knew Adrienne. It would be unjust to anyone else, dead or living, to think that the responsibility for this were not in large part her own. And even if we could know, might not the uncertain payment for a few weeks' madness be the worst possible thing for the child? I'm sorry—I know I shouldn't—but I distrust most human minds, my own included.

"There's one thing, though, that I must tell you. I found some scraps of letters among Adrienne's things. Perhaps I should have read them, but I didn't. I kept them until I had talked with Ann, and then I destroyed them. I couldn't bear to perhaps discover things in them which belonged only to her. I was no help to her in all her suffering, and I felt I had no right to unearth things which I had never been allowed to know. People take too much unfair advantage of the dead. It's the one thing, though, that troubles me a bit. Perhaps I should have read them."

"I'm glad you didn't," he said.

He looked at her sitting there before the glowing fire, her fingers playing with the crucifix of her beads. She was very pale, he thought, so much whiter than years ago when he had first noted the whiteness of her face. But still that long perpendicular line between her brows was whiter. He could see it there as her face worked while she talked.

"These marshmallows were really very good," she said. "Suppose you toast a few for me. I'm sure I'd be as bungling as Julie at it. Toasting marshmallows must be a purely American pastime. I'm sure we never did it in France, or perhaps there weren't such things as marshmallows when I was a child. What a pity!"

A marshmallow on a pointed stick, he thought. Could any object be more mundane and completely useless than a marshmallow? The wind outside, less harsh now, not wailing, swinging in toward the northwest, behind the house. Children asleep. Sea gulls in the barn. The approach of Death. Mr. Pumblechook and François Villon. What a collision of worlds! And yet he was aware of no collision.

"Thanks," she said. "You did that one excellently."

"Another?"

"Two more, and then I'm finished. Reluctantly. They're very good. To return to the child. She knows her father died in France—God forgive me if he didn't!—and that her mother died when she was born. That's all she knows. As you know, I took her back home when she was six. I wanted her to know her mother's country and my own, and a child stores up impressions. I took her to Brittany, to some nuns there, good simple women in a convent in the country. They were good to her. She was happy there. I think she's always been a happy child. But one year in Le Couvent de Sainte-Croix has been enough, perhaps too much. Most of my Sisters knew Adrienne, and pity is bad for a child even if she doesn't understand it as pity. Moreover, things leak out, though I don't believe they have thus far."

"She seems a thoroughly nice child."

"She is. She's sensitive and honest and thoughtful. I'd tell you, you know, if she were not. She is not perfect, thank God, but I've not seen a thing in her that I dislike or distrust. She loves books, reads both French and English well. If I didn't feel sure she'd grow into something fine, I'm sure you know I'd never ask this stupendous thing of you."

He knew from the nervous way she had begun to intersect her fingers that there was something of which she had not spoken and perhaps found hard to talk about. He understood what it was.

"Is she a religious child?"

She gave him a look of gratitude.

"Thanks. You always make things easy. She's reasonably so, like most children given a chance. I suspect overly devout youngsters. It's not natural, except in the saints, I suppose. But she has a nature that can be religious in the best sense. I'm not looking for spiritual gifts, they're there or they're not, but I should be unfaithful to the best in my own life if I allowed her to be deprived of the things that are her heritage. I believe that roots matter terribly in one's life, one's faith, one's country, one's language, one's home, and I know you feel the same way. I couldn't leave her in France, but I don't want her to forget it, and I know you'll see that she doesn't."

"I'll do my best."

"I know that. There are many people of my faith who would say I was doing wrong to leave her here with you, but I can't believe that. I know from Adrienne that there's a church not far away. She can go with those good people, Jan and Philomena. They can take her. If they get too old, she'll soon be able to take them. The rest is up to her."

"What do you want most for her?"

"Just what you've always wanted for your own children, the building up of her imagination so she'll have no quarrel with life. It can be done, as we both know, only so many people find out too late. She's got a good start. She sees things, and she somehow knows that there's more to them than just what she sees. And you'll know enough to let her alone. If we could only find the right places for children and then let them alone, we wouldn't need all this nonsensical talk about education."

"I believe this is the right place," he said.

"I know it is. I've seen your children, and I know you, God be praised! I know something else, too. It's true, mad as it sounds, that people have odd visions of the future when they're about to begin life somewhere else. Besides, even without visions, the best of us ought to be able to see where we're tending in all this frenzied pursuit after things that don't matter. You can't build a safe future with hatred and revenge and blindness on one side of the ocean and with people following false gods on the other. When Roderick and Julie are ten years older, or a bit younger or older than that perhaps, they're going to have to pay for the things we've done and left undone. I know these things are true. Julie's the prey of one mad world. I want her to be able to face another and not go down under it."

They sat for some time without talking.

"The wind has almost died," John Marston said. "Sometimes it does as suddenly as this."

He opened the door, letting the cold, rain-washed air flood the room.

"You'll see my land and sea tomorrow under the sun,"

he said. "I want you to have a good omen to take away
with you."

She smiled at him.

"I've had nothing but good omens from Windswept,"
she said, "since that scapegrace Villon began them a
quarter of a century ago. Who would deprive him of
glory? I only hope I'll have the chance to thank him myself."

Ann Marston came into the room with hot chocolate
on a tray.

"Mother says you're to have two cups of this, both of
you," she said. "It'll make you sleep. And Philomena
made the toast. She wouldn't trust me. You'll be glad
to know you're a holy visitant to Philomena, Mother
Radegund. You don't really mean to say that you two
have been toasting those wretched marshmallows!"

"Guilty!" said Mother Radegund.

Ann poured out the chocolate.

"Julie's sound asleep. I heard the prayers and did the
tucking up. Rod's still awake. He's been twice to the
kitchen to order a special breakfast for Julie."

Mother Radegund took a piece of toast and raised her
cup.

"To François Villon!" she said. *"Aux neiges d'antan!"*

8

It was almost a year before Julie Chartier felt Windswept taking her to itself as it had taken other children in
the past. Its very freedom at first baffled, almost fright-

ened her. With her it was not as it had been with Philip,
Ann, and Roderick, whose first conscious sight had been
of its wide land and wider sea and sky. It was weeks before she could get used to its days, stretching before her,
unordered, hers to use as she liked. There was almost
terror in this very fact. Her days in France and in Le
Couvent de Sainte-Croix had been snug and tidy, so ordered and arranged by bells and seemly manners and the
soft, but rigid tread of black-robed Sisters that they had
removed one from the necessity of decision. It had been
easy to do as one was told; it was hard to do as one wished.

The new dresses hanging in her closet cost her almost
painful decision every morning when she got up. Should
she wear the blue one with white socks, or the red skirt
with sweater to match? Should she wear the round comb,
which her Aunt Eileen liked, or a ribbon to match her
sweater.

"We're waiting breakfast for you, Julie."

"I'm sorry, I'll hurry. I didn't know just which dress to
wear."

"Slip on anything, dear. It doesn't matter. You forget
it's Saturday, and you and Roderick will be playing all
day."

The playing was easier. Rod knew all manner of things
to do, and she was beginning again to have ideas of her
own.

"Let's play Norsemen, Julie, at the anchorage."

"No, let's play French ships."

"All right then, but you chose last time."

"Well, I like French ships better than Norsemen."

"I'll be Champlain then, sailing up the coast into the

bay. We'll rig a sail in the dory. You can hold the rope, and I'll stand at the bow looking at all the new things."

"What'll I be then?"

"You can be a sailor whom I've chosen to write down all the things. Run and get some of those long sheets of paper father has while I get a piece of canvas from Jan."

"I'm not going to be a sailor. I'll be a French lady that Champlain has rescued from the Indians."

"I don't believe there were any French ladies around here all those years ago."

"Yes, there were. At Port Royal. Your father said so. And even if there weren't, I'm going to be one anyway."

"All right. I don't mind. But you'll have to write down things all the same. When I say, 'Mark the channel' or 'Three great spruces on that headland,' you must write it all down."

"All right. I'll write it down in French the way a French lady would. That's more than you can do. If you like, I'll teach you to say 'Three great spruces on that headland' in French, the way Champlain did."

She did not know exactly what *spruces* would be in French, but she had the superior and comforting sense that Rod would not know the difference, whatever she might say.

It was hard to get used to the school at Heron Cove, to the boys there who had neither Rod's imagination nor manners; hard to get used to the walk home when in November the darkness fell long before they saw the lights of the house glowing through the last trees. She did not feel Rod's friendliness for the shadowy road, the sudden sound of a rabbit scurrying through the underbrush.

It was hard to get used to Sundays, driving the miles to church between Jan and Philomena, who at first, she knew, did not like her very much, who looked at her oddly and with some suspicion.

"You don't look like your mother then," said Philomena.

"Did you know my mother, Philomena?"

"Yes, I did, one summer, twenty years ago."

"When she was a little girl, do you mean? When she was at Windswept with Ann?"

"Yes, that's what I mean."

"Did my mother like Windswept? Did you like my mother?"

"Of course," Jan said. "Everyone likes Windswept. Your mother had nice manners, Julie, and a pretty voice. We're almost there, Philomena. Make your hat straight."

It was hard to get used to the cold and snow, bitter cold with even the gulls gone into the bays, and the whole land white with snow. Or to days before the snow came, gray with cold winds and little sun, so that when she looked from her window in the morning, she looked upon a dull, almost black stretch of cold, frozen land behind a gray sea white with foam. There were no companionable houses, no friendly smoke from chimneys, no street sounds, no chatter of familiar voices as there had been in the white dormitory of Le Couvent de Sainte-Croix.

Julie! Maman est venue aujourd'hui—elle m'a apporté des bonbons!

Donne-moi un mouchoir, Julie! Je n'en ai même un seul!

Julie, je crois bien que c'est toi qui seras l'ange à la fête de Noël!

Only Philomena's voice calling:

"Dress up warm, children. The wind is cold. The snow coming. Jan will take you to school today."

Hardest of all was that January day when they called her into John Marston's study and told her Mother Rade-gund was dead. For beyond the sadness that filled her eyes with tears and her body with sobs was the dark, chok-ing knowledge that she was now cut away from the things which she had known and loved, from their shelter and safety, from France again, from the red capes and hoods of her friends, from Sisters Angela and Cécile with the shy kisses which they had sometimes given her, from old Sisters Hélène and Ste. Geneviève and their cautions for her always to be good so that the Blessed Virgin would never fail her in her hour of need. Not even Philomena's sudden affection or the new sled that Jan made for her or the new comfort of Eileen Marston's room at night could make her forget that she was alone in a strange, still un-familiar place.

Not until one miraculous spring day, eight months after she had come to Windswept, did she really feel that this rocky, lonely land, this great tumbling stretch of ocean, was hers as well as Rod's. She would never forget that day and the healing which it had brought.

She and Roderick had gone to the sea-wall, their first journey there since the autumn because of the pools of water which always made the path impassable after the melting snow and heavy spring rains. Rod was eager to see what the winter and early spring tides had thrown up against the high wall. There might be anything, he said, lobster-buoys, bits of rusted iron, even an abandoned row-boat. The day was warm and soft, the sea smooth, pale blue like the sky. In the woods the frail blossoms of the wild pear and the tight buds of the cherry hung white among the dark trees.

"There's a jack-in-the-pulpit, Julie. Take care! There's an awfully wet place."

"I don't care. My feet are soaked already."

"So are mine. Here's some white violets. Are there any white violets in France?"

"Of course, there are, silly. There's every flower in the world in France."

"See the buds on the iris by the pond. Ann loves them. They'll be out when she gets home. We'll pick a heap for her room. Shall we?"

"Sure. It'll be fun to have Ann at home."

"She'll teach you to swim better. Then we can play French ships with a real sail, not that old piece of cloth on the dory."

"That'll be fun. What are those white flowers like little candles?"

"They're Canada mayflowers. They change to little berries by and by."

"Who taught you all the flowers, Rod?"

"My father. He'll teach you, too, or I'll teach you myself."

"What's that bird way off in the woods? Listen!"

"It's a white-throated sparrow. It says, 'Swe-et, swe-et, Canada, Canada, Canada.' "

"So it does. Wait a minute. I want to listen to it."

"Philomena doesn't like it. She says it says, 'My home, Bohemia, Bohemia, Bohemia.' It makes her homesick."

"Does it make Jan homesick, too?"

"No. Anyhow he doesn't say so. Philomena always says more than Jan says."

"I love Jan, don't you?"

"Of course. Jan's my best friend in all the world."

"Is Jan old?"

"Jan? Why I don't know. I never thought. He's not so old as Philomena anyway."

"Of course he is, stupid. Jan and Philomena are twins, aren't they? Then they have to be the same age."

Roderick stopped in the path, beset with sudden fear. Perhaps Jan was old. Perhaps he would die some day. The very idea was beyond his grasping. Even on this thrilling spring day it made him cold with dread.

"I never thought of that," he said.

"Well, he doesn't seem a bit old," Julie said with sudden comfort. "And I'm sure he doesn't feel old. You're just as old as you feel. That's what Sister Hélène used to say in the convent."

Rod felt better.

"Do you wish you were back in the convent, Julie?"

"No," said Julie, and all at once she knew how true it was. "No, I don't, a bit."

"That's good!" said Rod.

The winter tides had been generous. They had spent an hour filling their pockets with shells, gathering lobster buoys into a pile to take home later, piling driftwood in a safe, dry place for picnic fires during the summer. Rod found an old spoon half buried in the sand, silver once, now tarnished and rusted.

"Look, Julie!" he cried. "It's yours! It's got *Julia* printed on it."

She looked, excited, feeling happier and happier, the sun warm on her legs and hair.

"Jan can change the A to an E, and then it will be really yours. Jan can do anything. You can eat your blueberries with it. What a find!"

"Wonderful!" said Julie. "Thanks, Rod."

"Let's go around the point by the rocks and home by the new road Jan's made. Philomena always has such a fit when we come in dripping. Jan's been cutting trees there. I helped him the autumn before you came, and you'd never guess what we found there one day. We found part of an old compass made of brass near the roots of a stump Jan was prying out. He hit it with his pickaxe. Jan cleaned and polished the compass, and we tried to find some writing on it, but there wasn't any, only he and my father said it was very old. So there was a path there once, Jan says, and people walked there. My father says there used to be people here long ago, French people who traded with the Indians, not just French ships. There used to be a man named Caleb Perkins when my father was a boy. He built our house. He was an awfully good man, my father says. He died just before I was born, and he knew about the French being here in the old days."

Julie felt warmer inside her at every moment. If only all the days could be like this one, with no high, strangling winds, with no surf crashing when she woke in the night, she would never want to live in any other place than Windswept.

They were tired when they reached the road that Jan had made for getting out his winter wood. Julie had fallen and scraped her knee. They sat down on a great fallen spruce to eat their cookies and to wash her bleeding knee in a convenient pool of rain water.

"There must have been a big wind to make this tree topple over," Rod said. "Look at the worms in the hole, Julie. I'm going to dig for some more and put them in the cookie bag. Flounders take worms better than clams, Jan says, and we can go fishing off the anchorage rocks tomorrow."

He began to dig with a sharp, pointed stone in the big hole which the falling tree had made, in the soft brown earth beyond the interlocked, soil-filled roots.

"There are never worms like these at home," he said. "Even behind the barn there are never big fellows like these."

Julie was washing the blood and dirt from her scraped knee when she heard his excited cry.

"There's a handle of an old pot here! There is, Julie! Come quick and dig! It's really a handle. It's iron."

Julie subjected her injured knee to more dirt as she knelt beside him. Now he had the handle in his grasp. They dug frantically with their hands to free the earth around it. Their fingers met stones, hundreds of beach pebbles beneath the brown soil and the rusted handle.

"It's a pot filled with stones. Pull, Julie! Pull!"

When they had once raised the small iron pot, one end

of the handle gave way, throwing them backward into the moss and ferns. But they were on their knees again in an instant, staring at their treasure, breathing hard with suspense and excitement. Rod pulled off his sweater and spread it on the soft ferns below the great roots of the tree.

"It can't be just stones," he said hoarsely. "No one would bury beach stones, would they? Of course, they wouldn't! Turn it over with me, Julie."

They turned over the small pot, rusted to the colour of the brown earth, coated with the dampness of years of rain and snow. They had to dig with their stones to free the pebbles massed tightly with hard soil. The pebbles came out at last in ungainly lumps of caked earth.

At the very bottom of the pot beneath layers of some papery substance which had once perhaps been bark from birch trees were coins, coins of gold, coins tarnished and damp, cold, coated with green. They did not speak to each other as they drew out the coins one by one, placing them on Rod's red sweater. One, two, five, ten, twelve, twenty, twenty-three, thirty, thirty-four, forty. They broke the caked lumps of stone and earth; they dug about in the now deep hole. There were no more. They lifted the coins from the sweater, one by one. They were all gold coins, some large, some smaller, gold, gold coins in a Maine wood-path, beneath an old spruce tree not old enough to have stood there when they were placed in that iron pot, how many years ago? Placed by whom? Buried by whom? Why? When?

"Here's one that's not so tarnished, a big one," Rod said, speaking for the first time, whispering, his breath dulling his words. "Let's scrub it in that pool, Julie. Let's—"

He's going to cry, thought Julie. Rod's going to cry.

She seized the coin. She moistened the hem of her cotton dress in her mouth, scoured the round piece of gold, the green of it staining her dress, coming off on her fingers. She looked at it.

"It's got a man's head on it," she said, "a man's head in a wreath of leaves."

She scoured some more, rubbing now with her handkerchief which she had taken from her bleeding knee. They went to the pool of water, leaving their wealth on the red sweater, jealously looking back upon it lying there in the May sunlight. They found some sand in the crevices and hollows of some rocks near, which was helpful in scouring and which saved their unsteady legs even the short run to the shore. Julie scooped the sand up in her new spoon, which now in comparison held little interest. They knelt by the pool in the wet soggy grass and ferns.

"Now I can see," Julie said. "It's a French coin, Rod. The king—he's a king with the wreath—is Louis XIII. There are words around him in Latin. *D. G.*, that means the grace of God. I learned that in the convent. *Fr.* that means France. *Rex,* that means king. So it says, *Louis XIII by the Grace of God, King of France.* And on the other side, Rod, there are crowns and fleur de lis, the flower of France."

She gave the coin to him and sat down suddenly upon the fallen tree. Now she was going to cry, she thought.

"Most of them are just the same," she heard Rod saying from the red sweater where he was kneeling. "They're most of them just this size, Julie, but there are some that aren't. Jan has something at home that takes off rust. Then we'll know. What will they say when we show them, Julie,—Jan and my father, Philomena and my mother? What will they say? Why don't you talk, Julie? What do you think they'll say? You're crying, Julie! Whatever for?"

"I don't know," she said.

She was glad that Rod was too busy with his treasure to try to comfort her, scouring more of the coins, going to the pool, rubbing them one by one. He had forgotten she was crying.

She had found more than the coins, she thought, sitting there on that fallen tree, dishevelled, dirty, looking out to sea, her tears drying on her soil-stained face. This point of barren land, these surf-swept rocks, other trees like this fallen one, had once heard French words spoken by people who came from France, from Brittany, perhaps, where sailors lived, from Provence where her mother had been born and spent her childhood. This Windswept, then, was not a foreign land. It was hers as well as Rod's. Long before his grandfather had found it, French people had known it, anchored their ships beyond this point, walked in these woods, buried their money against the time when they should return to it.

"Let's go home, Julie," Rod was saying. "It's yours as much as mine, you know. It's not mine any more than it's yours. You're not crying any more, are you, Julie?"

She looked at Roderick. He had replaced the gold coins in the iron pot, stuffing his sweater in over them. He was

brown with dirt, holding the rusted pot against his blue
blouse, stained now black and red. His yellow hair was
blowing in the strong wind from the open sea, his gray
eyes were big and round. Suddenly Julie thought, how
young he is. He's just my age, she thought, but it's like
Philomena and Jan. It's like Sister Hélène. It's whether
you feel old or young. Sometimes you feel young; sometimes you feel old.

"No, Rod," she said, "I'm not crying any more, ever!" *

9

"Mother, do you know what?"

"No, dear, of course I don't know what."

"Well, Julie and I have a swell idea. We're going to
put on a show for father's birthday. We're going to have
it right here on the terrace if there isn't a wind. You and
father and Jan and Philomena will be the audience. We're
getting out programs on my new typewriter. And we'll
have posters, too. Julie'll do those."

"That's splendid, Roderick. He *will* be pleased."

"Will you help us with the costumes?"

"Of course. What costumes?"

"Here's Julie. Julie, mother'll help us."

"Wonderful! What'll we have first on the program,
Rod?"

"Camilla, I guess."

"Camilla who? Who's Camilla?"

---

* In case this incident sounds incredible to my readers, may I remind them
that such discoveries of treasure are not unheard of on the coast of Maine?
In Hancock County, in the middle of the last century, a pot containing 2000
gold coins, mostly French of the 17th century, was found buried in a hillside.

"Mother, didn't you ever hear of Camilla?"

"No, I can't say I ever did. Who is she?"

"Don't be so high-hat, Rod! You know you never heard of her yourself till you read my book."

Roderick looked embarrassed.

"Well, you never knew yourself either."

"I didn't say I did, did I?"

"No, but I thought mother'd know. Maybe father won't know either."

"I don't know much, dear, but if this Camilla is in a book, your father'll know all about her. Whoever was she?"

"She's in Vergil."

"Well, then, depend upon it your father'll know. He and Vergil are thick as thieves. I read Vergil once, but it was a long time ago. And if I ever heard of this Camilla, she's quite slipped my mind."

"She's in a book called *Stories from Vergil*, Aunt Eileen. Sister Angela sent it to me for my birthday."

"Oh, yes, so she did, dear. I remember."

"Rod and I read it together. It's terribly interesting."

Roderick put another stick of wood on the fire and sat down with Julie on the stone shelf opposite his mother. It was a dull early September day of fog and high wind, two years after Julie's arrival at Windswept. How tall she's grown, thought Eileen Marston, swinging her feet by the fire, watching her children. What nice long legs she has! Good legs are an asset with dresses like this, and hers will always be nice. What nice eyes and skin! If Mother Radegund could see her, Eileen thought, I know she'd be pleased.

"Camilla," continued Roderick, "was a girl in ancient Italy, who'd been brought up as a warrior ever since she was a baby in a war-like tribe. She could fight while she was yet a child."

"How terrible!" Eileen Marston said.

"What tribe did she belong to, Julie? I keep forgetting those odd names."

"I can't remember. Anyway, when she was a baby, her father tied her to his arrow and shot her across the river."

"Whatever for?"

"Oh, to get her used to wars and fighting. We're going to have that scene. Julie's got an old doll to use for Camilla, and I'll be her father. Jan's going to make me a big bow and arrow, and I'll practice shooting the arrow with the doll tied to it. Our first number is going to be called, Scenes from the Life of an Ancient Maiden. The audience will have to guess. Of course, you can't guess, mother."

"I should never think of such a dishonourable act, only I'll likely enough forget her name anyway long before you shoot her across the river."

Julie laughed. There was no one like Aunt Eileen, she thought, sitting there with them, swinging her legs like a girl, always saying things which made one laugh, always ready to help.

"Well, Jan and Philomena won't be able to guess, so father'll have to. Do you suppose he can?"

"Well, if he can't, I've been monstrously mistaken in him for nearly fifty years."

"The next scene is where you come in, mother," Roderick said. "Camilla loved pretty clothes, you see."

"Good!" said Eileen. "She's right up my alley! She's beginning to sound quite human, this Camilla."

Julie laughed again.

"Camilla loved pretty clothes so much," she said, "that they caused her downfall."

"They've done that to me more than once. My downfall, not to say your father's!"

"Don't interrupt, please, mother," said Roderick. "I'll tell the rest, Julie."

"Put some more wood on the fire, darling, those small spruce sticks, before I hear this tragic tale. I'm cold."

"Camilla loved pretty things so much," continued Roderick, sitting down again on his mat, "that she went to her death because of them. One day while she was fighting on her horse, she saw a man among her enemies all dressed up in purple."

"He was a priest," put in Julie. "That's why he was dressed in purple."

"Well, when Camilla saw the purple silks, she forgot everything and went after the priest to kill him and get his fine things. And a horrid little furtive man pursued her when he saw her leaving the main body of her army and killed her. So she died because she forgot everything but going after the purple clothes which she wanted."

"Poor Camilla!" Eileen Marston said. "I surely feel for her!"

"Don't forget Diana, though, Rod," said Julie.

"Diana was goddess of the hunt and the moon and— what sort of maidens, Julie?"

"Chaste," said Julie.

"Even *I* have heard of Diana," Eileen said.

"Well, Diana couldn't bring Camilla back to life, but she could kill the man who killed her, and she did."

"Fine!" said Eileen. "Where do I come in?"

"I'm the priest dressed up in purple, fleeing for my life with Julie after me with her spear. Have you something purple for us, mother?"

"I shouldn't wonder at all. Yes, come to think of it, I've the very thing. I've got a purple evening wrap your father gave me years ago in Italy. Wait a minute—I know exactly where it is. I'll get it for you."

She got up quickly from the stone shelf. Roderick and Julie, intent on their programs, did not see her stumble and fall. When they looked up, startled by the sudden noise, she was lying on the floor, white and still.

Roderick Marston always remembered how the sun came through the fog, seemingly at that very moment, so that when he and Julie saw her there, the sunlight lay full upon her face, on her mouth with its eager smile.

10

That evening John Marston took them both for a long walk. The surf ought to be fine, he said, after these days of wind. When they turned the corner of the house and set off down the shore path, they passed Jan and Philomena sitting outside the kitchen door, on the ground. They were sitting farther apart than usual. Philomena was crying, her apron raised to her face. Jan was sitting quietly, looking out upon the water.

They are old, thought Roderick. Philomena and Jan are not young any longer. They are twelve, thirteen years older than my mother was. To cry a great deal as Philomena had cried all day, her sobs sounding from the kitchen through the quiet house, makes one old and tired. Not to cry at all like Jan makes one old and tired also.

Crying makes one ill, he thought, stumbling after his father down the path, ill as well as old and tired. He tried to remember when he had ever cried before. He had cried when Friday had been run over by that stupid man, bringing fish from Heron Cove, struck down in the road when she was bounding for a squirrel. He had cried when Jan had refused to take him somewhere because he had told a lie to Jan. There must have been other times, many other times, but he could not remember them. He had been ill at supper from crying, hurried out to the kitchen door, lost his supper, to Philomena's distress.

"He's sick. He ought to go to bed," Philomena had said to his father.

"The air will do him good," his father had told Philomena. "Come on, Rod."

He did feel better in the cool, twilight air. It was better to walk than to go to bed. Did life ever slip back to be the same? he wondered. Would things go on again, lessons and hauling traps, games, sailing, reading at night? Or would things never be even partly the same again?

Ann would be here at midnight. She was coming by the plane to Bangor. Jan would bring her home, driving long miles through the night. But it would be different. She would not say tonight: "Well, old yellow-top! How's everything?"

His father was saying something.

"See how purple the shore is in this light, Rod. See how purple Cadillac is, Julie."

I wish I could comfort Rod, Julie thought. I wish I could give him something he would like awfully, not my book, though Sister Angela would never know—he wouldn't want that now. Perhaps all my share of the gold coins that didn't go away to that museum. By and by he might like those to keep, only he probably wouldn't take them. I wish I could say something to help him. It's worse for Rod. I didn't know my mother, except that she was beautiful and very good, an example even to nuns, who are always good. I could pray for Rod, only prayers take so long to help. Pray always, my child, old Sister Hélène had said. Like the poem they learned at school, reciting it after Sister Cécile, *More things are wrought by prayer than this world dreams of.* But one could not hold prayers in one's hands, like gold coins or books. It was now that she wanted to be of help to Rod, stumbling there before her in the path, so sick at supper time.

Maybe, if tomorrow were fine, they could pick cranberries in the sun, crouch in the sun and wind on the headland above the sea, filling buckets with the round, hard berries, red, tangled in the grass. Perhaps Rod would like that, perhaps that would help.

"How many have you got, Julie?"

"Not half what you have. You're a faster picker than me, Rod. I can never pick like you."

"I thought the surf would be fine tonight," Rod's father said, standing there on the high red rocks, an arm around each of them. He's so tall, Julie thought, but Rod's getting tall, too. By and by, he'll come above his father's shoulders. If Rod goes away to school now, the way we've thought, people will think he's fourteen instead of only twelve.

The surf caught the last light of the sun. There were pink and lavender lights in the great pale green rollers that bounded like horses with white manes over the red rocks, thundering with their hoofs. When the spray dashed up as the rollers spent themselves, the drops caught the light. It would have been lovely on any night but this.

The smaller pebbles on the beach below, at one side of the great rocks where they were standing, were being pulled back with every receding wave, flung up again, with a harsh grinding sound. They listened to it above the noise of the surf.

> *Listen! You hear the grating roar*
> *Of pebbles which the waves draw back, and fling,*
> *At their return, up the high strand,*
> *Begin, and cease, and then again begin,*
> *With tremulous cadence slow, and bring*
> *The eternal note of sadness in.*
>
> *Sophocles long ago*
> *Heard it on the Aegean. . . .*

A small log was caught there in the waves, sometimes flung almost upon the beach, rolling there among the pebbles, then drawn back again far from the shore. That's like Rod, Julie thought suddenly, tossed about in his mind, unable to find a firm, safe place.

"Let's go home, father," Rod said. "I don't like it here."

When they walked homeward across the now shadowy land, the curlews were circling in great sweeping flocks, calling their sharp, sad cries. Their wings, so pale and golden in the sunlight, were now almost black.

"Their wings are like curved knives," John Marston said, "like those Arabian scimitars we've read about, two joined together with their bodies for the hilts. Look, Rod."

"Yes," said Rod. "Yes, they are like that."

"I read in the paper this morning," his father said, "that some white herons have been seen about, not far from here. I've looked for one about here all my life, but I've never seen one. The books all say it wanders sometimes in late summer to Maine. I'd give a good deal to see one."

When they reached home, Jan and Philomena were still sitting out of doors, on the ground, in the gathering darkness.

11

Young Roderick Marston woke suddenly and early on the morning after his mother's death. He had been dreaming that he and Julie were heaping gold coins into his mother's lap, by the fire, the gold coins shining in the light. When he woke, he found himself sitting up in bed, staring out of his window. The eastern sky was dark, almost a purple colour over the dark trees of the distant woods, over the still, gray sea.

He stared at the sky, half awake, not yet remembering things, until he saw his father asleep in the bed next his own.

"I'll sleep in your room tonight," his father had said. "If you wake in the night, I'll be there."

He was glad that his father was asleep, that he was not yet feeling that sickening rush of remembrance which was now sweeping through his own body, quickening his heart. He would lie down quietly again in order not to wake his father. It must be very early. There was no sound in the house. But he still sat up in bed, staring at that dark, yet clear, expanse of sky, with no clouds upon it, with no trace of sunrise. He had never seen a sky just like it except perhaps before a thunder-storm, purplish black in the west, holding wind behind it.

He did not know why he did not lie down, try to go to sleep again like his father. The morning air was cold through his open window. He drew the covers to his chin, about his shoulders, still sitting there in bed, looking at that odd eastern sky.

Was that a moving white cloud on its dark smooth surface, a mist slowly taking shape against its purple, now leaving the sky, now more white against the blackness of the distant trees? It was coming closer, this white shape, straight through the morning air. Now it was far past the trees, now it was flying over the land, over the blueberries and juniper, low, just clearing the alders, straight toward his window. He rose on his knees, forgetting the cold.

He should call his father, he thought, while there was yet time. This was what his father had been waiting many years to see. Why was he suddenly unable to speak? Why did he suddenly know that this was his, to hold and to keep? Why was this moment something that one could not share, this sight of a solemn white bird floating from out the purple sky?

The wings of the heron spread wide, the tiny soft feathers between its wings and its slender body were ruffled into white foam by the swiftness of its flight. Now it was near him. He could see its long yellow bill, its neck held closely to its shoulders, its great wings poised, still, not now beating the air but floating there for a brief moment upon the morning stillness, turning just before his window in a wide half circle, going back now above the edge of the still sea, back toward the dark woods, becoming fainter and fainter, now like a single white feather, lost at last in the distance.

12

Julian Lassiter came on from California for his sister's funeral, flying in a trans-continental plane which allowed a man to dine sumptuously somewhere in the firmament and breakfast in New York. Julian at sixty-nine was, John Marston thought—well, just Julian at sixty-nine. It had been a long time since he had seen Julian. After the advent of young Roderick, Eileen had gladly spent the winter months at Windswept so that they had missed seeing Julian and Lucy in California or keeping harried dinner engagements with them in Europe in places where, John Marston said, one would know Julian would be, Claridge's in London, the Ritz in Paris, the *Hotel de Paris* in Monte Carlo. He and Julian had not met since James Lassiter had died seven years before, and then under the most formal and unsatisfactory of circumstances.

Not that the circumstances differed now, yet Windswept was a more companionable place, even in sadness, than the old Lassiter home in New York. There were common memories at Windswept, of summers spent there during years at Harvard, of pleasures and experiences shared.

Julian liked being at Windswept in spite of the distressing reason for his visit. And he was not without his moments of vision.

"I'm glad Eileen went out like that if she had to go," he said to John Marston. "Eileen was always getting ready for some play or other. She'd have liked to go that way."

He stayed on a fortnight after Eileen had been placed in the little churchyard which Jan and John Marston had made some years before beyond the chapel, clearing away some of the smaller trees, enclosing it with a wall of beach stones. It was pleasant there above the quiet water of the anchorage, the boats swinging at their moorings, the sun there almost all day.

Just as in the old days Julian improved with time, John Marston thought. The stock market crash; the enormity of unpaid war debts; the increase of unemployment, of all those good-for-nothing men who would not work even if you gave them a job; the alarming inroads which communism was making among the young; the equally alarming breaking up of party lines; the unholy mess in Europe where everything was at sixes and sevens so that business was perilous at best—these after a few days lost, at least in measure, their stranglehold on Julian.

"The trouble with me is," he confided to his brother-in-law on one of their first long evenings by the fire, "that I've never had the sand to take what I really wanted and to pay the price for it. Remember how I used to dabble round with those old paints of mine? I'd have liked to study art, believe it or not, but I always felt so sort of foolish about it that I never had the nerve to stand up to my father. There are thousands of men like me—I know a good lot of them myself—making money and playing golf on Sundays, belonging to clubs and ranting round about the same old subjects, when they'd really like to have done some fool thing that would probably have paid them better in some ways in the end, no matter how many rows they weathered to get what they wanted. But the trouble with me is I've never had the guts to weather the rows. Now you're different, John. You've always been different. I don't mind telling you I envy you for sticking to your guns."

"What guns? I'm not aware of sticking to any guns at all. My father did it all for me. I don't deserve an ounce of credit."

"I'm not so sure. You gave up a tidy berth with Marston, Cobb, and Lassiter to come off away down here. There was more than one man in the firm who called you crazy, but you didn't mind."

"I wasn't there to hear them," said John Marston. "Though I can't say it would have mattered much if I had."

"Well, that's what I mean. I just didn't have your guts. If I'd once told Lucy I'd rather look at pictures in Europe instead of going in classy clothes to Wimbledon or Ascot, she'd have died of shock. And still, maybe, when it comes to that, she's had her own hankering, out of sight somewhere. Sometimes when I look at people I say to myself: 'Just what are you hankering for, too?' For all I know, Lucy's had times of wanting something instead of dinner parties and bridge and those garden clubs that fool all these society women into thinking they're doing something, getting rural, going back to Nature, or what have you? God! How I hate those garden clubs with women in big hats prattling fancy flower names in Latin. It seems to me Lucy's gone six days out of seven inspecting a garden either in Europe or some place in the U. S. A."

John Marston laughed.

"I'm not strong for garden clubs myself," he said, "but we're not bothered with them much away down here. They flourish in Bar Harbor and places like it. There are too many such places on this coast to suit me. Mt. Desert Island from the headland here is the way it ought to be."

"There's young Jim, though he's not young any longer, thirty-eight when I stop to think. I hounded him just the way my father hounded me, telling him he'd got to line up with the old firm and get into harness once he got through flinging my money around in Cambridge. I drove him into taking engineering at Harvard. Would you believe it, he preferred Latin! And if I had it to do over again, I'd prefer Latin, too, by God, much as I hated the stuff. When he got back from France, he stood me up to the wall and told me where to get off. I had a sneaking respect for him, much as I tore my hair. Now he's out there at Berkeley teaching Latin to those that have got sense enough to study it or aren't made by fathers like me to study something they've no knack for.

"I've got to give it to him that he's getting more out of life than I've got. He married a nice college girl with a lot of brains but good-looking, too, and they get a lot of fun out of things. They've got five nice kids, and they're always lighting out for somewhere in the mountains, the whole parcel of 'em together in an old station wagon."

John Marston looked at Julian sipping his whiskey by the fire, seeing him again in a checked suit and club tie in the red plush seat of a dirty New Haven train, hearing him say:

"Harvard's just a putrid sink with a lot of dead fish floating in it!"

How even inconsequential words can last through the years, he thought, when they have bred either extreme discomfiture or extreme happiness!

Julian's clothes were even now up-to-date, bespoke a successful man of the world. One would notice Julian anywhere, his well set-up figure, his heavy, almost white hair, his smooth, good-humoured face with few lines of either care or thought upon it. Julian was a man who in club cars would offer drinks to good-looking, well set-up men like himself, talk politics with men of his own stamp till far into the night, cursing the way things were going in America, lamenting that the good old days when a man could earn his wealth by his own brains and do what he liked with it were threatened, but only, of course, for the time being, only, of course, till these addle-pated fellows could be put in their places by men like himself.

"I always liked young Jim," he said, "when I used to see him in Cambridge and when Philip brought him here. Philip was keen about him, too."

"Well, I'm fond of Jim in spite of his notions. I don't see him so often as I'd like even though he's just across the bay, for we always stage a row, and I don't want to die of rage at the hands of my own son. He's one of these half-baked liberals, down on capitalism and all the rest of it. I tell him I'd like to know where he thinks he'd be now if it weren't for capitalism, but I can't get him to think straight. He voted for Al Smith, if you'll believe me, and he signed a petition to save the miserable skins of those two Italian blackguards. He did as sure as I'm sitting here. His mother went to bed over it, and the house wasn't worth living in for days. He made speeches, too, about joining the League of Nations and cancelling the war debts. And he's got all kinds of half-baked ideas about getting out of this depression. If you put this country into the hands of men like him, we'll have another Russia here before we know it."

John Marston smiled to himself in the shadowy, fire-lit room. This was clearly not the time or occasion to confess certain similar shortcomings of his own.

"If you admire Jim for standing up to you and choosing the life he wants to live," he said, "why be upset when he chooses his own thoughts? After all, a man's life is his thoughts, isn't it?"

Julian looked puzzled. He had never liked abstractions, but the point of his brother-in-law's contentions was clear enough.

"I don't think it's the same thing at all," he said. "If a man wants to teach Latin instead of designing ships, then I say more power to him. But when these young fellows take it upon themselves to question one hundred years of good, solid American experience, when they're forever harping on throwing over institutions that have made this country what it is today, then I say, watch out for them. I'm sick of hearing all this talk about our duty to Europe and all the rest of it. We've got enough trouble on our own hands without messing around with a lot of nations that don't pay their bills and that are always out to grab what doesn't belong to them. There are too many of these theoretical college professors around if you ask me. What we need is good, practical common sense. Now take the war. What did we get out of it, I'd like to know?"

"I for one got a great deal out of it," John Marston said. "I got thoughts I like to think."

He regretted his words as soon as they were spoken, noting Julian's evident embarrassment. It was vastly safer to keep off certain subjects.

"Jan's no end pleased to have you here," he said.

"Good old Jan!" Julian said. "There's a man that's weathered things well. Jan's got a lot inside him that most men don't have. Even I can see that. He's terribly keen on young Roderick and that pretty little French girl. You've surely had some outfit here, John, through all these years—Mrs. Haskell and Jan and poor old Anton and that terrifying Philomena, whose eyes scare me half to death, and now this Julie. Jim would like this household. He's always harping on our not seeing America as she really is, and having all of Europe and half of Asia messing around his house in something called a Cosmopolitan Club. Yes, Jim would call this a piece of America as it ought to be. With anyone but you running the show, I'd call it crazy."

"It's always suited me," John Marston said.

Julian was at his best when they left ideas alone and enjoyed reliving the experiences they had known as boys in the past.

"Mrs. Haskell now. She *was* a woman!"

"She certainly was."

"When Eileen wrote ten years ago that she'd gone to her reward, I couldn't get her out of my mind for days. I remembered how mother used to say that Mrs. Haskell made her feel like a soggy piece of driftwood."

"Well, she had nineteen years with Caleb Perkins, saw him through just as she would have wished. Mrs. Haskell was a genius at seeing things and people through."

"Perkins was a fine fellow, too. I guess they used to make good stuff out of this coast stock. When I first went West and was tempted to shirk matters, I used to see Caleb with a piece of wood in his hands."

"We owe a lot to both of them."

"Will I ever forget how Mrs. Haskell dressed me down when old Dick Foster left her a five dollar bill! God! How she laid me out! And, do you know, she wasn't far out of the way about most things at that."

Julian was not a great walker. The golf links did for

him, he said, and just now he was laying off a bit even on golf.

"I'm reading the Sunday paper now, just like an old man for fair. Of course, no one goes to church nowadays. Sometimes I wish they did, but if I proposed it, Lucy'd have a stroke. I have my times when I wish things were different, but, there, it's too late to change my ways. I may as well jog along. But I do want to last out to see this damned depression over and a stronger Republican than Hoover in Washington."

Nevertheless, he made the rounds of Windswept with John Marston, in good tweeds, swinging his stick.

"That old pine's still standing," he said, "and I can't see that the sea-wall's any higher than it used to be. See those ospreys there. They stick around just as you have done."

They stood one clear morning on the high summit of the land just above the cove. The tide was full, the sea a deep blue, the outlines of points, islands, and horizon distinct and vivid. How many September days have I seen it just like this, John Marston thought.

"Poor old Dan!" Julian said. "Do you know some nights even now I dream of him, lying down there with a smile on his face. Well, perhaps he had the best of it after all, going out with a big dream in his mind of all the mighty things he was going to do in the world, never knowing that in nine cases out of ten a man can never make his dreams come true."

He paused, embarrassed. Why are we always embarrassed, John Marston thought, over things that matter most, regardless of how old we are?

"Do you know," Julian said, "I've never gotten over being pleased that it was I who made the big dream possible for Dan?"

13

September's my month, thought Julie, sitting on a big flat rock at the anchorage, her brown knees drawn up to her chin, her brown hands clasping them. I came here in September.

Goldenrod and white asters tangled among the raspberries and alders, growing paler, not lasting so long now in the great jars in the living-room. Fireweed, brilliant in August, that great tract of it in the open space above the cove, flaming there, purple, violet, pink—rose bay they called it in England, Uncle John said, growing by the slow streams there. In September its blossoms gone, its long seed-pods smooth like long, slim fingers, pale rose, bursting into silvery wisps of mist, blown away in the wind, catching on the raspberries, caught in one's hair.

"Julie, your hair is full of silver."

"It's the fireweed, Rod. You ought to see it at the cove."

Scarlet bunchberries in the damp woods, already faded in the open stretches, still fresh and glowing among the ferns, tucked in the napkins at night to give a festive air to supper. Tiny sea-asters, pale lavender, growing even in the sand; the last of the pale pink bind-weed; a solitary blue iris here and there; the rich burgundy of the wild strawberry, three tiny brilliant leaves flat against the ground. Cranberries ripe and red; the leaves of the blueberries crimson, purple, rust, bronze, so that whole patches of the long land flamed like some rare Eastern carpet.

The ripe grasses just outside her window when she woke at sunrise, frail, bending with dew, growing lavender in the light, gleaming among the juniper. Ducks in startled, silent flight across the pond, black against the leaden water. A green and purple dragon-fly, its frail, transparent wings one pair above the other, spread above a gray sprig of bayberry.

"See, Julie, like a tiny plane, for all the world!"

The sea pale blue at dawn, the very colour of thin milk, azure as the sun rose, sapphire at nine o'clock, a Mediterranean blue at noon, purple at night. The moon rising like a great ripe fruit, swinging higher, the land and sea silver. Northern lights sweeping the sky. Windy days, still days, days of soft blue haze.

September's my month, thought Julie. It was in September that Ann had said, not as one says to a child, Ann was never like that, but as one says to a friend:

"I don't know how I'd make out without you, Julie, to help with Rod, to be here always with us, part of Windswept."

They had been sewing name-tapes on Rod's things that day, hundreds of tapes, with Uncle John and Uncle Julian walking somewhere and Rod off with Jan, getting Rod ready for St. Paul's, sewing together on the terrace.

September's my month, she thought, hearing the ropes slap in the light breeze, waiting for Rod to come to sail. Slipping out of the bay, catching the stiff northwest wind, flying before it past the point, past the light, on toward the open sea, the spray in their faces, cormorants skim-

ming the water, the long neck of a loon above the green
swells.

"Haul in a bit, Julie."

"All right!"

"Steady does it! Here we go!"

Idling home in the late afternoon, the wind from the
south, sitting aft together, sunburned and hungry. Rod
reciting poetry:

> *Life like a dome of many-coloured glass*
>
> *When to the sessions of sweet silent thought*
>
> *Like as the waves make toward the pebbled shore*
> *So do our minutes hasten to their end.*

"Where's that from, Rod?"

"Shakespeare. I told you yesterday. You've got a mind
like a sieve, Julie."

"I know it. I like the things all the same, even if I
don't remember where they're from."

Going away in late September, to school, to college.
With all the sadness of leaving there was always the in-
expressible excitement of going away. They always left at
dawn, driving to Bangor for the early train. The weather
had never once been bad, thought Julie, never once
through all these years.

"If we had any sense at all," Ann always said, "we'd
take the sleeper."

"Let's not have any sense," said Julie. "I hate sense."

In the half-darkness at five o'clock Rod pounding on
her wall.

"It's five, Julie. Get moving!"

"I've been awake for hours."

The stars at four o'clock. Orion in the east, his belt a broken line of dazzling light; Aldebaran red; Sirius glowing; and some great brilliant planet just to the right of Orion which she did not know. From her western window the Great Bear now almost touching the horizon, reflected now, she thought, in those coves of Schoodic, which we've always meant to explore and never have.

The stars fading, that last bright one sinking, losing its yellow, now a mere prick of white in the sky.

Ann at the table above the lighted candles, dressed as she had not been dressed all summer, looking young and handsome in her dark suit, gloves and purse on the table beside her.

"Well, see who's here!"

"You're looking swell, Ann."

"You're not so bad yourself, darling. That tweed's just the colour of your face. That hat's fetching."

Philomena coming in with muffins, brown and hot. A red shawl over her shoulders against her rheumatism. Rod appearing with a thump of luggage left on the kitchen floor, in a gray suit which set off his fair hair, in a collar and tie, placing his arm around Philomena, kissing her on her cheek.

"Muffins, Philomena! Swell! There's life in the old girl yet!"

"You needn't have, Philomena. Toast would have done very well."

"When you go, you get muffins, and now you eat them. A long drive it is."

"That's a nice suit, Rod. Wear it when you come to see me, will you?"

John Marston appearing in the doorway, shaved, dressed.

"Father, you're hopeless! Why in the world can't you let us go at this unholy hour without your getting up?"

"Don't try to run other people's lives, my dear. If you don't mind my saying so, it's a habit that's growing on you with mine. This has been my chief indoor sport for years. Mind you haskell things well. It's a long, cold drive."

The light coming over the sea, the candles glowing white before it.

"A good day. You couldn't have a better."

"We always have a good day."

The sound of the car outside.

"Rod, your clubs! You put them in the hall closet. And after all this fuss!"

"Are you sure you've plenty of money, my dear?"

"Take care of your old bones, Philomena. Remember we couldn't make out without you."

"I'm so glad you have that nice girl to help, father. I like her."

"She's all right. Her father's been my friend for years. Now whatever you do, don't worry about us here."

"I know I've forgotten something."

"Well, we can send it on."

"Rod, I wish you'd make a point of seeing Dr. Rush and telling him how much I liked his Chaucer pamphlet."

"I will, father."

"Is that youngster a good driver?"

"I don't know. I'm driving myself."

"Let me drive part of the way, Rod."

"Don't forget Jan's waiting at the barn."

"I'm not likely to forget Jan."

The sun just rising, round and red in the clear sky, streaming across the drenched grass, touching the gulls' wings. Jan at the barn door, stooped a bit more, but still young, eyes only for Rod.

"Take care of yourself, Jan."

"You, too, Rod."

"Till Advent, Jan. Set a trap for that porcupine. Old Giles will never weather another."

Rod was coming down the path, whistling, calling to the dogs, old Pippin and Giles, ten and twelve years old, still going strong. They would wait all day, lying in the sun, dreaming of by-gone rabbits, ready to bark in welcome when *The Sea Hawk* slipped again into the bay.

"So you're here. I've hunted everywhere. I might have known you'd steal a march on me."

"I told Ann to tell you I'd come ahead. Isn't she coming?"

"No, she's got letters for father. Some day for our last sail!"

"It'll be swell tomorrow, too."

Rod pulled on the tender rope. It swung shorewards, breaking its still shadow. How brown Rod was! He should always wear a blue sweater and white slacks. They were nice with his yellow hair.

"Eh bien, Mademoiselle Chartier. Bâteaux français aujourd'hui?"

14

It was a blustering spring day in March, 1939, when Jan and Philomena prepared to celebrate their eighty-fourth birthday. Philomena had been recalcitrant for days over the proposed festivities, but at last she had yielded. It was only acute embarrassment masquerading under the guise of fractiousness, Ann Marston told Julie, as they watched the two drive away in the back seat of the car, the boy who now helped Jan about the place at the wheel. While they were away in the village, buying Jan's present of a new pair of shoes, seeing the film of *David Copperfield*, Ann and Julie, just home for spring vacation, would make ready the birthday supper, prepare the table, do up the gifts. There was a cake made in New York, three tiers of it, necessary to hold eighty-four candles, Julie said. It was to be placed when lighted on a music box which revolved slowly as it played "Happy Birthday to You!" This last was Julie's gift, and she was no end excited over it.

"Fortunately there are other tunes, too," she told Ann.

"I'm almost prepared for Philomena's complete collapse," Ann said. "Too bad we sent Sally home today. I'm not too sure about these blasted chickens."

Jan and Philomena sat solemnly in the back of the car. It was such an unwonted experience for the two of them to go on a holiday by themselves that they felt almost embarrassed.

"Take these holes slow," Jan said to the boy. "We'll have to get busy with gravel before long."

When they had seen the film, a nice one, Philomena thought, only she'd never forget that poor David being so monstrously treated by Mr. Murdstone, they went to buy Philomena's new shoes.

"What now do I want of new shoes?" Philomena said. "New shoes at eighty-four. Why now, Jan?"

"Because your stockings are almost on the floor," Jan said. "I'd thought of two pair, Philomena. Some black for everyday, and some nice white shoes to wear in summer time. They are early with their white shoes. Only last week I saw them."

"Jan," said Philomena, "you grow more mad with each year."

But she smiled, liking Jan's arm guiding her across the street. She had liked the film, and there would be a lot to think about. That Peggotty, for instance. She was a kind woman. She had David to care for as Philomena had had Philip, and then Roderick, so far away now in England.

"We will look at new shoes for this lady," said Jan to the shopkeeper.

How well Jan says things, thought Philomena. Eighty-four years, she thought, and how many years without shoes at all except in the winter, and they made at Jakob, the cobbler's, stiff and likely to have nails in them after a short time. Whatever would their mother say at the very thought of new shoes? At the thought of two pair she would have covered her eyes in that old way she had of doing in moments of surprise or grief or pleasure—covering her eyes there beneath the hollyhocks of the cottage door that day when Kaspar told the lie to the priest, that day when Jan sent his first money home, that day when Philomena first said:

"I shall really go to America, *matko*. Jan says in this letter that I shall really go."

"Do these fit well, then, Philomena?" Jan was saying. "If they do fit well, we will have them done up for you."

"They fit very well, Jan."

"May I say you have pretty feet, Miss Pisek?" said the shopkeeper, who knew Jan well. "Not many a young girl has such pretty feet as you."

"Thank you," said Philomena. "My feet, they have lasted well."

How well they have lasted, she thought. How many long rows of grain her feet had followed, how many long rows of beets and peas, carrots, onions, her toes digging into the soft earth, making smooth circles as she moved onward on her knees. How many long miles her feet had carried her, bare in Bohemia, well shod in America. Feet, thought Philomena, the aching feet of so many still in the old country!

That radio, she thought. She was almost tempted to ask the nice shopkeeper to turn it off, blaring there from out that stupid box.

"I'm afraid the news is not so good today," the shopkeeper said.

"I think we'd best go now, Philomena," said Jan.

Jan's face looked odd, Philomena thought. Then she heard:

The German swastika now floats above the old castle of Prague.

This was what was coming from that box!

Philomena's face grew white with fear, then red with anger.

"Turn off that box!" she screamed at the shopkeeper. "It's a lie, I tell you. I do not believe it. Turn off that box, I say!"

"I'm sorry," the astonished shopkeeper said. "What's wrong, Mr. Pisek? Is she ill?"

"It's Prague," Jan said, his arm about Philomena's shaking shoulders. "It's Bohemia. It's our old country. We do not like the Germans. For many years they oppress the Bohemians. It's too long a story to tell you now. Come, Philomena."

"I'm sorry," said the shopkeeper again. "I guess there's no one likes the Germans overmuch. I guess some day we'll all have to stand together to beat that man Hitler."

That's true, thought Jan, when he was once on the street with Philomena. That's very true, no doubt, but first there is Philomena to be seen to. Not the castle at Prague now, thought Jan, above its river, so old and gray that morning long ago from the market-place with geese and chickens, and gay bodices, and Jonas Jurka trying to sell his bad ox Krok. Not the German swastika flying there in the night wind, but Philomena to get home to her birthday party.

Philomena did not dry her tears till they were well on the road home. A birthday party, thought Jan, for he had guessed the secret. And they at home not knowing of the Germans, since they had no voice-filled box, like the shopkeeper's. If Philomena were only young again, she would understand, pull herself together, guard Ann and Julie and John Marston against her sorrow. One was always guarding others against sorrow, thought Jan. But Philomena was old.

When they turned from the trees into the road and the puzzled boy shifted his gear for the long even drive to the house, Philomena took her gloved hands from her face.

"We cry no more, Jan," she said. "They must not at home know our sadness until the newspapers tomorrow. Tonight we are gay, and if we go to bed with hate, it is only eighty-four years of hate, Jan, instead of eighty-three."

The music box played that night for Jan and Philomena, slowly revolving the cake with its many candles. John Marston sat at the head of the table with Philomena on his right; Jan sat at the foot. They drank some old French wine, kept for years for just such a festive occasion as this.

"To Bohemia, the old country!" said John Marston, rising in his seat. "To the good land that gave us Jan and Philomena. Help from its friends and peace at last!"

They drank the toast, unsurprised at the tears which ran down Philomena's cheeks. Philomena was old and sometimes homesick. They expected the tears.

"And to Prague, that old city!" John Marston continued. "Saints Cyril and Methodius defend it! Drink, Philomena, to your old Saints!"

Philomena rose in her chair then, her gray eyes flashing, dry now, yet full of fire. There was hatred in her eyes, cruelty, revenge. She drew up her old shoulders, raised her old head. She can't be eighty-four, thought

Ann Marston. She looks mad, like one of the Furies. Has she drunk too much wine? She might be Hecuba before Troy, calling down the wrath of Pallas Athene upon the Greeks, or Tisiphone at the gates of Hell with her whip.

"I drink this wine to the death of the enemies of Prague," Philomena cried. "May the good God and the blessed Saints kill them all!"

She drank her wine, she raised the empty glass above her head. Then, to the amazement of them all, she hurled the glass upon the floor and trod upon its fragments with her new black shoes.

"Philomena!" cried Jan, "Philomena Pisek!" He spoke to her in their old language then, the odd words, Julie thought, adding the last touch to this strange dinner. He was imploring her not to ruin the party, such a party as they had never known in all their eighty-four years.

Philomena had no intention of ruining the party. She sat down quietly in her chair when the sound of crushed splinters of glass was stilled. She ate her cake. She laughed. It was the happiest night of her long life, she said.

"Philomena," Ann Marston asked, "do you remember how you used to tell Philip and me that Judas Iscariot was a German?"

Philomena looked suddenly at Ann, at Julie, at John Marston, at Jan. There crept again into her eyes all that had been in them when she had made her mad outburst, but she spoke quietly.

"And why not?" she said. "In our country we know he was a German. That is what we learned when we were young, is it not so, Jan? And tonight in the city of Prague they will say the same. Jan, tell them it is true!"

15

The last day of August, 1939, and they all with one accord, in one place.

"I'm sure I don't know why we do it," Ann had said at breakfast. "The cellar shelves are full. We've given jars to every food sale in Washington County and supplied Heron Cove for years. It's carrying coals to Newcastle at best."

"Well, I'm not going off to England tomorrow without doing what I like best today. The wind's just right for winnowing, and they've never been thicker. They'll keep for weeks. I'm going to take back a box of them to my gyp and another to Mrs. Wyatt. We'll sail this morning, Julie, and pick this afternoon."

How many years had they picked the highland cranberries, thought Julie. Eleven, she thought, with this one, every year except last year when they had left Rod in Cambridge after those weeks in England and Scotland, driving from Land's End to John o' Groats, before she and Ann had gone to France and Germany. Ten years, ten clear days of picking, the sea a deep blue, the sun strong, all of them on the headland, wandering slowly down the high shore.

"They're much thicker here, Julie. Big bouncers, too! How many have you?"

"Not half what you have. You're a faster picker than me, Rod. I can never pick like you."

"Do you get scared, Julie, when you think of school?"

"I guess so. Do you?"

"A bit. I s'pose it's terribly different from Windswept."

"I'm afraid so. Is St. Paul's a big school, Rod?"

"I guess. My grandfather went there, and my father, and Philip, and now me."

"Well, there's Advent coming."

Rod growing taller with every year, at Harvard now, a bit strange at times, going off by himself now and then to read poetry. She at Smith, listening to her friends, in her house, after Spring Dance.

"He's terribly nice, Julie."

"Well, didn't I tell you?"

"Yes, but you didn't say he was as smooth as all that!"

"Well, I hate all this everlasting blah about dates!"

How many years it had been, she thought. One could depend on these last days of August to be fine, leading up to September.

"I believe they're thicker than even last year, Julie."

"I guess you're right. They look like drops of blood in the grass."

"Not a very poetic thought! Do you know what I've done this summer in my off hours?"

"No. What?"

"I've written some sketches about Jan and Philomena, Bohemia and all the rest of it. I'm going to hand them in for my theme course. Last year I got an A on the themes I did about Windswept."

"Well, an A's too much for me to hope for. But I got a B myself."

"I'll tell you a secret if you'll keep it dark. No one knows but father and Ann."

"Of course, I will."

"Well. I might get a fellowship to Cambridge. If I do,

I'll go to England next year instead of back to Harvard."

"To England, Rod!"

"Sure. Father's awfully pleased. He's worked a lot in Cambridge. He loves it there."

Had it been only two years ago that Ann had come up with her filled pail to pour the berries into Rod's basket, hearing what Rod said, saying:

"If he goes, Julie, we'll go along in June. We'll take my car. Maybe we'll even have a new one. We'll all drive in England and Scotland, and after we leave Rod in Cambridge, we'll go to France. You can see the Sisters in Brittany."

Today, picking near Rod, on the headland, she remembered it all. There was nothing like picking cranberries in the sun and wind to make one remember: the coast of Cornwall so like this very coast, surf rolling in, no higher, no stronger than surf at the cove; the walls in Devon pink and white with valerian; all those hundreds of villages in Somerset, in Wiltshire, in Dorset, with their cottage gardens and quiet fields, slow streams with rose bay and white bedstraw and campion, old gray churches; the Strand and Fleet Street and the pigeons at St. Paul's.

"Dr. Johnson ate here, Julie. And Goldsmith and Fielding. Gosh! I don't deserve all this."

Tomorrow Rod would go back, to New York late tonight, on the ship tomorrow. In spite of all this awful threat of war, every day more menacing, he was going back. To his rooms at Emmanuel looking out over the gardens, to King's Chapel which he loved. *Music lingering on as loth to die.* To those flat green fields, and hedges, and Milton's river. To Grantchester, where they had had tea last summer beneath the orchard trees, with airplanes circling in the close gray sky.

"Can't we ever get out of the sound of those planes, Rod? I heard them all night. They make me nervous!"

"I'd like to be up there! England needs thousands more of them, Ann."

Rod, picking near her, filling his dipper, pouring its red berries into his basket, was thinking of England, too.

"Remember that night last summer, Julie, when we drove up from Cambridge to London? Remember how the moon flooded those harvested fields, all those shocks and ricks of grain?"

"Yes, 'twas lovely!"

She had gone from those harvested fields to France, she and Ann driving, from Dunkerque to Chartres over those wide fields, by those still canals, the towers of the cathedral rising while they were yet miles away. They had gone to Brittany, stopping the car one morning before the high white walls of a convent enclosure, a heavy black door opening to a courtyard, a white cross above the door.

"Here we are, darling. You'd rather go in by yourself, wouldn't you?"

"I'm not sure. Yes. I think so."

She had crossed the plot of grass; she had stood before the door. It was open a bit so that she could see into the courtyard, which ought to have seemed old and familiar even after twelve years, but which instead seemed new and strange. Looking in through the door, she had seen a nun working the handle of a pump by the convent well, the wide skirt of her blue habit drawn up a bit under her big white apron, the broad wings of her white cap flapping in the wind. She had stood there, unperceived, seeing in a long moment the nun, the white-washed walls, the small, grated windows, hearing the sound of children's voices through the open windows, conning their lessons, saying their tables in French.

She had come back to the car.

"I'm no end of a fool, Ann, but I can't, really. It's all so strange. Do I have to? They'll never know. Can't we go on?"

She had never ceased to be grateful to Ann.

"Of course, you don't have to. Tumble in. Let's see the stones at Carnac. You drive. I'm no good in these alleys."

Jan came up with his baskets filled.

"I've made Philomena go in," he said. "This wind's bad for her. She says not so many more. She can't use them all, she says."

"All right, Jan. Julie and I'll take a walk by and by, but I'll be back to help with the chores before supper."

John Marston was following Philomena's good example. At seventy-three, he thought, even picking highland cranberries can be too much of a good thing. He came up to Roderick, bringing his spoils of the afternoon.

Julie, listening, heard.

"I think I'm through, too," he said. "There's news at five, and since I've at last succumbed to a radio, I think I'll listen. You're still set on going back, Rod?"

"Yes, father."

"It's not too late to change your mind. I don't like the looks of things."

"I don't either. That's one reason I want to go. I'll have three weeks before term begins, in Somerset with the Wyatts. Hugh and Michael are in the R.A.F. They'll know how things are blowing."

"I'm afraid they're blowing badly, or perhaps blowing well, who knows?"

"Well, England's through with appeasing, thank God! I could see that at Cambridge last year. The best men there are all set to go, see the thing through. And it's got to be our war, too, before we're through."

"I hope that's true."

"I'll maybe not get another chance, father, to tell you. If England goes, I'm going, too, if she'll have me. You won't mind?"

These young things surely deal in understatements, John Marston thought. He said:

"I'll be proud, of course."

"Thanks. I expected that from you."

"What'll it be? The R.A.F.?"

"I think so. I took lessons last year. I'm not too bad, Hugh says."

"Well, I'll be going in. If you have a chance, walk out to Grantchester—along the river, and take a look at the fields by the last stile there. Your mother and I always liked that spot the winter before you were born, and I was working in Cambridge."

"Sure, I will. I'm dotty about Grantchester myself."

"The ale's good at *The Red Lion* there. And they used to have a nice garden, even late in the autumn, with a pleasant smell at night."

One was always desultory in one's mind while picking cranberries, Ann Marston thought. What went on in one's mind then was not so much thinking as feeling, getting at the essence of things. I've been at this for years, she thought—is it really forty years?—and I've never ceased to get a thrill out of it. It's a good way to start the year, she thought, getting hold of things that matter.

"Hello, Miss Marston! Nice summer?"

"Wonderful, thanks! And yours?"

"Swell, only I didn't get much reading done."

"Nor did I. How did *Tom Jones* and the influence of the classics come along?"

"I've just scratched the surface, I'm afraid. Can I see you soon?"

"Of course. Come around for tea."

"Thanks, loads! I'd love to. It's swell to see you. Four o'clock?"

I'd like to live forever, just as I am now, she thought. Not young like Rod and Julie. Heavens, no! Not facing all the bewilderment and suffering and confusion they're bound to face, but going on with these things, having them already a part of me, suffering, perhaps, but not stunned any more, waiting, working for a new world.

There have probably been other generations with the gifts of my own, she thought, but I don't know of them. The women of my generation—what we've had handed out to us! An old world and a new! An old world of horses and country schools, kerosene lamps and even a relative orthodoxy, stability, peace, complacency, Browning, God's in His heaven! Then the catapulting into a new world, with humour enough to keep one's head, curiosity enough not to get bitter, excitement enough not to go yearning after the past. And now this grim descent into an older past of blood and tears, greed and cruelty, forged with new weapons. Young people not knowing where they are in their minds, brought up on sentimental unrealities on the one hand, and, on the other, with too much of Mammon, needing understanding, faith. I'm glad I'm forty-six, she thought, glad I have a good chance to see a better world, even to help to make it.

She looked at Rod and Julie a few yards away, picking in the same spot. They've at least escaped unrealities, she thought. We've all escaped them here. She remembered a still day in Germany, just a year ago, driving through a seemingly deserted countryside, a vision she had had of things she had known all her life, but never before entirely perceived in all their simplicity and strength. This sea, this shore, these minutes and hours, red berries in the tangled grass. If faith were gone, the old, simple faith in a design for one's life, not forged on earth by one-self, but framed in Heaven, yet one could, if one would, build one's own design through an awakened conscious-ness even of material things, the visible and the temporal holding within themselves the means to the invisible and eternal. One can, even in these new, sad days, rise to the life immortal, she thought; one can find the golden branch among the shadows.

"Ann!" Rod was shouting. "Don't pick any more! We're winnowing. Come on!"

Will Rod always be winnowing cranberries, she thought? A small boy in bare legs and shorts, fumbling with the buckets, spilling half the crop; taller, in his first long trousers; now, still winnowing, about to sail back to England—England, its fields and streams, village churches and hedgerows, in danger.— She watched him place the big basket on the ground, raise the buckets one by one, laughing as the red stream fell.

"Careful, Julie! Wait till this gust is over. Now!"

"A full bushel!" said Rod. "What a day! Five o'clock, Julie! An hour before chores. Come on!"

She watched them run down the long shore path. Julie stumbled in the juniper. He caught her hand. They ran on together.

The wind is lessening, she thought. It will be a still night. It is growing cold. There's likely to be a frost.

An early frost would colour the blueberry bushes deeper, yet they could hardly be more bright. From the headland, as far as she could see, the land glowed with patches of scarlet and crimson, rust and gold, above the green and purple sea. The flames at Pentecost, she thought, coming with a mighty rushing wind, still touching men so that they may speak in other tongues than their own, still enabling their sons and their daughters to prophesy, their young men to see visions and their old men to dream dreams.

THE END